COLIN CLEVELAND AI
OF THE WOR

by the same author

Disappearer

Colin Cleveland and the End of the World

Girl's Rock

The Eternal Prisoner

Rogue Males

Mark Hunter series

Beautiful Chaos

Sixty-Six Curses

Trouble at School

Mysterious Girlfriend

The Beasts of Bellend

Countdown to Zero

Colin Cleveland
and the
End of the World

Chris Johnson

Samurai
West

Published by Samurai West
disappearer007@gmail.com

This paperback edition published 2025
ISBN-13: 9798293744831

Disclaimer

To forestall any complaints that Colin Cleveland, the hero of this tale, is just another Murray Leinster, the author would like to make it clear that the first draft of this book was written prior to the writing of *Mysterious Girlfriend*—so in fact it is Murray Leinster who is just another Colin Cleveland.

Assassination plots never hurt Hitler. The only way he could have been eliminated was by a woman or a whore who snuck in a knife, who gained his trust and then stabbed him as he drowsed off.

Courtney Love

If I was a Jewish girl in Hitler's day, I would approach him and become his girlfriend. After ten days in bed, he would come to my way of thinking. This world needs communication. And making love is a great way of communicating.

Yoko Ono

And poor old Goebbels has no balls at all.

old song, author unknown

Prefatory
A Word About Colin Cleveland

Before I begin this chronicle of his odyssey, there is something I have to tell you about young Colin Cleveland, something that I need to make clear in order to put the whole story into context:

Colin Cleveland suffers from acute End of the World Anxiety.

End of the World Anxiety? I hear you echo, with an audible shrug of the shoulders. Not exactly unusual in this day and age. Lots of kids are worried about the future of the planet: in fact, they are being actively encouraged to be worried about it. And while this is true, you have to understand that Colin's End of the World Anxiety is of a particularly refined nature, because it's not so much the melting icebergs, rising temperatures, the droughts and forest fires etc, that trigger his anxiety; it's the loss of stability, the collapse of law and order that he is convinced this will lead to; it's the idea that the precariously balanced edifice that we call civilisation is about to come crashing down around our (and more specifically his) ears. Having reached the ripe old age of twelve, Colin can no longer take his own personal safety for granted; he has lost that instinctive childhood belief of being cocooned in a nurturing environment; he has come to realise more and more that the world is actually a very dangerous place populated with dangerous people, and that there are lots of things that even his mother can't protect him from.

And that's what scares the bejesus out of him.

Even here in his home town of Eastchester, Colin sees signs of coming disaster. Looking at the local newspaper and reading of incidents of violence, of destruction of property, of burglary: to Colin, all these seem like alarming indications of the imminent collapse of society.

And what makes things worse, psychologically speaking, for our Colin is the fact that he has never been able to share his anxiety with anyone; he keeps his fears bottled up inside. His fears locked away inside his head, they grow, they fester, and they become acute. And of course, believing himself to be the only one who can really see the impending end of the world, he feels isolated; even at home with his loving parents, there is a part of him that feels cut off and alone.

What follows now is the story of how all of how all young Colin's worst fears very suddenly and unexpectedly come to be realised.

Part One
The Incident

Chapter One
'The End of the World!'

On the afternoon that the world ended, Colin Cleveland was lying in bed, delirious with fever. Influenza can hit us hard when we're children, and it is pummelling poor Colin right now.

Here in his fever-bed, one moment burning, one moment freezing, his mind is in turmoil, his body suffering and restless. In the throes of his *delirium tremendous*, he has tossed and turned so much, first lying on his back, then lying on his left side, then lying on his right side, vainly searching for that vaguely-recalled condition known as physical comfort, that Colin's fevered mind now believes that he has multiplied, that there are in fact three Colin Clevelands, all equally tormented, and sharing the one bed. There is the Colin lying on his back, Colin Number One; there is the Colin lying on his left side, Colin Number Two; and there is the Colin lying on his right side, Colin Number Three.

None of these Colins can find anything resembling physical relief in their respective positions. Colin Number Three, lying on his right side, shivering and aching, will think that perhaps he might find more comfort by turning onto his back, but then he will remember that if he rolls over onto his back, he will come into collision with the Colin Number One, who already occupies that position.

All three of these Colins dread the prospect of being sick. Of all the torments of his ordeal, being sick is the worst. He has already vomited about half a dozen times today. A washing-up bowl lies on the floor by his bed, patiently waiting for the next deposit.

His mouth is parched. A glass on the bedside cabinet mocks him with its emptiness. He needs water. If only he had more water…

Mum! Mum!

What time is it? It's getting darker. It must be late afternoon. School will be over for the day. They must be wondering what's wrong with him. He's been sick for two days now. What day is today? Wednesday? Colin is at big school now, Year Eight. Wednesday: Maths with Mr Peters. Colin hasn't done his homework. Long division. Colin can't do long division. What will Mr Peters say? Will he shout at him? How can anyone do long division? Mr Peters always wears those jackets with patches on the elbows. Colin doesn't like being shouted at. There's Bradley sitting at the table at the back with his gang. Bradley has always had it in for Colin. Why does it have to be him? Colin never did anything wrong to Bradley Why can't Bradley choose someone else to pick on? Why does it have to be him? There was that time Bradley and his gang chased him into the One Stop on Bitmore Street. They just waited outside, knowing he'd have to come out sooner or later. But Colin out-foxed them. He went through the door marked 'Private' at the back of the shop and got out through a storeroom and out into another street. Wait. Did he actually do that? Or did he just dream it? Where was Nigel that day? Of course; he's not talking to Nigel at the moment. Sometimes Nigel is Colin's best friend, but then they will fall out and don't talk to each other at all, sometimes for weeks and weeks. Colin can't remember what they've fallen out over this time. Was it something to do with *Doctor Who*? Might have been. Colin loves *Doctor Who*. But Natasha; she doesn't like it. Natasha is Colin's crush. Natasha sets Colin's heart pounding. She's so nice and so beautiful! Natasha is a mixed-race girl. Colin's not sure precisely what mix of races, but her skin is brown like coffee with milk and her hair is black and long and straight. She has the nicest smile in the world and the palms of her hands are a rosy pink. They look even pinker than Colin's, the palms of her hands, and he's always liked looking at them. The soles of her feet are the same; he knows cuz he's seen them in swimming lessons, all pink and wet and shiny…

Water!

He needs water!

Where's Mum? Is she making dinner or something? It's ages since she last checked up on him!

Has she gone and forgotten about him?

Mum! Mum!

Colin turns and now becomes the suffering Colin who is lying on his back, Colin Number One. Long division. He can't do long division. Or long multiplication. Doctor Who could do those sums in his or her head. Natasha is good at maths. Natasha is the new Doctor Who companion. Colin walks down the street past the fridge and the cabinets that used to be in the kitchen but have now become buildings. What's he doing outside? He's shivering, burning. He has to get to Natasha's house. Natasha will make him feel all better. Stupid David said he saw Natasha one night walking arm-in-arm with Paul Mitchell from Year Eleven. That's not true. Can't be. David tells fibs. And he's a chicken, too. The old World War Two bunker. Colin went down into it first. David was too chicken to go first. He bossed Colin into going first cuz he was too chicken. Nothing down there but Nigel's front room. Nigel's front room with his big, stupid dog. 'You need to learn to stand on your own two feet, Colin. You're a young man now.' That's what Mum said. Why did she say that? Was she telling him she wasn't going to look after him anymore? That he'll have to go away and live somewhere else like his big sister?

Mum! Mum! You're not allowed to leave me! You're not allowed! Don't make me go! You're supposed to look after me and give me a glass of water! That's all I want Mum! Just one glass of water! Please!

Mum!

MUM!

Suddenly there is fire and chaos all around him. He sees flaming bottles being thrown, buildings set on fire. Plate glass windows smashed and shops ransacked or destroyed. A seething crowd armed with crowbars pours howling along the streets, smashing all the cars, turning smooth, sleek bodywork into the brittle angles of road-smash. Smashing everything. Smashing everyone. No-one is safe anymore. The buildings burn and the streets seethe with rampant bloodlust. The sound of jet engines fills the air, loud horribly loud; the vast form of a passenger airliner falls stricken from the sky, a huge, terrifying mass of metal and doomed human lives falling onto the town, performing a giant cartwheel of devastation, erupting into flames and turmoil—

'The End of the World!'

Silence.

It's really dark now; night dark. Colin stares up at the ceiling. The end of the world. It sounded like it was someone outside, out in the street. Or was that just part of the dream.

'The End of the World!'

It *is* someone out in the street, someone sobbing, wretched with despair.

'It's gone! Everything's gone!'

Mum! Mum!

He looks towards his bedroom door. There's no light, no comforting thin rectangle of light. Have Mum and Dad gone to bed? Is it that late? He reaches for the glass on his bedside cabinet. Still empty. Mum would have refilled it if she'd been back since before. Why hasn't she been back?

What's happening?

Mum! Mum!

'It's gone! Everything's gone!'

Mum!

Mum!

MUM!

Chapter Two
'Mum! Mum!'

The next time Colin awakes it is broad daylight and his fever that has broken. He feels a blessed sense of release, as though he has hacked his way through a stifling jungle and emerged into fresh, clean air at the other side.

At first he just lies there, his body enjoying its renewed good health.

He recalls his delirium of the night before, his visions of chaos and destruction… It *was* all a dream, wasn't it? None of that stuff really happened, did it? No, of course not! He was lying right here in his bed, wasn't he? It was all in his head, wasn't it? It was the 'flu! Yeah, it was the 'flu making him dream and see those things, all those horrible things…

But still… That voice outside… That sobbing voice claiming the End of the World… Had he really heard that…?

Well, there's no noise outside now. Nothing. Complete silence.

He takes his watch from the bedside cabinet. Eight o'clock. Mum and Dad should be up by now, he should be hearing the usual sounds of the radio playing in the kitchen, and the sounds of cupboards and crockery.

He hears nothing.

Is it Sunday? Course not! Yesterday was Wednesday; he can't have slept for four days!

So why aren't Mum and Dad up? And his glass; it's still empty. Why hasn't Mum refilled his water glass? She *must* have come in to check on him since yesterday afternoon…

No… he has no recollection, not even a confused one, of his Mum coming in to see him; he feels sure he hasn't seen her… She must have come in when he was asleep then… She must have… But why didn't she refill his glass? Even if he'd been asleep, she would have refilled it so that it was there for him when he woke up…

And why aren't Mum and Dad up right now? Why doesn't he hear those reassuring breakfast sounds? Why does he feel so lonely and neglected?

He pulls back his duvet. He still feels weak and woozy from his illness. He puts his feet into his slippers, wipes the film of sleep from around his eyelids. The washing-up bowl is still there, empty.

Let's pause to describe the boy and the bedroom. Colin is a smallish boy, slender, with tousled fair hair and large blue eyes. From his aura of guileless innocence, 'baby blue' might be an apt description for those peepers. 'Mother-me eyes' would be another.

His bedroom is a smallish one, being part of a smallish, semi-detached house, and like most bedrooms, especially those of youngsters, it is a fair index of its owner. The bed on which he sits is up against the wall and at the side of the room furthest from the window, which looks out (when the curtains aren't drawn) on the Clevelands' small front garden, the street, and the identical row of houses opposite. There is a desk on which sits Colin's games console, a chest of drawers for his clothes, a small bookcase, and to the right of the window a built-in wardrobe full of the toys he is starting to out-grow now, but is still loath to part with.

It goes without saying that the walls are decorated with posters. There is a poster of Spider-Man, that perennial children's favourite. (Colin also has a box full of Spider-Man comics which he has been reading for years in spite of the fact that they carry a 'teen' age recommendation.) There is a film poster for Star Wars Episode 16. And there's a Doctor Who poster, featuring the current Doctor, Sue Perkins.

Noticeably absent from Colin's walls are any football posters. He is not a sporty boy and he's not interested in either playing or watching the beautiful game. As for the bookcase, it ought really to be called a 'media storage unit' as it holds as many Blu-rays, CDs and video games as it does books. Colin doesn't read that many books, and when he does he usually goes with the flow, reading whatever fantasy or adventure novels are popular at the moment. (Frankly, he doesn't understand those non-adventure books they have to study in English now at big school. What's the point of a story with no adventure in it?)

Colin stands up. There's still no sound of movement from within the house.

'Mum!' His voice is dry and cracked. He clears his throat and tries again. 'Mum! Mum!'

Nothing. No answer. No sounds of movement.

They can't both have gone out, can they? Both his parents work, but his Mum has been taking time off while he's been ill. She wouldn't have just gone back to work, would she? Without even knowing if Colin is better or not?

Maybe she's just gone to the shops. Yeah, and she'd have to walk too, if Dad has already taken the car to go to work...

But it's still a bit early for his dad to be setting off ...

Colin crosses to his bedroom window and pulls back the curtains to see if the family car is still parked in the drive.

The car isn't parked in the drive, but that's not the first thing Colin notices. There is smoke in the air. Coils of smoke rising slowly up into a cold, cloudless February sky. Three grey fingers, rising up into the sky from the centre of town.

Fires!

Colin's delirious visions of rioting and burning return to him. Did it really happen, then? Did he really hear that voice? Did the world come to an end last night?

Something happened.

Those coils of smoke... They don't look like the thick smoke you'd see coming up from raging fires... More like the aftermath; the smoke still rising up from smouldering embers...

The familiar queasy fear grips his entrails. End of the World Anxiety.

He looks for signs of disturbance in the street immediately below, but there is nothing; Murdoch Way looks just as it's always looked. One thing he notices: the front door of number 36, one of the houses across the road, is wide open. Somehow it looks wrong, that open door. Apart from the fact it's winter, you'd only expect to see a front door open if someone was about to walk in or out through it; but there is no-one, no sign of movement...

In fact, the whole street is empty; not a car passing by, not a single pedestrian. Murdoch Way looks like you'd expect to see it on a Sunday morning, not on a weekday morning...

And the car isn't there...

Colin bursts out onto the landing.

'Mum! Mum!'

He runs to Mum and Dad's room. The bed is empty, the curtains open. He runs downstairs, into the living room. Here the curtains are drawn, the light is switched on.

Into the kitchen. Here the light is also on, the blind drawn. There are preparations for a meal in this room, but it looks like the preparations for an evening meal, not breakfast. There are vegetables on the dresser, meat from the freezer. This isn't right! Why would Mum be making dinner at breakfast time? Breakfast should be toast and cereals!

What's going on here? Dad already left for work, and Mum starting to make dinner at breakfast time!

Wait a minute. If something *has* happened; if the End of the World *has* happened... Then maybe something's happened to Mum and Dad! Yes, he hasn't seen Mum since yesterday afternoon... Was she starting to make dinner yesterday tea-time when the world started to end? And Dad: maybe the car's not in the drive because he never came home yesterday! Then what's happened to them? They wouldn't leave him on his own like this, not for this long, not if they could help it!

But what could have happened? If the End of the World started when Mum was making dinner, what would she have done? Would she have gone outside to see what was happening? Did she go looking for Dad?

Colin runs through to the hallway. All of Mum's shoes are on the shoe-rack, and both of her coats are hanging on the pegs. She can't have gone out then! She wouldn't go out in her slippers and without a coat! No, she wouldn't! But if it was the End of the World...

The front door is locked.

That proves it! If she went outside the door would be unlocked, wouldn't it? But then; where is Mum?

Was she taken away? Was everyone taken away? Evacuated? Maybe something happened and everyone had to be evacuated... But then, why did they forget him? *How* could they have forgotten him?

They wouldn't just leave him... They *wouldn't*...

The news! He needs to turn on the news to find out what has happened!

Colin rushes into the living room and switches on the telly.

First the manufacturer's logo appears, but then a blank screen and a message: Weak or no signal. Check your cable connections.

He returns to the kitchen and switches on the radio. Static. Colin stabs the search button, but the tuner can find no stations; only static right across the wave-band.

What does it mean? Are the radio signals being blocked by some sort of interference? Or are there just no radio signals being broadcast for the receiver to pick up…?

Next he tries the den, the small room which houses the Cleveland family's PC. Colin powers up the computer and logs on. The internet. The internet news will tell him what's happening.

But when he clicks on a web-browser a 'not connected' window pops up. He tries the other browsers and with the same result. The internet connection is down! No radio, no TV, no internet: it really is the End of the World!

What is he going to do? With Mum and Dad gone, what is he going to do?

Colin starts to cry. He can't help it, poor soul! The world has ended, nowhere is safe anymore, and he's all on his own.

But wait! There's still his big sister. She's away at university up north, but he can still call her up on the phone. Maybe everything's still alright where she is.

The landline telephone is here in the den. He picks up the receiver, tries dialling a number, but it doesn't connect; just static on the line…

He runs upstairs and picks up his mobile. (Not a smartphone; his Mum won't let him have one!) He switches it on and stabs his sister's number. It doesn't connect.

No TV and Radio. No internet. No telephone signals.

Everything's gone! Everything's been taken away! Is it the same everywhere? Is it the same as this all over the world?

Colin remembers hearing about the Millennium Bug. How back at the turn of the century they thought that some glitch on computers might cause all computers to crash. People thought if this happened it would lead to global chaos… It had been a false alarm; nothing had happened then—but something a lot worse must have happened now!

He pulls off his pyjamas and hurriedly dresses himself. Downstairs again, he puts on his trainers and his coat. He opens the front door and steps outside.

Silence.

Half past eight on a weekday morning and not a sound.

Colin walks down the garden path and out onto the street. He looks up and down the road. On the right, the street intersects with the main road going into town. There are always cars going up and down that road in the daytime... But there aren't today. Not a single car passes by.

Above the rooftops those three thin coils of smoke still rise into the steely sky. The fingers of smoke barely move. Once again, those visions from his delirium spring to mind; visions of rioting, smashing and burning...

His eyes drop from the sky to the houses across the road. They seem somehow dead, abandoned. Have all the people in those houses gone away like his Mum and Dad have? The front door of number 36 still gapes open...

But then, in the front window of number 32, the house right across the street, he sees a face! Just above the level of the sill, a girl's face, looking at Colin, as he stands in the middle of the empty street. He knows the girl. Her name is Hayley, she is aged eight and goes to the same primary school Colin used to go to.

So there hasn't been a mass evacuation! Not unless that girl got left behind as well...

She continues to stare intently at Colin, her expression unreadable. Colin starts to walk across the road. The face suddenly disappears; it looks as if unseen hands have just dragged her forcibly away from the window. This pulls Colin up in his tracks. He stands on the pavement in front of the house. The windows remain tenantless. He wonders if he should go up to the door and knock, held back by the feeling that he will not be a welcome caller.

And then a sound reaches his ears. It's the sound of one of

those musical car-horns. The sound draws closer, coming from the main road. Car engines become audible, cars driving very fast; and something else: the sound of wild screaming and yelling.

A car, driving at speed, turns into the street from the main road. The car races past Colin. He only has a brief glimpse of the occupants, but enough for him to see that they are a family and that their expressions are terrified. And now two more vehicles turn into the road, a car and a pick-up truck. Both vehicles are packed with whooping, war-crying youth. They race noisily past, in hot pursuit of the first car. Colin stands rooted to the spot with fear.

When the cars have disappeared from sight and silence returns to the street, Colin comes back to life. The wolfpack is hunting, and he has only one thought, one imperative thought—and that is to initiate the Colin Cleveland Doomsday Defence Plan.

And with young Colin, to think is to act: he pelts back across the street to his house, slams and locks the front door, charges up the stairs to his bedroom, pulls off his shoes and coat, throws himself onto his bed, pulls the duvet over himself and curls up in a ball.

Doomsday Defence Plan initiated and now fully operational!

Chapter Three
'You Don't Think You're the Only One, Do You?'

It's hunger that eventually drives Colin to abandon the Doomsday Defence Plan and to venture out of doors.

At first he's too terrified to even think about food, and then, when his appetite does return, he survives mainly on snacks. There is plenty of food in the house, but unfortunately Colin doesn't know how to prepare a meal. He can operate the microwave, but that's about as far as it goes.

Days pass, and the supply of ready to eat snacks and

microwavable food begins to dwindle.

Most of this time Colin just spends in his room cocooned under his duvet. Now that the worst has happened, his End of the World Anxiety has increased from chronic to acute, aggravated by the fact that he doesn't even know exactly *how* or *why* the world has ended, only that it has.

And now, more than a week has passed, neither of his parents have returned, there's still no internet, no television or telephone signals, his stomach is starting to rumble and he knows no more about the whys and wherefores of the situation outside than he did on that first day.

From time to time he has peaked cautiously out of his window to see what's happening in the street outside. Most of the time nothing has been happening at all, but sometimes he has seen activity. Once he saw Hayley from across the road drive off with her parents in their car. At first he had thought they must be leaving for good, but then he'd heard the car come back and he'd returned to the window in time to see them hurriedly unloading bags full of groceries and rush with them into the house. Had they bought all those groceries? Colin wondered. Or had they stolen them? Were the shops still open after the End of the World, or were they just being looted?

During the daytime the town has been quiet, but at night it's another story, because then the wolfpacks come out of their dens and take to the streets, and the howling of their revels can be heard, sometimes distant, sometimes alarmingly close. On one occasion one of these packs had swept through Murdoch Way and sent Colin quaking beneath his duvet; but they had surged past without stopping, and left only minimal damage in their wake.

The street is silent, motionless when Colin, well wrapped-up against the cold, the earflaps of his furry hat securely buttoned beneath his chin, steps out through the front door of his house. Nothing has really changed since that morning over a week ago when he last ventured outside, the morning after the End of the

World. The sky was blue then, today it is blue as well, flecked with broken cloud…

Down the garden path and out onto the pavement. He looks down the street towards the intersection. No sign of traffic on the main road.

He feels unsafe. He doesn't want to be out here. If he had food he would go straight back inside. But his hollow stomach makes its own demands. He has to find food.

And then he sees that he's being watched. That little girl Hayley again, observing him from the front window of her house.

An idea. Should he go up to Hayley's house? Knock on the front door? Tell them he's lost his Mum and Dad? Tell them he's hungry?

Colin doesn't know Hayley's mum and dad. He's never spoken to them, and Colin isn't good at talking to grown-ups, except for grown-ups he knows really well—but he decides to try his luck anyway. He crosses the road to Hayley's house, hesitates at the end of their drive. The girl hasn't moved from the window; she still regards him with an expressionless face. Is she expecting him to come up to the door? Why doesn't she make some gesture, smile at him or something?

Swallowing his shyness, Colin walks up the drive and rings the front doorbell. He steps back to look at Hayley in the front window, just in time to see someone pull her back into the room, out of sight. Same as happened the last time.

Are they going to pretend they're not in?

He already feels like he's not wanted but he gives the doorbell a second ring. No response.

After this he gives up and walks away.

The door of number 36 is still wide open. There's no car in the drive, so Colin thinks the people there must have gone away after the world ended. He scans the houses on both sides of the street, wondering how many of them have also gone away, and how many of them are holed up indoors.

He sets off towards the main road. This road used to be a busy thoroughfare, but now it is a still-life picture.

Onward he walks, through the unnatural silence that. His plan is to make his way to the car showroom where Dad works, armed with a ragged notion that both Dad and Mum might be there. His theory is that Mum, when the world ended that afternoon, was worried when Dad didn't come home, and so she set off (without stopping to put on shoes or coat) to find him, and that she had made it to the showroom and they are both still there because for some reason or other they haven't been able to leave.

I did say it was a ragged notion.

Colin's Mum has always been the dominant presence in his life, the proactive parent, the voice of authority, the voice of instruction, the soother of tears, the solver of every problem; omniscient, infallible and indestructible.

One factor of Colin's End of the World Anxiety as it had started to emerge, was the growing realisation that actually his Mum *wasn't* indestructible, that the things in the world that even *she* couldn't protect him from. Amongst the horrors he had absorbed from the television news were those accounts of children killed in front of their mothers and (even worse!) mothers killed in front of their children. Perhaps it was for this reason that Colin was never able to confide in his mum about this particular problem; why he was never able to tell her about his End of the World Anxiety.

Colin's Dad's role, conversely, has always been a minor one, an ancillary parent whose main function is to crack bad jokes. Back when he was little, Colin had actually thought Dad's jokes were funny, but he has long since outgrown that phase. His Dad's jokes are groaners. (According to Colin's sister, it's normal for dads to make bad jokes, and that people even call those groaners 'dad jokes.')

As he proceeds along the road into town, Colin starts to see the first signs of the violence ushered in by the End of the World: a house across the street, a burnt-out shell. This blackened corpse is a stark sign of the ravages of the marauding wolfpacks.

Other signs follow. A car, over-turned, smashed up, in the middle of the road. A convenience store, its plate-glass windows shattered, the interior looted.

But still not a soul in sight. Not a sound.

He reaches the turning onto Larch Street. His friend Nigel lives down this road. Should he take a detour and call for Nigel? Just to see if he's okay? Maybe Nigel can tell him more about what's happened… Of course, technically he and Nigel haven't made friends again since their last falling out—but things are different now, aren't they? Nigel will come to the door, won't he?

Yes. He'll give it a go. He turns down Larch Street and comes to Nigel's house, number thirteen. He goes up to the front door and knocks.

His knocking elicits the familiar barking of Nigel's mongrel dog, just like it's always done. And if the dog's home, its owners must be home! And sure enough, a shadow against the frosted glass and the door opens cautiously. It's Nigel's mum. She regards Colin with an expression that isn't encouraging.

'What do you want?'

Her voice doesn't sound encouraging either.

'Is Nigel in?' ventures Colin.

It's the usual line, the thing he's always said whenever he's called round for Nigel and his mum has answered the door. Of course, when he says this, he really means 'Does Nigel want to come out and play?' or 'Can I come in and see Nigel?'; but on this occasion, Nigel's mum chooses to take the inquiry literally.

'He's *in*, yes,' she says. 'What about it?'

Colin doesn't know how to deal with this unexpected hostility. He starts to cry. 'My Mum and Dad have gone,' he sniffles. 'I've been on my own for *ages*. I haven't got any food…'

'Well, *we* can't feed you,' is all the answer he gets. 'We've only got enough for ourselves.'

'But what's *happened*?' blubbers Colin. 'Where are my Mum and Dad?'

'Nobody *knows* where they've all gone! The world's just gone to hell in a hand-basket, hasn't it?'

Nigel's face appears beside that of his mother in the half-opened doorway.

'Hey! You should go to the school, Colin,' he says, flashing an encouraging smile. 'They'll look after you there.'

'The school? You mean our school?'

'Yeah. They've got food there and places to sleep for people who've lost their parents.'

'You mean other people have lost their parents?' wonders Colin.

'*Of course* they have!' snaps Nigel's mum. 'You don't think you're the only one, do you?'

'Well, *I* don't know! I haven't been out since it happened! I don't even *know* what's happened!'

Nigel opens his mouth to say something but his mum cuts in. 'Look, we can't stand here talking; it's letting the cold in. Just go to the school.'

'Yeah, they'll look after you,' confirms Nigel. 'You'll be alright there.'

The closing of the door cuts off any further valedictions.

Colin decides to take the advice and sets off schoolwards; he's already heading in the right direction for it, and it's much nearer than the car showroom.

That brief colloquy has given Colin much food for thought. So other kids have lost their mums and dads! And they're looking after them at the school...! But what's happened to all those mums and dads? Where have they gone?

He arrives at the school gates. They are firmly closed. Between the vertical bars he sees the schoolyard and the surrounding buildings, typically grey and functional. There is not a soul in sight. How's he supposed to get inside? The back entrance...?

An intercom panel is built into one of the gateposts. Colin presses one of the buttons experimentally. Will it even work? Intercoms are like telephones, aren't they? And the phones aren't working...

But then the speaker crackles into life. A male voice speaks tinnily.

'Hello? Can I help you?'

'Er, yes; they said you were looking after people who've lost their mums and dads…'

'Yes, that's correct. Are you a student here?'

'Yes. Colin Cleveland.'

'Good. Hang on and we'll open the gates for you, and when they open go straight to main reception. One of us will be waiting for you there.'

'Okay,' says Colin.

The speaker falls silent. Colin isn't sure, but the voice sounded like it was Mr Brandon, his form teacher and one of the science teachers. So it must be the teachers who are looking after the orphaned students…

A loud click, and the gates slide open. Colin enters and, as directed makes his way across the schoolyard to the building on the right, in which the main reception area and administrative offices are located. The doors open obligingly and he steps into the foyer with its freestanding display boards of students' artwork. Colin walks inside. It's warm here; the heating is switched on. The reception office is empty; there doesn't seem to be anyone here…

'Hey, you!'

Colin spins round, galvanised by the musical voice, and sees a girl with brown skin, silky black hair and the warmest, most beautiful smile in the world.

It's Natasha! Natasha, the love of his life!

Chapter Four
'What We're Looking at is a Global Catastrophe'

The girl of Colin's dreams advances, still smiling at him. She is dressed in jeans and a woollen jumper, trainers on her feet.

'I… I…' begins Colin. He always gets tongue-tied around Natasha.

Natasha's smile of greeting turns to one of compassion, and

then her arms are around him, hugging him tightly, and the tears are streaming down Colin's face.

'I... I...' he blubbers.

They separate. Natasha wipes a tear from Colin's cheek.

'Your mum and dad disappeared, did they?' she asks.

'Ye-yes...'

'Same here,' says Natasha. 'Both my parents vanished when it happened. How did you find out we were here?'

'N-Nigel. I... I called for Nigel...'

'Well, I'm glad you found us. You're the twenty-first. We're all camped out here. Safety in numbers, right? Mr Brandon and Miss Lantier are looking after us. They're waiting for us in the staff room. Come on.'

They set off along the corridor. So it *was* Mr Brandon on the speaker! And Miss Lantier's here as well...

'So, where have you been since the Incident happened?' asks Natasha.

'What incident?'

'*The* Incident. That's what they're calling it. You didn't even know that? Where have you been since last week?'

'I... I've been at home...'

'At home, all this time? You haven't talked to anyone?'

'N-not till t-today...'

'Blimey. You can't have a clue what's going on then, can you?'

'The world ended, didn't it?'

'Well, yes. Pretty much.'

They walk into the staff-room, the lounge where the teachers of Park Lane Comprehensive gathered during breaktimes for their much-needed caffeine fix and air their grievances about their jobs and their students.

Two teachers rise from their chairs to greet the newcomer: Mr Brandon, dressed in brown tweeds, a short, stocky man with a square face and a crown of wild, wiry hair; and, as advertised, Miss Lantier, a French teacher in both senses of the word. Short-haired and elfin-featured, with a beauty mark just above her chin, she has long been considered by the male half of the student body one of the most shaggable teachers in the school.

There is a third person present, not advertised, and who is something of an unwelcome surprise to Colin. Paul Mitchell, a Year Eleven boy. Paul Mitchell, who David said he once saw walking arm-in-arm with Natasha.

'A new recruit,' announces Natasha. 'And guess what? He's been hiding away on his own since the Incident happened. Hasn't got a clue what's going on.'

'No more do the rest of us, when it comes down to it,' says Mr Brandon. 'Come in, come in… Hargreaves, isn't it?'

'Colin Cleveland,' says Colin. 'I'm in your form.'

'Yes, yes, so you are. So, you haven't ventured out till today? We'd better fill you in then. As much as we know ourselves, at any rate. Take your things off and have a seat.'

Removing his hat and his coat, Colin lowers himself onto one of the chairs.

'You'll know about the loss of radio signals, I assume,' continues Mr Brandon. 'And no doubt you'll have heard some of the racket that's going on during the nights.'

'Yes,' confirms Colin.

'And you know about the disappearances?'

'No,' says Colin. 'Not really.'

Mr Brandon scratches his tousled hair. 'Oh. Well, to put it in a nutshell, about half the population has gone.'

'Gone?' echoes Colin. And then his stomach rumbles loudly. He blushes.

'Oh, are you hungry?' asks Mr Brandon.

'Starving,' admits Colin.

'Of course you are. Stupid of me. That's why you came out of hiding, was it? No food left.' He gets up, looks vaguely around. 'Could someone pop over to the canteen…? Rustle up a sandwich or something for young Hargreaves…'

'Cleveland.'

'Ah, yes, Cleveland.'

'I'll go,' offers Natasha brightly.

She departs. 'Food's all in the canteen, but I can offer you a hot drink,' says Mr Brandon. 'Tea or coffee?'

'Tea, please,' says Colin.

Mr Brandon shambles over to a dresser where there is a kettle, mugs and the other appurtenances for making hot drinks.

'Black or white?'

'White, please. And two sugars.'

Mr Brandon switches the kettle on and takes a carton of milk from the mini-fridge. 'Two sugars, eh? Y'know, George Orwell argued there was no point adding sugar to tea, because if you did you just tasted the sugar, and not the tea. But I suppose you youngsters like your food to be strongly flavoured...'

'So, you have been all alone since the Incident 'appened?' speaks up Miss Lantier.

'Yes. Mum disappeared and Dad never came back from work.'

'And you have no brothers or sisters?'

'I've got a sister, but she's away at university.'

Mr Brandon returns with Colin's mug of tea. He reseats himself.

'Right,' he resumes, clearing his throat. And then: 'Where were we?'

'You were telling him about the Incident,' supplies Miss Lantier.

'So I was. Well, the Incident occurred Wednesday last, at precisely four fifty-nine p.m. I assume you know that much.'

'Not really,' says Colin. 'I had the 'flu that day. I was really ill in bed.'

'Oh, I see. You really were out of it then. Well, it was at exactly that time that the electromagnetic interference started up; suddenly there was no TV, radio, internet or telephone signals. And at that same instant half the population disappeared. Literally vanished without a trace.'

Colin wasn't expecting this. 'Half the population?'

'Well, nobody's conducted a census, but as far as we can work out it's about half the population. One moment they were there, the next they weren't.'

'Except nobody actually saw anyone vanish,' speaks up Paul

Mitchell.

'Yes, that's the curious thing,' affirms Mr Brandon. 'It seems that nobody who was actually being looked at disappeared before another person's eyes.'

'I'm not sure I understand…'

'Well, say you had two people in a room: two people looking at each other, talking to each other. When the clocks turned four fifty-nine and the Incident occurred, either both of them would have disappeared or neither of them. But, say if you were in a room with someone and happened *not* to be looking at them at that moment, then either that person or you yourself would have vanished. Do you see what I'm saying? As Mitchell here said, nobody actually saw anyone vanish. But it must have been instantaneous, though. No flash of light. No puff of smoke. One second they were there, the next they were gone.'

'That must be what happened to Mum!' cries Colin. 'She was downstairs and I was upstairs! I thought she must have gone out, but her coat and her shoes were still there. And she was just starting to make the dinner…'

'Yes, I'm afraid your mother must have disappeared,' confirms Mr Brandon.

'Bu-but…' Colin stammers, struggling with this revelation. 'Wh-what happened to her…? All the people who disappeared… Are they… are they… dead…?'

Mr Brandon sighs. 'I'm sorry, Hargreaves, but that's just what we don't know. What we do is that the mass-disappearance occurred at exactly the same moment the internet went down and the radio and television signals were lost. The exact same moment. As far as I see it, the people who disappeared were either killed on the spot or they were taken away. Personally, I incline to the latter theory, because as a scientist I find it much harder to credit the idea of a force that could completely destroy living matter without leaving any residue, than I do the idea of mass-teleportation to some unknown location.'

'So, the people who disappeared could be still alive and okay?' eagerly, from Colin.

'I think it's possible, yes. But whether they'll ever be returned to us is another matter.'

It is at this moment Natasha returns, bearing a generously-filled sandwich on a plate.

'Here you go,' she says, presenting it to Colin.

'Thank you,' says Colin.

He tucks into it hungrily.

Mr Brandon smiles at this display of appetite. 'Yes, we still need to eat, don't we? Whatever life throws at us, we still have to keep our bodies up and running.'

'We have just been telling Colin about the Incident,' Miss Lantier tells Natasha.

'And now for the aftermath,' says Mr Brandon. 'Well, it doesn't take a genius to work out what would happen after half the population suddenly disappeared and all means of mass communication was cut off. Panic set in. Insanity. Total breakdown of law and order. People took to the streets with the usual results. And those who didn't take to the streets just barricaded themselves into their houses, just like you did, Hargreaves.'

'Cleveland,' says Natasha.

'Cleveland. You know all about the street violence, because you will have heard it even if you haven't witnessed any of it. What you won't know is that over the past week the street violence has resolved itself into gang warfare; two rival gangs have emerged, and they've colour-coded themselves: the yellows and blues. The good news is that they've taken to only coming out at night, so it's fairly safe to move around during the day. Not that many people are taking advantage of that fact. No, most people are staying dug-in in their homes—and if they're waiting for help to arrive, I'd say they're waiting in vain.

'You see, the odds are that what has happened here has happened everywhere. It isn't just here in Eastchester. We've heard from people who have been to other towns and villages since the Incident, and we've had visitors from other towns and villages as well. The same thing has occurred everywhere that we know of. Mass disappearances and total electro-magnetic disruption. And I don't think it's confined to just this country, either: I believe what we're looking at is a global catastrophe.'

'What we don't know is who's behind it,' says Natasha.

'Yes, that's the million-dollar question. Or rather it's three questions: *Who* did it? *How* did they do it? And *why* did they do it? Have we been softened up for an invasion? Then where are the invaders? It's over a week now since the Incident, and nothing further has happened. As to *how*: well, to blanket the entire world with electromagnetic disruption, you'd have to have tampered with the Earth's ionosphere itself. And then the disappearance of half the population: was it just timed to coincide with the commencement of the signal disruption, or was it somehow part of the same phenomenon? And then *who* did it? Well, I know that everybody in the room agrees with me on this, but considering the level of technology that must have been used to effect the Incident, I'm inclined to believe that an extraterrestrial force must be involved.'

'Aliens?' gasps Colin.

'In a nutshell, yes.'

Miss Lantier is clearly one of the dissentient faction here. 'Then where are these aliens of yours?' she demands. 'Why 'aven't they landed?'

'You're thinking in human terms,' Mr Brandon tells her. 'These beings may not have caused the Incident because they want to invade and occupy us; they may have other motives, motives we couldn't understand. As for where they are, perhaps they're observing us even as we speak, from somewhere out in space—or perhaps they *are* already here on Earth, only we can't see them.'

Aliens. This strikes a nerve with Colin. His Dad has always had an interest in the paranormal (although Mum was a sceptic), and the bookcase in the den at home contains a whole shelf devoted to his collection of books on the subject: books on UFOs and the surrounding conspiracies, books on ghosts and haunted houses, books on cryptids and mythical creatures—in short, all the usual material fans of the occult thrive upon.

Colin had once made a very serious mistake: He had started reading some of these books, and he had started reading them at a time when his mind was already disturbed by his emerging End of the World anxiety. The result was, reading these accounts of the paranormal, and believing every word of them, they had just added fuel to the fire of his anxiety. To think that all this stuff actually existed! Just out of sight, just under the surface, hiding in the darkness, lurking in the shadows, on the borders of perception; it terrified him.

And now, here's Mr Brandon, a figure of fun for both his students and his colleagues on account of his scruffy absent-mindedness and inability to remember people's names; a figure of fun, but still a physicist, a teacher of science, and here he is calmly saying that he thinks aliens *do* exist, and that they're the ones who caused the Incident, the End of the World!

Miss Lantier now speaks up. 'I think this is enough talk for now. Colin has more than enough to process, I think.' To Natasha and Paul. 'Why do not you two show Colin around the sleeping and living areas we have set up. He can meet the other students who are staying with us, and this afternoon we can assist Colin with moving his belongings to the school.'

Voicing their acquiescence to this plan of action, Natasha and Paul have risen from their chairs, and Natasha holds out to Colin a hand, brown on the back and with a rosy-pink palm and finger-pads, and offers him a smile which expels, at least for the moment, all worrisome thoughts of extraterrestrials from his mind.

Chapter Five
'Beep-Beep, Beep-Beep...'

Is Natasha going out with Paul Mitchell?

Colin just isn't sure. On the 'she *is* going out with him' side there's the fact that David said he once saw them walking along together, arm-in-arm; there's the fact that David plays guitar in an indie rock band, and that Natasha's into indie rock herself, so it'd make sense that she'd fancy a boy who was in a band; there's also the fact that they seem pretty chummy together from what he's seen of them today…

However, on the 'she *isn't* going out with him' side there's the fact that David is a fibber, and he might just have told Colin he'd seen Natasha out with David to make Colin feel jealous; in addition to this there's the fact that Colin's never seen the two of them hanging out together at school; and to crown it all there's the fact that Natasha is a Year Eight student, while Paul Mitchell's all the way up in Year Eleven—which, by secondary school standards, would make it one heck of an age-difference relationship!

But even if Natasha isn't going out with Paul Mitchell already, she might easily end up going out with him, now that they're spending so much time together—and with Paul Mitchell as a rival, Colin knows he hasn't got a chance! But then, Colin never considered he had a chance of going out with Natasha anyway; he has always looked up to the girl as being unobtainable, out of his league. Natasha is one of those grown-up-for-her-age girls, while Colin is (and let's be honest here) the complete opposite. Natasha is into all those indie rock bands that no-one's ever heard of, while Colin listens to download chart pop music.

Of course, one easy way to resolve this dilemma would be for Colin to simply ask Natasha whether or not she's going out with Paul Mitchell, and right now, when he happens to have Natasha all to himself, might be considered the ideal time for it—but actually putting this particular question to her is, as Colin now discovers, going to require more courage from him than he can lay his hands on at the moment.

The two of them are heading into Eastchester town centre. Colin has insisted that he still wants to visit his original intended destination, the car showroom where his dad works. That ragged notion that his Dad might still be there persists. He has accepted now that his Mum must have been one of the people who disappeared when the Incident occurred; all the evidence points to that: but he doesn't know anything at all about what happened to Dad; all he knows is that he never came home. The others keep telling him that the chances are that he also disappeared—but what if he didn't? What if something else prevented him from coming home…?

So, in the end, Natasha announced that she would accompany Colin into town to check out the car showroom, and hopefully set his mind at rest.

Colin has been given the guided tour of the set-up at the school. It was weird seeing the place, usually teaming with noisy adolescent life, so quiet and empty. Two first floor classrooms have been turned into dormitories: one for boys, and one for girls. The tables and chairs had been stacked at one end of the rooms, and the space filled with mattresses. The students' mattresses and bed linen were their own, brought from their homes to the school. They would be doing the same for Colin this afternoon: Colin will also be packing up his clothes and everything else he will be needing for his extended stay at the school.

The students themselves were in the school library, which has been turned into a sort of common room. There were twenty in number, twelve boys and eight girls, none of them people Colin knows very well. In fact, it so happens there were no other Year Eight boys amongst the refugees, and with it being the case that Colin's (small) circle of friends are all (on account of his geeky interests and chronic shyness) boys, and all (because at school students of the same year tend to herd together) in Year Eight, the absence of any Year Eight boys from the group, meant that none of his friends are amongst the refugees.

'No, I think this is all some big experiment,' says Natasha.

Colin has just asked her whether she believes Mr Brandon's theory that the Incident was caused by aliens. (A much safer question than asking her whether she and Paul Mitchell are an item.)

'An Experiment?'

'Yeah. The Incident and everything that's happening now. It's all part of some great big experiment. And us, we're all the guinea pigs.'

'Who's doing this experiment?'

'The Government. That's who it is. I mean you've noticed that we've still got water, electricity and gas, right? All the utilities. That means there must still be people at the power stations and whatnot, and they're still doing their jobs, keeping everything running. You see? There's organisation behind it, isn't there? It's the Government. I bet it's all the G7 countries working together. You know what the G7 is, right?'

Colin doesn't, but not wanting to appear stupid, says that he does. He says: 'But what about what Mr Brandon said? About how the technology they used to make the Incident happen was too advanced for humans?'

'It might be more advanced than any technology we *know* about—but I bet they've got all this secret technology as well; stuff they don't *want* us to know about. Like all the radio signals being jammed: Brandon says they'd have to mess around with the ionosphere or something to make that happen: but me and Paul, we think it's satellites that are doing it. They've got a whole network of special satellites in orbit, and they're sending out these jamming signals.'

'Why are they doing that?'

'That's the experiment they've set up, isn't it? They want to see how we'll get on now, with no internet, no computers, no news, and no police or army or anything.'

'And where d'you think they've taken the people they teleported away?'

Natasha puts her arm around Colin's shoulder. 'I don't think Brandon's right about that, either, Colin. I don't think they've been teleported away; I think they're all dead; I think they all got zapped out of existence; my parents, yours, all of them.'

As they proceed through the empty streets heading further into town, Colin, absorbing Natasha's sombre prognosis, sees more and more signs of the nocturnal unrest; more burnt-out cars and buildings.

He's never talked to Natasha before as much as this as he has today. Not once! He's impressed with how mature she sounds with all her opinions about the Incident.

They turn onto one of the main shopping streets. Here the destruction is even worse. Not a single plate-glass window has survived unbroken; some shops have been gutted by fire, others looted and vandalised, their contents thrown out into the street and smashed up. Colin's heart misses a beat when he thinks he sees corpses in the road ahead. But then he sees that they are mannequins, thrown into the street from a big clothing store.

The sight of all this destruction unnerves young Colin. This is just the kind of wolfpack violence that has always fuelled his anxiety, and here it is, right in the centre of Eastchester, in the shopping streets he knows so well.

'Do the gangs come out every night?' he asks Natasha.

'Yep, regular as clockwork,' she confirms. 'Old Brandon says the rioting is like a disease; and he says it's still spreading. He might be right. We've already lost some people from the school. There were thirty of us kids to start with.'

Colin is alarmed. 'People staying at the school have been killed by the rioters?'

'No, not killed: joined them. Ran off in the night to join the gangs. It's contagious, you see.'

They turn a corner. Colin's heart leaps. He sees people! At the far end of the street, in the middle of the road: a large group of people!

'There they are! One of the gangs!'

'It's not one of the gangs,' Natasha assures him. 'I know who these people are. They're harmless; don't worry.'

Reassured, but still confused, Colin stares hard at the advancing crowd as the distance between them closes. There's something strange about them. They are all walking slowly, awkwardly, shambling along, and each of them holding one arm aloft.

'They look like zombies!' exclaims Colin.

'They are,' confirms Natasha. 'Smartphone zombies we call them.'

'But zombies are dangerous, aren't they?' argues Colin.

'These zombies aren't, believe me.'

As they approach the group, Colin sees that it's smartphones being held in those hands held up in the air. The zombies walk with slow, jerking steps, not looking where they're going, faces expressionless, eyes fixed on the skies.

A low murmur becomes audible. The zombies are intoning something under their breaths. As they draw alongside, Colin makes out the words (or rather the one word):

'Beep-beep, beep-beep. Beep-beep, beep-beep...'

'What's wrong with them?'

'They're smartphone addicts,' explains Natasha. 'They've turned into lost souls since the interference started and they lost the internet. Now they just wander the streets all day, trying to get a bar on their phones...'

'Beep-beep, beep-beep. Beep-beep, beep-beep...'

The car showroom where Colin's dad worked hasn't escaped the carnage. The huge plate-glass window facing the street has been smashed; the instrument of this destruction, a van, is still lodged half in the showroom and half on the pavement.

Negotiating the splintered glass, Colin and Natasha step into the showroom. From previous visits Colin remembers what it used to be like here: the latest-model cars on this display, the sleek, polished bodywork gleaming under the fluorescent lights... Today, the cars in the showroom all look like exhibits from motorway pile-ups: windscreens smashed, bodywork contorted, upholstery ripped out and strewn across the floor like spilt innards...

But in spite of this destruction, the showroom is still open for business. At least, the manager and Colin's dad's boss, Mr Newton, is on the shop-floor. He stands beside a wrecked coupé, and removing a card reading £20,000 from the dented bonnet, listlessly replaces it with a card reading £5,000.

'Mr Newton!' calls out Colin, as they approach the man.

'Oh, hullo Colin,' replies Newton.

He seems rather vague, thinks Colin. He must be upset about all his cars.

'This is Natasha,' says Colin.

'Hullo,' again. 'Are you here to buy a car? We've got some lovely—'

'We're here about my dad,' interrupts Colin. 'What happened to him? Is he here?'

'Your dad?' echoes Newton. 'Oh yes, Brian. No, no... He's not here... He's gone...'

Colin's heart sinks. 'Gone. You mean he disappeared?'

'Disappeared? Yes, I suppose he must have...' says Newton.

'Can you tell us what happened?' asks Natasha practically.

'Let me see... Oh, yes. I remember... I sent him upstairs to the office. He never got there... Yes, that what happened..."

Natasha puts a hand on Colin's shoulder.

'I did warn you...'

So, it's official, then. Both his parents are among the disappeared. He's an orphan.

'Can I interest you in a car?' ventures Newton, indicating the coupé. 'This year's model, turbo fuel delivery, automatic transmission, cruise control. Comes with a three-year warranty... Some minor shelf-wear...'

Chapter Six
'Now Pack It In Or You'll Get Worse Next Time!'

If only Miss Lantier had stayed with Colin that afternoon.

If only she had stayed with him after driving him back to his house in the school minibus, Colin would probably never have met Chorley at all and his story would have been a very different one. But fate can play these tricks on us, and fate decreed that

Colin would be left alone; that after dropping him off, Miss Lantier would decide to leave Colin to start packing his things while she went to a nearby service station to fill up with petrol and scavenge for supplies.

Nothing bad is destined to befall the French French teacher when she heads off on this impromptu expedition; she will return, but she will return too late and Colin will already be gone, snatched away by cruel fate.

It's not safe in post-Incident Eastchester for youngsters like Colin, people who've lost their natural guardians, to stay by themselves in their homes. Aside from the nocturnal menace of the blue and yellow gangs, it is known that untenanted houses are being targeted by looters, people who would not consider one lone child much of an obstacle. At the school the orphaned youngsters can be supervised, looked after. As Natasha has said: safety in numbers.

Arrived at his house, Colin goes upstairs to his room and he opens the drawers and starts sorting out his clothes. He has a sports bag and a wheelie suitcase, and he is to pack as many of his belongings that can be fitted into them.

Living at his own school… It seems strange, but then everything is strange now that the world has ended; everything is turned topsy turvy. At the school he will have to have his mattress on a classroom floor, along with all the other orphan boys; it'll be kind of like camping.

At least he won't be alone.

He recalls that talk he had had with his Mum not that long ago, that talk where she had told Colin he needed to start learning to stand on his own two feet. Because although in many ways a stern and exacting parent, Colin's Mum had also spoilt him rotten, basically doing everything for him. (It was only very recently she stopped running his baths for him!) Belatedly she must have realised her mistake: hence the talk. But unfortunately, what with Colin already being in a precarious state of mind, the result of being told by his mother that he was too clingy and dependent, that he had to stop relying on other people all the time, that he should start learning to stand on his own two feet; the result was to send Colin into a state of panic, convinced that his Mum was about to abandon him completely!

And now she has abandoned him. Not intentionally, but the result is the same. Colin has always craved feminine protection; he misses being mothered by his mother and being big-sistered by his big sister—and now that have been removed from his life, is he actually going to follow his mother's advice and start being more independent? Nope, because he's found two substitutes to cling to instead: Miss Lantier as a replacement mother, and Natasha as a replacement sister…

The sound of voices outside now breaks into Colins thoughts.

Young voices. And coming from the back garden.

Fearful, Colin crosses the landing to his sister's bedroom, cautiously pulls back the curtain and looks down from the window. The Clevelands' back garden is a small one. Boxed in by flimsy creosoted fencing, flowerbeds along the borders, an expanse of turf with a hopscotch path of slabs leading from the patio to the garden shed at the far end. An eight-year-old silver birch spreads its branches over the roof of the shed, a tree Colin brought home from school in a margarine tub when he was four, and which, against all expectations has actually thrived. (All the class were given one, but nobody else's did.)

The garden has been invaded. Three young people are there; three young people Colin knows only too well. The leader of the trio is Bradley, school bully, and bane of Colin's life. And with Bradley are his two cohorts, skinny little Ferret, and big Janice, the scariest girl in Year Eight.

And what's more, they're armed. Bradley is handling a scissor-knife, flicking it in and out of its sheath; Janice carries a big hatchet, the haft resting on her shoulder; while the Ferret is swinging a bicycle chain in the air.

What are they doing here? Have they come to get him?

'You sure this is the place?' asks the Ferret, neatly beheading some plants with his bicycle chain.

‘’Course I’m sure,’ comes the answer from Bradley.

‘But you don’t know if he’s here,’ pursues the Ferret. ‘He might’ve disappeared.’

‘Curtains are closed,’ remarks Janice.

As her eyes turn to the upper windows, Colin quickly drops the curtain and crouches down on the floor. Did she see him?

‘Let’s see what’s in here,’ comes Darren’s voice. ‘Janice?’

The next thing Colin hears is a fearful splintering impact. And then another.

Dizzy with fear, Colin peeps through the window again. As the others watch, Janice is swinging the hatchet at the shed door, the blade splintering the thin wood around the lock. She heaves the hatchet again and the door is open.

The three intruders go into the shed. If he wanted to, Colin could now take an inventory of the contents of the shed as they come flying out through the door: first Colin’s (punctured) bike, then the lawn-mower, the garden furniture, the gardening tools, tins of paint; all are thrown out into the garden by the laughing trio.

The desecraters now emerge from the shed. Janice lays into the lawn mower with her hatchet. Bradley prises the lid from one of the paint tins with his knife; he then hurls its contents across the garden, leaving a swathe of pastel-shaded enamel across the turf. Ferret and Janice join in and the other cans are soon opened and their contents sent flying, making a Jackson Pollock of the whole garden; the fence, the turf, the bike, the deck chairs, the silver birch tree.

The three laughing vandals step back to admire their handiwork.

‘Nice bit of decorating,’ declares Bradley.

Please go now, thinks Colin, mourning his ruined bicycle. You’ve had your fun; just go.

But Bradley now turns to face the house.

‘Now we’ll have a look inside,’ he says.

‘You think he’s in there? He *can’t* be,’ opines the Ferret. ‘If anyone was in, they’d have come out to shout at us by now.’

'Not if it's just him,' retorts Bradley. 'If it's just him, he'll be hiding, the little chicken-shit. Anyhow, even if he's not in, we can still have a look to see if there's anything worth nicking.'

The trio now cross to the patio, moving out of Colin's field of vision.

He sinks to the floor again. Oh no. They're going to come in here! They'll find him!

'Door's locked,' he hears. 'Go on, Janice.'

Thwack! comes the sound of an impact. Colin can picture it; big Janice pitching the hatchet into the door frame.

Thwack! Thwack! Thwack!

The house door is much sturdier than that of the shed; it takes more and heavier blows of the hatchet. But finally, jubilant cries announce success. The door is open!

Colin has been sitting paralysed with fear, but now he is galvanised into action. He runs out onto the landing.

'Hello, hello, anyone home?' calls out Bradley's voice. 'We've come to read the meter!'

Can he make it? Can he make it down the stairs and out through the front door?

'See, I told you,' comes the Ferret's voice. 'There's no-one here. They all must've vanished.'

They're in the front room! He's too late! His retreat is cut off.

'Never mind,' says Bradley. 'Let's find Cleveland's room. I wanna mess his stuff up.'

Now they're coming upstairs! Panicking, Colin runs into his own bedroom. He knows that when there are actually intruders inside the house, his previous Doomsday Defence Plan of cowering under the duvet just isn't going to cut it. There is only one possible hiding-place left to him: the built-in cupboard, where all his old toys are stored: a much better place to cower in! Quick as a flash he is inside, fingers between the slats of the Venetian door to close it behind him. He hears footsteps thudding up the stairs as he huddles down in the furthest corner, behind a stack of boxes, making himself as small as he can.

'This is his parents' room,' he hears.

'What about this one?'

'Nah. Looks like a girl's room. His sister.'

The footsteps come closer.

'Ah! This is it! Look at all that Spider-Man crap on the wall; I knew his room'd be like this!'

Colin cowers in his ineffectual hiding-place. His domain has been violated; the barbarians have arrived. He hears the sound of tearing paper. They're ripping the posters off his wall!

'Star Wars. Doctor fuckin' Who. What a load of bollocks.'

He hears the sounds of more destruction. It sounds like Bradley and the Ferret have swept all his DVDs and video games off the bookcase and are now stomping on them!

And then comes the dreaded moment.

'Let's see what's in there,' says Bradley.

The door swings open. Colin squeezes his eyes shut. (A futile reaction, but an instinctive one.)

A pregnant pause, and then a low, nasty chuckle. 'Come here, you two. Look what I found.'

Forced now to acknowledge the futility of the closed eyes, Colin opens them and sees Bradley stands there, leering at him triumphantly, flanked by his two lieutenants.

'Look at him hidin' in the corner,' chuckles Ferret.

'Little Miss Muffet,' sneers Bradley. (Bradley is in error here: it was Little Jack Horner who sat in the corner. Little Miss Muffet sat on her tuffet, whatever one of those might be.)

He flicks his knife in and out of its sheaf. 'Come out of there.'

Colin has little recourse but to obey. His legs feel like jelly but he manages to rise to his feet. He steps over the boxes and out of the cupboard, his assailants making room for him. He sees that his bookcase has been stove in; his games and DVDs litter the floor, the cases crushed and broken.

Bradley eyes him speculatively, toying with his knife. 'What are we gunna do with you…?' Bradley sounds thoughtful.

'Y-you shouldn't hurt me,' stammers Colin, suddenly remembering his one source of reprieve. 'You-you'll get in trouble if you do! M-Miss Lantier is coming here to pick me up!

She's just gone round the corner! She'll be here any second!'

'Whaddaya mean she's picking you up?' demands Bradley.

'In the school minibus.'

'Oh, I get it,' says Bradley, with a look of comprehension. 'You're going to the school, are yer? Lost your parents, but don't wanna join the gangs. Might've guessed you'd go running there.' Turning to the others: 'Grab him. We'll scarper with him before Lantier gets here.'

'B-but I don't want to go with you,' protests Colin, feebly.

'Yeah, and I don't care what you want!' Bradley tells him. 'You're comin' with us and that's that. Now shift.'

'But, I—'

'I said shift!'

Ferret and Janice grab Colin's arms and he is dragged down the stairs, and out through the front door onto the street. Colin looks eagerly towards the end of the road, hoping to see the white school minibus come around the corner. There's no sign of it.

'So, she'll be coming from *that* way, will she?' says Bradley, noting the direction of Colin's anxious. 'Then we'll go the other way. Come on.'

They set off along the path, Bradley pushing Colin from behind him, Janice at his side and Ferret in front, taking occasional swipes at the hedges with bicycle chain.

'Down there,' says Bradley, when they come to a cycle path leading off between two of the houses. Colin casts one last hopeful look back towards the intersection. Still no sign of the van, and a moment later they are going down the cycle path and the road is out of sight.

'What are we gunna do with him anyway?' asks Ferret, as they emerge from the jinnel onto the next street.

'We'll take him back to the base,' says Darren.

'What for?' demands Ferret. 'We don't want him in the gang, do we?'

''Course not. We're taking him as our prisoner.'

'What about Chorley?'

'What about him? He'll still be out when we get there, anyway.

We'll have the place to ourselves.'

'And what are we going to do with Colin?'

'We're gunna have a bit of fun with him, that's what.'

It's now that Colin makes a bid for freedom. He breaks into a run, charging down the middle of the road leaving his surprised captors behind.

'Get after him!' yells Bradley.

Colin puts every ounce of effort into his running. He's never been one of the fastest runners on the athletics field at school, but today he has more of an incentive to run as fast as he can: he doesn't know exactly what Darren's idea of 'having some fun' with him entails, but he knows that whatever it might be, it will not be anything conducive to his continued physical health and wellbeing!

Miss Lantier! She must have made it back to his house now; if only he can double back to Murdoch Way…!

But then, something impacts with the back of Colin's head. Stunned, he tumbles to the ground. Almost immediately Bradley and Ferret are on top of him. (Dumpy Janice, not so fast, and encumbered with her heavy axe, is still catching up.)

Ferret swings his bicycle chain triumphantly; it is a blow from this that has felled Colin.

'Get him up,' orders Bradley.

Colin is dragged to his feet.

Bradley punches him in the stomach. Colin doubles up, retching.

'Now pack it in or you'll get worse next time!' snarls Bradley.

Chapter Seven
'What Did I Tell You Little Bleeders?'

It's an old part of town, narrow streets and soot-blackened Victorian factories, a few of them still in use, the remainder closed-down or used as warehouses. Colin and his captors turn through an open gateway into a cobbled yard hemmed in by towering, unscalable walls. A grim, three storeyed factory building stands before them, rows of grimy windows looking down into the yard. Colin sees smoke rising from one of the chimneys.

'This is it,' announces Bradley. 'Our headquarters.'

'So, are you the blue gang or the yellow gang?' asks Colin.

The question provokes derisive laughter from his captors.

'We're not with the colour gangs, you twat,' Bradley tells him. 'We're Chorley's gang. He's the boss. 'Cept that he's not here at the moment.'

Crossing the yard, they pass through a pair of double doors into a dimly-lit cavernous room, once the factory floor, but now serving as a storeroom, piled high with cardboard boxes.

'This is our stash,' declares Bradley, indicating the stacked boxes with acquisitive pride. 'Know what's in all these boxes?'

'Things you've stolen from people's houses,' says Colin.

'Right,' confirms Bradley. 'But not just any old rubbish. We specialise, we do. We only take "home entertainment" stuff: Blu-rays, DVDs, video games; that sort o' thing.'

'Why's that?'

'Cuz that's what Chorley says. He says that this stuff's got a "high market value" at the moment. It's us that goes round looking for the houses with no-one in, and if they have anything worth nicking in 'em, we tell Chorley, and him and his pal go round in the van and pick the stuff up.'

'If you steal DVDs and video games, then why did you just smash up all of my stuff?' demands Colin, still aggrieved at the destruction of his possessions.

Bradley looks at him. 'I did it cuz it *was* your stuff and I don't fuckin' like you, that's why. Now, come on. Upstairs.'

The party crosses the room, passes through an open doorway and up a staircase. At the top of the stairs is a dim passage lined with doors. Bradley turns in through the first door, Janice and the Ferret following with Colin.

A welcome fire burns in the hearth of this room, which is further illuminated by a large-screen LCD TV, placed atop a couple of packing crates. Three people, seated on the miscellaneous chairs and sofas placed before the TV, look round to survey the newcomers. Colin recognises them; they are all kids from his school. There's Goobie, who, although in the same year as Colin, is six foot two in height, shaves every day and looks older than most Year Eleven boys. Also present are Jason and Jake, identical twins with matching sour dispositions.

'Look what we brought home,' says Bradley, pulling off his coat and throwing it on a chair.

'Colin Cleveland?' snorts Goobie. 'Whad you bring *him* for? We don't want *him* in our gang.'

'I know we don't,' says Bradley. 'He's not a recruit, he's a prisoner.'

The circumstances of Colin's capture are explained to the other gang members.

'So what are we gunna do with him now we've got him?' asks Jake.

'Whatever we fuckin' well like,' is the answer.

Bradley drags a plain wooden chair from against the wall and places it in the middle of the room. Colin is made to sit down in the chair.

Bradley looks pensive. 'He should be tied to the chair, really,' he says. 'That's how they normally do it. We got any rope around here?'

'There's some in the next room,' offers Goobie.

'Then go'n get it.'

Goobie obeys, returning with a coil of rope.

'Right. Tie him up.'

Janice and Ferret set to work, tying Colin's ankles to the chair-legs, his wrists together behind his back and lashed to the uprights of the chairback—and with Goobie holding him in a headlock, Colin can offer precious little in the way of resistance. Soon he is bound to the chair and completely helpless, surrounded by his captors.

Bradley stands toying with his knife, a calculating look on his face, like he hasn't quite decided what he's going to do with his prisoner. Ferret looks eager, like he can't wait for the entertainment to start; while Janice just looks at him with her usual sulky expression, like she doesn't really care one way or another what happens to him. Further back stand the twins, smirking at Colin's plight. Goobie looks uninterested; a straight-forward punch-up is more his idea of satisfying violence.

'Please let me go,' whimpers Colin, tears streaming down his face.

'Shuddup snivelling,' snaps Bradley. 'You little chicken-shit.'

'How about we cut his knob off?' suggests Ferret.

Everyone (Colin excluded) chuckles at this suggestion.

'No thanks,' demurs Bradley. 'I don't wanna be touching his wedding tackle. Anyway, we'd probably have trouble finding it.' More laughter at this one. 'I know: who's got a lighter?'

Goobie, a twenty-a-day man, hands over his cigarette lighter. Bradley tests the lighter, adjusts the flame to its maximum output, which on these cheap disposable models is like a small flame-thrower.

He leans in close to Colin, holding the inactive lighter close to his face. Colin strains his head backwards. The flame ignites; Colin scrunches his eyes shut. Much appreciative laughter.

Bradley swipes the flame back and forth past Colin's face a few more times.

'Stop it!' pleads Colin.

'"Stop it!"' echoes Bradley, derisively. 'God, you're a complete fuckin' pussy, aren't you? I've never liked you, Cleveland. Your whiny voice pisses me off. Your stupid soppy baby-face pisses me off. Your crappy Spider Man comics piss me off. If you weren't always in the way, I bet Nigel would've hung around with us lot instead of with you—and *that* pisses me off, an' all.'

'Nigel wouldn't hang around with you,' says Colin bravely. 'He doesn't like any of you lot.'

'Shuddup,' snaps Bradley, slapping him round the face. 'Know, what? Reckon you could do with a haircut. But since I ain't got any scissors, how about I just use this to do the job?'

He holds the lighter up to Colin's fringe.

'No,' gasps Colin.

'What's goin' on 'ere?' demands a new voice, a booming grown-up's voice.

Everyone looks round. A man stands in the doorway. A man in a brown leather jacket, wearing a red baseball cap.

The boss is back. Chorley has returned.

Bradley backs guiltily away from Colin.

Chorley advances into the room.

''Oo's this, and what the 'ell are you doin' to 'im?' he demands.

Bradley musters up a smile. ''E's a mate of ours, that's all. We was just playin' around with him.'

'Playin' around, were yer?' echoes Chorley. 'Funny idea you 'ave of playin' around. Looked to me like you were tryin' to set 'is 'air on fire. Now, if there's one thing I can't abide, then that is disrespectin' a feller's 'air. That gets me that does; that really gets me. ''Air is precious, an' somethin' to be cherished while you still got it.'

And to emphasise his point, Chorley removes his hat, revealing a completely bald crown.

'Did someone set fire to your hair, Mr Chorley?' ventures Janice. (From anyone else this question would have been sarcasm.)

'No they bleedin' didn't!' retorts Chorley. 'It fell out, all of its own accord. But you set fire to this poor bugger's 'air, chances are, it won't grow back. I can't abide that. People've got to respect their 'air, and they've got ter respect each other's. You never know when you're gunna lose it, see?'

They see.

Colin gazes at Chorley as though upon a saviour. He sees a man in his mid-thirties, tall and loose-limbed, with a smiling face, all mouth, chin, and beaky nose, like a Mr Punch doll. What hair he possesses is brown and wavy. Chorley looks at him, smiling encouragingly.

'What's yer name, mate?'

'Colin Cleveland,' replies Colin.

'An' 'ow old're yer?'

'Twelve.'

'So, you was at school with these scrotes, were yer? An' let me guess: they was always pickin' on yer, right?'

'Yes, they were.'

'Well, don't you worry, cuz they won't be pickin' on yer, no more. Ol' Chorley'll look after you. You'll be safe 'ere.' He turns to the others. 'D'you 'ear that, you lot? 'E's to be treated nice an' proper; got it?'

Mumbles of assent.

'Well, then,' says Chorley, impatiently.

'Well what?' says Bradley, sulky.

'"Well what?" 'e says. UNTIE HIM FROM THE BLEEDIN' CHAIR. That's not been hospitable like, is it? Tyin' people to the blinkin' furniture. Thad's unlawful restraint, that is.'

Bradley signals to Janice and the Ferret, who set about loosening Colin's bonds. Janice, stooping to free his ankles, discovers that their captive's bladder has betrayed him during his recent ordeal.

'He's pissed 'imself!' she crows.

Guffaws all round.

'Shuddit, you lot!' snaps Chorley. 'Any of you lot would've pissed yerselves too, if you'd be tied to a chair an' threatened with actual bodily 'arm. So you can can the bleedin' laughter.'

Colin stands up, totters. Chorley grabs him by the shoulders.

'Woah there!' he says. 'Bit shaky on yer pins, aren't yer?'

'It's my head…' says Colin, feeling the back of his head. He winces. The injury is tender and has swollen up, the surrounding hair sticky with blood

'What's up?' Chorley inspects the wound, feels the matted hair. He turns angrily on his gang. 'Which one o' you bleeders did this to 'im?'

'We didn't do nothing!' says Bradley. 'He just fell over.'

'It was his bike chain!' declares Colin, pointing at Ferret.

'Snitch!' retorts the accused.

'I'll bloomin' throttle you wi' that chain o' yours, one o' these days!' Chorley, glaring at Ferret.

'Can I go now, please?' Colin asks Chorley.

'I reckon the first thing we gots to do is take care o' your injuries,' replies Chorley. 'That's a nasty bump you got. An' was you plannin' on goin', anyway?'

'To the school; Park Lane Comprehensive. There's two teachers there, looking after pupils who've lost their parents.'

'Oh, yeah,' says Chorley. 'I've 'eard about that. Stayin' there, were yer?'

'I was about to be staying there,' answers Colin. 'I was at my house packing my things up, and they were going to pick me up in the van, but then *they*,' pointing an accusing finger at Bradley *et al*, 'broke in and they grabbed me and brought me here even though I didn't want to come.'

Chorley glares at Bradley. 'You broke inter 'is 'ouse?' he challenges. 'What did I tell you little bleeders? You only break into them 'ouses what you knows to be untenanted—an' by that I mean the bloody 'ouses what ain't got bloody no-one inside of 'em!'

'His house *looked* like it had no-one in it,' protests Bradley. 'All the curtains was closed and no-one answered the door when we knocked.' (Presumably the blows of Janice's hatchet are to be considered knocking on the door.) 'How was we to know he was there, when he was hidin' in the back of his cupboard like a scared rabbit?'

'You dragged me here to torture me!' accuses Colin.

'We was only messin' around,' sulkily.

'Well, there'll be no more o' that kinder messin' around,' asserts Chorley. He puts a hand on Colin's shoulder. 'Listen, mate. Less go upstairs an' I'll see to that there bump on your noggin, an' I'll treat yer to a nice 'ot cuppa tea, eh? I want ter make it up to yer for your mistreatment at the 'ands of my honourable bloody associates, see?'

Colin hesitates. He is grateful enough to Chorley for saving him from Bradley, but the man still is a criminal, the head of a gang of looters, and he would much rather be at Park Lane with Natasha and Miss Lantier to look after him. But he doesn't want to offend the man by seeming too eager to leave, either.

'Whaddaya say, then?'

'Okay…' agrees Colin.

He follows Chorley to the door.

'An' you lot, be'ave yerselves!' fired back at Bradley and Co.

Chapter Eight
'From Now On, Yer One Of Us'

Chorley takes Colin up the stairs to the second floor and into another furnished chamber. This one is also supplied with a fire, but it has only just been lit and has yet to warm the room. A man, tending the fire, rises as they enter. He is tall, thickset and sports a doleful expression. His hair is loose and curly.

'Colin, meet me friend an' colleague, Maclean,' introduces Chorley. 'Got the fire goin', 'ave yer?'

'Well, it didn't get itself going,' is the surly response.

'No, I don't suppose it did,' agrees Chorley. 'Lookee 'ere, Maclean, old son. My new mate Colin 'ere is in need of a fresh pair o' strides. Now, 'ow about you just nip dahnstairs and borrow a pair off one o' the twins? They should be abaht the right size for Colin.'

'Yes, I'll go'n get him some trousers,' replies Maclean wearily. 'It's not as though you could've done it yourself when you were down there, is it?'

And with this he departs.

Chorley winks at Colin. ''E's a real card, ain't 'e?' he says. 'You can't 'elp likin' ol' Maclean, can yer? We goes back a long way, we do, me an' 'im.'

'It's alright about the trousers—' begins Colin.

'No, no,' demurs Chorley. 'We can't 'ave you walkin' around in wet strides. But first, less 'ave a look at that bump o' yours. Sit yerself dahn.' Chorley goes to a sideboard, returns with a first-aid kit. Gently, he cleans Colin's head-wound with ointment. 'That'll do. Can't stick a plaster on it cuz yer 'air's in the way. Got yerself a nice 'ead of 'air, ain't yer, son? Real silky like. You only get that with blond 'air like you got, that silkiness.' Chorley replaces the first-aid box. He claps his hands. 'Now ter put the kettle on for a brew.'

Colin sits back in the armchair. It's nice and cosy close to the fire, and Colin finds himself relaxing. Yes, he'll just have this drink with Chorley, and then he'll be on his way.

Chorley returns to the sideboard, which is supplied with tea things. The soft rumble of a kettle starting to boil fills the room, adding to the friendly atmosphere.

''Ow'd you take yer tea, then?' asks Chorley.

'Milk and two sugars, please,' replies Colin.

'Nice polite boy, aren't yer?' observes Chorley. 'I likes that, I does.'

Maclean returns bearing a pair of jogging bottoms.

'Are they clean?' demands Chorley.

'Yes, they're clean.'

'Smashin''. You jest step inter those, Colin me old son.'

'But, no, I—'

'Now, now.

Colin stands up to receive the bottoms. He would rather have changed in another room but it looks like they expect him to change in here. Turning his back on the two men, he first pulls off his trainers, then takes off his wet jeans. He is about to step into the jogging pants when—

'Well take yer pants off, then! They're gunna be wetter than yer jeans, ain't they?'

'But, I—'

'Now go on. There's no ladies present, is there?'

Reluctantly, Colin pulls off his pants and quickly pulls on the jogging bottoms. They are very cold and he has that uncomfortable feeling that comes from putting on clothes that are not your own (and especially when they belong to someone you don't like!) And with no pants on underneath them, feels like he's in his pyjamas.

'That's better,' says Chorley. 'Now, Maclean 'ere 'll take away yer wet things an' put 'em in the wash.'

'But I can just take them with me—'

'Wouldn't 'ear of it,' dissents Chorley firmly. 'We'll wash 'em for yer.'

Maclean takes up Colin's wet things and leaves the room with them. Colin watches them go with a vague feeling that his escape is being cut off.

Chorley now comes forward with two steaming mugs and places them on a table between two of the chairs facing the fire.

''Ere we are. Nice 'ot cup o' char. Sit yerself dahn.'

Colin resumes his seat and Chorley lowers himself into the neighbouring armchair.

'Nice an' cosy, ain't it?' he says appreciatively.

Colin starts to relax again. Chorley isn't such a bad person, he thinks. He's just making up for what Bradley and the others did to him. As for his jeans and pants, he can always come back and collect those tomorrow. He'll need to bring back the jogging bottoms anyway.

He sips his sweet tea.

'So whaddayer think abaht all this then, Colin?' asks Chorley.

'All what?'

'All this what's 'appened, I mean. The Incident, as they're callin' it. Arf the people disappearin' an' the internet and telly an' everythin' goin' off. What do yer think abaht it?'

'I think it must be aliens,' says Colin.

'Aliens, eh? Well, that's one idea. Although if aliens is be'ind all this, you'd've thought that they'd've come down from space ter 'ave a look at their 'andiwork, wouldn't yer? Unless o' course they're watching us from up there in their spaceships.'

'Don't you think it was aliens, then?' asks Colin.

'Well, I tell yer, Colin old son, I don't know, an' that's the truth. I mean I ain't sayin' you're wrong: it could be aliens. It could be the government. It could be the flamin' Russkies and Chinks workin' in cahoots. I don't know 'oo did it, no more 'an anyone else does. What I'm thinkin' is more abaht results than causes. I mean the way things is now, an' what it all means ter us. It seems ter me that the biggest diff'rence is that the playing field 'as been levelled, if yer see what I mean?'

Colin doesn't see what he means and says so.

'Well, what I mean is this: what was the biggest diff'rence between people before all this 'appened? It were money, weren't it? Some people 'ad lots o' money, some didn't 'ave so much, 'an some didn't 'ave any at all. But now, money's no good, is it? Fer the time bein' at least. At the moment all the money what's in circulation is all jus' worthless scraps o' paper. An' the money what's just on computers: well that's gone, ain't it? No-one can get at the computer money. So basically, there's no rich an' there's no poor anymore, is there? Yeah, you might say the rich man is still livin' in 'is big mansion. But now, someone 'oo was poor could just come along an' kick 'im right out of it. Y'see? An' there's nothin' 'e could do abaht it cuz 'e 'asn't got the power anymore what went with 'is money, 'as 'e?' Colin watches Chorley as he speaks; watches the man's hawkish profile as he stares into the fire. 'Yes, we's all equal now in this new world o' ours. People jest take what they wants. Like this 'ere 'eadquarters o' ours. We found the place empty and there weren't no-one around to tell us we couldn't 'ave it, so we jest moved in an' set up shop.'

'Did you move here because your house got burnt down?' wonders Colin.

Chorley frowns. 'Our 'ouse got burnt?—Oh! I sees what you mean. No, you is sufferin' under a misappre'ension there, Colin me lad. Maclean and me, we don't come from Eastchester. We used to be—well we lived out in the country like. Yes, we jest sorta drifted into town; a day or two after the Incident, it was. Then we some'ow 'ooked up with them young delinquents downstairs and started up our little operation.'

'Stealing from people's houses?'

'Stealin's an 'arsh word there, Colin. I mean ter say it's all finders keepers these days, an' even then, we got principles we

’ave, in this operation of ours. We only takes from them ’ouses what we know ter be empty, them ’ouses where all the residents ’as disappeared like, or else as left town lookin’ fer greener pastures.

‘Y’see? I look upon meself as a businessman. An’ what we’re doin’ ’ere is providin’ a service. Y’see, we specialise. We only takes home entertainment products, we do: DVDs, Blu-rays and the like…’

‘Yes, Darren told me that.’

‘Did ’e? An’ did ’e tell yer why? No? Well, y’see, what’s most o’ the people been doin’ since the Incident? They’ve been stayin’ put indoors, ’aven’t they? Stayin’ indoors an’ watchin’ the telly. But what can they watch? They can’t watch normal TV, an’ they can’t watch them streamin’ channels neither. None o’ that stuff’s workin’. So, all they’ve got ter watch is DVDs an’ Blu-rays. But not everyone’s got any DVDs or Blu-ray’s, ’ave they? Cuz when those streamin’ services took off, a lot o’ people got rid of all that stuff, thinkin’ they didn’t need ’em anymore. Ha! Bet there’s a lot of people around now who’s wishin’ they ’adn’t done that! Well, that’s where we come in. Y’see, we’re liberating all the DVDs an’ Blu-rays from the ’ouses what’s been abandoned, an’ then we’re gunna sell ’em to all them people who’s sittin’ at ’ome getting’ bored to death cuz they ’aven’t got anything to watch on the telly. That’s the service we’re providin’.’

‘You’re selling them to people?’ says Colin. ‘You mean, for money?’

‘O’ course I mean for money. What else would be sellin’ ’em for?’

‘But you said money was just waste paper now.’

‘So it is, right *now*—but it won’t *always* be, will it? Money’ll come back sooner or later; whether they get the computers back on-line or even if they can’t. Yeah, it’s bound to ’appen sooner or later. Like I say, we’re providin’ a service. An’ that’s why we only pinch the home entertainment stuff; everythin’ else we leave be’ind.’

‘Bradley and the others smashed up my DVDs,’ says Colin,

sulkily.

'Did 'e now? Then that's somethin' else I shall 'ave to 'ave words abaht wi' that young shaver. No vandalism: that's another one o' my rules. We got enough senseless destruction o' property wi' them blue and yeller gangs runnin' around. No need ter add to it. 'Well, it won't 'appen again. I'll set 'im straight abaht that one. From now on, yer one of us, and you'll be treated wi' respect.'

Colin stands up, alarmed. 'But I don't want to be one of you! I'm going to stay at the school!'

'Stay at the school? What d'yer wanna do that for? 'Ave they got anythin' there that we ain't got 'ere? No, you'll be safe as 'ouses 'ere. You don't wanna go to no school.'

'But they're *expecting* me,' protests Colin. 'So I've got to go; I've got to go now.'

Colin makes a dash for the door. But as he reaches it, it slams shut and Chorley is standing in front of it, arms folded.

'Now, now. I can't let you just toddle off like that; I jest can't. Y'see, I've taken I liking to you, I 'ave, Colin old son. You're a nice, polite, well-be'aved young feller, and I wants you to be in our gang. And seein' as 'ow what I say goes around 'ere, that means you *is* gunna be in our gang. End of bleedin' story.'

Chapter Nine
'She Ain't Gunna Look Twice at Yer, Mate'

Colin sits staring into the fire, whose flames provide the only illumination in the room. Outside it is night and a blizzard is raging.

Chorley enters the room and seats himself in a vacant armchair.

'So this is where yer 'idin' yerself, is it?' he begins. 'Proper little lone ranger, ain't ya? They's all watchin' a film downstairs; one of them shoot-'em-up action films, it is. All-star cast.

Sylvester Stallone an' that mob. Looks like a good flick, it does. Why don't you come dahn and join 'em?'

'Don't want to,' says Colin, sulkily, his eyes on the dancing flames.

Chorley heaves a sigh. 'Are you still sulkin' on account o' me not lettin' you go to that bloomin' school o' yours? Is that what all this is abaht?'

'Yes,' answers Colin, seeing no reason to conceal the truth.

He has been a reluctant member of Chorley's gang for several days now. Reluctant and uncooperative. He has been fed, clothed, and generally well-treated. Even Bradley and his cohorts have been friendly towards him. At first Colin thought this was only because Chorley had ordered them to be friendly, and was expecting the knives to come out the moment the boss's back was turned—but this hasn't been the case; with the fickleness of youth, it seems that Colin's erstwhile tormentors have genuinely accepted him as one of the team.

The only thing he's been denied is his freedom. And after the prospect of Park Lane School as a refuge, with the feminine ministrations of Natasha and Miss Lantier to comfort and console him, Chorley and his gang and his chilly Victorian warehouse seem a pretty grubby substitute.

'I'll tell yer what,' say Chorley: 'I don't geddit. I jus' don't geddit. Why do yer think you'd 'ave been better off there than you are 'ere? Explain that one. Iss not like any o' yer best mates is there; you told me yourself they ain't. So, what's so bleedin' good about that school? They got food. Well, we got food an' all an' we got Maclean to cook it for us, an' you can't say he isn't pretty handy in the kitchen. An' what's more *I* let yer eats whatever you want ter; at that school they'd proberly be imposin' an 'ealthy diet on yer, and you'd 'ave to be eatin' lots o' them vegetables what I know you don't like. An' I'll tells yer somethink else: that place is bein' run by teachers; so they're proberly makin' the kids there do all their schoolwork. Yer don't 'ave ter do school-work 'ere, does yer? Yer can do what yer wants 'ere. That bein' the case, then what, by all that's 'oly, is so bloody good about that school, that yer pinin' fer the place like a bleedin' lost dog?'

It's embarrassing, it's personal; but Colin decides it's time to tell the truth.

'There's a girl there…' he says.

'Oh, so *that's* what it is, is it?' says Chorley, enlightenment in his voice. 'There's a girl there, is there? Let me guess: it's a girl what you fancy, innit? Thought so. An' what's this girl's name?'

'Natasha.'

'Natasha, eh? An' this Natasha, does she reciprocate your feelin's?'

'Does she what?'

'Does *she* fancy *you?*'

'Not sure. Don't think so…'

'Does she even know you fancy 'er?'

'Don't think so…'

'What, you ain't told 'er?' And then: 'No, I don't suppose you have. It's cuz you're shy, ain't yer? Shy arahnd girls, an 'specially arahnd girls what you fancy? Now am I right or am I right?'

'Yes…'

'An' what's she like, this girl? What sorta girl is she? One of the quiet sort? Or is she outgoing?'

'Outgoing?'

'Yeah. Friendly, chatty? Popular, got lots of friends?'

'Yes! That's what she's like!'

'An' clever, is she? What you'd call mature for 'er age?'

'Yeah!'

Chorley shakes his head sadly. 'Then it ain't gunna work, is it? She ain't gunna go out wi' you; not a girl like that. No, them girls, they go for boys what's a bit older than they is. Boys like you, they just think you're still kids, they do. They might be all nice to yer, like a big sister, but they ain't gunna see you as boyfriend material. An' I bet you know that really, don't yer? Always thought she was too good for yer; out of league, right? Come on: 'aven't you always thought she was out of yer league?'

'Yes…' admits Colin.

'See? You admit it!' triumphantly. And then: 'No, she ain't

gunna look twice at yer, mate. Not in the way you want. Girl like that: she'll only go for the older boys; ones what're confident an' outgoing like she is. An' 'as she already got a boyfriend? Come on: 'as she?'

'I'm... not sure...' says Colin. 'There's Paul Mitchell...'

'An' 'oo's this Paul Mitchell, then?'

'He's one of the others staying at the school...'

'Older than her?'

'A lot older: Year Eleven. He's in a band...'

'A band! Well, there yer goes, then! A band! Might as well pack up an' go 'ome. A band. Girls ''er age is mad for boys what's in bands—it's like bleedin' catnip to 'em! An' 'e's there with 'er at the school right now? She'll be 'ookin' up with him, then! Bound ter be. And jest think: if you was there, jest think 'ow yer'd feel wi' all that goin' on right under yer nose, day in, day out. You'd be miserable, you would. It'd be bleedin' purgatory for yer. Drive yer to bleedin' suicide. No, mate: yer better of where you are. Take it from me; take it from old Chorley. An' pinin' for 'er ain't gunna do you no good, neither. You need ter forget about that girl, you do. Get 'er right out o' yer mind.' Chorley stands up. 'So, why don't you stop mopin' 'ere all on yer tod, an' come downstairs an' watch the film?'

Colin has been put in charge of sorting and cataloguing the gang's merchandise. He has to work through all the countless boxes of DVDs and Blu-rays 'liberated' from people's houses, and sort them all into categories. First, the Blu-rays have to be separated from the DVDs; then they have to be divided into 'film' and 'TV'; and after that arranged into their respective categories. A row of boxes, labelled with marker pen, has been laid out across the floor to store the items for each separate category: thus, there are boxes labelled 'DVD Drama TV,' 'Blu-ray Sci-fi Film,' 'DVD Comedy TV,' 'Blu-Ray Children's TV,' etc, etc.

Now this is just the kind of task that Colin Cleveland can apply himself to, and in spite of himself, he's starting to enjoy the work. It's cold down here on the factory floor, but he's well wrapped-up, and the nature of his task keeps him active, having to keep moving around for box to box. Also, the work interests him because it involves film and television entertainment; the gang has amassed an impressive haul, and a lot of it is just the kind of thing that Colin likes to watch himself.

However, there are two particular boxes whose designated contents Colin would never watch, and he does not at all like having to handle: and those are the boxes marked 'DVD Adult' and 'Blu-Ray Adult'—if it were up to Colin, he'd throw the filthy things straight into the bin! For Colin, unlike many boys his age, not only does not view pornography, but he has always made a point of avoiding it. Dirty stuff it is; filthy; only for dirty people with dirty minds. Fortunately, when he's sorting through the contents of each newly-opened box, the dirty films are nearly always already separate from everything else (because those who possess it obviously like to keep their pornography apart from their more mainstream entertainment), and because of this, these things can just be picked up in bulk, carried to the boxes marked 'Adult' and dropped into them with as much noise as possible—and thus eye-contact with those offensive covers is kept to the bare minimum.

There was one cover that *had* caught and held Colin's attention, though: a cover which had featured a pretty girl who looked a lot like a slightly older version of his still beloved—in spite of Chorley's 'pep-talk'—Natasha. Intrigued, and wondering if Natasha looked like this when she didn't have any clothes on, Colin had turned the box over, but then had been repelled an image on the back featuring the same pretty girl in the arms of a very muscular black gentlemen who was clearly behaving very violently towards her, judging from the (what appeared to Colin) pain-contorted expression on her face. And what seemed even worse to Colin was that she was hugging the man who was hurting her so much. Why would she do that? And why would she let herself be *filmed* doing that? It all seemed vile and wrong and confusing to Colin, and he'd thrown the DVD into the box and quickly buried it under more of its filthy kind.

And now Colin keeps thinking about that picture; it has burned itself into his inner eye, and keeps intruding itself in his thoughts. He can't help connecting the girl with Natasha, who she so strongly resembled, and wondering if Natasha would ever let anyone do things like that to her; if she'd ever let Paul Mitchell…

'Workin' 'ard, are we?'

It's Chorley, stepping in from the yard, just arrived back in the van. Grinning, he crosses the factory floor and joins Colin.

'Got some news for you,' he announces. 'It's about that school of yours.'

'What about it?'

'Only that it got attacked last night. The Yellow gang, it was. They torched the place.'

'They set fire to the school?' says Colin, horrified. 'W-what about… what about…?'

'The people what was there? Well, from what I 'eard, some of 'em got out, and some of 'em didn't. And them what did get out: they've scarpered. Skedaddled. Left town, they 'ave.'

'W-what about Natasha…?'

'I tell yer, *I don't know*. Maybe she was one o' the lucky ones; one of the ones what got out. But jest think: if you 'adn't been 'ere all safe an' sound; if you'd been at that school like you kept sayin' you wanted to be: maybe you *wouldn't* have been one of the ones what got out. Think about that, mate, an' thank yer lucky stars that ol' Chorley kept you safe an' sound right 'ere.'

Having dropped this bombshell, Chorley leaves Colin to recover from it. He has a lot to process. Natasha. Either dead or left town. He finds that the latter alternative hurts him more: it feels like desertion. True, they were talking about the possibility of leaving Eastchester even that morning when he was with them at the school; they were saying it might become necessary if the gang violence continued to escalate… But that Natasha, Miss Lantier and the rest would just abandon Colin like that… Miss Lantier must have seen that something had happened at Colin's house while she was gone; she must have worked out that he was taken away by force, against his will… Why hadn't they tried to find him? Why hadn't they come and rescued him from here? It seemed like they'd all just shrugged their shoulders and forgotten about him; like they didn't care, like they'd never really cared…

Colin sits between Chorley and Maclean in the cab of the white van, Chorley on his left, Maclean on his right and at the wheel. The thaw has set in and it's a dry, overcast day and they are on their way to another empty house with a stash of DVDs, located by Bradley and his scouting party.

Colin hasn't been allowed to join these scouting parties so far; Chorley doubtless thinking he might try to escape if he went outside with only Bradley and his cronies to keep an eye on him. (Not that Chorley need have worried on that score: Colin has already sounded Bradley out about letting him escape from the factory and has been met with a flat refusal. 'No fuckin' way! If I let you escape, Chorley'd have me guts for garters!')

'This is the life,' says Chorley, attempting as usual to infect Colin with some of his own enthusiasm. 'Free enterprise. That's what I calls it. Free flippin' enterprise.'

'Another word for it would be stealing,' says Maclean dryly.

'It ain't stealin' when there's nobody there ter be stolen from,' declares Chorley. 'Abandoned property, that's what it is.'

'Unless all the people who disappeared suddenly come back,' says Maclean. 'The moment that happens our "capital investment" turns into stolen property.'

'Them people what disappeared ain't comin' back,' says Chorley, confidently.

'And how do you know? Nobody knows where they went, how it was done. They could all just suddenly pop back the way they popped off.'

'They ain't comin' back,' insists Chorley. 'I reckon it was some new weapon what did for 'em. Dead people don't come back to claim their goods 'n chattels.'

Turning a corner they see ahead of them a group of smartphone zombies, shambling along the middle of the street, phones held aloft.

'Oh, not this flamin' lot again,' groans Chorley. 'Why can't they keep on the flamin' pavement like normal people?'

'Because they're not bloody normal people, are they?' responds Maclean, slowing down as he approaches the group.

'Bloody cattle blockin' the road is what they are,' says Chorley. 'Why can't they stop at 'ome an' watch the bleedin' telly like everyone else? Give 'em a blast of the 'orn.'

'Whatever your lordship says,' says Maclean.

He beeps the horn.

The zombies don't turn to look at the van approaching behind them, but by some herd instinct they divide and start moving towards the edges of the road, opening a passage for the vehicle to pass through.

Chorley winds down his window as he passes them.

'Why don't you give it up, you lot?' he calls out to them. 'There's no bleedin' internet anymore! It's not there anymore, an' it ain't bloody coming back, either! So forget abaht it! You ain't gunna get any bleedin' bars on yer bleedin' phones. So go 'ome an' find some other bleedin' form o' recreation! Watch the telly; and if yer ain't got nothing ter watch, then come to our next DVD sale! Market Square, Saturday!'

The smartphone zombies make no response to this exhortation; just continue to point their useless devices at the empty sky.

'Beep, beep. Beep, beep. Beep, beep…'

A few streets later and they are passing one of the town's main supermarkets. There are a great number of cars parked in the carpark, and a flow of customers going into and out of the shop, the latter laden with heavy-laden shopping bags.

'What are 'ell's goin' on 'ere?' demands Chorley. 'That shop got cleaned out weeks ago. It should be bloody empty!'

'Looks like they've got new stock in,' says Maclean.

''Ow could they've got new stock in, you pillock?' retorts Chorley. 'There 'asn't been anythin' like that since the Incident 'appened! Pull in, I wanna 'ave a look at this.'

Maclean parks the transit van in a vacant parking space. They get out and make their way to the supermarket.

'Black marketeers; that's what it's gotta be!' declares Chorley. 'Some gang from out o' town must've found a ware'ouse full o' supermarket goods, an' now they've come 'ere to flog 'em to people! What a bloody liberty!'

'You'd be taking the same liberty if you'd been the one who'd found the warehouse full of grub,' sneers Maclean.

'That's different, ain't it?' replies Chorley. 'I'm local, so if it were me doin' that, I'd jest be performing a service for my community.'

'Local? Before the Incident we were—'

'Never mind where we was before the Incident. That was then, an' speaking for meself, I already feel like I'm a fully-integrated citizen o' this 'ere burrer, an' with the civic pride what goes with it: an' I say that these black marketeers, comin' in from outta town and flogging their goods is jest taking a liberty, exploiting the needs o' the community.'

A surprise is awaiting them when they step inside the supermarket.

The surprise is grey in colour, and there's a lot of it.

The supermarket has been completely restocked; merchandise has returned to every shelf in every aisle—and all of it is grey. The cereal boxes, the frozen food packaging, the crisp packets, the chocolate wrappers, the labels on the cans, the jars, the bottles: all of them are a uniform neutral grey.

'What the bleedin' 'eck...?'

Chapter Ten

'Old Chorley'll Look After Yer...'

They walk up to the nearest aisle, the first section of which happens to be breakfast cereals. The grey boxes are emblazoned with legends in bold black lettering succinctly describing the product: CORN FLAKES, WHEAT BISCUITS, BRAN FLAKES, FROSTED CORN FLAKES, TOASTED RICE CEREAL, PORRIDGE OATS. No brand names, no artwork; just these basic descriptions in bold black letters. The same font (Arial Black; you'll find it on the cover of this book) prevails on every product in the supermarket.

'This ain't black market stuff,' declares Chorley. 'This is official.'

He picks a box of corn flakes from the shelf. The back of the box is identical to the front; the top, bottom and side panels are bare. No ingredients or nutritional information; not a traffic light to be seen.

'Look at this,' says Chorley, aggrieved. 'No maker's address; nothin' about where it was made are 'oo made it; and no flamin' barcode neither…!'

They look around the shop. The customers move around the shop, calmly pushing their trollies, filling them with goods, and then when they have taken all they need, wheeling their trollies straight out of the shop and to their parked cars. There is no staff walking the shop floor or stacking the shelves; no-one at the checkouts to tally up the price of the goods and demand payment for them.

By some mysterious agency the shelves have been restocked, and customers have been tacitly invited to just come in and help themselves to whatever they need.

Chorley, Maclean proceed along the aisles of the shop, taking it all in. Everything is there. Toilet paper, cleaning products, bath products. Tobacco and alcohol have not been forgotten, either.

'Look, they've even got fresh food!' says Chorley. 'Dairy stuff, meat, fruit and veg… Where's it all come from? And why aren't they chargin' anything? What about the bleedin' economy?'

'The economy's offline,' says Maclean.

'I don't like it,' avers Chorley. 'If people get used to getting stuff for free, they soon ain't gunna wanna pay for anything, are they?'

'Not even their DVDs,' smirks Maclean.

'Well, I don't like it,' repeats Chorley. 'I don't bleedin' like it.'

They are watching another horror film this evening. The whole juvenile section of the gang is sat around the large-screen television in the common room: Colin, Bradley, Ferret, Janice, Goobie and the twins. The horror film is the usual gory type favoured by Bradley and his friends: this particular one features a group of hapless American teenagers dying in various horrible ways at the hands of a group of redneck demons.

Colin himself is not such a big fan of horror films; in fact, before the Incident, this was just the kind of film that his mum wouldn't have allowed him to watch! But not wanting to be the odd one out, he has been getting accustomed to these films which are usually more yucky than scary, and trying to cultivate a liking for them.

At least tonight's film hasn't got any nudity in it. Colin doesn't like it when they have nudity in them—it's just embarrassing!

So, Colin sits on one of the sofas, Bradley by his side, watching the film and chewing on a chocolate bar whose plain grey wrapper announces it to be a 'Peanut and Nougat Chocolate Bar,' and which prior to the End of the World had been known as a 'Snickers' bar.

Colin's viewing is interrupted by a tap on his shoulder. He looks up to see Maclean standing over him, the usual morose expression on his face.

'Chorley wants to see you.'

Bradley looks round. 'See us about what?'

'I didn't say all of you, did I?' retorts Maclean. 'He just wants to see Colin.'

'But I'm in the middle of eating this,' says Colin, holding up the chocolate bar.

'Well, bring it with you. It's not chained to the floor, is it?'

Colin gets up and follows Maclean. They ascend the stairs to the second floor, designated Chorley and Maclean's domain, just as the first floor is for the kids.

'Why does Chorley want to see just me?' asks Colin.

'Well, you're the blue-eyed boy, aren't you?' says Maclean. 'Sun shines out of your bloody backside, doesn't it? He probably wants to give you a medal, seeing as how you're such a valuable, hard-working member of the team. The rest of us, we're just a bunch of layabouts compared to you, aren't we?'

When Maclean says this sort of thing in front of Chorley, Chorley always bursts out laughing and says what a card Maclean is; but to Colin it has always seemed there was more malice than humour in Maclean's humour—and right now he feels that the malice is being aimed squarely at himself!

They arrive at the upstairs living room, where Chorley sits in his shirtsleeves, glass in his hand, looking even more jolly than usual.

'Come in, me old mate, come in!' he greets Colin. He pats the chair beside him. 'Sit yerself dahn.' To Maclean: 'An' you: you got something to do, ain't yer?'

'Oh yes, I've got tons of things to do; a whole bloody shopping list of things to do.'

And with this, Maclean stomps out of the room, slamming the door behind him, leaving Colin alone with Chorley.

''E's a card ain't 'e?' chuckles Chorley, with a nod towards the door. And then, patting the chair again: 'Come on, Colin. You jest sit yerself dahn next to old Chorley. Old Chorley'll look after yer…'

Colin shares a bedroom with Bradley, Goobie and the twins. The bedroom, another previously empty upper room of the factory building, has been supplied with beds 'liberated' from local furniture shops.

Colin lies in his bed, wide awake, listening. The sound of deep regular breathing tells him that the room's other occupants are asleep. Colin now pulls back his duvet, swings his legs out of the bed. The air is freezing cold, and he quickly removes his pyjamas and puts on his clothes, his shoes, his coat.

Colin has made a resolution which he is now determined to carry out: he's getting out of here. He doesn't want to stay in Chorley's gang a moment longer. Not a moment longer.

Now dressed, Colin creeps across the room to the door. This is his first obstacle. The door creaks when you open it; it might wake one of the others; and if they catch him trying to escape, they will stop him.

Colin takes hold of the handle, turns it and very slowly—and discovers that opening the door slowly only makes it creak more slowly. The noise is very loud in the pitch darkness.

Wincing, Colin, stops, listens. No sound of movement from any of the beds.

Colin insinuates himself through the gap in the door. He gropes along the corridor towards the stairs; the walls are like ice to the touch. Down the stairs he enters the storeroom. There is a modicum of light here, filtering through the row of tall arched windows. He tries the yard door first, but finds it closed as expected. He moves over to the windows. These windows are placed very high in the wall, and boxes in irregular stacks have been piled against the wall beneath them. Colin, when he has been working down here during the daytime, has often idly mused on how easy it would be to climb up one of the stacks of boxes to look outside through the window. He has never actually tried the experiment, firstly because the windows only look out into the yard, and secondly because the glass panes are so dirty that he probably wouldn't have been able to see much anyway.

But today he has a different motive, and he now makes his way up one of the stacks of boxes and reaching the summit, finds himself level with the window embrasure. Up close he now sees that the glass is indeed filthy with the accumulated grime of years, and very little can be seen through them. Colin starts feeling along the edges, fingers gathering up the dirt as they explore for a catch or a handle.

'Those windows don't open.'

The voice, rising suddenly from the darkness startles Colin so much he nearly falls from his perch.

Caught!

'Bradley?' in a frightened whisper.

'Yeah, it's me,' says Bradley. 'Come on. Get down here.' There is no anger in his voice; he speaks quietly and in the same friendly tone he has used with Colin since their reconciliation.

Colin climbs back down and faces Bradley, whose form is dimly visible in the darkness.

'And even if you could've got the window open and you didn't break your leg jumping down into the yard, how were you gunna get out through the gates? They're locked, y'know, and you could never've climbed over the wall. You're not fuckin' Spider-Man.'

'I don't care,' sniffles Colin, tears streaming down his face. 'I've got out of here. I'm not staying!'

'It's Chorley, ain't it?' says Bradley. 'He did something to you: when he called you up to his room. Started messing around with you, didn't he?'

'He's a dirty old man!' explodes Colin with sudden fury. 'He's filthy! I'm not staying here with me anymore and you can't make me! So don't try to stop me!'

'I'm not gunna stop you, I'm gunna help you,' is Bradley's reply. Resting one hand on Colin's shoulder, he raises the other and Colin hears the jingling of a set of keys.

'Chorley's keys! Where did you get them?'

'Me? Wasn't nothing to do with me,' says Bradley, all innocence. 'You pinched 'em, didn't you? Just now, before you come down here. You snuck into Chorley's room, didn't you? And you found the keys in his jacket and you swiped 'em, didn't you? And you never woke Chorley up, cuz he was snoring his head off the whole time. And now you're gunna unlock that door over there, get across the yard and open the gates, and then when you've done that you're just gunna chuck the keys back into the yard and make yourself scarce. Now, come on: before it starts getting light.'

They go to the door. Bradley unlocks and opens it. They step out into the frosty pre-dawn and hare across the yard to the gates. Here the numerous bolts are pulled back with as little noise as possible, the padlock opened and the chain removed; and finally with the largest key of the bunch, the lock of the gate itself opened. Bradley pulls one of the gates open.

'Now go on, get out of here,' he says, throwing the bunch of keys back into the yard.

'H-how do you think I should get to Norton-Braisley?'

'Norton-Braisley?' Bradley looks bemused. 'Why would you wanna go there? Other end of the country, ain't it?'

'Yes, b-but my sister's there, and I haven't got anywhere else to go—'

'You go to the school, you pillock.'

'The school? But it got burnt down—'

'No, the school *didn't* get burnt down. It never got attacked by the yellow gang. That was all a lie. It was just a story Chorley told you cuz he wanted you to stop moping.'

Colin can hardly believe his ears. 'Then they're still there? The teachers and—?'

'Far as I know they are, yeah. So just you go straight there. You'll be alright; it's nearly light, so the gangs will've packed up for the night and gone home by now.'

'Thanks, Bradley…' says Colin, sniffling.

'Yeah, yeah. Just shift your arse already.'

With a slap on the arm from Bradley that is both a shove and a valediction, Colin slips out through the gate and starts running down the street.

Chapter Eleven
'That Miscreant Has Told You Nothing but Lies!'

Colin practically flies along the streets.

He had been bracing himself for the gargantuan task of making the journey alone all the way from Eastchester to Norton-Baisley in search of his sister; something he would have considered completely impossible before the world ended, but which had seemed like his only option: and now it turns out that Natasha and others are all still at the school, that they've been there all the time, and that story about the school burning down was all a big fat lie!

He had thought his only hope of safety and sanctuary were in the far north of England, when all the time safety and sanctuary had been just around the corner!

Daylight spreads itself across the sky, expelling the darkness, as Colin makes his joyful way through the silent streets.

He reaches Park Lane and the familiar buildings of the school come into view; still standing and intact, just like Bradley has promised. It's still early, though. Will anybody be up yet to answer the intercom at the gate?

Colin soon discovers this question to be an academic one: the intercom beside the gates has been vandalised, the metal panel staved in and clearly inoperative. However, this setback is a minor one: the railing walls fronting the schoolyard are easy enough for a nimble youth to scale, and this Colin now does, dropping safely down into the yard.

Fizzing over with thoughts of his reunion with Natasha, Colin hares across the yard to the main entrance. If nobody's up yet then the doors will probably be locked—well if they are, he'll just have to try knocking; and if that doesn't work, he'll just have to wait!

The doors prove to be unlocked. Colin steps into the foyer. It was here that Natasha came to meet him the first time he came here; when she had hugged him and it had felt so good, so comforting…

He goes to the staffroom and the staffroom is empty.

Colin moves onto the library, the common room for the refugee students. Empty.

Yep. Everyone must be still in bed, then.

Still unconcerned, Colin makes his way up to the first floor, where the two classrooms that had been turned into dormitories are located. He would really like to see Natasha first, but she'll be in the girls' dormitory and he can't really go in there—that'd be like going into the girls' changing rooms! No, he'll have to go into the boys' room and wake up Paul Mitchell, his (possible) rival for Natasha's affections. Or maybe he could just wake up one of the other kids… Doesn't really matter who he wakes up first, does it…?

It certainly doesn't, because when Colin walks into the classroom the first thing he sees is that there's nobody there to wake up. Moreover, the mattresses that had been set out on the floor last time he was here are now stacked up against the wall; and of the students' bags and belongings that had littered the place before, there is no sign.

Now Colin *does* start to worry. He remembers Bradley's words, that 'as far as he knew' they were still at the school. But he didn't know for *sure*; he hadn't actually seen them here; he just *assumed* they were still there because he knew that Chorley's story about the school being burned down was a lie. But Colin knows, from what was being said that day he was here, that they *were* thinking about possibly leaving Eastchester if things didn't get any better—and that was *weeks* ago.

Colin goes to what was the girls' sleeping room and finds the same story: mattresses stacked against the wall, no sign of personal belongings.

That's it. They've gone.

Crushed by this fresh disappointment, Colin aimlessly and tearfully wanders the vacant corridors of his school; they echo with the sound of his solitary footsteps. All his hopes of comfort and protection, he finds himself thrown again upon his own resources—and these, it must be confessed, or an unreliable set of resources at best, and in very short supply.

He returns to the ground floor, thinking how the school was before the Incident, all noise and bustle, and how much he'd hated it, and how he'd often come home from school with a splitting headache… Now it seems like a halcyon time; now he just wishes that things could go back to being like they were then… The world now it has ended is a terrifying place, where everything keeps changing, and nowhere is really safe, and no-one is there to save you from the bad people…

His footsteps have taken him to the back regions of the school building, where the woodwork and metalwork classrooms are located. He hears a sound; the ringing sound of something small and metallic striking the ground; the sound comes from outside. The corridor windows here are high up in the wall, so Colin cannot see outside, so he pauses and listens. There is no repeat of the sound. He runs to the nearest exit doors. The doors are glass-panelled and look out on a courtyard formed by the rear wall of the school building and two single-storey extensions.

Parked in the courtyard is the school minibus. The bonnet is up and somebody is bent over the engine. From where his present vantagepoint Colin can only see the rear of this somebody; a denim rear and unmistakably female in configuration.

Colin opens the door and steps outside. Alerted by the sound, the mechanic rises from her work and turns to face Colin, and Colin sees that the owner of those denim hindquarters is Miss Lantier, his French French teacher.

'Colin!' she exclaims.

Her face lights up. Dropping the tools she is holding she rushes forward and, cupping his face between her hands, kisses him noisily on the mouth—and her hands being the worse for grease and engine oil, leaves sticky black handprints on Colin's cheeks.

'Ah, *mon chéri!*' she gushes. 'I thought you were lost! And it was all of my fault! I was so distraught! Where 'ave you been all this time?'

Colin is every bit as ecstatic as his teacher at this unexpected reunion. 'I got captured by a gang! A gang of looters! And they told me that the school got burnt down and you'd all gone away!'

Breathless explanations follow.

'So that is what happened! We just did not know! And when I saw that my letter to you had gone, I was even more at a loss!'

'What letter's that?' asks Colin, confused.

'Why, the one I left at your 'ouse! You did not receive it? Ah! Then I will explain: when I come back to your 'ouse that afternoon and see that something has transpired, I drive around all over the neighbourhood, up and down the streets, hoping to find some trace of you. But, no! There is no sign. Finally, I 'ave to admit defeat. So, I return to your house, and you see, I do not know if you 'ave been captured, or if perhaps you have just fled from the vandals who enter your house. Hoping this might be the case and that you will return later, either to your house or to ze school, I decide I will take your things back with me, just as we had planned. So I pack all your clothes, and I take your mattress and your bedding and I put them in a van, and I bring them back to the school. But first, I write a letter to you, saying what I have done, and I leave the letter in your bedroom, yes? But then, when I come back the next day, the letter 'as gone!'

'Yes, but by the next day my whole house had been looted, hadn't it? They came that night and stole everything, so they probably stole your letter as well.'

Now it's Miss Lantier's turn to look confused. 'What is this you say? Looters did not steal everything from your 'ouse. When I come back next day, my letter to you is all that is missing.'

'You mean…?' Colin is dumbfounded. And then: 'Chorley! He lied to me about that as well! He went back there and he must have read your letter and not told me about it!'

'Ah, this Chorley!' says Miss Lantier, pronouncing it 'Surely.' 'That miscreant has told you nothing but lies! Ah, if only I had not left you alone, and none of this would have 'appened! I thought you would be safe, that there would be no danger during the hours of daylight. I was wrong. The others, they blame me as well. 'You should not have left him on his own!' cries Natasha. She was furious with me, that child. M Brandon, even he admonishes me. 'You make a bad decision, Miss Lantier,' he say.'

'Where *are* all the others?' wonders Colin. 'When I came in just now there wasn't anyone in the staffroom or the library, and the sleeping rooms looked like you weren't using them anymore. I thought you'd all gone away!'

'Ah, of course! You do not know; how could you? Our numbers 'ave been greatly depleted since you were here previously. We are only four now: M Brandon and myself, Natasha and Paul. The other students: they have all gone!'

'Gone where?'

'Gone to join the colour gangs! Yes, they vanish in the night—

run away. It is contagious; a madness. That is why we are departing this town.'

'Depar—What, you mean you're going?' Colin struggles to keep up. He's glad that Natasha is still here, although not so glad that Paul Maxwell is here too—and now it turns out they were about to leave after all.

'That is so. We depart tomorrow,' Miss Lantier tells him. 'Today, we make our preparations. I, you see, am giving the minibus the service to ensure she is in good working order. We are going on a journey. So you see, you pick the right time to escape from this Chorley, Colin. You might have miss us, otherwise.'

A day later and he might have got here to find they really *had* gone! 'So where are the others? Have they gone out?'

'The others? No, they are all here. M Brandon, I think he is on the roof, checking his Geiger-counter. And Paul and Natasha, they are around here somewhere; they take their morning constitutional.'

Colin has barely opened his mouth to inquire what a 'constitutional' might be, when Natasha and Paul appear in person, from the direction of the playing fields. For a moment it looks like Natasha and Paul are holding hands—but then the thought is swept from Colin's mind when he sees the look of joy that transfigures Natasha's face when she catches sight of him.

'Colin! Oh my God; it's you!'

In a moment she has crossed the intervening space and she's hugging him ecstatically, repeating 'Ohmygod, ohmygod!' over and over and both of them are crying and Colin is as happy as he's ever been in his life.

And when she finally releases him: 'Look at you, scruff-pot: you've got oil all over your face, and now you've bloody got it on mine, as well!'

The day is devoted to making their preparations for leaving Eastchester. Tasks have already been allocated, and Colin is told he can 'have the day off' and just sit in the library and watch TV;

and normally he would have been quite happy to do this, but he feels he ought to be helping, so he drifts around, assisting with tasks here and there.

Most of the work revolves around packing the supplies they will require for their journey, which might end up being an extended one. Clothes, food, camping equipment—everything they might possibly require. (The minibus is a twenty-seater, and as there are only five of them in the group, there's plenty of spare room for storing supplies.)

Colin spends a portion of the day assisting Natasha sorting and packing the party's clothes, which have just been laundered. In the off-limits-to-students nether-regions of the school there is actually a room housing several washing machines! Colin had never known before that there even *was* a basement to the school, let alone that it had washing machines…

Over breakfast, Colin had given a full account of his time as a member of Chorley's gang. The events of last night which prompted his bid for freedom, Colin, embarrassed and ashamed, had only stutteringly described in the vaguest of terms—but this was more than enough for his companions to join up the dots. Natasha had been all for going straight to the gang's headquarters and inflicting summary justice on Chorley, but Mr Brandon had quietly vetoed this idea, arguing that it might lead to consequences, and it was best for the group to stay together on campus and not endanger their intended departure of the following day. For his own part, Colin will be satisfied if he just never crosses paths with Chorley again; but still, he likes how Natasha got all indignant on his behalf; it showed that she cared about him, didn't it?

Before breakfast, Mr Brandon had returned from the roof with the information that radiation readings were still at their normal background level.

'A lot of this country's electricity is generated by nuclear power, young Hargreaves,' he had explained. 'Now, if any of those nuclear power stations had been abandoned by its operators for any amount of time, the nuclear reactors would have gone into meltdown; there would have been a major nuclear incident by now, and we would all be dropping like flies from radiation sickness. This hasn't happened, ergo the nuclear power stations are still being staffed. In fact, all power stations, water supply stations, gas supply stations, must still be running smoothly—it's been a month now since the Incident, and we haven't lost any of the basic utilities. Not here in Eastchester we haven't, anyway.

'So, who's running everything? And now the shelves of the supermarkets have been restocked as well. Where's it all coming from? Who's producing all these anonymously-packaged food products? We don't even how or when or by whom the food is being delivered. Nobody seems to have seen anything. It's as though the stuff just materialised on the supermarket shelves overnight.'

Colin suggests that perhaps the aliens made the food materialise on the shelves.

'Well, *someone* is in control, it seems. And whoever it is, they obviously don't want us to starve to death. But yet nobody has shown themselves, nobody has made any announcements. Yes, I know that the signals are still out, there's still no television, radio or internet; but there are other ways of broadcasting the news. Before the advent of electronic communication news travelled very slowly, but it still travelled. They could have printed up a newspaper of some kind and delivered it to the shops along with the food; leaflets could have been dropped by aircraft; messengers could have been sent out across the country. But no, whoever is pulling the strings seems determined to keep us in the dark. No-one's made any attempts to establish law and order—we've all just been left to our own devices. I would very much like to find out why.

'Something else: they've restocked the shelves of the supermarkets, but one thing that *hasn't* been replenished are the fuel supplies at the service stations. True, not many people are actually using their cars much at the moment, but even so, there's going to be a petrol shortage very soon. Apparently our unseen overlords don't want us travelling around. I wonder why? I wonder what discoveries we're going to make when we set off on our grand adventure…'

Colin has been keeping an eye on Natasha and Paul during the day, looking for anything that might suggest they're going out. Chorley's words about teenage girls and rock musicians have lodged in his mind, and even though he knows Chorley's a big fat liar and that he just said those things because he wanted to get Colin to stop liking Natasha… there still might be something in it… He *thought* he'd seen Natasha and Paul holding hands this morning when they'd first appeared; but now he's not sure if they were or not; it was only a glimpse… One thing that's clear enough is that Natasha and Paul are very chummy; they seem to have a lot of things in common, opinions about this and that, theories about the Incident, and they like talking about them together. When they're in the middle of one of these conversations Colin feels very left out; he feels small and inadequate, because Natasha talks like she's way above him, like she's as brainy as Year Eleven student Paul Mitchell, even though she's really only Year Eight like Colin and only six months older than he is—but that six months *does* make her thirteen and officially a teenager, while Colin is still only twelve and not yet a teenager. It must make a big difference, that extra six months…

By teatime they've finished their preparations and they could have set off there and then if they wanted to; but it's getting dark and they decide it's best to stick to the original plan and set off first thing tomorrow morning.

It's a decision that nearly proves fatal.

Chapter Twelve
'We've Got to Get Out of Here!'

Colin dreams of the wolfpack. The savage gestalt, smashing, burning and destroying everything in its path. The wolfpack howl fills the air while the city burns.

And then he is awake and surrounded by darkness. Lying on his own mattress, under his own duvet, wearing his own pyjamas, for the first confused moment, he thinks he is in his own bedroom; but then he remembers: he is in the English teacher' staffroom adjacent to the classrooms that had previously served as the girls' and the boys' dormitories. His mattress is on the floor, and next to it Natasha's and Paul's mattresses.

And he can still hear the sound of the wolfpack; it wasn't just a dream: they are outside right now. At first he tries to convince himself that they are only passing, passing along the street outside the school—but the sound is too loud, too sustained: they're not just passing, they are here, inside the school grounds.

He scents a sharp smell in the air, the acrid tang of smoke.

The school is on fire. They've set fire to the school!

The End of the World has come back with a vengeance.

Colin sits bolt upright in bed and by the moonlight he sees that the two vacant mattresses have been vacated, covers thrown back in a hurry. Natasha and Paul have gone! They've run away! They've abandoned him, forgotten about him!

Now, many people, upon finding themselves situated as Colin now is, would blindly have given into their instincts of self-preservation and made for the nearest exit, regardless of any perils that might intervene—but not Colin Cleveland: he rises above these dubious instincts inherited from our primitive ancestors; he, the thinking man (or boy), triumphs over the brute beast, Colin's reaction is swift and prompt: instead of flight he abandons hope, initiates his Doomsday Defence Plan, and buries himself under his duvet.

Even cocooned under his duvet the smell of smoke grows rapidly stronger, and if Colin still harbours any lingering hope, it is the hope that the smoke will finish him before the flames reach him, and that dying of smoke-inhalation is one of those painless, if not downright pleasant deaths, as drowning is reputed to be.

But now he hears the approach of running footsteps in the corridor outside. They're getting closer… The wolfpack is inside the school! And now it looks like Colin might not even live longer enough to succumb to asphyxiation. You'd have thought (thinks a detached part of Colin's brain) that having set fire to the building, the attackers would have preferred to watch the conflagration from without rather than within…

But then, they can't know that he's here in this room, can they? Yes, maybe they'll just run straight on past…

But they don't because the door bursts open, and Colin, curled up in a tight foetal ball, braces himself for the worst. And then hands are laid upon him and start to drag him from the mattress, and Colin starts to struggle and scream.

The duvet, the one tangible barrier between himself and reality, is yanked away from him.

'Colin!'

That voice! Natasha!

'Stop struggling, you idiot! We've got to get out of here!'

'No! Leave me alone!'

'Don't be stupid! The whole place is on fire! Colin! COLIN!'

'We haven't got time for this!' snarls a new voice and Colin is dragged roughly to his feet.

Paul Mitchell.

'Come on!'

Taking an arm each, Natasha and Paul exit the room and start running, and Colin has no choice but to fall into pace with them. As they approach the stairs, the smell of smoke becomes much stronger.

'What's happening?' sobs Colin.

'It's the yellow gang!' reports Natasha breathlessly. 'They've broken in and they've torched the place! We've got to get out of here!'

The yellow gang! It's the yellow gang who've attacked the school and set fire to it—Chorley's made-up story has suddenly come true!

Colin sees two figures appear out of the haze, standing by the doors to the staircase. The figures resolve themselves into the forms of Miss Lantier and Mr Brandon, the latter looking a lot more agitated than the former. Colin sees that they also, like

Natasha and Paul, have had time to get dressed. Why wasn't he? He feels exposed having to run around in his bare feet and just wearing his pyjamas. (But at least, with the school burning down around him, it's not cold.)

'You've got him! Good!' says Miss Lantier, and leads the way down the stairs. The smoke is much thicker now. It attacks Colin's throat, making him cough; and assails his eyes, making them water.

'We can still make it to the minibus!' urges Miss Lantier, when they reach the ground floor. 'But we must 'urry, while ze gang are all still in ze front yard!'

'Yes, but even if we make it to the minibus, the only way out is through the front gates!' coughs Mr Brandon. 'I'm afraid we'll have to abandon it and make our escape on foot, across the playing fields!'

'Nonsense!' retorts Miss Lantier. 'We would be fools to sacrifice the minibus!'

'I agree!' says Paul. 'The van's our only chance!'

Natasha voices her concurrence, and Colin silently adds his own. For one thing he doesn't fancy running out into the cold night in nothing but his pyjamas—and all his clothes are in the minibus!

They race along the corridors towards the rear exit, holding sleeves over their mouths to protect their throats. The smoke is now much thicker, and Colin can't even tell which way they are running. He still hasn't seen any flames, because the fires must be at the front of the building, but he can feel the heat from them. But now they are moving away from them, the heat diminishes, the smoke thins out and finally they are out through the doors and the cold night air.

At first it looks like they've made it to the minibus before any of the raiders, but then three figures appear from behind the vehicle. Youths in their late teens, each with a yellow bandanna tied around his head. All three are armed with makeshift weapons: a crowbar, a machete, a baseball bat studded with nails. The yellow gangers, with feral rictus grins, eyes wild and intense, advance on their prey.

The face of the wolfpack, just as Colin has always imagined it.

What happens next is as welcome as it is unexpected. Miss Lantier launches herself at the first attacker with a flying kick. Even as the ganger staggers under the impact, she follows up with a rapid series of kicks, felling him. She turns to the ganger with the crowbar, smashing his nose with a vicious rabbit-punch before toppling him with an uppercut. The third yellow ganger takes a swing at her with his porcupine baseball bat. Miss Lantier ducks to avoid the blow, then kicks the bat from the man's hand. Before he can either run or retrieve his weapon, he is poleaxed by a barrage of swift kicks.

Miss Lantier turns to her friends, wiping the imaginary dust from her hands.

'Let us go!'

She leads the way to the minibus. Everyone piles inside, Miss Lantier taking the wheel, Mr Brandon the front passenger seat.

'I didn't know you did karate, Miss Lantier' says Natasha, impressed.

'Savate,' Miss Lantier corrects her. 'French kick-boxing, yes?'

She turns the ignition key.

'Are you sure we can do this?' questions Mr Brandon. 'The schoolyard is thick with those maniacs; how do you propose driving through them?'

'By driving through them,' replies Miss Lantier simply. 'Fasten your safety-belts, *mes enfants!*'

Natasha, seated beside Colin, buckles her seatbelt; Colin follows suit.

The van accelerates forward along the access road which skirts the playing fields before turning to run alongside the gymnasium, taking them to the main schoolyard where both their way out and largest concentration of their enemies awaits them. The road is hedged in on one side by the gymnasium and on the other by the perimeter wall. Colin sees scattered groups of yellow-gangers in front of them, picked out by the vehicle's headlights. Some of them move to block the progress of the minibus, but when Miss

Lantier makes it very clear she has no intention of even slowing down, they scatter out of its path. A few missiles are hurled at the bus, but none with any effect. Colin sits gripping the armrests of his seat, and as Natasha is doing the same and with the centre armrest belonging to both of them, Natasha has her right hand clasped firmly and reassuringly over Colin's left hand.

They've nearly made it, thinks Colin.

But then they come to the end of the access road, and they turn into the schoolyard and before them is a vision of Pandemonium.

The whole front of the school is ablaze, a solid wall of flames from which thick plumes of smoke rise up into the clear night sky. This curtain of fire throws a lurid light across the entire schoolyard, floodlighting a scene of wild revelry. There must be hundreds of them: yellow-gangers, dancing, yelling and whooping, glorying in the fire and destruction they are wreaking. Gang-members on motorbikes weave in and around their comrades. For Colin the scene is terrifying: one of his nightmare visions of the End of the World come to life.

But Miss Lantier doesn't hesitate—she floors the accelerator and heads straight for the gaping entrance gates, directly into the thick of the crowd. The minibus ploughs right through them, the crowd screaming and throwing themselves aside to avoid being hit—but not all of them are quick enough, as testified by the numerous heavy thumps against the bodywork of the bus.

And then they are through the crowd and out through the main gates. The minibus slews to the left, and Colin sees, just as they turn, a van, a white transit van surrounded by a crowd of gangers who are in the process of tipping it over on its side. Even in that brief moment as they pass Colin is able to distinguish the two terrified occupants in the cab of the van: Chorley and Maclean!

And then the van is out of sight, and the minibus is hurtling down Park Lane, towards the main road.

'Oh lord... oh lord... oh lord...' groans Mr Brandon, invoking a deity for whom he generally never spares a thought. 'That was... that was terrible! You must have hit at least a dozen of them...!'

'I know!' enthuses Miss Lantier. 'Just like Bastille Day, yes?'

'We've got trouble,' announces Paul Mitchell. 'They're after us.'

Colin looks back, sees the headlights of several motorbikes, closing in on them.

'Oh lord…' again, from Mr Brandon. 'They're not just going to let us go, not after we just ploughed through their friends like that. Oh lord, oh lord…'

'Have faith, M Brandon,' says Miss Lantier. 'I will do my best to take us safely from this town.'

Skidding wildly, the van turns onto the thoroughfare. The motorbikes, four in number, start to close in. The leading bike overhauls them on the left, and Miss Lantier deliberately swerves across the road towards it. The rider, instinctively swerving to avoid a collision, sends himself and his machine straight off the road and into a wall. A second bike overtakes them on the right. The rider, steering one handed, a length of pipe in his other hand, cuts in front of them, and throws the pipe back at them. Miss Lantier swerves again, and the missile, intended to smash the windscreen, bounces harmlessly off the metal framework.

And then flames suddenly leap up across the road ahead. A barricade across the road, soaked with flammable material, has just been ignited. Figures swarm out from behind the barricade, armed with petrol bombs.

'Christ!' yells Paul. 'How did they get in front of us?'

'They didn't,' tersely, from Miss Lantier. 'It's the other gang; the blues. They are attacking their rivals.'

And it's true. The yellow gangers' motorbikes, as well as themselves, come under fire from a barrage of missiles. The motorbike in front of them skids to avoid collision with the flaming barricade, and the bike falls on its side, shedding its rider, who is immediately set upon by blue-gangers.

Miss Lantier turns the wheel and hits the brakes, and the minibus slews across the road, skidding sideways to a halt. Now they are facing back the way they came and the two remaining yellow gang motorbikes shoot right past them. Miss Lantier guns the engine again and they accelerate away from the flaming barricade. A few projectiles are thrown after them, but there is no attempt at pursuit, the ambushers being more concerned with dealing with the yellow gang riders.

Natasha squeezes Colin's hand.

'Looks like we've made it,' she says. Colin looks at her and she smiles at him in the dark. Colin smiles back and then blushes because he's only wearing his pyjamas.

'And now, we will head straight out of town,' comes Miss Lantier's voice. 'And we shall not stop until we are well clear.'

Mr Brandon has nothing to say to this; he appears to have gone into shock.

Part Two
The Journey

Chapter Thirteen
'You Have Seen Something You Did Not Wish To, Yes?'

Colin awakes to broad daylight. At first he is confused as to why he is lying on an upholstered seat instead of in a bed, but then memory slips back into place and he remembers he's in the school minibus.

He can hear the sound of stertorous breathing emanating from the front of the bus, otherwise all is quiet. He pulls back the blanket that covers him and sits up. The source of the snoring is Mr Brandon, asleep in the front passenger seat. Apart from Colin and him the minibus is empty. Colin scans the surroundings outside. A gravel carpark, surrounded by trees. There is just one other vehicle parked in the carpark: a car, a hatchback. The hatchback was there when they arrived last night (or early this morning) and it had been deduced that it had most likely been there since the day of the Incident, and that its owner or owners would never be coming back to claim it. Colin can see no sign of the others members of the group. They must have gone to the picnic area.

He looks at his watch. Half past eight, just gone. He needs to get dressed. He looks over the back of the seat, wonders how he's going to find his stuff amongst all the luggage and equipment piled on the back seats of the bus, but then he remembers Natasha putting his sports bag under his seat when she tucked him in last night. He pulls the bag out, opens it and is grateful to find, thanks to Miss Lantier, everything he needs, even a pair of trainers. Where should he dress? Right here? He surveys the carpark again. Still no sign of the others. But even so… clutching his clothes, Colin retreats under the blanket, and had there been any observer present, they would have seen the squirming, writhing form of a boy dressing himself while lying horizontal across a bus-seat and covered by a blanket, and they would probably have wondered what he was up to under there.

Having performed this operation with the ease and facility of nimble youth, Colin throws back the blanket, runs his fingers through his hair and puts on his trainers. He rises from his seat and opens the sliding side door, which has been left ajar, being careful not to wake the still snoring Mr Brandon. He steps down onto the gravel car-park.

It is a brisk, sunny morning, much milder than the day before; a spring-is-in-the-air morning. This particular brand of air is invigorating, especially to the young, and Colin inhales it appreciatively. He feels buoyed up this morning, feels like he's ready to face the world (even though technically the world has ended.) What an escape they had last night! He finds that he can enjoy that frantic drive now that it is safely in the past.

Colin sets off along the access road which leads from the main road to the picnic site, passing the large illustrated signboard displaying a map of the pathways through the nature reserve, as well as, for the benefit of bird-watchers, line drawings of some of the avian species that are to be found here. The picnic area comes into view. Colin knows this place well from family outings, when he and his big sister had both been much younger. It looks as though it has been unvisited since the Incident; there is an absence of litter and none of the picnic benches have been defaced or vandalised in any way.

And there is Miss Lantier, sitting at one of the benches, reclining against the table, smoking a cigarette. (Colin didn't know she smoked!) No sign of Natasha and Paul…

'Bonjour, Colin!' Miss Lantier greets him as he walks up to her. 'I trust you slept well? But then you youngsters always do, yes?'

Colin assures her that he has slept well. A spirit lamp, kettle, mugs, and all the other appurtenances for making morning tea and coffee have been set out on the table.

'And is M Brandon coming?' inquires Miss Lantier.

'No, he's still asleep,' says Colin. And then, trying to sound casual: 'Where's Natasha?'

'Oh, she has just gone for 'er constitutional,' is the reply.

That 'constitutional' again! Must be a French word.

He decides to take the plunge and confess his ignorance. 'What's a... what's a constitutional?'

Miss Lantier looks surprised. 'Why, a constitutional is a walk; an invigorating stroll, yes?'

Colin looks around, still sees no Natasha.

'Which way did she go...?'

'Over zhere, along the nature trail.'

Miss Lantier points with her cigarette off to the left where the footpath into the woods commences. Close to this path is the functional brick building which houses the public conveniences.

'Would you like a cup of tea, Colin?' asks Miss Lantier.

'No, I... er, I need to go to the toilet first...' says Colin.

Colin makes his way to the toilets. The toilets are open, and while he is relieving himself at the urinals, it occurs to Colin that most public toilets will have been left open like this, with the Incident happening as it did at four fifty-nine, before these places were locked up for the night.

Just as he is washing his hands, Colin hears a cough, a clearing of the throat, emanating from one of the toilet cubicles, and looking in the mirror sees that indeed one of the row of doors behind him is closed. For a moment he is alarmed, imagining a stranger, possibly hostile. But then the solution presents itself: Paul Mitchell! This thought is very welcome to Colin, who had been entertaining powerful suspicions that Natasha had not gone for her morning stroll alone. But no, Paul is in fact right here, and judging from the spreading aroma, will be here for a while longer. The field is clear! Time to seize the moment!

Not wanting to lose a precious second, Colin scorns the hand-dryer and hurries outside and straight onto the beckoning nature trail. Of course! He should have guessed Natasha would be on her own: Miss Lantier would have said so if Paul had gone for a walk with her! Yes, he'd just assumed Paul would be with her because Paul had been with her that time they appeared yesterday, when they may or may not have been holding hands.

Colin hurries along the path, eager to catch up with his

beloved. The only problem is that there are occasional forks in the path, and having no Native American blood, Colin is not an expert tracker.

However, in the end it transpires that Colin only needs a working pair of ears in order to track down Natasha, and these he possesses.

The sound is unexpected, and comes from off the path and amongst the trees to his left. Audible gasps in rhythmic sequence; like someone engaged in a set of vigorous exercises; push-ups or something... Colin is momentarily confused, but the sounds are definitely female, so it must be Natasha… But then, why not? Natasha's a sporty girl, always has been, so why shouldn't she be doing a morning workout? Maybe she'll ask him to join her!

Blithely, Colin strikes off the path and towards the source of the sounds. Almost there now… There! Just past those bushes…

Colin skirts the bushes and behold! There across a small clearing is Natasha, performing her morning exercises in the vertical position, back against a tree, and in close partnership with Paul Mitchell, that self-same Paul Mitchell Colin was sure he'd left back in the toilets.

Natasha. Natasha as Colin has never seen her before, jeans around her ankles, brows contorted, teeth bared. Natasha, with her very audible breathing exercises perfectly synchronised with Paul Mitchell's vigorous pelvic thrusts—altogether a stimulating physical workout, just the thing to set you up for the day.

But very much *not* what Colin Cleveland wanted to see. And when Natasha gasps the words: 'Oh, fuck…! Yes… YES…!' that is the last straw. He turns, he runs, he flees from the awful spectacle, stumbling and crying.

How could she? How could she let someone do that to her? Just like her porn-star counterpart on the back of that DVD! It was like she was totally transformed; like she wasn't the same person; wasn't a human being anymore! And she said the F-word as well! She never normally says the F-word.

Colin stumbles on, all but blinded by his tears, thoughts of Natasha and Paul colliding with memories of that night with

Chorley. Chorley and his violating hands. *Ol' Chorley'll look after you.*

It's all dirty! It's all vile, dirty stuff!

He stumbles suddenly onto the main footpath—and into the arms of Miss Lantier. He looks at her, sees both amusement and sympathy on her elfin face.

'Ah, my poor boy,' she sighs. 'You have seen something you did not wish to, yes? There…there…'

She hugs him, pressing his face against her chest, and the floodgates open Colin cries his heart out into his teacher's warm angora sweater, and she soothes and caresses him with her voice, her arms, her scent…

The deluge over, Miss Lantier wipes Colin's eyes and taking him by the hand, leads him back down the path towards the picnic site.

'Yes, they have been lovers for some weeks now, those two,' she tells him. 'Natasha informed me of this herself when she wished to consult me on sexual health matters; but even before then I had surmised how things were. It was only to be expected…'

Taken up with the sight that he has seen, and the flurry of emotions it has thrown him into, Colin has forgotten something very important, something that's been tugging at the back of his mind… Its sudden arrival at the *front* of his mind stops him dead in his tracks.

'There's someone in the toilets!'

Chapter Fourteen
'You Mean You've Seen UFOs?'

Colin and Miss Lantier arrive at the picnic area at a run. The first thing they see is Mr Brandon, conversing affably with a bearded man, a complete stranger.

'Ah, there you are,' says Mr Brandon. 'This gentleman is Mr Forbes. He tells me he's been travelling around the country on foot. I'm sure he'll have much valuable information to share with us.'

Mr Forbes turns to the newcomers and doffs his porkpie hat. He is a middle-aged man, with pale eyes and a placid expression. His clothes are rustic and he carries a rucksack.

Mr Brandon performs the introductions. 'These are two of my friends. My colleague Miss Lantier, and one of my students Colin Hargreaves.'

'Cleveland,' says Colin.

'That's right; Cleveland. Where have Natasha and Mitchell wandered off to?'

'Just taking a stroll,' says Miss Lantier. 'They will be along presently.'

'Well, let's organise some breakfast. I don't know about anyone else, but I need my morning cuppa. Would you care to join us, Mr Forbes?'

'The offer is a most generous one and I would be honoured,' replies Forbes.

They are seated at a picnic table. The kettle has boiled and drinks have been dispensed. Colin, munching on a cereal bar, sits at the end of the bench; next to him sits Miss Lantier, and next to *her* Natasha. On the opposite seat the newcomer Forbes sits facing him; beside Forbes sits Mr Brandon and beside *him* sits Paul Mitchell, facing Natasha.

Colin hasn't looked Natasha in the eye since her return to the picnic site. For one thing, he has decided he's going to give her the cold shoulder treatment; but in addition to this, another question nags at him: Did she *see* him? When he discovered her doing what she was doing with Paul, did she see him? Colin just can't be sure. She was certainly facing in his direction, so she *could* have seen him; but she had clearly been preoccupied with what she was doing, and her eyes had looked like they were closed, or at least half-closed… The idea that she might have seen him tortures him; even if he hadn't decided on giving her the cold shoulder anyway, he would be just be too embarrassed to look her in the eye if he knew for sure that she'd seen him.

Meanwhile, their guest, Mr Forbes, has been telling his story. 'I hail from a small northern hamlet named Huffy. I am a poet and I have always preferred to live in pastoral surroundings. I resided with my dear wife Lydia; alone, because we have never been blessed with children. Lydia disappeared on that fatal afternoon. She had just repaired to the kitchen to brew a pot of tea—alas, she never returned.'

Says Mr Brandon: 'Yes, from what we have been able to determine, nobody actually disappeared while they were in view of anyone else. The person was always out of the room, or at least not in anybody else's line of vision.'

'Quite so. I arrived at the same conclusion when confabulating with my fellow villagers; after the Incident, we were a greatly diminished community.'

'So, what made you decide to take to the road, if I may ask?'

'You may. It was simply that having lost my beloved wife I felt cast adrift. Feeling thus, and impelled also I will confess, by a sense of curiosity, I decided to cast myself adrift entirely. I packed my bag and said farewell to the village of Huffy, with no fixed goal or destination, but merely to observe this altered world of ours, and perhaps gain some knowledge as to the true facts behind the Incident.'

'Isn't it dangerous to be wandering around the countryside?' inquires Natasha. 'I mean, with no police or anything, aren't there lots of gangs around?'

'I have encountered no aggressive gangs,' is the answer. 'Only the occasional wayfarer like myself. But then, in my wanderings I have tended to avoid the larger population centres, so I cannot speak for the conditions in those.'

'You say you have met other people,' says Miss Lantier. 'But what about traffic? Is there much traffic on the roads?'

'Very little at all from what I have seen,' is the reply. 'But then, I have not felt obliged to follow these man-made highways in my travels. No, I often strike out directly across pasture or heath, ignoring those artificial pathways.'

'So, from what you have seen you don't think people are travelling about much?' questions Mr Brandon.

'That would be my impression. There was one occasion, however, when I happened to come across one of the main artificial causeways of this country: I believe it was the Great North Road. There I observed a whole fleet of articulated lorries proceeding along the otherwise deserted dual carriageway. Container lorries they were, and identical in conformation: all of them painted grey and bearing no markings.'

Mr Brandon is intrigued. 'Lorries, eh? I wonder if it's these trucks that have been delivering the food that's starting to appear on the supermarket shelves?'

'I cannot answer that for sure, but I can say that the lorries I saw were the identical shade of grey in hue as the packaging of the new supermarket products; one cannot help but make the connection.'

'That proves it then,' declares Natasha. 'It's people behind all this, not aliens.'

'Yeah, if trucks are bringing the food to the shops, then we know it's not being beamed onto the shelves by aliens,' says Paul.

'True, but I would say it's still too soon to assume that there is no extraterrestrial involvement here,' cautions Mr Brandon.

'What? Aliens driving lorries?' scoffs Natasha. 'Little grey men? Their feet wouldn't be able to reach the pedals.'

'I too would not be too hasty in ruling out the other-worldly from the equation,' says Forbes. 'Since setting off on my travels, I have observed strange vessels haunting the skies, both during the day and in the hours of darkness.'

Everyone is staring at Forbes now, but the man remains placid.

Aliens! thinks Colin. He knew it had to be aliens!

'You mean you've seen UFOs?' challenges Paul. 'Alien spaceships?'

'Unidentified craft, certainly. Whether they are actually of extraterrestrial construction, I could not say.'

'This is astonishing news, Mr Forbes,' says Mr Brandon. 'We have seen nothing of the kind in Eastchester; no aircraft at all.

Can you tell us what these craft looked like?'

'I have only seen them from a distance, but they appeared to be saucer-shaped objects, like many of those allegedly witnessed over the years. Seen at night, they appear as bright lights, and like many previously-reported phenomena they possess the ability to hover motionless in the air and then to instantaneously move off at great speeds.'

'You've witnessed this yourself?'

'I have indeed.'

'Well, no propulsion system known to human science can produce that kind of instantaneous acceleration.'

'Doesn't prove it's aliens,' insists Natasha. 'It could be people who've got secret technology.'

Says Mr Brandon: 'What about you, Mr Forbes? Do you attribute the signal disruption and the mass disappearance of people to extraterrestrial or to human intervention?'

'I confess to having been unable to form any definite opinion on the subject. There are arguments in favour of and against both hypotheses. All I can say is the world is now a much-altered place, and I do not predict that things will ever return to how they were before.'

After breakfast, they pack up their things and set off in the minibus. Colin had planned to make it clear to Natasha he was giving her the cold shoulder by deliberately not sitting next to her—but upon getting into the bus, discovered his plans had been forestalled: Natasha had already taken a seat next to Paul!

As they were preparing to leave, Mr Brandon had invited Forbes to join their party; an offer the man had politely declined, for which Colin for one is glad. He doesn't want any stranger joining their group.

Only a few hours before Colin had woken up feeling great. Relieved at their escape from Eastchester, and that they were together and heading out on a great adventure, with the minibus as their 'base,' their safe haven (kind of like the TARDIS, but not bigger on the inside)—but now his mood has completely soured.

Mr Brandon, who has placed himself firmly back in charge now that there are no immediate dangers to be confronted, has proposed making the nearby town of Kettleworth their first port of call. The route they are taking will take them past a village called Orville Green; they can stop there first, and speak to the inhabitants, if there are any. (According to Forbes, some of the smaller villages have been abandoned completely.)

Emerging from woodland into more open country, a church-tower becomes visible in the distance, and presently they are driving into the village of Orville Green. A single street leads them to the green which (presumably) gives the hamlet its name. A square plot of grass, with a pond in the centre and a single tree of great antiquity, looked upon on all sides by rows of neat cottages. Beyond the green, the single village street continues towards the church and then out of the village.

Miss Lantier parks the minibus on the edge of the green. All is quiet; not a soul in sight. The ground rises sharply beyond the cottages in front of them; a green hillside on the summit of which a large stately home commands the village.

'Looks deserted,' is Paul's comment.

'Perhaps it is,' answers Mr Brandon.

'Or per'aps they are all just shut indoors watching ze television, as they were in Eastchester,' says Miss Lantier.

'Yes, but in a small community like this, you would expect the residents to have banded together more.'

'Well, they can't be outside all the time,' points out Natasha. 'And they might just be keeping out of sight cuz they don't know who we are.'

'Well, let's try and show them that we're harmless,' suggests Mr Brandon.

They get out of the minibus and—looking harmless—stroll along the perimeter of the green. Colin studies the windows of the cottages as he passes them. In one he sees a net-curtain fall back into place. Natasha has seen it as well and announces the fact.

'Then we can assume we are indeed under observation,' says Mr Brandon.

They are, and as will shortly transpire, not only from the village residents.

They come to a shop, a typical village post office cum general store. The sign reads 'closed,' but the door, when Miss Lantier tries it, proves to be unlocked. A quick look inside reveals that the shop has been stripped bare; the shelves are destitute of goods of any kind.

'Hm. I wonder if this means the shop hasn't been restocked since the Incident, or if it's just that the new stock has already been taken away,' says Mr Brandon. 'Let's try knocking on a few doors. If no-one answers, then we'll just have to accept that they're not going to trust us; and then we might as well be on our way.'

They knock on the door of the cottage adjacent to the Post Office.

No answer.

They move on to the next cottage with the same negative result.

'Oh, let's go,' says Natasha. 'They obviously don't want us here.'

'Let's just try just one more house,' responds Mr Brandon. 'I'm puzzled as to why they're being so cautious. We can't exactly look threatening to them, can we? Which is the cottage where you saw the curtain move, Natasha?'

Natasha leads them back to the house in question. This time their summons is answered. The door opens slightly and an elderly man peers at them through the crack, a troubled expression on his countenance.

'Get out of here, you idiots,' he hisses. His eyes look past Colin and friends, scanning the green, as though looking for danger.

'What's wrong?' asks Mr Brandon. 'Are you in some kind of trouble here?'

'*You're* the ones in trouble, you idiots!' snaps the man urgently. 'Unless you get back into that van of yours and get out of here right now!'

'But, what—?'

'Look, *they* will have seen you! They see everything that goes on here! They'll be on their way here by now! Just get into that bloody van of yours and get out of here while you've still got time!'

'Who are you talking about? Who's watching you?'

'Look, stop asking—Oh, forget it.' The man's voice switches to a tone of resignation. 'You're too late now. They're here.'

The door slams shut. They turn and see a group of figures marching onto the green in precise military formation; double-file, a leader at their head. At first Colin thinks they must be soldiers, but as they draw nearer, he sees that they are in fact teenage boys wearing old-fashioned public-school clothes: black blazers and short trousers, black and red striped ties and caps.

The Orville College Boys have arrived.

Chapter Fifteen
'Keep Your Hands Off Her!'

The platoon of schoolboys fans out in a rough semi-circle, surrounding the visitors from Eastchester. They ought to have seemed absurd, these schoolboys in short trousers marching like soldiers, but the villager who had tried to warn them off had sounded terrified of these people, and Colin for one has been infected with that fear.

The leader, tall, and with the physique of a rugby player, steps forward. He carries a swagger stick, and on his face sits an insolent smile which looks very much at home. He coolly surveys Colin and his friends.

'Well, well, well, what do we have here?' is his opening gambit; very unoriginal, but nobody takes him up on this. 'And where might you lot have come from?'

'We're from Eastchester,' Mr Brandon tells him. 'We were just passing through. We're not here to bother anyone, so if we're not welcome here, we'll be happy to—'

'Yes, but you're *weren't* just passing through, are you?' cuts in the boy. 'Because you stopped your van and got out.'

'We were just curious to ascertain the situation in this village; that's all,' says Mr Brandon. 'Who might you be, young man? I see you're wearing—'

The boy interrupts him again. 'I *might* be lots of things, *old* man, but my name is Pendennis Major, head pupil of Orville College. That's Orville College, up there,' indicating the building on the hilltop. 'And as for the situation here you say you are so curious about; well, it's quite simple: *we're* in charge around here. The village of Orville Green has been annexed by Orville College, and everyone in it is subject to our commands; and I do mean *everyone*.'

'And why would the people 'ere kowtow to an *enfant* like you?' sneers Miss Lantier.

Pendennis Major walks up to the French woman, coolly surveys her from head to toe. She meets his insolent appraising look with a scornful one of her own.

'In spite of your impertinent tone, I shall answer your question on this occasion, *mamzelle*, because you're new here and you don't know the ropes,' says Pendennis. 'The good citizens of this hamlet obey us because if they didn't, they would starve to death. We control the food supply around here, and if the people want their quota, they have to come to us for it.'

'So that is why the village shop has no stock,' says Miss Lantier. 'You take it all. Ha! If it was me, I would just leave this place and go somewhere else.'

'Yes, but the villagers here aren't going to leave this place and go anywhere else, because we happen to have their women up yonder in the school.'

'You 'ave them as 'ostages?'

'*Oui*, *mamzelle*, we 'ave them as 'ostages,' mimicking the French accent. 'In a manner of speaking, anyway. We haven't got them all locked up in the cellar or anything; no, no, that would be a shocking waste of material assets. They are all gainfully employed, working as our maidservants. They keep the place spick and span, cook our meals, and well… generally cater to all our needs.'

'You have all of the women of this village working as your maids? Your slaves?' Miss Lantier, with renewed contempt in voice and visage.

'Well, not quite all of them. We only find employment for the females of between the ages of eleven and forty who are able-bodied and of presentable appearance.'

'Between eleven and forty?'

'That's right. Secondary school to menopause, or thereabouts. We do have one or two over-forty exceptions up at the school, but she has to be a real smasher for us to bend the rules like that. As for you, *mamzelle*,' says Pendennis, looking Miss Lantier up and down again; 'I think you will make a topping French maid. Togs are different for French maids, aren't they? Short skirt and fishnets.'

'You think I'm going to—?'

'Yes, I *do* think I'm going to. You weren't invited to come here, but now that you have arrived, you are all our subjects. Here you are and here you stay.' Pendennis turns to Mr Brandon, holds out a hand. 'Keys,' he says.

'Keys?' echoes Mr Brandon

'The keys to your van, you old fossil. Hand them over.'

'I don't have the keys. Miss Lantier is our driver.'

He turns back to Miss Lantier, extends the same hand, this time with mock-courtesy.

'If you would be so kind…?'

This is it, thinks Colin, who has been watching this exchange with bated breath; if Miss Lantier is going to launch into a display of those ruthless fighting skills she demonstrated the night before (along with her equally ruthless driving skills), it will be now that she does it.

But nothing happens. Miss Lantier just hands over the car keys without protest. Pendennis Major pockets them.

'*Merci*. So tell me, who are you people? That bus of yours says Park Lane Comprehensive. That's the peasants' school over in

Eastchester, isn't it? Are you actually from that school or did you just nick their van?'

'We all belong to that school,' answers Mr Brandon; 'Miss Lantier and myself as teachers, and these three as students. But about our staying here—?'

'Not open to negotiation.' Pendennis now turns to face Colin, Paul and Natasha.

'So you three are all students at the peasants' school. How quaint.' He walks up to Natasha, eyeing her approvingly. 'And what's your name, dusky maiden?'

'Natasha,' says Natasha, voice and expression neutral.

'And from which of the colonies do you hail?'

'England.'

'And your ancestors? Where were they from?'

'Several places. I'm mixed race.'

'Oh! One of those exotic combinations, are we? Splendid. You know, I think I might take you on as my personal maid. How does that sound? Not that you have any choice in the matter.'

Paul now steps forward. 'Keep your hands off her!'

Pendennis faces him calmly. 'And who do we have here? The jealous boyfriend? Surely Natasha has better taste than to go for a puny pretty-boy like you.'

'Fuck you, you public-school ponce.'

Pendennis slashes Paul across the face with his cane. Paul launches himself at Pendennis. Pendennis sidesteps and trips him. Turning to his minions, who have remained silent and motionless spectators. 'Carter. Stubbs. Wilks. Sort this fellow out. I'd do it myself, except I don't want to sully my hands.'

The three students summoned step forward. Pouncing on Paul before he has time to even pick himself up off the ground, they start kicking him.

'Stop it!' screams Natasha.

'Alright! That's enough,' says Pendennis Major.

The three students desist, and return to their positions, leaving Paul, battered and bleeding on the tarmac. Natasha tries to go to his assistance, but Pendennis holds out a restraining arm. 'Stay where you are, my dear.' To Mr Brandon: 'You: you can take care of the pretty-boy.'

And now, the moment Colin has been dreading: Pendennis Major now turns his attention to him.

'What's your name, boy?'

'Colin Cleveland,' says Colin.

'What year are you?'

'Eight.'

'Eight? Oh yes, second form. My brother, Pendennis Minor, was in the second form. He was one of the ones who disappeared that day. You look nervous, Cleveland.'

Colin answers in the affirmative.

'Well, don't be. I'm not going to hurt you. Yes… I like the look of you Cleveland. You remind me a bit of my brother. Yes, I think I can make something of you…'

Chapter Sixteen
'We Don't Allow "Buts" Around Here'

In its tree-top nest a mother sparrow is feeding its young. The naked fledglings chirp with shrill voices as they raise their pink heads, beaks parted, instinctively begging for food. And the mother sparrow herself similarly operates on pure instinct as she drops the food into the gaping mouths of her hungry brood. There is no room for anything like conscious maternal love in the sparrow's tiny brain; instinct alone compels her to care for her young, just as instinct has compelled her to build the nest in which she laid her eggs. What we see here is simply nature at work, the everlasting cycle of birth, nurture and growth.

At least that is what we see until a gunshot rings out and the nest and its occupants are suddenly extinguished, blasted into a miasma of twigs, gore and feathers.

Pendennis Major heaves a huntsman's sigh of satisfaction as he lowers his shotgun and hands to his lackey for reloading.

The sun-dappled beech woods that form the southern perimeter of the grounds of Orville College. Present are Colin Cleveland, Pendennis Major and a third Orville student performing the office of gillie. I say a third because it seems that Colin himself has now been enrolled in the college, as he wears the same uniform as the two other boys.

'Why did you do that?' asks Colin, in a voice of appalled protest. 'They weren't hurting you.'

'I never said they were hurting me,' responds Pendennis. 'This isn't war, Cleveland; this isn't kill or be killed. This is sport; this is huntsmanship. There's only one rule when one is out hunting: if it moves, give it both barrels. Hunting for sport,' he proceeds; 'is a man's prerogative, Cleveland. Hunting for sport is man asserting his superiority over the rest of nature by blasting it into atoms. These lesser creatures exist solely for our benefit or amusement. Our superior intelligence gives us the right of life or death over the lesser animals. It has always been that way, and it jolly well always will be. That's what you've got learn, Cleveland, now that you're one of us.'

'But I don't really want to kill animals…' says Colin.

'Do you eat meat, Cleveland? Or did your parents force a vegetarian diet on you?'

'No, I eat meat…'

'Well, then. You shouldn't have any qualms about killing animals, should you?'

'Yes, but—'

'No "buts" Cleveland. We don't allow "buts" around here. Anyway, I won't be teaching you any shooting today; you can just observe, because now I'm going to proceed with your indoctrination lecture. You're new, so you need to understand how we do things around here. So, pay attention.'

Colin's face assumes what he hopes is a suitably attentive expression.

'It started with the Incident, of course,' commences Pendennis, as they proceed through the woods. 'The day everything changed and all the old rules went out the window. By a lucky fluke, when the Incident took away half the population, here at Orville

College it took away nearly all of the teachers and only a handful of the students. That's what triggered it. You see, the balance of power had shifted. The teachers who were left, they couldn't cope with the situation; they had no more idea than we did what had happened, and they were a jolly sight more worked up about it than we were. Well, we didn't waste much time taking advantage of the situation, and we soon made ourselves top-dogs in the school. The teachers didn't put up much of a fight. A couple of them we killed as examples, and the rest soon fell into line.

'So there we were. We could do what we pleased and we had the teachers waiting on us hand and foot. It was jolly enough for a while, but it wasn't enough. We had other needs to satisfy, the teachers were all chaps, and the internet had gone west. Now, where could we find what we wanted? The answer was there right under our noses: Orville Green. We needed to extend our dominions to cover the village as well as the school itself. So that's what we did: we marched on the village and it didn't take us long to subdue the population. And then we just rounded up all the eligible females, brought them back here, and enrolled them as our staff of maidservants; the teachers we relegated to gardening duties.

'So, Cleveland, this is the world we've created for ourselves, a world of the young and the strong—and you're going to become one of us, okay?'

'Couldn't I just stay down in the village with Paul Mitchell and Mr Brandon?' inquires Colin.

'No, Cleveland, you could not. I've decided to make you one of us, and that's what I'm going to do; so get used to the idea. I know you're still wet behind the ears, and you've been mollycoddled and brought up to believe in equality of the sexes and all that rot; but we'll soon knock all of that nonsense out of you. That pussy-whipped pretty-boy Mitchell: he's a lost cause; we couldn't have him disgracing our uniform. But with you, it's not too late. I can do something with you, Cleveland; I know I can. I can make a man of you. I see a lot of potential in you, but you're soft; not your fault, just the way you were brought up; you just need toughening up, that's all. You've been mixing with the wrong crowd, but now you're with the *right* crowd, and we'll soon lick you into shape.

'It's that infernal mixed school they sent you to. Coeducation was one of the worst ideas anybody ever had. That and letting women go to university. And giving them the vote. *That* was when the rot really set in. Women never should have been given the benefit of a full education. I mean it's alright teaching them to read and write and play the piano and draw pretty pictures; but that's all they need, the basics; and the domestic stuff, of course: plying the needle and cooking and all that sort of thing—but nothing more. Women, you see, were intended to be men's servants, not their equals. That's the number one rule, Cleveland. Women were never meant to be our intellectual equals. It's just not possible. They *think* they are, but really all they're doing is imitating us, the men. They try to be like us, doing all the things that only men were allowed to do before all this emancipation rot came along. But all that's going to end now: and it starts right here at this school. We're putting things back to how they should be, the men the masters, the women the slaves.'

'Rabbit at ten o'clock,' says the gillie.

They have emerged into a clearing in the forest. Colin sees the rabbit, white and stark against the background of foliage. Standing on its haunches, it looks towards the intruders, but makes no move to flee, clearly thinking itself a safe distance away from them.

Pendennis aims his shotgun.

'That's it my beauty,' he purrs. 'Just you stay right there…'

Run, stupid! thinks Colin as loudly as he can—but not loudly enough; the rabbit stays where it is.

Colin pushes Pendennis just as he fires; just a nudge to the elbow, but more than enough to spoil the shot.

The gun roars, the rabbit disappears into the bracken.

Pendennis turns on Colin, and the look of fury on his face is enough to make Colin take a step back.

'You little worm,' he grates, quivering with rage. He levels the gun at Colin's face. 'How dare you? Nobody spoils my shot, do you understand? *Nobody.* I took you on because I thought I could make something of you, Cleveland. You reminded me of my brother and I thought it wasn't too late to make a man of you. And here am I, taking the time to instruct you in our ways, and you have to go and spoil my shot, all because of some silly sentimental feelings about a stupid lump of fur. What have you got to say for yourself, Cleveland?'

'I...'

'Answer me, boy!'

'I-I'm sorry...'

'Well, you'd better be. And there'd better not be a repeat of this incident, or anything like it. Don't make me regret my decision about you, Cleveland.'

He lowers the gun.

Chapter Seventeen
'Never 'Ave I Been Groped With Such Consummate Naughtiness!'

Colin Cleveland sits disconsolate on a bench in the gardens of Orville College. His seat is on the brow of the hill and the ground slopes down before him, offering a picture postcard view of the village below, with its steepled church and the village green with its venerable oak basking in the morning sunlight.

But neither the view or the fragrant spring air does anything to lift Colin's spirits. He has been a 'student' of Orville College for several days now, and he is not enjoying the experience. If he knew what purgatory was, he would apply the word to his present surroundings. He'd never even liked going to school when he was at Park Lane Comprehensive, but compared to this place, Park Lane had been paradise. Here at Orville College, it's like the boys' changing rooms at Park Lane, except that the *whole school* is like the boys' changing rooms!

And he's stuck here.

A procession of people appears, walking up the grassy acclivity from the village to the college. The villagers, coming to collect their food ration. As they draw closer, Colin espies Paul Mitchell and Mr Brandon amongst the file of people. He envies Paul and Mr Brandon. *They* get to live in a nice cottage down in the village. *They* don't have to play rugby every day. Colin has bruises all over his body from all these obligatory 'rugger' games which Pendennis Major insists will 'make a man of him.' Colin thinks it's more likely they will make a permanent invalid of him.

(Rugby is currently the only lesson on the Orville College curriculum, and Colin finds himself actually pining for silent classrooms, ticking clocks, textbooks, and long division!)

Miss Lantier has been a real disappointment. She seems to have just rolled over and accepted the situation. Why hasn't she used her French karate (or whatever it's called) on the Orville College Boys and rescued everyone from this place? Instead, whenever Colin has seen her around the school, she's had a feather duster in her hand and a happy smile on her face, like she actually enjoys being a maid! And Natasha, she's a maid here too. Colin has not seen much of her, and when he has seen her she always looked tired and disinclined for conversation. (All the women working in the school wear these Victorian maid outfits, white aprons over grey dresses with very long, full skirts; the single exception being Miss Lantier, who wears fishnet tights and a dress with a really short skirt, because she's supposed to be a French maid, and apparently that's what French maids look like.)

The villagers have made it up to the school gardens now, and Colin gets up from his bench and walks over to them as they head towards the rear of the school building, where they have to queue up outside the school kitchens to receive their food rations. He's going to ask Mr Brandon if he can get Pendennis Major to let him live down in the village instead of in the school. Pendennis has already vetoed this idea once when Colin himself requested it, but he hopes that maybe Mr Brandon can convince the head boy that Colin just isn't cut out to be an Orville College Boy.

Paul and Mr Brandon have joined the queue outside the kitchens when Colin walks up to them, feeling very uncomfortable because the villagers are all looking at him.

'Hullo there, young Hargreaves,' Mr Brandon greets him, affably enough. 'And how are they treating you up here?'

'Oh, he's alright,' declares Paul, before Colin even has a chance to commence the very roundabout approach to requesting Mr Brandon's help, which he has been rehearsing in his mind. 'He's that prick Pendennis's blue-eyed boy, isn't he?' (ignoring the anxious 'shushes' provoked by the 'prick' epithet.) 'He's living in clover, isn't he? Waited on hand and foot; all the food he can stuff his face with.'

'But it's not nice here at all!' protests Colin. 'They make me play rugby all the time!'

'Oh, you poor thing…!'

'And what about Miss Lantier and Natasha?' asks Mr Brandon.

'No, they don't have to play rugby…'

'I mean are they both in good health?'

'I don't see them that much, but I think so,' replies Colin. 'A bit tired, maybe…'

'Oh, I'm sure they are!' Paul, with a humourless laugh. 'A tough life being a maid, isn't it? Poor Natasha!'

All this time the queue has been moving forward and now it's nearly Paul and Mr Brandon's turn. Colin decides to abandon his plan of requesting Mr Brandon's aid; Paul Mitchell's hostile attitude has put him off.

He mumbles his excuses and walks off.

What's up with Paul Mitchell, anyway? When they first got here, he was so much against Natasha becoming a maid that he got beaten up over it; but now it's like he doesn't care about her at all—and he's supposed to be her boyfriend!

Colin wanders into the oak-panelled entrance hall of the school building, where two maids are down on their knees scrubbing the parquet floor at the foot of the grand staircase, watched over by a number of Orville students. (More supervisors than there are people actually doing the work; it's heartening to see that, even after the End of the World, these time-honoured English institutions still manage to survive!)

Colin espies Miss Lantier, conspicuous in her fishnets, dusting the plaques on the wall with her bright purple feather duster. He decides that she, not Mr Brandon, might be his best hope. He'll go up to her and try and convince her she ought to rescue everyone and get them out of this place. The minibus is still parked down in the village, all they need is to get hold of the keys...

'Miss Lantier...?'

'Ah, Master Cleveland! *Bonjour!*' she greets him, tickling his nose with her duster. 'And how may I serve you thees morning?'

'Well, I was thinking that maybe we should be trying to esca—'

'Anything you wish, master! It is for you to command, and for me to obey!'

'Yes, but I'm saying don't you think it's time we—'

'Time for me to prepare you the bath, yes? *Bon!* It would be my honour to do this! And shall I scrub your back for you, my master?'

'No, really! I just think if we could get the keys—'

'Or perhaps you wish me to massage your feet with aromatic oils? Or any other part of your anatomy you may wish to have lubricated—?'

'No, no, nothing like that! I just think we ought to try and esca—'

'Oh!' Miss Lantier springs into the air. 'Oh, Master Cleveland, you are so naughty! You just give me the pinch on the bottom! Oh my goodness! Naughty, naughty, Master Cleveland! I feel giddy! I will swoon!'

'But I didn't touch you!' squeaks Colin, alarmed. 'I didn't do anything—!'

By now, the attention of the boys across the hall has been drawn to them.

'What's this?' says one of them. 'Young Cleavers just pinched the French minx's *derriere*?'

'Didn't think he had it in him!' chimes in another.

Grinning from ear to ear, the boys advance towards them.

'No, I didn't do anything!' protests Colin. 'Miss Lantier's just joking—!'

'Don't be so modest, Cleveland!'

'Splendid work, Cleavers! Bravo!'

'I do believe old Pendennis's training is starting to pay off!'

'No, I didn't, I didn't touch her!' insists crimson-faced Colin. 'I didn't touch her! She—!'

'Ohhh!' Another jump in the air. 'Oh, Master Cleveland! You do it again! You pinch my bottom a second time! Oh, goodness! Never 'ave I been groped with such consummate naughtiness! Oh! Your fingers, they send the tingles coursing through my body! My nipples, they are erect! I am on the verge of the orgasm! Oh, Master Cleveland! One more time! I implore you, do not leave me like zis! Finish what you 'ave begun, I beg of you! Fondle my buttocks one more time!'

'The minx is right, Cleveland! Finish what you've started!'

'Strike the final blow, old man!'

'Put the poor hussy out of her misery, you old teaser!'

Mortified, Colin flees the building, pursued by the students' taunts and the Frenchwoman's supplications.

Having gained the sanctuary of his favourite bench, Colin strives to recover his scattered wits. (As for his dignity, this is going to take much longer to reassemble.)

What on earth is wrong with Miss Lantier? Saying he was pinching her bum and acting up like that when all he was trying to do was have a serious conversation with her! After that exhibition, there's no way he's going to trust that woman with even assisting in, let alone leading, any escape plan! She's gone completely mad!

'Ah, there you are Cleveland!'

Oh no. Now it's Pendennis Major! He's probably heard about the incident in the hallway and now he's come to 'congratulate' him about it!

However, it soon becomes clear that this is not the case and that Pendennis knows nothing of the Miss Lantier incident. He sits himself down on the bench next to Colin.

'What are you doing, sitting here all on your own, Cleveland?' he inquires briskly. 'You look like you're moping, and we don't allow moping around here.'

(Another one for Colin to add to the growing list of 'things we don't allow around here' at Orville College.)

'We only have team players around here,' proceeds Pendennis. 'None of your lone wolves, thank you very much. That's one thing the rugger should be teaching you: you're part of a team here, and the team's got to pull together. No letting the side down, d'you hear?'

Colin hears.

'How are you cracking on with that maid of yours?'

'What maid?'

'The maid who comes to your room every day, Cleveland. Satisfactory, is she?'

'Yes. She's good.'

'"Good"? That's a rather weak compliment, Cleveland. Can't you be more precise?'

'Well, she does a good job of cleaning the room.'

'I suppose she does, but what else? What else do you do with her? It's more that side of things I'm anxious to hear about.'

'What side of things?'

A sigh. 'I just said, Cleveland. I'd like to hear the gen about what you get up to with your maid aside from watching her clean up your bally room.'

'Oh, I don't watch her doing it!' says Colin, surprised. 'I always go out when she comes in.'

'What! You leave the room when the maid arrives?'

'Well, yes. I'd be in the way otherwise, wouldn't I?'

Pendennis looks hard at Colin. 'You know…' he says slowly, 'if it was anyone else, I would be starting to suspect mockery here. But you… Do you mean to tell me you don't…' He trails off, at a loss for words. And then: 'Well, what do you think of her? Do you think she's a looker?'

'Thinks who's a looker?'

'The maid, Cleveland,' through gritted teeth. 'The bloody maid who comes into your bloody room every day.'

Colin thinks about this, and clearly for the first time. 'Well, she looks nice, I suppose. A bit old, maybe…'

'Well, yes she is in her thirties,' concurs Pendennis. 'But that was why I picked her out for you, really. I thought a greenhorn like you could do with a maid with a bit more experience, who could show you the ropes… Seems what I didn't realise though, is just *how* bally green you are… Okay, so you'd prefer a maid who's nearer your age; splendid. Are there any you like? Come on, you must have had a look at them all by now, Cleveland; anyone who particularly takes your fancy?'

'Out of the maids? Well, I… I kind of like…'

'Yes? Come on: spit it out, laddie…'

'Natasha…'

'Natasha? The girl from your school…? Oh, I get it! You were always spoony on her? Even before all this happened? Back when you were at that peasants' school together? Ha, ha! I always thought it was just that Mitchell creature who was spoony on her…! But you were spoony on her as well, were you?'

'What does spoony mean?' asks Colin.

'I mean you "fancy" her; that's how you oiks put it, isn't it? You fancy the dusky Natasha, do you? Dash it, Cleveland, why didn't you tell me this before?'

'Well, yes… I *did* use to like her… But…'

'But what?'

'Well, she's going out with Paul Mitchell.'

Pendennis laughs out loud at this one. 'Going out with him… Listen, Cleveland: maybe she *was* going out with Paul Mitchell, but she jolly well isn't anymore. That relationship is well and truly over; you can take my word for that one.'

'Are you sure?' queries Colin, unconvinced.

'I am very sure, Cleveland,' replies Pendennis. 'Surer than anyone else. Believe me, the field is clear for you, old fellow; you do not need to worry about Paul Mitchell.'

Colin perks up. Pendennis seems very sure of his facts; and it would certainly explain Paul Mitchell's attitude when he met him just now. So, Paul and Natasha aren't together anymore! But still…

'But still…' says Colin, verbalising his last thought. 'She might… she might not… like me…'

'What are you on about, Cleveland? Of course she likes you. She always asks me how you're doing.'

'Yes, but I mean… she might not *like* like me… You know… love me…'

'Love you?' Pendennis sounds incredulous, nay positively affronted. '*Love* you? Don't you go all soppy on me and start talking about love, Cleveland. We don't talk about love around here.' (Another one to add to the list.) 'Natasha is a *maid*, Cleveland; and a maid is a servant. You don't expect your servants to love you, do you? You expect them to obey you. What is love, anyway? Affection? Well, if you want affection, then you order her to be affectionate. Hugs and kisses? If you want hugs and kisses, then you order her to hug and kiss you. And so on and so forth. You give the order and she obeys; simple as that. Master and Servant.'

'But I can't just order Natasha to do stuff—!'

'That's just what you *can* do, Cleveland. You need to forget about the past; forget about when you were at school together, acting like equals; because you're *not* equals anymore: you are the master and she is the servant. That's how it is now. *She* knows that; *she* didn't need much breaking in; it's just *you* that still needs to adjust, Cleveland.' Pendennis looks at his watch. 'But enough of this chinwagging; time to get a move on, Cleveland. Come on!'

'What for?'

'What d'you mean "what for"? Rugger practice!'

Night is falling. Having spent the afternoon being bounced around the rugby field and now feeling more roughly-handled than even the ball would own to if it could speak its mind on the subject,

Colin has reached a decision.

He's getting out of here.

He has given up any hope of joined in this endeavour by any of the others: Miss Lantier's off her perch; apparently even Natasha has got used to being a maid; Paul Mitchell's gone all stroppy; and Mr Brandon's no good in a crisis—so he's going to escape on his own. He's going to escape and then he's going to make his way across the country to Norton-Braisley and find his sister.

Actually, "escaping" doesn't really even come into it in Colin's case. He's not a prisoner here; he's not being guarded or watched. It's true that if he asked Pendennis if he could go, Pendennis would say no. So then he just won't ask him, that's all. He'll just pack his bag and sneak out of school after it gets dark. He doesn't even need to worry about the front door being locked: the room he has been given is on the ground floor, so all he has to do is climb out the window.

And that's what he's going to do.

Dinner is over and he makes his way back to his dorm. He opens the door, steps inside, closes the door and bolts it. He switches on the light and turning to face the room is surprised to see it is already occupied.

A maid sits on his bed and the maid is Natasha.

Chapter Eighteen
'Miss Lantier Knows Best'

'Your new personal maid reporting for duty,' says Natasha briskly, smiling and saluting.

Natasha: his new maid! Colin had thought this wasn't going to be happening till tomorrow! And here she is now, right when he was all set to escape from here!

What can he do? How can he get rid of her? Pendennis says the maids have to do whatever you order them to, and that even Natasha will do whatever you order her to because she's a maid as well. Well, that's easy enough: all he's got to do is order her to leave the room!

Then another thought occurs to Colin, an even better one: why doesn't he just order Natasha to escape with him? Yes, and then, after they've escaped together, he can order her to stop being a maid and to go back to how she used to be!

Brilliant! This second plan is the better one, because he would much rather escape with Natasha than without her; because in truth, although he has done his best to expunge the girl from his heart, seeing her here now, right here in the same room with him, he realises he still loves her as much as he's always done.

'Well, are you just going to stand there gawping at me all night?' inquires Natasha, still smiling.

Natasha's demeanour strikes him as being not quite authentically maid-like. Shouldn't it have been 'Well, are you just going to stand there gawping at me all night, *my master*?'

'Well, I—'

'Look, Colin. Just sit down here,' patting the bed beside her. 'I've got a lot to tell you and not much time.'

'*You've* got a lot to tell *me?*' echoes Colin, obeying her nonetheless, and seating himself beside her.

'Yes. Cuz y'see, we're getting out of here tonight.'

Colin is dumbfounded.

'You mean... we're escaping?'

'Yes. You want to get away from this place, don't you?'

'Yes!' cries Colin, delighted. 'And I've got it all planned! We'll just climb out through the wind—'

Natasha holds out a rosy pink palm. 'Woah, woah, woah. Slow down, boy. We've already got a plan. When I say *we're* escaping, I don't just mean us two, I mean everyone. Miss Lantier's—'

'Miss Lantier! You mustn't have Miss Lantier in your escape! She'll ruin it for you! She's gone completely mad!'

'She's gone ma—?' Natasha bursts into laughter, quickly smothered. 'Oh, I get it! You mean from what happened with you and her today?' More smothered laughter. 'No, y'see, it was...' Another splutter. 'Y'see, it was... God, I wish I'd been there to see that!'

The floodgates open again.

Colin, feeling rather nettled, watches Natasha as she shakes with stifled laughter, which erupts afresh whenever she seems on the verge of getting it under control, and she flaps her hand at him in a 'just give me a minute' gesture.

Finally, and with an effort, Natasha overcomes her mirth, wipes the tears from her eyes and takes deep breaths of air.

'Right,' clearing her throat. 'About Miss Lantier: what happened, y'see, was that we'd got our escape plan all ready and it was all set to go off tonight—and then you come along and walk up to her in and, right in front of everyone, you try to start a conversation with her about escaping from here! So, she had to do what she did; she had to do it to shut you up, didn't she? You could've ruined the whole thing!'

'Well, I did try to talk to her quietly,' says Colin, in his own defence.

'Yes, but you still picked the worst time and place to do it. Miss Lantier couldn't take any chances, could she?'

'Well, I couldn't really choose the time and place; I don't get to see her that much… Anyway, why couldn't you have told me about your escape plan before? Then I would've known!'

'Same reason. *We* haven't been able to get to see *you* much, either. I'm only here now cuz Pendennis told me to come here—so it's worked out very nicely, cuz now I can fill you in now. Otherwise, you wouldn't have known anything about it until we came to get you after we'd set the place on fire.'

'Set the place on fire?' exclaims Colin.

'Yeah, that's basically the plan: we're going to burn the whole school down. Y'see, it's not just you, me and Miss Lantier who are escaping tonight: it's everyone; I mean all the women they've got up here working as maids. And we're not just escaping, either. We're staging a coup.'

'What's a coup?'

'Coup means a revolution, a takeover. We're going to sort out these Orville College bastards once and for all.'

'By burning down the school?'

'Pretty much, yes. Here's the plan. Zero Hour is twenty-one hundred hours. Nine o'clock in old money, so it's not long now. First, we'll meet up with Miss Lantier; she'll be in Pendennis's room. And that's the other piece of good luck we had: when he ordered me to come here to you, Pendennis also ordered *her* to come to *him* in his rooms—and that happens to be exactly where she wants to be. So, she's going to take care of Pendennis; then she's going to get the keys to our van, which he's got in the desk in his room. So we meet up with her, and then we go down to the kitchen where all the other maids'll be waiting; and that's where we'll start our bonfire.'

'And then what?' asks Colin.

'Well, then we get out of the school before it burns down around our ears.'

'What about all the students?'

Natasha waves a dismissive hand. 'Oh, we'll take care of them. They lose the school, they lose their empire. They won't be able to do much after that.'

'Really?'

'Really. Don't worry; Miss Lantier's got it all sorted out. She planned this whole thing; she's really clever, Miss Lantier.'

'And it all starts at nine?'

'Yes, so we'll be going soon; and you need to take everything you want to take with you, cuz we won't be coming back.'

'I was going to change back into my old clothes before I escaped…'

'Well, go on then: get changed.'

Colin stands up, looks at Natasha, looks uncomfortable.

Natasha puts two and two together. 'Come on, Colin, you're not shy about getting changed in front of me, are you? God, we used to always get changed for PE in the same classroom, back in primary.'

'Yes, but that was a long time ago…'

Natasha giggles. 'Alright then; I'll close my eyes, okay?'

She closes her eyes. Colin sheds his Orville College uniform and resumes his own street clothes.

And then it's nine o'clock and they step out into the corridor, and proceed to their rendezvous with Miss Lantier. Pendennis has appropriated for his own use the erstwhile headmaster's suite of rooms. This suite, comprising study, living room, bedroom, bathroom, is up on the first floor, and Colin and Natasha make their way there without encountering any opposition. In fact, the school seems strangely quiet to Colin. It's as though everyone's decided to have an early night—unheard of the college's recent history.

Reaching the suite, Natasha taps on a door. It opens almost instantly, and Miss Lantier beckons them inside. The room is the study, where the old headmaster once sat behind his imposing desk, the terror of all students summoned to his presence. Through an open doorway Colin hears the sound of loud snoring.

'Excellent, Natasha,' says Miss Lantier. 'You have advised Colin of our plans.'

'Yes, I told him everything he needed to know,' confirms Natasha.

'*Bon*. And I have just acquired the keys,' holding them up.

'Who's that snoring?' Colin wants to know.

'Why that is Pendennis,' answers Miss Lantier. 'It was necessary for me to render him unconscious. I knocked him out: so!' miming a karate chop.

Colin frowns. 'I didn't know people snored when they get knocked out. They don't on TV.'

'You can't believe everything you see on the telly,' Natasha tells him.

'*Oui*. The airbrushing of reality,' says Miss Lantier. 'But enough of this; let us proceed. The other maids should have all assembled in the kitchens by this time.'

They exit the study, and just as they do, a door further down the corridor opens and an Orville student—Colin recognises him as Carruthers—appears.

'I say! What are you three—?'

Miss Lantier launches herself at Carruthers. She strikes, Carruthers groans, crumples to the floor. The hand that Miss

Lantier withdraws holds a knife, blade dripping red.

'You stabbed him!' exclaims Colin.

'Shh!' urges Miss Lantier. 'I know, and it is most regrettable; but he left me no choice. You saw that he was about to kill me, yes? It was him or me.'

Actually, it had looked to Colin like Carruthers was taken completely by surprise and never stood a chance. But as he opens his mouth to say this, Natasha nudges him in the ribs.

'Miss Lantier knows best,' she tells him.

They make their way downstairs to the main hallway. Still the school is unnaturally quiet.

'Where is everybody?' whispers Colin.

'Oh, in their rooms, I suppose,' replies Natasha.

They make their way to the back of the building and into the kitchens, where the rest of the maids, about thirty in number, are waiting for them. They stand in a tight group amongst the polished metal fittings. They look eager, expectant.

Miss Lantier claps her hands. 'Excellent. We are all 'ere. On to the next stage.

In response to this, industrial sized containers of cooking oil are produced from cupboards and the maids proceed to douse the room with the pungent flammable liquid, pouring it over walls, fittings and floor.

'*Bon*,' says Miss Lantier. 'And now we depart.'

The party now makes its way back to the main entrance, maids with cans of cooking oil leaving a liquid powder-trail in their wake, all the way up to the doors. They step outside into the cool night. Miss Lantier produces a box of large matches.

'But if you start the fire right here at the front door, won't that make it hard for the students to get out?' questions Colin.

Natasha nudges him again. 'Miss Lantier knows best.'

The match is struck, ignited and tossed through the doorway. Flame leaps up and instantly the trail of oil is ablaze. The escapees retreat further into the grounds.

Fire alarms start to cry out. As Colin watches the fire spread, Miss Lantier takes Natasha aside. After a brief whispered conversation, Natasha returns to Colin. She takes him by the hand.

'Come on, Colin,' she says. 'Let's get down to the village. The others can take care of things here.'

'But we can't leave without Miss Lantier!' argues Colin. 'She's the one who drives the bus!'

'We're not taking off in the bus tonight, silly,' Natasha tells him. 'There's no hurry now. We'll sleep down in the village and head off tomorrow. Come on.'

Hand-in-hand, they walk down the hill, and when Colin looks back, he sees that the fire is spreading rapidly, displaying its flickering light in all the ground floor windows of the college. A thick plume of smoke rises into the night sky. Natasha tugging his arm, a mute reproval for dawdling, and Colin, eyes forward, obediently mends his pace.

Thankful to have been rescued from that disagreeable masculine environment, Colin is blissfully unaware of the innocent deception that has been practiced upon him: an innocent deception involving a cocktail of recreational drugs and sedatives introduced into the students' evening meals, Colin's excepted.

And as Orville College has ceased to observe strict dining hours, not all of the students will have partaken of this sleep-inducing repast, and so it is necessary that the maids, their former servants, must remain at the scene of the blaze, ready to lend a helping hand to any students lucky enough to escape the conflagration.

Chapter Nineteen
'He Must Have Been Run Over Dozens of Times'

Natasha sits beside Colin on the minibus today. In fact, they occupy the same two seats they had occupied on the night of their dramatic escape from Eastchester. As for Paul Mitchell, he sits in surly silence two seats forward and in the opposite row. They were arguing earlier this morning, Natasha and Paul; Colin had heard them, although they'd abruptly stopped as soon as they'd seen him approaching.

Paul Mitchell now seems diminished in Colin's eyes. The clever, charismatic rock musician he had envied has become sullen and bitter, with most of that bitterness directed at his former girlfriend—if former she is. Colin isn't entirely sure if indeed they have split up; even he is wise enough to know that people who are going out can have these blazing arguments, these falling outs, and then make up again. It used to be the same with him whenever he'd had one of his periodic falling outs with Nigel: they would ignore each other and not talk for a certain amount of time, and then in the end they would shake hands and make friends again. So he knows it's possible that Natasha and Paul are just in one of those ignoring and not talking phases right now, and that they might get back together again. Frankly he's at a loss to understand the cause of this rift between Natasha and Paul; when he's fallen out with Nigel before, the cause would be a dispute about something to do with *Doctor Who* or *Star Trek*—but it's doubtful that something like that will be the cause here with Paul and Natasha.

But whatever the cause of the rift, Paul Mitchell seems diminished in Colin's eyes, and as a result he himself feels elevated, like he's now closer to Natasha, that she's not so much 'out of his league' as she had seemed to be before… Could she become his girlfriend? Could Natasha start to like him the same way she liked Paul Mitchell…? Yes, she's sitting next to him right now—but there's always the danger she might go back to sitting next to Paul.

They have resumed their interrupted journey to Kettleworth.

Mr Brandon says it will be interesting to see what conditions are like in that town. He also has ideas about investigating the local power station, to see if they can discover who is keeping the place in operation.

They pass a road sign bearing the legend 'Kettleworth', and they are driving through a well-to-do residential district, detached houses with gravel drives and leafy front gardens on either hand. Everything looks peaceful; the street and the houses show no signs of the arson and destruction that has ravaged Eastchester.

Not a soul is in sign, and it is an indication of death rather than a sign of life that first claims the travellers' attention. An exclamation from Miss Lantier draws all eyes to the road ahead, where, vivid against the grey macadam, they see the red and pink exclamation mark of roadkill. Colin grimaces at the sight. He remembers family outings in the car, and those inevitable animal corpses he'd see along the country roads. On the telly, they didn't like children watching things with strong violence in them; but TV violence was made-up violence, pretend violence; while the blood and guts of roadkill, that was the real thing, and there it was, right out in the open, where little kids could see it!

This particular squashed corpse looks a lot bigger than the usual smear on the road; it must be a dog or something.

'Could you pull up, Miss Lantier?' says Mr Brandon in an odd voice. 'I'd like to have a look at this…'

Miss Lantier complies, and the bus comes to a halt beside the roadkill. They all get out. Colin doesn't really want to see this up close, but he follows the others anyway, staying in the rear, so the others are more or less screening him from the sight.

'My God…' utters Mr Brandon.

The others make similar exclamations, and curiosity overpowering his aversion, Colin forces himself to look at the mess in the road—and he sees that the splattered corpse is not that of a dog: not unless dogs have started wearing clothes. A pair of jeans, encrusted with blood and gore, lie flattened against the road surface, along with some rags that might once have been a shirt, and the fragmented remains of a pair of shoes.

Dizzy with nausea, Colin looks away, leaning against the side of the van for support.

'Who could have done this?' he hears Miss Lantier say.

'Hit and run,' suggests Natasha.

'It's more than a simple hit and run,' responds Mr Brandon. 'Just look at it. This body's been flattened. He must have been run over dozens of times.'

'Maybe the body's been here a long time.'

'No, this is obviously recent. You can see the blood's still wet.'

'Whoever it was must have got run over by a convoy—I know! Maybe it was those trucks! The ones that man we met said he'd seen.'

'Yes, that could be a possibility…' agrees Mr Brandon.

'Let us get back in the van,' says Miss Lantier. 'We are not safe out 'ere.'

They quickly get back into the bus, Colin still feeling queasy. Squashed corpses lying in the road… Even in Eastchester he'd never seen anything like this…

They proceed into Kettleworth. Still no-one in sight, no pedestrians or traffic. Further on they come upon another large smear in the road that was once a human being. This time they stop but don't get out.

'This one's much older,' declares Mr Brandon. 'The blood has oxidized. Been here for weeks, I'd say.'

'Weeks?' echoes Miss Lantier. 'Why has it just been left there? Why has no-one come to remove the corpse?'

No-one has an answer. In the next street they find the road partially blocked by a burnt-out wreck. This is a sight more familiar to Colin. Burnt out cars he has seen plenty of, back in Eastchester.

They approach the wreck. It is composed of two cars, locked in a terminal embrace, bonnets telescoped—and in the driver's seat of each car sits a charred corpse, both of them wearing crash helmets.

'These cars weren't attacked by rioters!' asserts Mr Brandon. 'Look at them: they deliberately rammed each other!'

'Joyriders,' says Natasha.

'Joyriders gone insane,' says Mr Brandon.

'Or under the influence,' says Miss Lantier. 'Alcohol or narcotics.'

She guides the bus around the wreck, and they proceed through the silent streets. An expectant fear fills the air. By now, they are all nervous, none more so than Colin.

'We should turn back,' he says. 'It's not safe here.'

'Courage, Colin!' urges Miss Lantier.

Natasha squeezes his hand.

'Perhaps nowhere is "safe" anymore. We are living in an uncertain world, Hargreaves,' says Mr Brandon portentously (in what will be the last time he ever gets Colin's name wrong.)

They move along a thoroughfare of terrace houses flush against the pavement. At the junction ahead they see another squashed corpse on the road, another burnt-out wreck.

'No parked cars,' observes Miss Lantier. 'We haven't seen a single one, apart from these wrecks.'

'You're right,' says Mr Brandon. 'I wonder what that could mean… A mass-exodus? Everyone who still had petrol in their car has just driven away…?'

And then it happens, just as the minibus slows at the intersection. The van seems to appear from nowhere and, roaring past, clips the bus on the starboard side. The impact sends the minibus spinning across the road. Miss Lantier hits the brakes, but before she can regain control a second assailant appears, a pick-up truck, and they rammed again, this time a full broadside collision. The force of the impact tips them up on two wheels. They have barely recovered their equilibrium when a third vehicle pounces from the right, and they are struck again and sent spinning across the intersection.

'Everybody out!' yells Miss Lantier. 'Quickly, while there's still time!'

Natasha unclips her seatbelt. 'Come on, Colin!'

The sliding side door won't open, so Paul, Natasha and Colin have to scramble over the front seats and tumble out through the front passenger door.

Colin, stunned by the suddenness of the onslaught, can barely process what's happening. He feels sick, giddy. There seems to be vehicles all around them, the feral cry of supercharged engines fills the air. They circle around them, launching sudden assaults, like sharks attacking a whale.

Miss Lantier shouts something. It sounds like an order. Now Natasha grabs his hand and they are running across the road. Colin catches sight of Miss Lantier and Mr Brandon fleeing across the road away from them. Even as he watches a van, their first assailant, screams past again, and Mr Brandon disappears under its wheels, instantly devoured by the metal monster. Devoured and then discharged in its wake, a bloody pulp smeared across the road.

The sight sends Colin into a panic. He hears Natasha call his name over the roaring of car engines, the squeal of brakes. He can't see her. He runs to the row of terrace houses. A black Porsche, singling him out for destruction, hurtles towards him, tons of furious metal, ready to smash him to a pulp, engines sounding murderous hatred. Colin throws himself at the nearest front door. Locked. He hammers on it, screaming. The speeding car mounts the pavement, and intent on murder, bears down on him. Colin can see the driver, anonymous under a mirror-visored crash helmet. He flattens himself against the door.

And then the door opens behind him and Colin tumbles backwards into the void of unconsciousness—leaving me with little choice but to bring the chapter to a close.

Chapter Twenty
'You're Not From Round Here, Are You?'

When Colin emerges from his state of oblivion, he is lying on a settee in a room rank with the combined odours of alcohol, tobacco and unwashed humanity.

He looks around and discovers in the room's single occupant to be the source of these smells, especially the last. A fat man of indeterminate middle-age, both chins grey with bristles, dressed comfortably but redolently in jogging bottoms and t-shirt, he sits in an armchair, glass in hand, regarding Colin with an amiable, but somewhat vacant, smile.

'Welcome back to the land of the living,' he greets Colin.

Colin, busy collecting his thoughts and assembling them in the right order, sits up slowly. He sees that the room is a small living room, rather tastelessly wallpapered. There are bottles everywhere: on the tables, the shelves, the floor, the furniture; wine bottles, beer bottles, bottles of spirits. Some of the bottles display the colourful labels of famous brands, while others exhibit the drab grey labels of the new, post-Incident merchandise.

'Sorry about the mess,' says the man, following Colin's eyes around the room. 'But I haven't been able to get to the recycling bins lately, and they've stopped doing doorstep collections.'

He chuckles at his own witticism, takes a swig from his glass.

'It was you... You opened the door... Let me in...'

'Yeah, I did, and just in time, too. That car went screaming past, and when you fell backwards like that, I thought it'd clipped you; but no, you're alright; still in one piece. You'd just passed out from the shock or something. Not surprising, really.'

'So... how long have I been passed out?' asks Colin.

The man looks at his watch. 'Hm...' frowning. 'What time was it when you started hammering on my door?'

'I don't know!' retorts Colin, regarding the question as a silly one.

'Hm. What time do you make it now?'

Colin examines his own timepiece. 'Eleven fifty-five.'

'Yeah! That's what my watch says, and all!' The man seems pleased.

'So how long does that mean I've been unconscious?'

'Not sure,' says the man. 'I lose track of time, to be honest...'

'Well, is it like five minutes? Or more than five minutes?'

'Oh, definitely more,' confidently. 'More like an hour, I reckon.'

'An hour?' squeaks Colin. 'But what about the others? Haven't any of them been here?'

‘What others?’

‘The people I was with.’

‘Oh, them? No, they’re dead, aren’t they?’

‘Dead?’ cries Colin, aghast. ‘You mean all of them?’

‘Yeah. Those cars don’t let you go once they’ve got your scent. Like I said, you were lucky—bloody lucky.’

‘I saw Mr Brandon get… So, what about Natasha and Miss Lantier…? They got run over as well? You saw them get killed?’

‘No, I didn’t *see* it, did I? You don’t think I went outside to look, do you? Soon as you fell into the hallway, I shut the door again, sharpish; so I didn’t see the end of it. But they’ll be dead alright, cuz the cars went away. Those cars don’t go away until they’ve finished the job they started. You’re not from ’round here, are you?’

‘No,’ admits Colin.

‘I guessed you lot must be visitors; no-one who lived here would be driving around in the open like you were. Haven’t introduced myself, have I? The name’s Len. What’s yours?’

‘Colin,’ says Colin. ‘Colin Cleveland.’

‘And where are you from, Colin?’

‘Eastchester.’

‘Oh! Eastchester, eh? And what brought you here to Kettleworth?’

‘Well, it was getting too dangerous in Eastchester. We were looking for somewhere safer.’

‘Well, you came to the wrong place,’ announces Len, in the tone of someone imparting good news. ‘However bad it was where you were, it’s ten times worse here. What was up in Eastchester?’

‘It was gangs,’ says Colin. ‘They came out every night, fighting and smashing things.’

‘And what about during the day?’

‘It was alright during the day.’

‘Well, that sounds like paradise on Earth compared to this place. Here it’s not safe outside anytime: day or night. No-one goes outside, not unless they want to get run over. The Road-

Ragers are everywhere.'

'Road-Ragers?'

'Yep, that's what we call them. It's like they've taken road rage and turned it into a sport; and it's a sport they're very passionate about. I don't know how many people have been killed by 'em since they started up.'

'But why do they do it? Running people over…'

'Well, that's the question, isn't it? But my educated guess would be they do it because they *can* do it; because there's no-one around to tell them they can't do it; not anymore.'

'Are they people from this town? Or—'

Len nods solemnly. 'Yeah, they're locals, alright. God knows what sent them off the rails… Well, it was the Incident, wasn't it? But it didn't happen straight away. No, first few weeks after everything shut down and all those people vanished, it stayed fairly quiet. We were all scared and confused, but people still went out, met up and talked to each other… And then this little girl got killed. I didn't see it happen myself, but other people saw it, including the girl's poor mum. She was playing out on the road, this girl was. A bit silly, but it was a quiet street, and not many people were driving about since the Incident. So there she was, playing in the road, her mum and some of her friends standing nattering on the pavement, when a car comes out of nowhere and runs the girl over. Zoom! Just like that. The car didn't stop or slow down, but they saw that the driver was wearing a crash helmet. That was the start of it. First more hit-and-runs, then there was this massacre in the carpark of one of the supermarkets. It was the day the new food first turned up in all the shops. More than fifty people got killed in this massacre, all run down by these cars that came up out of nowhere. After that nobody was safe on the streets, so here we are, on lockdown, and slowly starving to death cuz we can't even go out to get food. People try sometimes, they try to make it to the shops to get supplies. Nine times out of ten they don't make it back. That's what happened to Stevie and Bruce, my housemates. We shared this place.' He waves a hand around the room. 'After the Incident we stockpiled all the booze we could get hold of, y'see. But we weren't so careful about the grub. When it got too dangerous to go out, we just drank ourselves silly every day; y'know, to conserve the food supply. But it ran out in the end, and Stevie and Bruce, they went out one night to get supplies. They never came back.'

'The Road-Ragers got them?'

Len nods solemnly.

Colin stands up. 'I've got to go,' he says, not relishing the decision he has arrived at. 'I've got to see if my friends got away or not.'

'Are you bonkers? They're dead; they must be.'

'But you don't *know,*' insists Colin. 'You didn't *see* it, did you?'

'I didn't see Bruce and Stevie get killed, but I still know they're dead! Because they didn't come back! And you said yourself, if your friends were still okay, they'd have come here looking for you!'

'But they might not've *seen!* We were all running off in different directions; they might not have *seen* me come in here!'

Len shrugs. 'Well, even if by some miracle they did get away, they'll be long gone by now. They won't still be hanging around outside.'

'But I've still got to go outside and look. I need to know if they got away or not.'

'What for? That's just risking your neck for nothing. Stay here with me. You're safe enough here. And look: I've got plenty to drink. Just help yourself.'

'I don't want to drink, and I'm too young anyway. And you haven't got any food. I'm going out.'

Colin walks out into the hallway, Len following. He opens the front door. The street is quiet. He looks down the street towards the intersection where it all happened. He sees the minibus, battered and buckled; and he sees the remains of Mr Brandon…

But no-one else. There are no other corpses smeared across the road.

He turns back, looks at Len. 'I'm going to look.'

'I wouldn't. The coast might be clear right now, but once you set foot out there... They're like sharks, those people; they scent you, they sniff you out. I tell you, mate, you go out there, you won't make it back.'

'I'm going to look,' repeats Colin and he steps out onto the pavement. Keeping close to the wall, he makes his way towards the junction. Standing at the corner, he looks up and down the thoroughfare. No cars in sight. And no corpses either. Mr Brandon's is still the only body on the road. So the others did make it!

But where are they now...? Len said they would be long gone, but maybe they're not, maybe they're hiding somewhere nearby...

Colin steps off the pavement and onto the road. If any of the others are nearby, they're bound to see him...

Someone *does* see him. The revving of an engine makes him look around.

There, further down the street: the black Porsche. The same car that nearly got him before.

The Porsche leaps forward, bearing down on Colin. Across the road a jinnel between two houses beckons. Colin runs for it, reaches it just as the Porsche sweeps past.

Has it been out there all the time? Has it been waiting for him to step outside, just so it could finish the job it started before? They don't let go; that's what Len had said. This Porsche has selected him for its prey, and it's not going to give up until it kills him.

He peers out into the street. The Porsche has stopped and turned round, facing him, waiting for him. Colin turns and runs down the alley. It carries on for some time, before being intersected by a residential street.

He sees someone. A woman holding two small children by the hand. The children are crying and the features of all three of them look pale and drawn, their bodies emaciated. The mother's face holds a look of weary despair. She leads her children out into the middle of the road.

And then they just stand there. Waiting.

A squeal of brakes, and a car turns onto the street. The black Porsche! It accelerates towards the three figures standing in the street. The children, scared out of their apathy, start to scream and struggle, but the mother, using all her remaining strength, holds them firm as the car hurtles towards them.

Colin screws his eyes shut.

The car rockets past.

Silence.

Colin opens his eyes. Three fresh corpses. He darts across the road to the continuation of the pedestrian way. The Porsche, down the street, performs a skidding U-turn. The mother and her children are just an incidental treat; Colin is still the main prey.

Colin makes it across the road and into the alley. The sports car sweeps past.

And now Colin is able to proceed for a considerable time, without encountering any more roads. First the alley takes him between the ramshackle fences of back gardens, before becoming a dirt track running alongside the corrugated metal perimeter fence of a football ground. More backyards, and then he reaches an arched wooden door in a lichened wall. He tries the handle of the door. It opens. He finds himself in a stone-flagged passageway with a wall on one side and the buttressed wall of a church on the other. At the end of the alley, another arched doorway.

Colin passes through the doorway and finds himself out onto the pavement.

Immediately before him, over the roofs of a row of parked cars, is a marina filled with boats, their masts pointing up into the grey sky. Off to the left a pontoon bridge spans the river. Beyond the bridge, open countryside. He has reached the edge of town. If he can make it over that bridge, he's home free!

But what about his pursuer…? Another thing Len said was that all the Road-Ragers know the town like the back of their hands; his pursuer in the black Porsche will probably know that the pedestrian way he has followed comes out here…

He looks to the right where the road leading from the bridge into town curves out of sight… No sign of the Porsche… Not yet, anyway…

But then, the path he's just followed diverged at more than one point along the way. The Porsche wouldn't know which path he had followed; it couldn't possibly cover all the exits. He might be in luck…

On the left, where the road curves to join the pontoon bridge stands a riverside pub, *The Golden Swan* (formerly *The Saracen's Head* until someone complained that the name was Islamophobic.) Colin now proceeds cautiously along the footpath in the direction of the pub, eyes and ears alert.

He passes the last of the row of parked cars. Before him now the road curves towards the pontoon bridge. He just has to make it over that bridge…

He steps off the path and looks anxiously all around, resting his hand on the bonnet of the parked car.

The metal is warm… Black paintwork…

Colin looks at the windscreen and sees the unreadable automaton visage of the driver, seated motionless behind the wheel of his car.

Colin runs. He runs for the pontoon bridge as the metal monster hiding in plain sight comes to life, shattering the silence with its hunting cry.

Across the bridge and Colin is pelting down the road. Tall hedges bar his way, but up ahead is a gate, if he can just make it to the gate…

The metal predator bears down on him.

Colin trips and falls prostrate right in its path.

He braces himself for extinction, hoping it won't hurt too much.

The squeal of brakes.

Silence, comparatively.

Colin opens his eyes.

The car has stopped, engine idling, just a few feet away from him.

A change of gears and the car starts to reverse, right back over the bridge. Facing him on the verge there is a sign: Kettleworth. The town limits. He has passed the town limits.

Chapter Twenty-One
'No Colin, I Would *Not* Prefer It'

Climbing shakily to his feet, Colin has barely had time to consider his options when he espies somebody sitting on a gate further down the road. From the clothes, it looks like Paul Mitchell. Colin starts walking towards him. It *is* Paul Mitchell. He is looking in Colin's direction, but neither speaks nor makes any gesture, just sits there on the gate, eating something.

There's no sign of Natasha or Miss Lantier.

'You were lucky,' are Paul's first words as Colin walks up to him. His voice and expression are neutral. The food he is consuming is a chocolate bar in a plain grey wrapper: a 'Caramel and Nougat Chocolate Bar,' once called a 'Mars Bar.' Colin is suddenly reminded of the fact that he hasn't eaten since breakfast and is very hungry.

'They stop chasing you when you get outside the town,' Paul tells him. 'We found that out when we got out.'

'We?' eagerly. 'So the others are with you?'

'They *were* with me. Well, not old Brandon, of course: he's dead. Roadkill.'

'I know; I saw it. It was horrible.'

'Hm. We thought the same thing had happened to you. It looked like that Porsche got you. Climbed right onto the path.'

'Yes, but somebody opened their door and let me into their house, so it missed me. What happened to Natasha and Miss Lantier? Why aren't you still with them?'

Paul chews his confectionary, measuring his words. 'We had a… disagreement. Decided to go our separate ways. And good riddance to them, as well.' He mutters something that sounds like it might be 'pair of whores' but Colin isn't sure. 'Look, if you want to join up with them, and I'm sure you do, they went that way,' pointing down the road. 'They're heading towards Heatherly, the next town from here. If you get a move on, you'll catch up with them.'

'How long ago was it they set off?'

'About twenty minutes ago. So, like I said, get your skates on and you'll catch up with them.'

'But what about you? What are you going to do?'

'Haven't decided what I'm doing yet. I might just go back to Eastchester. It's better than Kettleworth, anyway. Don't you worry about me.'

'You think I should go after Natasha and Miss Lantier, then?'

'Yes, I think you should. And the longer you stand here nattering, the longer it'll take you to catch up with them.'

'Okay. You wouldn't prefer it if I stayed with you…?'

'No Colin, I would *not* prefer it.'

This is the answer Colin was hoping for, yet it still carries a sting with it.

'Okay, I'll get going then. Have you, erm… got any spare food?'

'No.'

The tone of the monosyllable and the look that goes with it, are both very definite.

Colin sets off along the road.

He soon leaves Kettleworth behind and is proceeding through the countryside, grazing land punctuated with the occasional grove of trees. He walks briskly, his thoughts on the two women ahead of him. It was all very well for Paul to say he can catch up with them, but if they've started twenty minutes ahead of him, they're going to *stay* twenty minutes ahead of him; they've both got longer legs than he has… Unless of course they decide to stop along the way…

Twenty minutes pass, and still no sign of the women on the road ahead. What looks like a much denser tract of woodland has appeared on the horizon. And now Colin hears a car approaching.

He looks back. A beige sedan, travelling at a moderate pace. Not a Road-Rager, of course, but it still could be anyone, so best not to try and solicit a lift.

To let the approaching car know that he's not interested, Colin stays on the verge, keeping his eyes ahead.

But in spite of this, the car slows to a stop as it draws level with him. The passenger door window slides down, revealing a grinning face wearing a red baseball cap.

''Ello there, me old mate!'

It is Chorley!

Chapter Twenty-Two
'C'mere, Yer Silly Sod!'

Colin had all but forgotten about Chorley, in so far as it's possible to forget the first person to have sexually molested you. The last time he had seen Chorley was during the night of the attack on Park Lane Comprehensive, when he had caught a glimpse of Chorley and Maclean in their van, while it was in the process of being tipped over on its side by members of the yellow gang. For all Colin knew that incident could well have ended terminally for the two men; but even if it hadn't, he had still come to regard Chorley as a bad memory he had left behind him for good when he had said goodbye to Eastchester; as someone he was never going to cross paths with again.

But here he is, greeting Colin like they are old friends mutually happy to have run into one another. Dimly, Colin is aware of Maclean occupying the driver's seat of the car; but his eyes are fixed on Chorley, mesmerised by that hateful face with its rictus grin.

'Fancy runnin' inter you out 'ere!' Chorley is saying. 'Now this is what I calls a stroke of bleedin' luck! Cuz, me an' 'im, we've been lookin' all over for yer, we 'ave. 'Aven't we, Maclean, old son?'

He turns to Maclean for confirmation.

That loss of eye contact acts like the breaking of a spell for Colin. He starts running.

'Oi!' calls Chorley after him. 'C'mere, yer silly sod! What you runnin' off for?'

A five-bar gate presents itself. Colin scrambles over it and into an overgrown meadow. The ground slopes down towards wooded countryside. He runs for the woods.

'Come back 'ere!'

Colin throws a glance over his shoulder. Chorley! He is over the gate and running after him! The shock nearly makes Colin fall, but he struggles on, arms and legs pumping.

As he gains the cover of the woods Colin snatches another look back. Chorley is gaining on him!

Colin charges through the arboreal twilight, weaving between the trees, crashing through the bracken. And then, without warning, his foot hits an obstacle. Pain shoots up his left leg and expecting solid ground, he finds himself instead pitching forward down a sharp declivity, a culvert concealed by the surrounding bracken. Unable to stop himself, he tumbles all the way to the bottom, coming to rest in a shallow streamlet of muddy water.

Colin pulls himself out of the water, and falls against the bank, catching his breath, nursing his ankle. He cannot run any more. The pain in his ankle is intense.

'Colin? Colin? Where are yer?' comes Chorley's voice, wheedling, coaxing. 'You don't 'ave ter run away from me, do yer? Ol' Chorley's not going to 'urt yer, is he? Good pals like us need ter stick tergether, don't we…?'

Colin grits his teeth, trying to control his breathing, fearful that the very sound of it might draw Chorley to him. At least this streamlet is well hidden, roofed over by foliage.

'Come on, old mate,' continues Chorley. 'I know yer 'idin' arahnd 'ere somewhere. You don't need ter 'ide from old Chorley… Was you thinkin' I wanted ter take yer back to Eastchester? Is that it? Izzat what made yer scarper? You think I want you back in the old gang with Bradley an' them lot? Then don't you worry, cuz there ain't no gang anymore, see? Went our separate ways, we did… Bradley and 'is mates 'ave proberly joined one of the colour gangs by now. An' as fer me and Maclean; well, we'd 'ad enough of Eastchester, so we took off. And we've been lookin' all over for you, mate. We thought you was with them others from your school, we did. Where was you goin', all on yer tod? Were you 'eadin' north to try an' find that sister of yours? Is that it? Well, then come with me an' Maclean! We'll drive yer there, we will; get yer there in no time! So why don't you come out? We'll look after yer! You can rely on yer old pal Chorley, can't yer?'

Colin hears heavy footsteps crunching through the deadwood.

'What're you doin' 'ere? You should 'ave stayed with the bleedin' car! Someone might come along and nick it!'

'I haven't left the key in the bloody ignition, have I?' comes Maclean's voice. 'Or do you think someone's going to come along and carry it off?'

Chorley guffaws. 'Did you 'ear that? Same old Maclean, eh? 'E's a bloomin' riot, ain't 'e? Never a dull moment with 'im!'

'And who do you think you're talking to?' inquires Maclean. 'The birds in the trees?'

'The birds in the trees,' chuckles Chorley. 'Tha's a good 'un. No, I'm talkin' ter young Colin, ain't I?'

'Funny, cuz I don't see him.'

'That's cuz 'e's 'idin', ain't 'e?'

'How do you know he's hiding? He could be miles away by now while you're standing here talking to the trees.'

'No, 'e's 'idin',' insists Chorley. ''E's got to be arahnd 'ere somewheres.'

'Well, if he doesn't want to show himself it's going to take a lot more than the two of us to find him in this lot. Let's get back to the car.'

'Get back to the car? An' leave poor Colin out 'ere all on 'is tod?'

'Well, maybe he prefers being "on his tod."'

'No, no… 'E's young an' 'e needs lookin' after. We can't leave

’im jus’ wanderin’ the countryside.’

‘Very noble,’ sneers Maclean. ‘Well maybe he’s not convinced of your good intentions. Let’s get back to the car.’

‘I can’t jest—’

‘Look, we know he’s in this area. We can pick up his trail again later, if we’re lucky; but we can’t search the whole bloody forest. Let’s get back to the car.’

Chorley sighs. ‘Alright, then.’ And raising his voice. ‘If you can ’ear me, we’re goin’ now. This is your last chance ter show yerself. Come on, mate! We’ll look after yer!’ A pause. And then: ‘Gunna be like that, are yer? Well, if you change yer mind later, we’ll be ’eadin’ dahn that road ter ’Eatherly. Got that? ’Eatherly; next town along. We’ll be waitin’ for yer there.’

Voices and footsteps recede.

Colin relaxes, as much as his throbbing ankle will allow this.

Pulling his sock down, Colin inspects the injured ankle. It has swollen alarmingly. Will he be able to walk on it? He stands up cautiously, tentatively trying his weight on his left leg. It hurts, it hurts a lot; but even so he doesn’t want to stay here; he wants to get moving and find Natasha and Miss Lantier; *they* will protect him from Chorley. Chorley wouldn’t stand a chance against Miss Lantier.

He crosses the rivulet and crawls up the other wall of the gully. And then, limping, he sets off on what he believes is a course parallel to the road. But Colin is not a human compass, and country roads do not always travel in straight lines, and so he is actually striking off obliquely away from the road and heading deeper into the woods.

Colin’s progress is slow and painful. He feels frustrated, by the return of Chorley, by the twisted ankle that’s slowing him down. If it hadn’t been for Chorley, he wouldn’t even *have* a twisted ankle! Events seem to be conspiring against him, conspiring to keep him away from the people he wants to be with.

The ground starts to rise, a fact which only increases his discomfort, and the by the time he reaches the clearing at the top of the acclivity, his ankle is throbbing so badly, he has to sit down and rest it. He removes his trainer and sock; the swollen area is now fiercely red and hot to the touch. He leans back against the bole of a tree, his leg stretched out before him, and takes stock of his surroundings—and the first thing he notices is that the road isn't where he left it; or rather, where what Colin believes to be his unerring sense of direction tells him it ought to be. And in fact, the road isn't anywhere. The forest—as it now appears to be—stretches off in all directions, and there is not a road in sight, nor even a file of telegraph poles that might indicate the presence of one; there is nothing manmade to be seen, just a lot of trees and a lot of sky.

And then something in that sky catches his eye. At first it's so small that it's just a black dot, and might be a stray bird—but as Colin looks the black dot grows larger, and he can tell by its smooth motion that it is a mechanical object, an aircraft of some kind. He listens for confirmation of this, but hears no sound of rotor blade or jet engine. Is it a balloon? Colin wonders. It draws nearer, takes shape, and the shape is elliptic. An airship? No, airships have engines, don't they? There is still no sound, and if it is an airship this one appears to be moving sideways…

And now it is close enough and clear enough that there can be no doubt anymore: what Colin sees is a flying saucer, a genuine Unidentified Flying Object.

It will be remembered (unless you've forgotten) that Colin's End of the World Anxiety embraces all aspects of the supernatural, and as this includes aliens, abductions and UFOs, the apparition now before him brings on a major attack.

Black in colour, or at least seeming so against the hazy pale-grey sky, the saucer glides silently past, looking so terrifyingly *wrong*. Feeling completely exposed on his hilltop, Colin dares not move a muscle. Who knows what kind of surveillance and detection devices the saucer might possess…! Judging from all the accounts he has read in his father's books, you can't hide from aliens; they always know exactly where you are.

But if the occupants of this particular flying saucer are aware of Colin's presence, they are apparently not interested; the saucer passes across Colin's line of vision without changing its trajectory, and moves out of sight. However, just to be on the safe side, Colin quickly moves into deeper cover, and, finding a suitable spot, curls up in a ball to ride out his anxiety attack.

Chapter Twenty-Three
'You Know Too Much'

By nightfall, Colin is well and truly lost and he knows he's lost. The Heatherly road—or any other road for that matter—remains as elusive as ever. He despairs of ever finding a way out of the forest, convinced that whichever direction he chooses to take will only take him ever further away from the four comforting arms of Natasha and Miss Lantier. He remembers having heard somewhere that people who get lost, especially in a forest or a desert where there are no landmarks to follow, will end up walking in circles. Colin doesn't *feel* like he's walking in circles, but then all those other lost people who ended up walking in circles probably didn't realise it either—if you knew you were walking in circles, you'd do something about it, wouldn't you?

And so, wretched, intermittently tearful, his stomach a hollow pit, Colin plods on, the pain of his injured ankle forcing him to take frequent breaks. And it is only now, after night has fallen, and he is starting to feel the cold (he left his jacket in the minibus), faint with hunger and exhaustion, his ankle throbbing more painfully than ever, that he makes the welcome discovery that he hasn't been walking in circles the whole time, when he abruptly finds himself at the edge of the woods, with arable farmland stretching away before him.

At last!

Wearily leaning against a tree, he pauses to take stock of the view. At first the landscape looks barren, no sign of life at all—but then he perceives a light; a solitary light, faint, small and close to the ground.

Colin makes his way towards it, tramping his way across the

fields. As he closes the distance, he perceives that the light is orange, flickering—the light of a campfire! Could it be Natasha and Miss Lantier? It might be! But wait a minute: what if it's Chorley and Maclean? It could just as easily be them.

He approaches cautiously. The fire is close to a small stand of trees, and he uses these as cover in order to approach unseen. He can hear the crackling of burning branches now, but no sound of conversation reaches his ears. He becomes conscious of the appetising smell of cooking meat. It smells like pork sausages. Could someone be cooking baked beans and pork sausages? That's something that campers eat, isn't it? You can cook them in the tin.

Almost there now, and Colin treads very carefully, keeping the group of trees between him and his target. Still no sound of conversation… He peers cautiously round the trunk of the tree…

A solitary man sits before the fire. A bearded man wearing a porkpie hat. He is eating a piece of meat from a tin plate, handling the food with his fingers. Colin recognises the bearded man: it is Forbes, the wandering poet they met at the picnic ground that day!

Colin wasn't particularly taken with Forbes at the time. He didn't like the man's funny way of talking. But right now, any familiar face is welcome. And that meat smells so good!

Colin steps out from behind the tree and into the light.

'Hello,' he says.

Forbes stiffens, stares suspiciously, but then relaxes.

'Good evening, young man,' he says. 'Your face looks familiar. Have our paths crossed before, perchance?'

'Yes,' affirms Colin. 'It was last week at the picnic area near Eastchester.'

'Ah yes. The party with the minibus. But you appear to be alone? Where are the others of your group? And pray, be seated.'

Colin gratefully sits down close by the fire. 'I've lost the others,' he says. 'Well, Mr Brandon's dead, and Paul's gone off on his own, but I'm looking for Natasha and Miss Lantier. Have you seen them?'

'The two women of your group? No, I haven't seen them.'

'They were supposed to be going to Heatherly.'

'Heatherly? I believe that settlement is not far from here.'

'It's near here, is it?' excited. 'Do you know which way it is?'

Forbes points. 'There is a road yonder; those bushes mark its course. I believe it will take you to Heatherly.'

Rising, Colin looks in the direction indicated. The Heatherly road. He's found it at last!

His stomach rumbles loudly.

'I perceive you are hungry, sir,' says Forbes.

'I'm starving,' confesses Colin.

'Then pray, sit down and help yourself, and take sustenance before continuing your journey. Pork cutlets, ungarnished, are all I can offer you; courtesy of an obliging farmer, who was good enough to present me with some cuts from an animal he had just slaughtered.'

Willingly accepting, Colin sits down again. Between himself and Forbes a large flat rock has been placed at the edge of the fire, and on this the cutlets are broiling.

'Alas, I possess no cutlery,' says Forbes. 'So please use your fingers.'

Forbes puts some pieces of meat on another tin plate and passes it to Colin. Colin picks up one of the hot cuts and transfers it to his mouth. It tastes good!

'It is to your liking?' asks Forbes.

'It's great,' affirms Colin, mouth full.

'I'm glad you approve. There are some people, certain religious denominations for example, who disdain the eating of swine flesh. I believe the reason for this lies in the fact that pigs are omnivorous creatures and there are some who maintain that only the flesh of plant-eating mammals is fit for human consumption.'

Colin, eating industriously, takes in little of this speech, and what he does take in he doesn't understand.

'I'm about to boil some water for tea; unfortunately, I only possess one mug, but you are welcome to share with me.

Alternatively, I can offer you a bottle of mineral water.'

Colin, feeling dehydrated replies, 'Can I have the water, please?'

Forbes passes a bottle, bearing the by now familiar grey label with black lettering: MINERAL WATER STILL.

Colin uncaps the bottle and gulps down the tepid water, while Forbes arranges an old kettle on the tripod over the fire.

'How did you manage to lose your friends?' he inquires.

Colin fills him in on his recent adventures.

'Well, you have certainly had an adventuresome day,' says Forbes, pouring the now boiling water into his tin mug. 'I would advise you to take as much rest as you can before moving on to Heatherly; you have been ambulating for far too long considering the injury you have sustained to your ankle; you need to rest it. I can offer you blankets if you wish to repose here for the night.'

I don't know…' says Colin. 'Should I…?'

'I would advise it… At least, repose yourself for the nonce, and give the matter some thought…'

Considering Forbes' offer, Colin shuffles backwards to recline against the trunk of the nearest tree, beginning to feel overheated from proximity to the fire. Forbes' rucksack being in the way, he moves it to one side.

Should he stay here, or should he move on…?

His hand happens to fall on something soft. Clothing. There must have been a pile of clothes under the rucksack. Mildly curious Colin looks down. He sees thick circles, light and dark. A cap. A striped cap. He picks up the cap. He recognises it. It is an Orville College cap.

What is Forbes doing with an Orville College cap? And not just the cap, he now sees: an entire Orville College uniform.

Strange…

A shadow falls across Colin.

He looks up. Forbes stands over him. His placid expression has hardened into one of menace; he holds a hunting knife in one hand.

'This is very unfortunate,' he sighs. 'I really should have

disposed of those clothes But alas, is too late now. You know too much.'

'How come you've got an Orville College uniform...?' asks Colin, both alarmed and mystified.

'Oh.' Forbes seems nonplussed. 'Perhaps you *don't* know too much. It appears I have been precipitate; that I have overestimated how much of the truth you would be able to deduce from your discovery of those clothes. This is rather awkward, because I fear that I have proceeded too far to withdraw now: I have revealed "my true colours" as it were. My menacing demeanour and the weapon I hold in my hand will have alerted you to the fact that something is amiss. Most unfortunate.

'Well, to answer your question, those clothes belonged to a student of the academy just named; he was, I believe, the only one able to escape unscathed from the bonfire you and your friends made of the premises. Our paths crossed earlier today.'

'Where is he now...?' asks Colin.

'Closer than you think. In fact, I could say that you have become intimately acquainted with him since partaking of your repast just now. You see, an interesting fact about the flesh of swine—and perhaps an additional reason why some people object to consuming it—is that in taste it bears a remarkable resemblance to the flesh of human beings.'

At first Colin doesn't get what Forbes means—but then he *does* get what he means and he realises what happened to the owner of that school uniform. His stomach performs a somersault and he is violently sick.

Chapter Twenty-Four
'Are You Going to Eat Me?'

'Perhaps you're wondering why I should have resorted to cannibalism? Food is still readily available, you would argue; there is no shortage. And what is more, since what we call the Incident, food is now entirely free. Everybody can take as much as they need. That is what you are thinking, is it not…? Well, to explain my motives I really need to take you back to when the Incident occurred; I need to take you to my native village of Huffy. As I told you and your friends on the occasion of our last meeting, I lost my dear wife Lydia to the Incident. Now I'm sure you have heard it said that we never truly appreciate something until we lose it? Well, that was the case with myself. Please do not think I used to take my wife for granted, or that I mistreated her in any way: nothing of the sort. I appreciated her at her full value, and was conscious of how fortunate I was to possess this woman for my helpmeet. But her loss made me realise something else, something of critical importance: to wit, my wife had been the one single thing that allowed me to maintain my slender grip on my sanity.

'Yes, I confess it. When I lost my wife I became completely insane—and the first manifestation of my insanity was, I regret to say, to the detriment of my fellow villagers. As I believe I said last week, Huffy is a very small hamlet, and the Incident took away one half of its already very small population. I am not sure how the thought first came to me, but I began to ponder more and more upon the idea of just how vulnerable my fellow villagers were. Many of them were elderly, and consequent upon the disappearances, many were now living alone. Yes, I kept on ruminating upon how vulnerable they were. I thought "never mind the possibility of some armed gang of youths descending on the village; one determined man could easily move from house to house and slaughter every one of the inhabitants." Yes, that is what I realised, and it took no great mental leap for me to decide that I myself could be that one determined person. In short, that is what I proceeded to do. Armed with this very knife you see before you now, I one evening progressed from house to house through the village of Huffy, and slaughtered all of my neighbours. And having accomplished this, I experienced the most enormous sense of achievement, of job satisfaction you could say.

'Well, it was after this that I commenced my wanderings, having nothing to detain me in Huffy. And so I set off. I believe I said before that I have encountered other solitary wayfarers during my travels, but what I neglected to mention was that I killed every single one of them. The first one I also devoured was out of simple necessity. I was hungry and at the time the supermarket shelves had yet to be resupplied. But I soon discovered that I enjoyed consuming my victims as much as I did the act of depriving them of their lives. It was not so much that I acquired a taste for human flesh, but the immense pleasure I felt at breaking the ultimate of human taboos—because surely cannibalism is even more of a human taboo than the act of murder itself.

'And really that brings us up to date. I killed that boy today because it pleased me to; I devoured him because it pleased me to. And then your arrival afforded me a further pleasure: that of ensnaring someone into unwittingly consuming human flesh. And you liked it, did you not? Yes, you confessed as much yourself. Your stomach only rejected the meat when you learned its origin. Rather hypocritical, I would say. If you enjoyed the meat at the time, you cannot really claim to dislike it in retrospect.'

'Are you going to eat me?' asks Colin, wretched, sitting tied to the tree by ropes.

'My dear boy, that is hardly any concern of yours, now is it?' says Forbes. 'Surely you should be inquiring whether or not I am going to kill you? That I would say is the more important issue, from your perspective. What I might do with your body post-mortem is hardly going to affect you one way or the other, is it? Yes, the question of whether or not I am going to kill should be your main concern at the present time.'

'And are you going to kill me?' asks Colin obediently.

'My boy, I can do nothing but kill you! Not killing you would be an act of stark defiance against my very nature. We can only live our lives according to our own lights. Nature intended me to be a homicidal maniac. I would have become one much sooner had I not married my dear Lydia. Completely unconsciously she acted as a control element, keeping my murderous antisocial impulses in check. She did not realise she was performing this function; for that matter neither did I. But now she has gone and my true nature has manifested itself. So, to answer your question: yes, I am most certainly going to kill you. The only remaining question is when I shall do this. You see, I am quite enjoying having someone to talk to like this, someone to really open up to. You see, I have never had quite the same experience with any of my previous victims. In most cases I pounced on them and slew them without warning, but with you I have had the opportunity to make you my prisoner and to have this conversation with you. Yes, and I have enjoyed it. So I do not think I will kill you immediately. Perhaps I will kill you before I retire for the night; perhaps I will wait until the morn. I shall consider the matter as I finish drinking my tea.'

Colin, lashed firmly to the tree, considers himself doomed. He can see no way out of this; no hope of escape and out here in the middle of nowhere, no hope of rescue.

As if expressly to contradict this pessimistic thought, a movement in the darkness catches Colin's eye. A shadowy figure, moving very slowly and carefully, advances towards Forbes from behind. As the figure draws closer, the firelight picks out the features of the newcomer. It is Natasha! Her eyes are fixed on Forbes' back as, lips pursed, she takes each careful step.

Natasha! And she clearly realises that Forbes is an enemy! His heart pounding with the return of hope, Colin mentally urges her on, praying that no treacherous twig will snap under her foot.

And then it occurs to him that he is staring at Natasha and that this is not a good idea. If Forbes chances to look towards him, the man will see that Colin's eyes are fixed on something behind his back. He quickly looks away.

Talk! Yes, he should say something to Forbes, keep his attention occupied.

'So is your tea alright?'

It's the best he can improvise.

Forbes looks at him. 'Yes, it is, as it happens,' he says. 'Although why that should be of any interest to you, I really cannot fathom. Is this perhaps the beginning of that bond that is supposed to form between captor and captive? Stockholm Syndrome, I believe they call it.'

Closer… Getting closer…

'I just wondered if it tastes alright without milk,' proceeds Colin.

'It tastes fine without milk. Adding milk to tea is a preference chiefly exclusive to the British. You will find that the people of most other countries drink the beverage unadulterated. In Japan for instance—'

Just what tit-bit of information Forbes was about to regale him with regarding Japanese tea-drinking practices, Colin will never know, because at this moment Natasha springs. She pounces on Forbes, grabbing the knife he has set down by his side.

The struggle is brief. Colin hears a strangled cry, and then Forbes subsides. Natasha pulls the knife from between his ribs and rushes over to Colin.

'You okay?'

'Yes!' says Colin, with feeling.

'I can't believe you're still alive,' she says, smiling and stroking his cheek.

'He was going to kill me later,' says Colin, misunderstanding.

'I mean from this morning! We thought you got run over.'

'No, I didn't get run over. You saved me. Thank you.'

'You're welcome. Let's get these ropes off you.'

She commences cutting the ropes that bind Colin.

'I heard most of what that sicko was saying to you,' she proceeds. 'But I couldn't jump in while he was still holding that knife. I had to wait till he put it down.'

Free of the ropes, Natasha helps Colin to his feet. She embraces him warmly. Colin starts to cry. He thought he was going to die and now Natasha has come along and saved his life.

'God, we've had a hell of a day, haven't we?' says Natasha when the hug has ended.

'How did you find me?' asks Colin, wiping his eyes. 'Are you with Miss Lantier?'

'Nope, I'm on my own,' is the answer. 'And I haven't got a

clue where we are, either. I've just been wandering around in the dark. I saw the light of this fire and I got here just in time to see you getting tied up by that psycho. Well, he's dead now, and he got what he deserved.'

'Actually,' comes a faint voice. 'I haven't expired yet, although I am in a considerable amount of pain…'

Forbes lies where he has fallen, one arm moving feebly.

'If you were to perhaps staunch the bleeding…' he continues. 'It's not too late… Both physically and morally… Yes, I feel that I am ready to turn over a new leaf, to renounce my criminal ways, if you were to assist me and give me another chance at life… So, if you would just…'

'Come on, Colin,' says Natasha, taking him by the arm. 'Let's get out of here.'

'The road's that way,' says Colin, indicating the direction.

They set off across the field.

'…The greatest saints have always been reformed sinners… Really… this pain is most disagreeable…'

Leaving Forbes to enjoy his slow and painful death in solitude, Colin and Natasha gain the road. They set off in what they hope is the direction of Heatherly.

'What's up? Have you hurt yourself?' Natasha, noticing that Colin is limping.

'Yes, I twisted my ankle.'

'Let's have a look.'

Colin sits on the verge, and more by touch than sight, Natasha examines the injury.

'You shouldn't be walking on that,' she says. 'First place we come to, we'll stop for the night.'

They resume their walk, Natasha supporting Colin. 'So, what happened to you? We all thought that black Porsche got you.'

Colin describes his adventures, up to his escape from Kettleworth and his meeting with Paul Mitchell.

'Bastard,' intones Natasha through gritted teeth, when he gets

'What's wrong?'

'Paul bloody lied to you, that's what's wrong. He sent you off on a wild goose chase.'

'What, you didn't go down the road to Heatherly?'

'Yeah, we did go down the road to Heatherly, but you'd never have been able to catch up with us, cuz we weren't walking, we were in a car!'

'A car! How come you were in a car?'

'Miss Lantier got hold of one,' explains Natasha. 'Look, let me tell you what happened to us when we all got split up. After Brandon got killed and we thought you'd been killed as well, we all ran off in different directions. First, it was just me with Paul, cuz Miss Lantier disappeared. We didn't see what way she went. Well, me and Paul got away from the Road-Ragers by cutting across gardens and keeping off the roads as much as we could. We ended up taking cover in this supermarket. We were there for a while, arguing about what we should do next. You'd probably noticed that me and Paul already weren't getting on very well today, and it didn't get any better. In the end I get fed-up with him, so I just walked out of the shop. Paul came after me and then this car came along. We thought it was those Road-Ragers come back, but it wasn't: it was Miss Lantier. She'd ended up at some petrol station, and while she was there, one of those cars came along and the driver got out to use the little boys' room. So, she just got into his car and drove off in it!

'So, after she picked up me and Paul, we made it out of Kettleworth. A couple of those cars chased after us, but they stopped as soon as we were outside the town. And then when we pulled up to decide what we were going to do next, Paul started acting up again, and this time it wasn't just me he was having a go at: he started calling Miss Lantier bad names as well. So basically, we just kicked him out of the car and went off without him.'

'If you drove off with Miss Lantier, how come you're not still with her?'

'Cuz something bloody weird happened. It was about half an hour later, we were driving along, talking about things, when suddenly the car packed up on us. It was like the battery had just died or something. So we got out to have a look under the bonnet—and then I don't know what happened. It was like one minute I was there, standing next to Miss Lantier while she was looking at the engine, and then the next minute it was pitch dark and I was standing in a field in the middle of nowhere!'

'Missing time!' exclaims Colin.

'Missing time?'

'Yeah! That's what happens when you get abducted by aliens. When they put you back, they wipe all your memories of being on their spaceship, so that you have this big gap in your memory. That's missing time! Yes! I bet you were in the same flying saucer I saw today!'

'What? You saw a flying saucer?'

'Yes! It was this afternoon!'

Colin now recommences his own narrative, describing his encounter with Chorley and then his getting lost in the woods and what he saw there.

'Yeah, that thing you saw could've had something to do with what happened to us,' agrees Natasha. ''Cept I don't think it was aliens: it was people. It's the people who're behind the Incident and everything that's happening... But what did they do with Miss Lantier? Did they put her back somewhere else, or have they still got her? If she is still around, I reckon she'd make for Heatherly, so that's where we need to go.'

'Don't forget Chorley said he was going to Heatherly, as well,' says Colin.

'Don't you worry about that creep. He's not going to hurt you while I'm around,' promises Natasha.

The two travellers proceed on their way. The road enters more wooded country, and it's not long before they encounter human habitation: a single-storeyed house, set well back from the road in a picturesque garden. No lights show in the windows of this dwelling.

'Just what we were looking for!' says Natasha. 'We can stay here for the night. Looks abandoned.'

'They might have just gone to bed,' suggests Colin.

'Bit early for going to bed. Well, let's just knock on the door and see.'

They walk up to the front door and Natasha knocks firmly.

They wait. No light comes on. No sound is heard from within.

Natasha knocks again. She calls through the letterbox. Nothing stirs. She tries the front door. It is locked.

'Let's try round the back.'

Here they meet with success. The back door is unlocked, and they step into the kitchen.

'Hello?' calls Natasha.

The house is silent, and a quick search proves that it is indeed untenanted. The rustic dwelling looks neat and tidy, undisturbed by any previous intruders. Whoever once lived here must have just quietly vanished from existence on that fateful day, leaving their empty home behind them. The house has two bedrooms, both of them have double beds, one of them having the appearance of being a guest bedroom. There are family photographs in the living room and the bedroom.

'I bet it was this old couple who lived here,' declares Natasha, indicating one of these photos. 'We'll be safe enough here for the night. We'll keep the lights out in the rooms that face the road, just in case, though I doubt anyone'll come along. Now let's have a look at that ankle of yours.'

In the bathroom bandages are found, and Natasha binds Colin's ankle. This done, they go to the kitchen. There's plenty of edible food, and Natasha, who is famished, sets about preparing a meal. Colin, however, has lost his appetite.

'I ate *person*,' he says dolefully.

'But you didn't do it on purpose, did you?' argues Natasha. 'Plus, you chucked it all back up again, anyway. And you can't go to bed on an empty stomach.'

Colin acquiesces, and Natasha makes them both a tasty (and meat-free) meal, which they sit down at the kitchen table to enjoy.

Chapter Twenty-Five
'You Know How You're Mixed Race...?'

The guest bedroom, being the bedroom facing away from the road, is the one selected for their night's rest. Colin had supposed that with their being two beds, they would be occupying one each, but Natasha soon set him straight on that score.

'We'll share,' she told him. 'It's safer if we stick together. And look, there's enough room in this bed for two elephants! And I don't snore, either!'

And so Colin, stripped to his underpants, lies on the left side of the bed, waiting for Natasha to return from her ablutions to join him. The room is cosily lit by the lamp on the bedside table on the other side of the bed. He lies on his back (Natasha has told him it will be better for his ankle if he sleeps in that position) with the covers up to his chin and his heart pounding with excitement.

He's going to be sleeping with Natasha! Actually sleeping with her! Girlfriends and boyfriends sleep together. He's often heard people talking about lovers sleeping together; so that means Natasha and him are going to be like girlfriend and boyfriend tonight, actually sleeping together—sleeping side-by-side in the same bed!

From the neighbouring bathroom, Colin hears the toilet flush, and then the click of the cord light switch. And then the bedroom door opens and in walks Natasha stripped of her outer clothes. Her bra and knickers are matching and white in colour, a beautiful contrast to her brown skin. White also are her teeth, which she displays in the generous smile she directs at spellbound Colin. He has never seen such a beautiful vision in his life; her navel in particular draws his attention. Her bare arms and her bare legs, seen before during swimming lessons, are not new to him—but the naked midriff: this is something new; the soft curve of her hips, the planes of smooth brown skin framed above and below by the white cotton, the enticing hollow of the belly button…

Carefully setting down her clothes on a chair, Natasha climbs into the bed beside Colin. 'I'm turning the light off, okay?' she says. Colin murmurs his consent and the room is plunged into darkness.

Natasha settles herself beside Colin, and he soon begins to feel the warmth of her body. His eyes adjusting to the gloom, he turns his head, discerns her profile.

'Natasha…?' begins Colin, hesitant.

'Yes?'

'Can I…? I mean, there's something I wanted to tell you about… Is it alright—can I tell you…?'

She looks round at him. He sees a smile in the darkness. 'Course it's alright. You can tell me whatever you want, Colin.'

'It… it's something that bothered me for a really long time… only, I… I couldn't tell anyone about it… I was worried people would laugh if I told them…'

Natasha turns on her side, reaches out her arm, squeezes Colin's shoulder, fingers transmitting soft encouragement. 'Well, I'm not going to laugh, Colin… If you've got something bottled up inside you like that, you need to get it off your chest… So go on, I'm listening…'

And so, Colin tells her. He launches into the story of the onset of his End of the World Anxiety (not that he calls it that himself), the story he has never told anyone before. Stumbling and awkward, helped along by Natasha, he unburdens himself.

And Natasha listens to it all, and she doesn't laugh.

'You poor thing,' she says, stroking his arm. 'Keeping all that bottled up inside you like that… But why didn't you tell someone what was bothering you? That just made it a million times worse for you, not telling. You should've gone to see the school counsellor. That was what she was there for, wasn't she?—to listen to things like that.'

'But I thought the school counsellor was just for people who were going mad…?'

This makes Natasha laugh. 'Going mad. You didn't have to be

bonkers to go'n see the school counsellor: you're thinking of psychiatrists; that's different. The school counsellor, she was just there to listen to students' problems. It didn't matter what; anything at all that was bothering you…'

'Oh…'

'Well, it doesn't matter. You've told me now, and I'm just as good as a school counsellor, aren't I?'

Colin meets her eyes in the darkness, smiles.

'That's it. You've got it off your chest now,' still stroking his arm. 'Poor thing… You must have felt really lonely, having all that on your mind and not being able to tell anyone…'

'But… but why was I like that…? Why was it just me who was worrying like that…?'

'Well, you just got this idea stuck in your head, didn't you? That happens to people sometimes. People get things stuck in their heads. Things that scare them. Doesn't mean you were mad or anything. And anyway, you were right, weren't you? The worst has happened now, and you know what? You were the clever one who saw it coming! Nobody else did. So, you don't have to worry anymore…'

'But I still get scared… about things… Like today when I saw that flying saucer…'

'That's anxiety. Having all that stuff bottled up in your head for so long: it's given you anxiety. That's not surprising, but when you've got anxiety, your friends can help you out with that. And that's me, right? *I'll* be here to help you out; and so will Miss Lantier, when we find her again. Okay?'

'Yes…' Colin, tearful, smiling his gratitude.

'Right. Well, let's just get to sleep now, so you can give that ankle of yours time to start healing. Okay?'

And, leaning over him, Natasha kisses Colin briefly on the lips, a Japanese kiss, gentle, meaningful.

'Goodnight, then. And don't you worry.'

'Goodnight…'

'…Natasha…?'

'Yes…?'

'Can I ask you something?'

'Yeah, course you can.'

'Well… you know how you're mixed race…?'

'Yes, I do know that.'

'Well, I was… I was wondering what races are you a mix of? If it's alright to ask…'

A sigh in the dark. 'Yes, it's alright to ask. Well, I'm one third Indian, one third Arab, and one third South Sea Islander; now get to sleep…'

'Okay…'

When Colin awakes it is abruptly and he is gripped by the feeling that something is very wrong.

Daylight filters in through the drawn curtains and the first thing he sees is that he is alone. He immediately attaches his sense of disquiet to Natasha's absence. Something must have happened to her.

He looks at his watch. Ten past nine. It's later than he thought, so actually it's not surprising that Natasha is up, he tells himself. He listens. No sounds of activity from either kitchen or bathroom.

He throws back the covers and swings his legs out of bed. A stab of pain reminds him of his injured ankle. He examines it. Still tender, but the swelling has definitely gone down. Dressing quickly, he goes to the kitchen. The room is empty, but a mug on the table and a still warm electric kettle tell him that Natasha was here recently.

He moves through the bungalow: living room, bedroom, bathroom. No Natasha. She must have gone outside. He tries the front door. Locked. He returns to the kitchen and tries the back door, and finds it open.

He steps outside. There's no sign of Natasha in the back garden, so he moves round to the front, and surveys the scene. The garden with its flower-beds a medley of colour under the bright morning sky, stretches out towards the road; and across the road rises the green wall of the surrounding woodland.

No Natasha.

The familiar feeling of rising panic starts to creep over Colin. He calls out Natasha's name.

His first treacherous thought is that Natasha has deserted him, that she's gone off on her own to find Miss Lantier, leaving Colin behind because she doesn't want to be slowed down by him and his bad ankle. A treacherous, ungrateful suspicion, which Colin dismisses when what seems to him a much more plausible explanation for Natasha's absence occurs to him. The aliens. The aliens who abducted Natasha yesterday. They've come back from her and they've taken her away again.

Colin drops down onto the front doorstep, buries his face in his hands. Natasha has gone. She has been taken away, maybe for good this time, and he has been left on his own.

He hates this new world. He hates the uncertainty of it; the constant fear and danger. This new world is a world with no rules, with no order to it, no neat and tidy routines to follow. Colin just wants to be safe and secure like he felt last night when he was with Natasha, and she listened to the story he's never told anyone else before. Natasha. Yesterday she had seemed indestructible; singlehandedly she saved his life—but today this new world has reached out and taken her away.

Crying and sniffling, Colin doesn't hear the car, doesn't hear the footsteps advancing up the garden path. He is only aware of the newcomer when a shadow falls over him and an all too familiar voice speaks.

'Well, fancy runnin' inter you 'ere!'

Colin looks up. Chorley grins down at him.

Galvanised, Colin springs to his feet, tries to run, but a hand clamps around his upper arm.

'No yer don't,' says Chorley. 'Yer not runnin' out on me this time, sunshine.'

Colin struggles frantically but uselessly as Chorley drags him along the path. Maclean sits at the wheel of the car, looking disinterested.

'Leggo of me!' screams Colin. 'I don't wanna go with you!'

'Well you've got ter come with us, 'aven't yer?' grunts Chorley. 'You need lookin' after, don't yer? Yer can't be all on yer tod, can yer?'

These rhetorical questions take the struggling duo to the road where Chorley opens the back door of the car and pushes Colin inside. He follows Colin onto the back seat, slams the door.

'Right. Move it.'

The car moves forward.

Colin continues to scream, kicking and punching Chorley.

Chorley defends himself from the futile blows.

'Nah, come on! Jus' you calm down. There's no need for the 'ysterics. Ol' Chorley ain't gunna 'urt yer.'

'Get off me you dirty old paedo!' screams Colin.

Chorley's expression turns savage. 'Now, don't *you* start callin' me bad names,' he hisses. 'Jest you settle down and do what you're told.'

Colin's only reply is to continue lashing out.

'I'm tellin' yer ter pack it in!' warns Chorley. 'Will you calm dahn or not?'

Colin does not desist. Chorley fetches him a stinging blow around the side of the head. Stunned, his ear ringing, Colin subsides, whimpering.

'Now that was your fault,' Chorley tells him. 'You forced me ter do that, didn't yer? Well, let's just calm dahn now. Let me get yer seatbelt on. We ain't either of us got our seatbelts on yet, 'ave we?'

He fastens Colin's seatbelt, and then his own.

'Now, that's better, ain't we? There was no need fer the 'ysterics, was there? We'll jus' drive along, all peaceable like, until we get ter 'eatherly.'

Colin says nothing.

'You 'eard what I said ter yer in the woods yesterday, din't yer?' proceeds Chorley. 'I wasn't talkin' to meself then, was I? Well, I meant what I said then. We can go anyplace yer like. We can 'ead back to Eastchester if you want, or we can 'ead north ter find that sister o' yours. Whatever you want, that's what we'll do?

You jus' say the word.'

'I want to get out of this car,' says Colin, sullenly.

'Anything except that,' is the flat reply. 'As a responsible adult, I ain't gunna leave you on yer own.' He sits back in his seat. 'So what do yer think o' the new set o' wheels? Nice little motor, ain't it? Yeah, I decided we didn't need that ol' van anymore. If we're goin' travellin' then we need a nice comfy automobile; ain't that what I said, Maclean old mate? Let's get rid o' the van, I said, din't I?'

'I thought we got rid of the van because the yellow gang tipped it on its side,' replies Maclean, sourly. 'As you may recall, we were both in it at the time.'

'Well, 'ow was I ter know the bleedin' yellers would turn on us like that?' retorts Chorley. 'You try ter do someone a favour and they turns around and bites yer!'

'Yeah, but you weren't doing them a favour, were you? You told them that that school was the blue gang's headquarters, just so that they'd get you inside the place. And a right mess that plan turned out, didn't it?'

'Well I wasn't ter know they'd go overboard like that! I didn't want 'em to torch the blinkin' place, did I? All I wanted was ter get me mate 'ere back.' Turning to Colin: 'Now, why did yer do that? Why did you run off like that?'

'You know why I ran away!' retorts Colin, hotly. So, it was Chorley who set the yellow gang on the school!

'Nah that's jus' what I *don't* know,' says Chorley. 'Why you should up sticks an' leave is a mystery ter me. I thought you were settlin' in, I did. Gettin' along famously, we were. So why did yer 'ave ter go an' sneak off like that?'

'You know why!' repeats Colin. 'It's because of what you did to me, you dirty paedo!'

'Stop callin' me them names!' snaps Chorley. 'Look, I'd 'ad a few drinks that night, that's all. I was tight an' I got a bit carried away. No 'arm in that, eh? Jest a bit o' fun.'

'It *wasn't* fun.'

Chorley heaves a sigh. 'Well, alright then. What if I was to say

I won't do anythin' like that again? 'Ow abaht that?'

'I don't believe you!'

'I mean it. I won't do it again.'

'You've got to promise.'

'Alright then, I'll promise. I swear on me mother's grave that I'll never do anything like that to yer again. Okay?'

'Cross your heart?'

'Cross me 'eart.' Chorley performs the act. 'Y'see, all I want is ter look after yer, that's what it is. I've come to think of meself as yer guardian, I 'ave. The world ain't too safe anymore, y'see. You need someone like me ter look out f'yer. And speaking of, how come is it, you ended up on yer tod? You was in that minibus that took off outer the school gates that night, weren't yer? 'Oo was with yer?'

'There were two teachers and two students with me,' says Colin. 'Mr Brandon and Miss Lantier, and Natasha and Paul.'

'Natasha…' Chorley wine-tastes the name. 'Natasha. Ain't that the name o' the girl you said you was soft on?'

'Yes,' says Colin.

'Yeah, I thought it was. An' what 'appened ter them? 'Ow comes you was all alone when I met yer yesterday? Did somethin' 'appen?'

Grudgingly, Colin gives an account of recent adventures.

'Ah! So that's why I found yer sittin' on the doorstep o' that empty 'ouse an' sobbin' yer 'eart out! She ran out on yer did she? Well, that's women for yer!'

'She didn't run out on me!' retorts Colin. 'The aliens took her away!'

'Aliens? And where do bleedin' aliens come into it?'

Colin explains.

'Well… well maybe you're right, then,' decides Chorley. 'Maybe them aliens did come back for 'er, like you say. Well, then! Lucky for you me an' Maclean turned up when we did!'

This is a piece of luck Colin could have done without; but at least they're taking him to Heatherly. Hopefully Miss Lantier will be there in Heatherly.

Chapter Twenty-Six
'Sod That for a Game o' Soldiers'

'The Great North Road!' pronounces Chorley. 'An' do yer know 'oo built this 'ere road, Colin old son? Julius Caesar, it was! Julius Caesar and the Roman bleedin' Empire!'

'Oh yeah,' from sarcastic Maclean. 'The Romans were well known for building north- and south-bound dual carriageways, weren't they?'

'Well, yeah, I know this ain't the actual original Roman road,' says Chorley. 'I admit it's been resurfaced once or twice since then. But it's still in the same place, ain't it? Y'see, Colin, them Romans always built their roads in straight lines, and Julius Caesar, he wanted a main artery runnin' north an' south so that 'is legions could march up to the Scottish border to do battle wi' the Jock McHaggises. 'Ad a lot o' trouble wi' the Jocks, the Romans did.'

They have the motorway to themselves. Not another vehicle is in sight. Colin has passed along many empty roads since leaving Eastchester, but on this vast motorway that emptiness is so much more apparent.

There was no Miss Lantier waiting for them in Heatherly; there wasn't anyone at all. The whole town was deserted. Either the Incident had taken away the entire population, or else those who were left had decided on a mass-exodus. There were no signs of violence or disturbance; no burnt buildings or looted shops; but not a single person to be seen.

And so, Colin has not been rescued from the clutches of Chorley, but that worthy has promised to drive Colin to Norton-Braisley to look for his sister, and he appears to be keeping his word. By following the M1 they should reach their destination by evening.

Chorley turns round in his seat. 'Know what I miss most of all in this new world?' he asks Colin.

'Football,' replies Maclean.

'Well, yes,' says Chorley. 'But I wasn't going ter talk abaht football wi' Colin, cuz I know 'e ain't interested in the Beautiful Game. No, the thing I miss in this new world is the takeaway grub. That's what I miss. A good Indian or Chinese takeaway.'

'You've been missing them for a long time, then,' says Maclean. 'We didn't get many takeaways where we were.'

Chorley ignores this comment. 'Are you with me there, Colin? Did you used to like a good takeaway?'

'We didn't have many takeaways at home,' says Colin.

'Didn't 'ave takeaways? How come?'

'Mum liked cooking the dinner. We had fish and chips sometimes.'

'Well, fish 'n chips are alright in their way, I'll grant yer that. In fact they're pretty much this country's only contribution ter world cuisine. Nah, I don't mind some fish 'n chips now an' then. An' them battered sausages they do is good an' all. But what about the curries and the Chineses, Colin, old mate? Didn't you ever 'ave them?'

'Mum made us curry sometimes.'

'Did she nah? Well, there's nothin' wrong with an 'ome-cooked curry, and don't think I'm slightin' yer Ma's culinary skills, but 'ome-cooked jest doesn't taste the same as a takeaway curry.' Chorley sighs reflectively. 'Beef curry; that's what I used ter like. Come to think on it, it's funny them places even did beef curry. I mean ter say, if you was in India, you couldn't 'ave a beef curry, could yer? Cows is sacred animals in India; an' yer don't go eatin' sacred animals. I wonder what they 'ad instead…? Maybe goat curry…'

'I'm sorry to interrupt this fascinating discussion,' says Maclean; 'but we've got company.'

'Eh? Where?'

'Behind us.'

Colin turns round in his seat. Behind them, a fleet of articulated lorries are approaching. The vehicles, about six in number, are uniformly grey in colour.

'Where the 'ell did they come from?' wonders Chorley.

‘I’ve heard about these lorries,’ says Colin. ‘They’re what deliver the food to the shops.’

‘Ah! Well, that makes sense,’ says Chorley. ‘That stuff ’ad to be comin’ from somewhere. So it’s them trucks what delivers it, eh? I wonder oo’s drivin’ ’em…?’

‘They’re moving faster than us,’ reports Maclean. ‘They’re closing in.’

‘Then they can overtake us, can’t they?’ says Chorley. ‘It’s not like there’s a shortage of bleedin’ room.’

Colin keeps his eye on the lead truck as it closes in. He too wonders who is in the cabs of these trucks… Presumably people who know the truth about what’s going on. People, or maybe *not* people… Colin looks into the cab. He can’t make out anything of the interior. Is it just the way the daylight is reflecting off the windshield? Or is the glass tinted…?

The truck is right on top of them now, all Colin can see are the headlights and the engine grill.

‘What’s ’is bleedin’ problem?’ demands Chorley. ‘Why don’t you overtake, you idiot?’

The truck seems to be inches from them. Alarmed, Colin looks round at Chorley.

‘Maybe we’re not supposed to be on this motorway?’ is his anxious suggestion.

‘We got as much right ter be ’ere as them,’ asserts Chorley. ‘This is a public bleedin’ ’ighway. No, that geezer’s jus’ tryin’ ter spook us cuz we’re the only other car on the road. Just messin’ around, ’e is. Surprised he ain’t tootin’ ’is ’orn at us.’

‘Incoming,’ says Maclean,

Colin wonders what he means, but soon sees. The second truck has overtaken the first on the outside lane and is drawing alongside them.

And then a bump jolts the car and its occupants. The lorry behind has grazed their bumper.

‘I take it back,’ says Chorley. ‘These geezers mean business. Step on it.’

‘I *am* stepping on it,’ Maclean tells him. ‘This isn’t a bloody racing car.'

Another impact.

'We need to get off this motorway and fast!' declares Chorley.

'No! You think so?' sarcastically.

And now the second truck cuts in front of them, while a third takes its place in the other lane. They are now completely boxed in. The three metal monsters loom over them, their full-throated diesel roars filling the air. Compared to these giants, their car is like a go-cart.

'They're gunna smash us to pieces!' yells Chorley. 'Do something?'

'Like what?' yells back Maclean. 'I can't jump over the bloody barrier, can I?'

'Then pull in at the next layby!'

'And how am I supposed to see when the next layby's coming up? In case you hadn't noticed, my view ahead is somewhat restricted at the moment. And I couldn't pull over anyhow: they're making us go too fast!'

'Look, *I'll* tell yer when there's a layby coming up!' says Chorley, stabbing the window regulator on the door beside him. The window slides down, admitting noise and fumes. Releasing his safety-belt, Chorley extrudes his head and shoulders.

'I can see ahead!' he announces. 'Don't see any layby…'

The car is rocked by another impact. Chorley cries out, coming into violent contact with the window frame, and collapses back into his seat.

'Watch what you're bloody doin'! You nearly broke me bleedin' neck!'

'It wasn't me, was it? It was the bastard in front—he suddenly slowed down!'

'Well, try and keep 'er steady,' adjures Chorley, craning his neck out the window again.

'I can see a bridge!' he cries. 'An overpass! There's gotta be a slip-roa—yeah, I see it!' triumphantly. 'We got us a slip-road coming up! Right; get ready! When I say now, you yank the steering wheel!'

'Right!'

Two more jarring impacts, front and then back, and another cry of pain from Chorley.

'Bloody bastards! Right! Just a few more seconds… Now!'

Maclean jerks the steering wheel, the car slews to the left. And they are on the slip-road, slamming into the barrier. Chorley's head strikes the top of the window frame; he falls back onto his seat. Maclean recovers control of the vehicle, and now they are climbing the exit ramp; it is too late for the lorry in front to move in and block them, and the pursuing vehicles make no effort to follow them.

'Well, sod that for a game o' soldiers,' says Chorley, rubbing his throbbing temple. 'From now on we're stickin' ter the bloody B-roads!'

Chapter Twenty-Seven
'Cheery Lookin' Barrack, Ain't It?'

They are lost.

Night has fallen, torrential rain lances down from the sky, drumming a furious rhythm on the roof of the car as they pursue their way through densely wooded country. Colin is reminded of a similar occasion driving with his family. That time there had been thunder and lightning as well as the rain, and he had been very young at the time and terrified by the noise.

'Speakin' of extra-terrestrials…' says Chorley, breaking a lengthy silence.

'We weren't speaking of them,' replies Maclean.

'Well we was a couple of hours back, wasn't we? Well, anyways, I was jest thinkin' 'ow that that Chupa-whatsit thing they got in Mexico, that goat-sucking thing—'

'Chupacabra.'

'Yeah, the Chupacabra. Well, I was jest thinkin' as 'ow that thing's got ter be an extra-terrestrial.'

'An alien? You're not suggesting that Chupacabras caused the

Incident, are you?'

'No! O' course I ain't! It's just an animal, ain't it? It ain't intelligent. But what I'm sayin' is, I reckon it must've come from outer space, right?'

'And how do you come to that profound conclusion?'

'Well, jest because it's recent, ain't it? It ain't got any 'istory, if yer see what I mean. Yer know, when they discovered America and catag'rised all the new animals what was there, they didn't mention that one, did they? And it weren't no legend'ry creature either, like the Abdominable Snowman in the 'Imalayas. No. Until a couple o' decades back, no-one 'ad even 'eard o' the bleedin' Chupacabra. But since then, people've been seein' it all the time, 'aven't they? An' now there seein' it in other countries round them parts; not jest in Mexcico. It's spreadin', ain't it?'

'And how do you deduce from all that that the thing must be alien?'

'Well, it stands ter reason, don't it? I mean, an 'ole new species can't jest suddenly materialise outer thin air, can it? So I reckon it musta been brought 'ere by aliens. It might be some alien's pet or somethin'. An' I reckon some UFO what landed in Mexico one time must've left one of 'em be'ind, by accident like; either that or they did it on purpose. So it got left 'ere an' now it's reproducin', ain't it? an' it's spreadin' an' that's why more n' more people 'as been seein' the bloomin' thing.'

'And how did it manage to reproduce if they only left *one* behind?'

'Well alright, they left *two* of 'em be'ind!'

They drive on through the darkness. The dimly-seen trees form a rampart on either side of the road; not a light is to be seen. It seems to Colin like the forest will go on forever, an eternal forest under an eternal downpour of rain.

'First town or village we come to we're stopping,' announces Maclean. 'I'm not driving through this all night.'

'Gettin' fatigued, are yer?'

'Yes, I'm getting fatigued.'

''Ello, we've got somethin' 'ere,' remarks Chorley.

The headlights pick out a tall brick wall closely bordering the road on the left. A pillared gateway appears, the two wrought-iron gates ajar.

'Well, well, well,' says Chorley. 'Must be a house or summat. Let's 'ave a butchers.'

'Right.'

Maclean slows and turns off the road and through the open gates. They now proceed along a drive flanked by trees and shrubbery, and then before them rises the bulk of a substantial mansion house. Not a light shows in any of the many windows.

'Looks like no-one's 'ome,' says Chorley. 'Not unless they all turned in early.'

As they swing round into the forecourt, the car's headlights pick out a vehicle already parked there; a large camper-van.

'Now that don't belong 'ere,' declares Chorley. 'Camper vans don't go with posh country houses.'

Maclean pulls up, close to the van and in front of the porticoed entrance to the mansion.

'Cheery lookin' barrack, ain't it?' remarks Chorley.

'Looks like a prison,' is Maclean's opinion.

'Well, we ain't seein' it at its best,' reasons Chorley. 'Not when it's pissin' down with rain like this. Come on: let's check out that van first. See if anyone's 'ome.'

They all get out of the car. The rain slants down onto them and Colin pulls up the hood of his new coat (liberated from a clothes shop in Heatherly.) He looks up at the façade of the mansion, and gloomy and uninviting it appears to his eyes.

Chorley has gone up to the camper van. He knocks on the door.

''Ello? Anybody 'ome?'

Receiving no answer, he tries the door.

'Locked,' he reports.

Maclean presses a hand to the van's bonnet. 'Stone cold,' he announces. 'Well, let's check out the 'ouse.'

They turn to the house entrance. Colin's heart skips a beat. The doors are wide open! A minute ago they had been firmly shut, but now they are both gaping open, and not a person in sight.

'Them doors was shut a minute ago, weren't they?' says Chorley, looking from Maclean to Colin for confirmation.

'They were,' affirms the latter.

'Well, 'oo opened 'em?'

'I don't know, do I?'

''Ello?' he calls out. ''Oo's there?'

No answer. No sign of movement from within the doors.

'Well, come on, then,' says Chorley. 'Let's go in. Someone's got ter be 'ome unless them doors opened by theirselves.'

'I don't think we should go in,' says Colin. 'I don't like it.'

'Well, we can't stand 'ere all night gettin' soaked, can we?' reasons Chorley.

'Then let's just get back in the car and go somewhere else.'

'Now, don't be daft, son. No-one's gunna 'urt you, are they? Not wi' me an' Maclean to look after yer.'

He walks resolutely towards the porch. Colin and Maclean follow.

The hall they enter is deserted, the only things visible dust and cobwebs, neglect and disuse.

'Nobody's lived here for donkey's years,' pronounces Maclean.

'Well that bleedin' campervan ain't been parked out there fer donkey's years, 'as it?' retorts Chorley. 'And these doors didn't open by theirselves.' Addressing the room: ''Ello? Anybody 'ome?'

As if in response to this the front doors slam shut behind them with a thunderous crash.

Three startled pairs of eyes question each other in the dim light.

Maclean runs to the door. He rattles the handles.

'I can't open them!' he reports. 'They're locked!'

Chorley joins Maclean at the doors and tries his hand at opening them.

'We've been 'ad,' declares Chorley. 'Some bleeder's gone an' locked us in. They must o' been 'idin' be'ind the doors.' He hammers the doors with his fist. 'Alright, you bleeders!' he calls out. 'You've 'ad yer lark, now open the bleedin' doors!'

Silence, save for the sound of the falling rain.

'D'yer 'ear me? Stop playin' silly buggers an' open the bleedin' doors!'

Still no response.

Chorley sighs. 'Come on, we're wastin' our time 'ere. Let's try getting' aht through a winder or somethin'.'

Chorley turns towards the doors to one of the front rooms, the others following. They are brought up in their tracks by a peal of high-pitched, maniacal laughter. The chilling sound reverberates through the hallway.

'Well, *that* didn't come from outside,' declares Maclean. 'Someone's in here with us.'

Chapter Twenty-Eight
'Once it lets You in, it Doesnae Let You Oot Again!'

While in most respects very responsible parents, Colin's mum and dad really have a lot to answer for when, arranging their books on the shelves of the bookcase in the den, they elected to place all those books on the paranormal where they were in easy reach of the most impressionable in of their impressionable offspring. Far better would it have been had they consigned them safely out of reach to the shop shelf, alongside the sex manuals and books on erotic art. (In fact those latter books, taken in relation to the development of Colin's End of the World Anxiety, would have done him far less harm!)

Thanks to those books, Colin as firmly believes in the existence of ghosts as he does in the existence of aliens. He had read and absorbed into his consciousness every one of those accounts of ghostly apparitions, poltergeist activity, and possession by malignant spirits. And while it is true that none of those books had included any stories of ghostly maniacal laughter, Colin is certain that ghostly maniacal laughter is what he is hearing now—especially when taken in conjunction with the phenomenon of the front doors mysteriously opening to let them in, and then just as mysteriously closing to *lock* them in.

The peals of laughter now expire.

'Alright, you've 'ad yer lark,' calls out Chorley. 'Now yer can bleedin' well show yerselves!'

'You still think this is all just some prank?' questions Maclean. 'A minute ago you said that someone locked us *in.* But that laughing didn't come from outside; it was in here with us.'

'I know it were; but we don't know 'ow many of 'em there are, do we?' says Chorley. 'Anyway, they could've locked the front door and then come back in through a winder or somethin'.'

'Yeah, but that laughing came from upstairs,' insists Maclean.

'So, one of 'em's upstairs, then!' says Chorley. 'And I'm gunna blinkin' well find 'im.' Raising his voice: 'You 'ear that? If yer don't bleedin' well show yerselves pretty sharpish, I'm gunna come lookin' for yer. Got that?'

The response to this is another burst of lunatic laughter.

'Right! You've asked fer it!' grates Chorley. 'You got me really pissed off, you 'ave; an' when I find you buggers, I'm gunna wring yer bloody necks for yer!'

He marches towards the stairs. Colin grabs his arm.

'No, don't go upstairs!' he pleads. 'Let's just look for a way out of here.'

'I'm with him,' says Maclean.

'No!' insists Chorley. 'I ain't jus' scarperin' wi' me tail between me legs. I ain't gunna give these bleeders the satisfaction. I'm gunna find 'em and I'm gunna give 'em a piece of my mind, that's what I'm gunna do.'

'But what if it's not people? What if it's a ghost?' urges Colin.

'It ain't a ghost, cuz there ain't no such thing as ghosts; no such thing. An' you can take ol' Chorley's word for that, young shaver.'

And with that he stomps up the staircase.

'Come on; we'd better follow him,' says Maclean to Colin.

Colin and Maclean catch up with Chorley at the top of the stairs. They are on a kind of gallery from which corridors branch off from this in both directions, receding into darkness. There is no sign of movement, but then, somewhere off to the left, they clearly hear the sound of a door slam shut.

'Ah! So there y'are!'

Forthright, Chorley sets off down the left-hand corridor.

Colin, as he and Maclean follow with much less enthusiasm, thinks that Chorley's confidence isn't going to do them much good if it really is a ghost they have to deal with here. Not believing in the existence of ghosts doesn't make you invulnerable to them when you actually run into one!

'It was arahnd 'ere somewhere…'

Chorley starts throwing open doors to the left and right. The rooms revealed are all similarly devoid of furniture and places of concealment.

'Must've been further down…' he says.

Maclean stops him. 'Something's wrong here,' he pronounces.

Chorley looks at him. 'Whaddaya mean "somthin's wrong"?'

Maclean points to his own face. 'What do you see?'

'Your ugly mug.'

'There! You see?'

'Yeah, I see! I just said I bleedin' see!'

'No. I mean, you see what's wrong?'

'With your phiz? It looks the same as usual ter me.'

'No. What I mean is, how come you can see my face?'

'Because I've got eyes, that's 'ow!'

'Yes, but we're not cats, are we? People can't see in the pitch dark.'

'That's because it's not pitch dark, you wally.'

'Yeah, and that's my point. *Why* isn't it pitch dark? It's night and we're in a corridor with no windows. Where's the light coming from?'

'What are you blitherin' on abaht?' snaps Chorley. 'It's not *light* light, is it? It's dark light. That's how it is at night.'

'Yeah, but any light at night has to come in from outside. How's it getting into this corridor?'

'It just is, isn't it? It's not the bleedin' Black 'ole of Calcutta, is it?'

Colin looks along the corridor. Is Maclean right? The gloom looks like the uncertain light you would expect to find in an unlighted corridor at night… But yes, where is the dim light coming from? Shouldn't they be in complete darkness?

And now the laugh repeats itself again, and this time coming from somewhere behind them.

'I've 'ad enough o' this!' announces Chorley. 'Stop pissin' arahnd and bloody well show yerselves!'

He stomps off along the corridor, Colin and Maclean following in his wake.

They proceed for some time; and then Chorley stops abruptly.

''Ang on a minute,' he says. 'I don't remember the corridor bein' this long. Where've the bleedin' stairs gone?'

'The stairs?'

'Yes! The stairs dahn to the 'allway. We should've come to 'em by now.'

'We can't have.'

'Well, alright then. Then they should be a bit further down…'

They resume their progress. The corridor just continues on and on, uninterrupted by anything resembling a landing or staircase.

Chorley halts again.

'Somethin's wrong 'ere.'

'That's what I've been trying to tell you!'

'Yeah, but that was just you wafflin' on abaht the bleedin' lightin' effects. I'm talkin' about an 'ole flamin' staircase what's disappeared!'

Colin hears a noise. A sort of muffled moaning sound. It seems to be issuing from beyond the nearest door.

'I heard something!' he tells the others.

'What?'

'Listen!'

They listen. It comes again, a sort of muted whimper.

'It came from in 'ere,' says Chorley.

He crosses to the door and throws it open.

This room is not empty like the others they have inspected. A jumble of paraphernalia litters the floor; and in addition to this, a pungent odour, unfamiliar to Colin at least, pervades the air—but far more interesting than all of this are the three ghosts standing at the back of the room. Yes, ghosts. That's what they look like: three quivering forms draped in winding sheets, dolefully voicing a wordless sepulchral lament. Strangely, on closer inspection there appears to be only the one winding sheet covering the three trembling forms. A three-headed ghost? Or three ghosts shroud-sharing?

Colin stands terrified, but Chorley's reaction is very different. Exclaiming 'Found yer, yer little bleeders!' he marches across the room and with a single sweeping movement pulls the sheet from the heads of the ghosts!

Or at least, that which Colin had taken to be ghosts. He now sees that they are nothing of the kind. He now sees three very alarmed and very corporeal human beings cowering against the wall. Two are women, one white, one black; the third a bearded man. They all look to be in their early twenties.

Chorley regards them triumphantly, hands on hips.

'So, what 'ave yer got ter say for yerselves?' he inquires. 'What d'yer think you've been playin' at, eh?'

'Who are you people?' responds the white woman, speaking with a Scottish accent; she seems the least frightened of the trio. 'How did you get here?'

'*I'll* ask the questions!' retorts Chorley. 'An' my next question is a repeat of the last one: what d'yer think you've been playin' at?'

'We havnae been playing at anything,' replies the woman. 'We were just hiding from you.'

'An' a lovely job you were doin' an' all,' congratulates Chorley. 'I'd never 'ave guessed you was there. Look, what I'm askin' yer abaht is all that other malarkey. I mean the lockin' us in this 'ouse, an' the laughin' an' the doors slammin'.'

'That wasnae us,' the woman tells him.

'Don't gimme that. You was playin' pranks on us, wasn't yer? Pretendin' ter be ghosts an' tryin' to scare us outer our wits, you was!'

'That wasnae us!' insists the woman.

'Then why were you 'idin' like that? Looks like a sign of a guilty conscience ter me.'

'We were hiding because we didn't know who you were.'

Chorley sighs. 'Look let's start at the beginnin' 'ere: is this 'ouse yours?'

'No.'

'Is that campervan what's parked outside yours?'

'Aye, that's ours.'

'Right. So you're visitors 'ere?'

'No, we're prisoners here.'

'Prisoners? And 'oo precisely is 'oldin' you prisoners, then?'

'The hoose is.'

'The 'ouse? 'Ow can the bleedin' 'ouse be 'oldin' you prisoners?'

'You'll find out soon enough when you try to get out of here,' speaks up the black woman.

'She's right,' affirms the first speaker. 'The hoose is haunted, and I mean *really* haunted. Once it lets you in, it doesnae let you oot again!'

'So that's why we couldn't find the staircase!' exclaims Maclean.

'The staircase?' echoes the Scottish woman.

'Yeah,' admits Chorley. 'The main staircase: it don't appear to be where we left it…'

'That's the hoose that's done that,' affirms the woman. 'It traps you inside. It trapped us, and now it's trapped you!'

Chapter Twenty-Nine
'Get Out Of My Head!'

Trapped! Trapped in a haunted house! Chorley should've listened to me, thinks Colin. We never should've come upstairs!

'Trapped?' scoffs Chorley. 'Don't gimme that. You tryin' ter tell me it was the 'ouse what locked us in, an' it's the 'ouse what moved the stairs, an' it's the 'ouse what we 'eard laughin' at us…'

'That might've been Derek,' says the black woman.

'Aye; if ye heard laughing, it might've been Derek.'

'An' 'oo the 'ell is Derek?'

'He's our team psychic. He's gone insane. The hoose has driven him mad.'

'Your *team* psychic? Just 'oo are you bloomin' comedians anyway?'

'We're ghost hunters,' announces the woman. 'I'm Zena, the team leader. This,' indicating the black woman on her right, 'is Annette. And this,' indicating the bearded man on her left, 'is Stoner. He's our cameraman.'

'Cameraman?'

'Aye, we broadcast our show on the internet: *Mostly Haunted.* Have you not seen it?'

'No, I bleedin' 'aven't,' replies Chorley. 'So yer ghost 'unters wot does an internet show. Right. An' I suppose you,' looking at the bearded man: 'bein' called Stoner an' all, is the one responsible for this stink of cannabis what's permeatin' the atmosphere in this 'ere room?'

'It helps him relax,' says Zena.

'Yeah, I reckon all three of yer 'ave been doin' a lotta "relaxing", 'aven't yer?'

'Well, so would you, if ye'd been trapped here as long as we have!' retorts Zena, defensively.

Chorley shrugs. 'So, you've been stuck 'ere for a few hours: it's not a bleedin' eternity, is it?'

'It's nae a few hours, ye lummox: we've been trapped here for days noo!'

'Days!' exclaims Chorley. 'Don't gimme that! Days? Jest 'ow many days are we talkin' about 'ere?'

'It's no' that easy to tell. It's always night in this place. Ye can't keep track of time. Our watches have all stopped…'

'Time means nothing in this place,' pronounces Stoner solemnly.

'Let me get this straight,' says Chorley. 'Yer sayin' you've been 'ere fer days, but it's always night? 'Ow the 'ell can that 'appen? There's a bleedin' winder right be'ind yer.'

'Try looking through it,' invites Zena.

The three ghost hunters stand aside from the window. Chorley peers through the glass. Colin and Maclean join him.

'Can't see a bleedin' thing,' reports Chorley.

'You see?' says Zena.

'But it's night right now, ain't it?' retorts Chorley. 'It ain't surprisin' I can't see nothin'.'

'Aye, but how do you knoo it's really night?'

'What're you talkin' abaht? Because it was night when we got 'ere ten minutes ago, that's 'ow I know. It was night an' it was chuckin' it dahn.'

'We haven't heard any rain,' says Zena.

'Don't gimme that! It may 'ave stopped now, but it was chuckin' it dahn when we got 'ere.'

'We havnae heard any rain,' insists Zena.

Colin speaks up. 'You mean the windows always show night, even when it should be day?' he asks.

'Aye, laddie. And it's no' just ordinary night. You cannae see a thing. There's only darkness oot there, only darkness.'

'That's ridiculous!' declares Chorley. 'This room faces front, right? So, if I open the winder an' stick my 'ead aht, I'm gunna see our car and your van dahn below, aren't I?'

He fumbles with the latch of the window.

'You won't be able to open it, man,' Stoner tells him. 'If I could open a window I'd've just *flown* out of this place, y'know? I'd be long gone.'

Chorley struggles doggedly with the latch, but finally he is forced to give up.

'It's solid. Yer can't move it a bleedin' inch.'

'Of course ye can't,' says Zena. 'We're all prisoners here.'

'Prisoners,' echoes Chorley. 'You talk like it's the 'ouse itself is doin' it. It's not a ghost, then? A ghost yer can see?'

'Oh, there are ghosts ye can see,' says Zena. 'We got plenty o' those.'

'So, it's the ghosts, then? Not the 'ouse?'

'The ghosts. The house. Both, maybe. Who knows? It's all because of the Incident, isn't it? Things have gone haywire since then. Everything's been disturbed.'

'The Incident?' cries Chorley. 'What's all that got to do with this 'ouse bein' 'aunted?'

'Everything. That's what I'm telling ye: since the Incident happened paranormal activity has sky-rocketed. That's why we're here, ye see? We've been going round some of the most haunted hooses in the country, and we've seen apparitions in every one of them!'

'So, the Incident's causin' all the restless spirits of the dead to start walkin' around, is it?'

'Ghosts are nae the restless spirits of the dead, ye lummox,' replies Zena. (Evidently, the *Mostly Haunted* team favour the 'stone tape' explanation of ghostly apparitions.)

'An' you lot 'ave been going rahnd getting all this footage fer your internet show that you can't even bleedin' broadcast because there ain't no bleedin' internet anymore?' summarises Chorley. 'You three really are off yer chumps!'

'We're filming for whenever the internet comes back!' replies Annette defensively.

'An' so yer came ter this place an' now yer stuck 'ere?' An' 'oo's this guy 'oo's lost his marbles? Your team psychic. What 'appened to 'im?'

'Derek? Well, he just went mad and now he's run off somewhere. We havenae seen him for days.'

'An' there's ghosts 'ere 'an all? Ones what you can see?'

'Oh aye. They can pop up anywhere. We think they're mostly the ghosts of inmates.'

'Inmates? What the 'ell was this place, then? A prison?'

'Nae, it was a private lunatic asylum, back in Victorian times. You didnae knoo that?'

'No, I "didnae knoo that." So this place was a loony bin? An' you lot 'ave jest been 'oled up in this room, smokin' yerselves silly, when you coulda been lookin' fer a way outta here!'

'D'you think we havenae tried? But how can you find a way oot when all the rooms and the corridors don't stay in the same places? Don't ye see? We're in a maze, and it's a maze that keeps changing.'

'Yeah, well, I can see you lot might've given up, but I bloody 'aven't,' declares Chorley. 'We're gunna find us a way outta 'ere.' Turning to Colin: 'What say you, Colin? We ain't jest gunna give up, are we?'

And everyone is looking at him: Chorley and Maclean; Zena, Annette and Stoner; all gazing expectantly at him, which Colin thinks is strange; strange that they should all think it so important to hear him voice his support for Chorley's plan… But wait a minute: they don't look expectant, they look alarmed. Yes, there is a look of horror spreading over each of their faces. And, he now realises, they are not looking *at* him, they are looking *past* him! They are looking at something behind him.

Colin turns cold. There shouldn't be anything behind him apart from the wall. But the others wouldn't be looking so alarmed if there was only a wall behind Colin. Colin feels a prickling run down the back of his neck and down his spine. There *is* something behind him. He can feel it. His back feels exposed and vulnerable. There is something there, a chill presence standing right behind him…

Galvanised, Colin jumps and turns like a startled cat. Eyes. He sees eyes glaring down at him from a cadaverous face. The face belongs to a tall figure dressed in Victorian clothing. A rectangular head with dead, pasty skin, sparse hair. The hollows of the eyes are in shadow but the eyes within them blaze like lamps; and those lamps are fixed on Colin with a look of insane, burning malice.

Panic seizes Colin with rough hands; and with a wail of terror, he turns and flees precipitately from the room, the image of those lunatic eyes in that cadaverous face propelling him along the corridor.

He runs, and finally he stops running. He turns to face an empty, silent corridor. The spectre has not pursued him; but there's no sign of the others either. What are they doing back there? Why are they so quiet?

He waits. Still nothing, not a sound. Cautiously, he starts to retrace his steps.

He reaches the open door. Silence. He looks into the room. The room is empty. No ghost. No Chorley or Maclean. No trio of ghost-hunters. Even the clutter on the floor has gone.

Colin looks up and down the corridor. Has he got the wrong room? But all the other doors are firmly closed; this is the only one that is ajar; the door that he had run out through... Experimentally, he tries the doors to either side of the empty room. Both are locked.

Like a maze that keeps changing. That's what the Scottish woman had said. This must be what has happened: everything has just changed and the room with the others is gone!

He is lost and alone.

No, not alone. A quiet chuckling reaches his ears from further down the corridor.

And then he hears footsteps.

Slow, deliberate footsteps, emanating from the gloom.

Colin runs. He runs to the limit of the corridor, where it rightangles. Concealed by the turning, he peers back down the corridor. The footsteps and the low chuckling continue. It doesn't sound the same as that insane laughter that greeted them when they first entered the house.

And now a shape, a human shape detaches itself from the deeper shadows, and, as it advances, becomes more distinct. Expecting another cadaverous apparition in Victorian clothes,

Colin is surprised when he sees a stocky young man dressed in jeans and pullover.

The fourth member of the ghost-hunting team; the psychic who had been driven insane! What was his name? Derek. Yes: it must be him!

Colin turns and runs. This man might not be a ghost, but he's still a madman, and the last madman he encountered had wanted to kill and eat him!

But at the end of this branch of the corridor he is confronted with a blank wall. A dead-end! He tries the nearest door. It opens and ducks inside the room, a much larger room than the one the ghost-hunters had made their shelter. And it has another exit, a door at the other end. Colin makes straight for this door, opens it—and finds himself face to face with the very man he has been fleeing from.

Colin springs backwards, forgetting in his fright even to slam the door in his adversary's face. (Even Scooby and Shaggy would've remembered to do that.)

Derek steps into the room, head cocked at an angle. He's no longer chuckling and his posture is unthreatening.

He regards Colin with a pensive look. 'Are you lost, little boy?' he asks, his voice calm, quiet. 'Lost little boy. Little boy lost. Well, we're all lost in this place, aren't we? Lost, lost, lost. Lost In an endless maze…'

Colin retreating before him, Derek saunters into the room, surveying his surroundings. 'Walls, walls, walls. Always walls… The walls speak to me, you know? Yes, they speak to me. All the history of this house is recorded in the walls, stored away… I just have to reach out and touch the walls; just have to reach out and touch… Then I can see, I can hear…'

Derek presses both palms against one of the panelled walls.

'It's all here. The misery. The despair. The terror. The whimpering, the screaming, and the laughter. The laughter of broken minds. Laughter with no meaning… A whole catalogue of sounds; an anthem of human suffering…'

And it's an anthem that Colin starts to hear. Barely audible at first, but rising in pitch; echoing screams, moans, crying, laughter... The sounds rapidly fill the air. Both doors suddenly slam shut, loudly and violently sealing the room.

Derek steps back, removing his hands from the wall. Face contorted, he clutches his head.

'Now they're in my head,' he gasps. 'I can see what they see, feel what they feel. The cold, dark corners... The unending misery...'

He spins round, stares at Colin.

'Got to get out of my head,' he says. 'Got to get out.'

He advances towards Colin, eyes glaring, threatening hands extended. Colin presses himself against the wall, terrified.

'Get out of my head! Get out! Get out!'

Something in the wall gives with an audible click and Colin falls backwards. The panel swings back and Colin finds himself in pitch blackness and silence, the horrible cries suddenly extinguished.

Climbing to his feet, he soon discovers that he is in a very confined space, two of the walls composed of bricks; the third, the one he fell through, wooden. Could it be one of those hiding places they used to have in these old houses? A what-do-you-call-it, a priest hole...?

His hands grope for the fourth wall that would prove this theory, but instead his foot encounters a ledge and his hands thin air. Colin quickly retreats, imagining himself on the lip of a yawning chasm.

Recovering from this shock, common-sense now puts forward the suggestion that what he has encountered might just be the first step of a downward flight of stairs. Testing this theory, he projects a foot over the ledge, and lowering it, sure enough encounters a solid surface.

A staircase it is. It might be a way out.

He descends cautiously, leaning against the wall for support. The narrow stairs are wooden, some of them creak underfoot, but they seem sound.

The air becomes noticeably cooler. Still no sign of a light. The flight of stairs terminates in what at first seems to be a dead-end, but turns out to be a switchback landing. Three more flights, two more landings, and Colin steps onto a stone surface. Solid ground. But is he on the ground floor of the mansion, or have those flights of stairs taken him down as far as the cellars? It's still pitch dark.

A tactile inspection reveals that he is in a narrow stone corridor. The walls are cold. Keeping his left hand against the wall, he feels his way along. Presently, his hand encounters wood. Damp vertical planks of wood. A door.

Should he try going through this door or continue along the passage? wonders Colin. The dilemma is solved when he finds that the stone passage abruptly terminates just beyond this door, with no other egress.

His hands find a rusty loop door-handle. He twists it. The door opens inwards. Cold, musty air issues from beyond the door.

He steps inside and into another stone passage, this one much colder and the walls oozing slime. He sets off along this new passage, still walking blindly, one guiding hand against the damp, stone wall.

The passage seems very long. He walks into clinging curtains of cobweb; he hears the squeaking of rats, and at one point feels something brush against his trouser leg.

And now he hears the door, far behind him now, slam shut.

He freezes in his tracks.

The door! Someone has shut it! Have they locked him in here? Does this mean he couldn't go back even if he wanted to; that he has walked into a trap? And then, another thought, much more alarming: what if the door has been shut by someone coming *into* the passage? Someone could be coming after him!

Colin breaks into a run, impelled by visions, vague and fearful, of who or what might be pursuing him. His ankle, carbound and rested for much of the day, begins to protest that it is not yet healed. Colin tries to ignore this, but the ankle is insistent, and his running soon develops a limp.

He sees light ahead, dim but discernible, and with the light comes the scent of the outside, of trees and grass and rain. He redoubles his speed, or tries to, and the light ahead takes shape, a rectangle of external night. He draws closer, and the rectangle becomes segmented with vertical divisions. Bars!

Colin closes in on them, not losing hope, because the bars are widely spaced enough for possible egress between them. He reaches the grill. Not stopping to look for latches or catches, he squeezes himself between two of the thick, rusty bars and finds himself on a steep hillside, wooded and weed choked. The storm has passed and the moon shines down. Colin makes for the nearest cover and throws himself onto the saturated ground. Ankle screaming, he can run no further.

He keeps his eye on the metal grate, brick-surrounded, emerging from the hillside. No flesh-and-blood adult pursuer would be able to squeeze through those bars—but what if the grate is a gate, and the gate not locked…?

But no-one appears, no-one emerges. Perhaps the pursuit had been imaginary after all…

When the pain in his ankle has subsided, Colin will limp down the hillside, still raining under the trees, and after traversing some fields come to a farm. The farmhouse will prove to be untenanted but locked, and as breaking and entering will not occur to Colin, he will seek shelter in a hayloft, and from the slumber which follows he will awake refreshed but flea-bitten, his ankle rested and on the road to recovery.

Chapter Thirty
'*Nazi* Flying Saucers'

Remembering his mother's words about learning to stand on his own two feet, Colin has formed the resolution to complete the last stage (or at least what he fervently hopes will be the last stage!) of his journey to Norton-Braisley alone and unaided. True, it could be argued that this decision has already been taken out of his hands by the fact of his having been separated from his last set of fellow-travellers, Chorley and Maclean; but frankly Colin has every intention of *staying* separated from them if he can help it. Yes, they possessed a car, which would have taken him to his destination much sooner and in much more comfort for a boy with a sprained ankle, but on the debit side, Chorley is a creep and a dirty old man and Colin doesn't trust him one bit, drunk *or* sober.

And so Colin has taken to the roads on a solo journey. He is not going to rely on anybody else; he is going to make his way to Norton-Braisley all on his own—and only when he gets there and finds his sister will he go back to relying on someone else. (The possibility that his sister might not actually be there at all is one that Colin has taken the wise precaution of dismissing from his mind, so as not to be discouraged by it.) And this is why we find Colin on this sunny forenoon, following the serpentine course of country roads, making his solitary way through cheerful pastoral scenery. You will notice that Colin no longer walks with a limp, and this is because several days have now passed since the ordeal of the haunted house. With spring advancing, the weather has become warmer, and Colin walks with his jacket tied by the sleeves around his waist. In fact, today is the 30th of April, a fact of which Colin is cognisant, because his watch is still working and it gives the date as well as the time, and the date is one which is all the more significant to him because tomorrow is his birthday and he will be thirteen! Yes, he will have finally caught up with Natasha (which makes it all the more of a tragedy that Natasha is not around at the moment to be caught up with.)

If you're wondering whether Colin is heading in the right direction for his intended destination—well frankly so is he. Having failed to get his hands on a road atlas—and he has passed several service stations and other likely outlets without being able to find one—he has been forced to fall back on the old Colin Cleveland Unerring Sense of Direction (and we know how reliable that one is) and is heading in what he hopes is a northerly direction. Ideally, he would like to follow the course of the M1 motorway; because while it may dangerous for motorised traffic, if he could keep it in sight, at least he would know for sure he was heading in the right direction—but unfortunately he hasn't been able to find the M1 motorway.

Another plan of Colin's which has so far not met with success, is that of getting hold of a bicycle, in order to reach his destination in more comfort and in a shorter space of time. After forming this plan, it just so happened that the first town Colin had arrived at had been the town of Hoopdriver, widely known as the Cycling Capital of the North. Now this would have been a stroke of luck worthy of the very best of coincidence-ridden novels, but had actually turned out to be anything but. And this was because, subsequent to the Incident, what with most other forms of recreation now denied them, the Hoopdriver mania for cycling had soon risen to even greater eminence, basically becoming the whole population's *raison d'etre.* The town's various cycling clubs had banded together and formed the Central Cycling Committee, and had basically taken over the running of the town, organising events and competitions, and basically keeping up the morale of the Hoopdriver community in these post-apocalyptic times. And at first things had gone swimmingly; but then, dissension had reared its ugly head. A dispute had arisen between committee members as to whether the three speed, thirty-two gear model was the best bicycle available, or if in fact the two speed, forty gear model was the superior machine. The dispute had soon escalated out of control and very soon it was open warfare on the streets of Hoopdriver, with the two opposing factions, the Three Speed Thirty-Twos and the Two Speed Forties bent on each other's total annihilation. This was the situation Colin had blundered into on arriving in Hoopdriver, and to cut a long story short, he had managed to escape from the town with his skin intact, but without a set of wheels.

For the time being at least, he has resigned himself to footslogging, and the sun rides high in the sky as Colin wends his way through a stretch of open meadowland; the pastures bordered by low stone walls instead of the brambly hedgerows familiar to Colin's neck of the woods. Towards the horizon, the grazing land gives way to wooded, more hilly terrain.

A sound now reaches Colin's ears. A sound he has not heard for a long time: the sound of a propeller-driven aeroplane. He stops in his tracks, searches the sky for the aircraft. He spots it. A high-winged, single-engined monoplane, cheerfully red in the sunny sky, circling as it begins to lose altitude.

Who can it be? In the months that have passed since the Incident, Colin has not seen a single aircraft (of Earth origin) in the sky. If he has wondered about this at all, he has just assumed that no-one has had any reason to use aircraft. Obviously planes and helicopters still exist, and (barring improbable coincidence) not all of the people qualified to fly them can be amongst the people who disappeared; but since the Incident a lot of people seem to be staying at home, so Colin has just assumed there are no aircraft in the skies for the same reason there are no cars on the roads. But still, if Colin could fly a plane, he would want to fly overseas; he would want to know for sure if the Incident had actually happened in other countries the same as it had here...

Could this be the answer here? Could the aircraft now descending be a visitor from overseas?

At this point in Colin's cogitations the aeroplane's engine starts to stutter. The machine is now at a low altitude, descending towards the fields as if for a landing. The engine coughs again, and then cuts out completely. Colin, never having read any Biggles books, expects to see the aircraft drop from the sky like a stone, unaware of the fact that a light aircraft, even with its engine dead, can still glide in for a safe landing.

And it seems that the plane is going to come down very close to where Colin now stands. He sees the machine appear over the trees, gliding low towards the large open meadow before him. It touches down, bounces, touches down again, losing speed in what looks like being a smooth landing; but then the undercarriage apparently encounters an obstruction, and Colin watches in horror as the aircraft spins, cartwheels, before finally coming to rest with a buckled wing and its tail in the air.

Colin stands frozen to the spot, anguished spectator of a tragedy. Is the pilot dead? They must be after a crash like that!

So thinks Colin, but then an offside door is pushed open, and a figure dressed in pilot's overalls hoists itself out of the cockpit and jumps down to the ground. The distance is too great for Colin to make out details, but the aviator is a Caucasian, dark-haired and as far as he can tell, male. Hands on hips, the pilot surveys his crashed plane, and then, turning to take in his surroundings, espies Colin standing at the roadside.

The pilot makes urgent beckoning gestures.

Obediently, Colin scrambles over the stone wall and jogs across the turf towards the plane. As he closes the distance it becomes apparent that the pilot is in fact a woman; a good-looking woman in her twenties, very tall, her hair a buzzcut, her facial features strongly defined.

Colin comes to a stop before her. 'Are you okay?' he asks.

She places a large hand on his shoulder.

'We must seek cover,' she tells him solemnly. 'It's not safe out in the open.'

And without further ado, she takes Colin by the hand and starts running for the treeline at the extremity of the field. Running hard to keep pace with her, Colin can't help feeling annoyed with his new acquaintance, glad though he is that she has emerged from her crash unscathed. If it's as unsafe as she claims to be out in the open, then why had she just beckoned him to join her in the middle of the field, a place where he was a lot more 'out in the open' than he had been in his previous location by the roadside?

It doesn't make sense, does it?

However, they reach the cover of the trees without incident. Here the woman throws herself flat, indicating that Colin should do the same. He lies down next to her, and looks at her as she stares intently at the field they have just left. He follows her gaze. Nothing has changed. The sun still smiles down on the verdant landscape. Even the crashed aeroplane, with its bright red bodywork, somehow looks picturesquely at home in his surroundings.

'So… why isn't it safe to be out in the open…?' he ventures to ask.

The woman fixes him with her intense gaze. 'Because of the Enemy, of course.' And before Colin can frame a question: 'What is your name, boy?'

'Colin,' says Colin. 'What's yours?'

'Julia,' replies the woman. 'What part of England is this?'

'The north…'

'Cannot you be more specific?'

'Well, the nearest town back that way is one called Hoopdriver—but you were just flying a plane! You should know where we are better than me!'

'Yes, but I am a stranger to this country,' Julia tells him, twisting from her supine position to sit cross-legged. 'I have only just arrived here from overseas.'

'You've come from another country?' excited, sitting up also. 'Which one?'

'Israel.' Julia unzips a pocket of her flightsuit, extracts cigarettes and lighter. Grey packet, the single word CIGARETTES. (Not even a health warning!)

'Oh…' Colin is a bit hazy as to where Israel is. 'And did the Incident happen there as well?'

'Of course it did,' lighting her cigarette. The Incident was a global event: it happened everywhere.'

So they were right, thinks Colin! Mr Brandon and Natasha and everyone; they were right when they said that the Incident must have happened all over the world.

'Do you know what caused it?' asks Colin. 'The Incident.'

'Yes. The Enemy caused the Incident. They are now in full control of the world.'

'You mean the aliens?'

'Aliens?' a look of surprise. 'What is this talk of aliens? Extraterrestrials, you mean? The Enemy are human beings, Colin; the very worst type of human beings: they are Nazis.'

'Nazis?' Colin wasn't expecting this. 'You mean like Germany in World War Two?'

'Yes, exactly like that. They have re-emerged: the new Third Reich. The Incident was their *blitzkrieg*. With it, they crippled the world in one swift strike, and now they have assumed total control. But some of us are fighting back. This is why I have flown here directly from Israel: I wish to make contact with the resistance movement of this country and to form an alliance between them and my own people.'

Third Reich? Blitzkrieg (whatever that is)? Resistance movements? This is a lot to take in, and not at all what he had come to believe. 'Bu-but… what about the flying saucers—?'

'*Nazi* flying saucers,' incisively. 'The Third Reich has been experimenting with such craft since the Second World War, and now they have perfected them.'

'Nazi flying saucers…?' Then Natasha, Miss Lantier, weren't abducted by aliens, they were abducted by Nazis?

Somehow, that sounds a lot worse.

'Natasha? Miss Lantier? Who are these people?'

'Two people I was with. They got abducted by alie—a flying saucer…'

'I see. Then they will have been taken to one of the concentration camps. I am concerned that a saucer may be sent out to inspect my crashed aircraft,' says Julia. 'We would do well to remove ourselves from the immediate vicinity. Why are you alone, Colin—what is your family name?'

'Cleveland.'

'Why are you alone, Colin Cleveland? To what destination were you heading?'

'I was heading for Norton-Braisley.'

'Excellent! My destination also. Come, we can continue this conversation as we walk.' She stands up, and Colin does the same. From another pocket she produces a compass. 'Norton-Braisley lies north by north-east of our current location. The swiftest route between two points is a straight line: we will follow a compass course. Come.'

Colin falls into step beside her as they move deeper into the woods. 'How come you want to go to Norton-Braisley as well?' he asks.

'I have already told you. My purpose is to make contact with this country's resistance movement; Norton-Braisley is where their main stronghold has been established. If you did not know this then why do *you* wish to go to Norton-Braisley?'

'My sister's there. My mum and dad got taken away in the Incident, so I'm going there to be with her.'

'Excellent! Then if your sister is still there then she will undoubtedly be a member of the resistance movement. You know, it is dangerous for a young boy such as yourself to be moving around occupied territory on your own; so it is fortunate that our paths have crossed like this, Colin Cleveland. I shall ensure that you reach your destination in safety.'

'Are you a soldier?' asks Colin.

'I have had military training, so in a manner of speaking, yes I am. To be precise, I am an operative of Mossad. You have heard of Mossad?'

'No…'

'Mossad is an espionage covert operations organisation belonging to my country. We have long waged war against the Nazis.'

'Why's that?' with the hazy notion that Israel is an Arab country.

'Really, Colin Cleveland, you ask me that? Did they not teach you about the Second World War at your school?'

'Well, we were doing twentieth-century history, but we'd only got to World War One when the world ended.'

'But you must know *something* about the Second World War?'

'I've seen a few films…'

'And you know of the Holocaust, yes?'

'No, what's that?'

'The Holocaust, Colin Cleveland, was the systematic extermination of millions of Jewish people at the hands of the Nazis.'

'Oh. Are you Jewish, then?' innocently.

'Yes, Colin, I am,' looking at him sideways. 'We all are in Mossad. Israel is the homeland of the Jewish race. But then, if your education in modern history ended with the First World War, then I suppose you can be forgiven for not knowing that, as well as the rest.'

Having smoked her cigarette to the stub, Julia discards it and immediately reaches into a zippered pocket for its replacement.

Chapter Thirty-One
'People *Change,* Colin Cleveland'

Israel is the only country not occupied by the Nazis, according to Julia. Her people at Mossad got wind of the impending Incident just in time to prepare their own country for the event, but too late to warn the rest of the world. (Exactly *why* it was too late for them to warn anyone else when they still had enough time to prepare themselves, is something Colin isn't quite clear on.) But Israel is not occupied by the Enemy, it is besieged by them, and they have to fend off regular attacks from squadrons of flying saucers.

'And every country apart from Israel has been taken over?' asks Colin, seeking clarification. 'Every single one?'

'That is correct,' replies Julia, now on her fifth cigarette.

'But there's got to be *hundreds* of countries in the world,' says Colin. 'How can just one country take over all those other countries? I mean, even with flying saucers and everything, you'd think they just didn't have enough people to be in all those countries at the same time.'

'Yes, but the Enemy is not just one country, Colin Cleveland,' Julia tells him. 'As in the last world war, Germany has formed an alliance with Japan, and the world has been divided between the two empires. Germany occupies Europe, Western Russia, Africa, the Middle-East and North America, while Japan occupies Asia, Eastern Russia, Oceania and South America.'

A German and Japanese empire! Just like *The Man in the High Castle*! But hang on a minute... That series was about an alternative reality where Germany and Japan won World War Two... But in real reality, they *didn't* win the war and plus that war happened a long time ago now…

'But Germany and Japan have been our friends since after the war…' says Colin slowly, verbalising his puzzlement. 'How could they just suddenly go back to being the baddies like that…?'

'There was a *conspiracy*, Colin,' replies Julia. 'I have already told you this. The Nazi faction in Germany conspired to take over their country, and they had formed an alliance with a far-right faction in Japan who staged a simultaneous takeover of *their* country.'

'I see…' says Colin. 'But… it's funny that all the people in Germany and Japan just went along with it… I mean, they were our friends until—'

'People *change*, Colin Cleveland,' interjects Julia. 'And sometimes they change very suddenly. The history of the world is full of examples of this happening.'

Clearly considering it superfluous to furnish Colin with any examples of these sudden changes, Julia, discarding the remains of her fifth cigarette, unzips a pocket to call into requisition the sixth. It has come to Colin's attention that every time she has done this, it has been from a different one of the plethora of pockets in her flightsuit that she has extracted the cigarettes and lighter. Either Julia is a conjuror who can magically move things from one pocket to another, or else she has a very large supply of cigarettes and lighters about her person.

Descending a wooded hillside they come to an A-road intersecting their path. Just as they reach it, the sound of motor vehicles suddenly separates itself from the silence, growing rapidly in volume.

'Down!' orders Julia.

They drop to the ground behind the foliage bordering the road. Moments later a fleet of grey articulated lorries thunders past them in rapid single file, shaking the ground and filling the air with the roar of diesel engines. The procession finally passes and pastoral calm returns.

'We think those lorries are the ones that bring the food to the shops,' Colin tells Julia, when they have risen to their feet.

‘This is so,’ confirms Julia. ‘They ferry the produce from the food production plants the Nazis have set up. These plants are staffed by slave-labour. Your two friends; those you said were taken by one of the flying saucers: they will have been put to work in one of the food plants.’

‘Do you think so?’

‘I am sure of it.’

The news comes as something of a relief to Colin, who, since Nazis had been brought into the picture, had been beginning to imagine much worse fates for Natasha and Miss Lantier. If they are being to work in a food factory then at least they’re both still okay.

‘Come, we must proceed,’ says Julia. ‘We will not make it to our destination before nightfall, so soon we must find shelter for the night, and then we will complete our journey in the morning.’

They proceed without further incident, and as the light fails, they chance upon a convenient isolated house, untenanted but undisturbed and with still-edible food in the cupboards and freezer cabinet. They enjoy an improvised evening meal at the kitchen table, which reminds Colin of a similar *tete-a-tete* meal with Natasha (less than two weeks before, but also an eternity) and he can’t help comparing his companion of the previous occasion with the one of the present. Yes, Julia isn’t as attractive as Natasha, she smokes cigarettes all the time and she’s too old to be his girlfriend; but she is still a beautiful woman, strong and confident, who brings hope with her—and in other words is a new rock for Colin to lean on.

At Julia’s request Colin fills her in on his adventures. Julia is unsurprised to hear about the haunted house incident. The Nazis, she tells him, will be responsible for the increase in the number of ghosts: they have long been known to dabble in the occult. She also promises to protect Colin from Chorley, should they chance to run into him. (Colin firmly believes that it won’t have taken Chorley long to find a way out of the haunted house—just how wrong he is in this assumption is something he will only discover much later.)

After dinner, and to complete the pattern of similarity with that last night with Natasha, Julia insists that they must sleep in the same bed! It is her duty to protect Colin, she tells him, and this is a duty she cannot adequately perform were they to sleep in separate rooms.

Announcing her intention of ensuring that the house is secure for the night, she leaves Colin in the bedroom they have selected. He undresses (leaving his pants on, of course) and climbs into bed. Presently, Julia returns. She sits down on a chair to remove her boots and then, rising again, unzips her flightsuit—and shedding which she hits Colin with a double whammy of jaw-dropping surprise because not only is she not wearing anything at all underneath it, but she's also very hairy! In imitation of a pair of stockings, hair covers her legs all the way up to the top of the thighs; it grows rampant around her groin, spreading out before forming a thin line extending to her belly-button; it forms a border around the nipples of her large, heavy breasts; and it grows in abundance in the cavities of her armpits.

Colin gapes, wide-eyed with astonishment. In his naivety, he has always believed that body hair was an exclusively male institution and that women just didn't possess it; he thinks of all the smooth female legs he has seen on television, in swimming lessons at school… Could it be that Julia is actually a transexual woman? Could this be the explanation of Julia's tall stature, the androgyny of her facial features, and most of all, all this alarming body-hair? But her figure; her breasts, her waist, her hips… Colin's knowledge of transsexualism is as hazy as his knowledge of most other things that have 'sex' in their name, but he does understand that men who want to become women can be furnished with breasts—but can they also be given a female pelvis? This would seem like a much more difficult operation for the surgeons to perform.

But then, maybe he's wrong. Maybe Julia isn't a transexual woman. Maybe it's just normal for women from Israel to be hairy…

Julia folds up her flightsuit and turning to place it on the chair, offers gaping Colin the full visual benefit of two large, powerful buttocks, the cleft between them a nest of hair. Straightening up, she offers Colin a brief smile; closed-lipped, not toothy like Natasha's, but still encouraging. She goes to the door, flicks off the light switch and climbs into bed, turning onto her side to face Colin.

'Well, Colin Cleveland,' she says, voice subdued; 'tomorrow will be your birthday. I wish I could bake for you a cake for the occasion, but I'm afraid I'm not much of a cook.'

'That's alright,' says Colin. 'Mum always used to make me a cake… This'll be the first time… my first birthday without… without…' Without his family being around, Colin wants to say, but tears, swift and sudden interpose themselves.

Julia's arm reaches out and draws him towards her, and then Colin is sobbing in her strong embrace, her arms holding him tightly, his face cushioned between her breasts. Her body odour is strong, but pleasant to Colin. The strength of her muscular arms, the warm softness of her breasts, the heat and the smell radiating from her skin, her whispered soothing words: they are all one, entwined together, enfolding, comforting, and protecting.

Colin's tears slowly subside, mind and body relaxing, and still locked in Julia's embrace he drifts into peaceful slumber.

Chapter Thirty-Two
'Many Happy Returns!'

Daylight, and Colin awakes to find himself alone in bed. Memory falls into place. Julia. He was with Julia, the woman from Israel… He is reminded of another morning, another empty bed…

A surge of alarm. Has Julia gone? Has she been taken away? Taken away like Natasha was?

He throws back the covers and hurriedly dresses himself. He runs out onto the landing and checks the bathroom. Nothing. He runs down the stairs and into the kitchen. Empty. He tries the front rooms. Also empty.

He runs out the front door, pulls up suddenly. Julia is just standing there in the garden, calmly smoking a cigarette. She looks round and smiles at him.

'Good morning, Colin Cleveland,' she says. 'Many happy returns!'

Thank goodness.

After breakfast they set off, resuming their journey. According to Julia they should be reaching Norton-Braisley by this afternoon. If Colin is lucky, he will be getting to spend the last part of his birthday with his sister.

They are crossing a meadow, approaching the margin of another forest. The treeline stretches off in both directions as far as the eye can see.

'Yes, this is it,' says Julia, compass in hand. 'We just have to traverse this forest and we should be within sight of our destina—down!'

Julia throws herself flat. Colin does the same, at a loss to understand the cause for alarm. But then he spots them: three flying saucers in tight formation flying swiftly and silently across the cloudless firmament, high above the trees. They pass by, the sinister black forms diminishing in size, finally merging into the horizon.

'If only we could capture one of those craft and learn its secrets,' says Julia, as they climb back to their feet.

'Haven't you done that already?' asks Colin. 'Couldn't you examine one of the ones you've shot down in Israel?'

'Unfortunately not, Colin Cleveland,' replies Julia. 'When they are struck by missiles, the saucers self-destruct completely, leaving only the smallest fragments of burnt wreckage. What we need to do is to attack a flying saucer when it is on the ground and its crew has disembarked. This is something I will suggest when we make contact with the freedom fighters in Norton-Braisley.'

Reaching the perimeter of the woods, they discover a well-defined path leading through the trees, one which according to

Julia's compass readings, will take them in exactly the direction they want to go.

They proceed deeper into the woods.

Presently, at a turning in the path, a strange sight appears ahead, one that brings the travellers up in their tracks. At first Colin thinks his eyes must be playing tricks on him. But he blinks and looks again and the sight he sees is still the same. Peering over the top of some ferns are the heads of a squirrel and a fox. Apart from the incongruity of seeing a squirrel and a fox in such close proximity, even more remarkable is the fact that the two heads are at least four feet above the ground and they are the size of human heads!

The two heads separate and, emerging from either side of the clump of ferns, reveal themselves to be perched atop two small but ordinary-looking human bodies. The squirrel is dressed in cords and a shirt. The fox wears a brightly-coloured, full-skirted dress. Both hold tambourines, which one shakes and the other drums upon as they advance, moving with dancing steps.

Children! thinks Colin. What are children doing dressed up like this in the middle of the woods?

'Can we help you?' inquires Julia.

The masked figures do not respond, but continue to skip towards them. More masked figures now emerge from the trees, closing in on Colin and Julia from either side. An owl, a hare, a badger, a stoat and an otter. All of them carry tambourines or drums, and all of them appear to be children, small but thickset in build.

The fox and the squirrel beckon, and the newcomers on either side make sweeping gestures. They clearly want Colin and Julia to continue along the path.

'What do you want with us?' demands Julia.

Again no verbal response, not even a ripple of childish merriment.

'We have no time for this,' says Julia. To Colin: 'Let us proceed.'

They resume walking. The masked figures frolic around them,

banging their drums and shaking their tambourines, but doing nothing to impede their progress.

'Who are they?' Colin wants to know.

'I do not know. Perhaps orphaned children who have sought shelter in the woods.'

This theory is soon proved wrong when the forest unexpectedly opens out and they find themselves approaching a tiny village. The path joins a road paved in stone-sett, which leads into the village, forming its main street. The houses on either hand are all very old, half-timbered, thatch-roofed dwellings. There is not a car in sight, nor any telegraph poles. In fact, there is nothing modern to be seen; it's as though they have stepped into the past.

As they near what they can see from its signboard is the village pub (*the Green Man*), a group of smiling people stand in the middle of the street, as though waiting to greet the newcomers and their dancing entourage. In fact, it soon becomes clear to Colin that the welcoming smiles of the villagers are all directed specifically at *him*!

A man and woman, both middle-aged and comfortably scruffy in appearance, step forward from the group. The man wears a loose shirt and baggy cord trousers. A beaky nose flanked by twinkling eyes project from the clearing between a thicket of tangled beard and a crown of tangled hair of the same colour and consistency. The woman is plump and wears a gipsy blouse and a long skirt with a tasselled hem. Her hair is long and dark, somewhat unkempt; a pair of old-maidish *pince-nez* rest on her nose.

'Greetings, visitors!' says the man, shaking first Julia's hand, and then, with much more enthusiasm, Colin's. 'Welcome to Wood Haven! We are so glad that you have made it here in time! Allow me to introduce ourselves; I am David, and this,' indicating the plump woman, 'is my wife Helen.'

Colin is confused and embarrassed by this effusive welcome, while Julia is frankly suspicious. 'You sound as though you were expecting us,' she says, her tone accusing.

'Indeed we were,' is the ready reply. 'Your coming was foretold. And that you should arrive today, the day of our Mayday celebrations, is most auspicious.'

'I don't see what our arrival has to do with your Mayday celebrations,' retorts Julia; 'and moreover, you seem to think that your village was our intended destination. You are in error: we are just passing through, and in fact we had no idea that your village was even here.'

'Nevertheless, your coming was foretold,' answers David equably. 'Our village elder had a vision: she foretold that on a certain day a virgin boy and his valiant protector would come to Wood Haven, and that his coming would mark the end of the curse that has afflicted our village.'

'What curse?'

'We can't have children,' speaks up Helen. 'That's our curse. No children have been born in Wood Haven for years and years now; and now we haven't got a single child left in the village.'

'No children?' sneers Julia. 'Then who are these people: midgets?' indicating the masked figures still standing beside them.

In response to Julia's question, these people now remove their animal masks, and reveal themselves to be indeed midgets, and all clearly adults. (Their smiling countenances suggest that they have not taken offense at Julia's use of a name for those with dwarfism that some now consider to be derogatory.)

'Very well. You have no children here,' accepts Julia. 'But I fail to see how you think that Colin's presence in your village will alleviate your inability to produce offspring. He has no intention of remaining with you; as I have said, we are just passing through.'

'We know, and we're not expecting either Colin or yourself to stay here,' says David. 'All we ask is that you allow Colin to take part in our Mayday festivities this afternoon. His presence there will be much appreciated. Just for today is all we ask. After that you can be on your way.'

Julia's scowl deepens. 'In what way is he to "participate" in these festivities?' she demands.

'Simply to preside over them,' is the ready answer. 'We would crown him our Prince of May and he would sit on the throne we have prepared for him on the village green where the celebrations are always held. It's simply a symbolic act, but as Colin's arrival here was foretold by our village elder, we believe his presence to be auspicious, and that it will mark the end of our period of infertility.'

'Yes, well I am sorry to disappoint you,' says Julia. 'But we really do not have the time to participate in your festival. We really need to be in Norton-Braisley by this afternoon.'

'Norton-Braisley?' echoes Helen. 'You'd never make it there by this afternoon or anytime today: it's over fifty miles from here!'

'You lie!' snaps Julia. 'Norton-Braisley lies just on the other side of this forest!'

'Other side of the forest? Why, it's not even in this county!'

'You lie!'

'She doesn't, you know,' says David. 'If you think you're close to Norton-Braisley, then you must have lost your way. But that doesn't matter: we will be happy to assist you! We can supply you with a map. All we ask is that you remain here for this afternoon and that you allow Colin here to be our Prince of May.' Turning to Colin: 'Would you like that, Colin? Would you like to preside over our celebrations?'

'Would I have to make a speech…?' asks Colin cautiously.

'No, not at all!' David assures him. 'All you have to do is sit in the chair of honour while we perform our Mayday dance. After that you will be free to mingle with the crowd and enjoy the attractions of the fair along with everyone else. There will be food and games; all sorts of things! How does that sound?'

'Well… today is my birthday,' says Colin.

David pounces on this news. 'His birthday! His birthday! Another omen! Happy Birthday, Colin Cleveland! Congratulations! I'm sure your being here today on the anniversary of your nativity will bring about an end to our troubles!'

'I wish you hadn't mentioned that it was your birthday,' mutters Julia out of the corner of her mouth.

Chapter Thirty-Three
'Who's Slumpy Feg?'

'Aye, that's him. That's the little bugger I saw in me vision.'

They stand in the front parlour of *The Green Man*, where the wizened crone sitting in the corner by the fireplace has put down her knitting to study the newcomers.

'You seriously claim to have seen Colin Cleveland in some kind of prophetic vision?' challenges Julia.

'Aye, and you an' all, ye barmy bint,' snaps the crone.

'Our village elder has spoken,' pronounces David.

'Aye, I've spoken. Now stop yer ruddy yappin' an' get the lad kitted out for the ruddy festival.'

'Kitted out?' questions Julia.

'Yes, Colin will be bathed and anointed and dressed in the raiment of the May Prince,' explains David. 'Perhaps you also would like to take this opportunity to refresh yourself? If you'll pardon my saying so, you are both of you smelling somewhat... well-travelled...'

'I wish to confer briefly with Colin,' replies Julia, and so saying, she puts an arm around Colin and guides him across the room away from David, Helen and the village elder.

'Well, Colin?' she says, low-voiced. 'Do you wish to participate in this festival? I would advise you not.'

'But it can't do any harm, can it?' argues Colin. 'And it'll be nice to do something nice on my birthday...'

'Yes, but if we proceed to Norton-Braisley you will be able to celebrate the remainder of your birthday with your sister. Isn't that what you wanted?'

'Yes, but they just said we're not as near to Norton-Braisley as we thought we were. They said it's miles away and we won't get there today at all.'

'That's what they *say*. But I do not believe them.'

'Why not? You might have been wrong about where we are, mightn't you? I mean, you're not from England, are you? You're from Israel and you've never been in England before…'

'Yes, but I have studied maps.'

'You might've remembered them wrong.'

'Look, Colin Cleveland, are you not at all suspicious of these people? Because I am. Living here in the middle of the forest, isolated from the rest of the world. They know nothing about the Incident. They have no television or internet connection, so they do not know about the signal-jamming; and they apparently haven't been affected by the disappearances… They are clearly a pagan community, and they perform strange rituals. These Mayday celebrations…'

'But lots of villages have Mayday and do maypole dancing. That's normal in England…'

'Yes, but I suspect that these people here take it much more seriously than most… Have you never seen *The Wicker Man?*'

'No; is it a TV series?'

'No, it's an old film with Edward Woodward, and I don't suppose you would have seen it… The situation we are in now reminds me uncomfortably of that film.'

'Why? What happens in it?'

Julia sighs. 'Never mind. Look: if you really want to stay for these Mayday celebrations then we shall stay. I shall remain by your side, and my protection should be adequate. Just as long as they don't make you wear a long white dress…'

Colin, wearing a long white dress, steps into the parlour where Julia, who has also performed her ablutions but has not changed her clothes, is waiting for him.

She marches up to him, alarmed by his appearance. 'What did I tell you not to wear?'

'But it's not a dress…!' protests Colin pathetically (and I use the word pathetic in its modern rather than traditional context.) 'It's a ceremonial robe. It just *looks* like a dress, that's all.'

'So did Edward Woodward's.'

Conducted by David and Helen, now dressed as a Morris dancer and a witch respectively, they leave the *Green Man* and follow the winding street to the village green where by now all the inhabitants of Wood Haven have gathered. Booths offering attractions, beverages and comestibles line the perimeter of the green along three of its sides, while the maypole, with its plume of brightly coloured streamers stands as the centrepiece. Facing this, the throne prepared for the May Prince stands at the summit of a log pyramid. The villagers, all in fancy dress, many of them masked, dance and frolic around the green, while a medieval beat combo, featuring strings (lute), woodwind (flute, shawm), and percussion (drums, tambourine) provides the music.

'*What* is that?' demands Julia, pointing to the pyramid, her expression registering something close to horror.

'Why that's the throne, the chair of honour, of course,' answers David.

'Yes, but what is that it is standing on?'

'It's the dais.'

'Dais? It looks more like a funeral pyre,' declares Julia.

'Well, yes, it is quite tall,' agrees David. 'But young Colin is our Prince of May, and we want him to be seen by everybody. I can assure it's structurally sound.'

'That is not what I am concerned about.' She takes Colin by the hand.

'Is something wrong?' asks Colin innocently.

'I am still unsure,' replies Julia.

Following in David's tinkling footsteps, Colin and Julia ascend the steps of the dais. Reaching the summit, Colin, at David's invitation, seats himself on the throne. David places a chaplet of flowers on his head. (Colin it is not at all sure about this new adornment, thinking it only adds to the girlie look of his ensemble already strongly suggested by the 'robe'.)

David now turns to face the green. 'People of Wood Haven!' he calls out.

At his stentorian tones, the crowd become still and silent. The music ceases, and all eyes, real and painted, look up at the throne.

'Behold!' proceeds David. 'As foretold, this young stranger

has arrived among us to be our Prince of May! Let us welcome him!'

Cheering, uproarious and sustained.

David motions for silence. 'His advent marks the end of the curse that has fallen upon us! This child has arrived and the end of our time of childlessness is now at hand!'

More cheering.

'We give thanks to Colin Cleveland for graciously accepting the role of Prince of May and of honouring these festivities! And to his protector Julia, who has guided him safely to be with us today!'

More cheering.

'And now, let the ceremony begin!'

The maypole dancers take up their streamers, the band launches into an instrumental rendition of 'The Safety Dance' and the maypole dance begins. David moves to descend from the dais, but Julia stops him, her strong hand gripping his arm.

'Where do you think you're going?'

'We should descend. It's customary for the monarch of the festival to remain here alone during the performance…'

'Yes, but on this occasion, I think both you and I will remain up here with him,' says Julia.

'If you insist…'

'I *do* insist.'

Colin, meanwhile, is enjoying himself immensely. Seated on a throne and being cheered by an enthusiastic crowd is enough to elevate most people, and Colin is no exception. And at first he sits watching the lively, choreographed maypole dance with great pleasure; but then a new player appears on the scene. A figure dressed in a brown costume covered with leaves, like the Green Man from the picture on the pub signboard, he capers around at the foot of the dais, sometimes stopping to wave a stick with a balloon on the end up towards the throne. There is something vaguely threatening about the gesture and Colin starts to feel uneasy…

It is only after the dance has concluded and Colin has been allowed to descend from his throne and mingle with the crowd, that Julia allows her suspicions to relax. She stays by Colin's side as, conducted by David, they move around the fair, viewing the attractions. Colin munches contentedly on a toffee apple.

'Of course, you are free to depart any time you wish,' David is saying. 'But if you were to stay for the rest of the day, I can promise Colin here a birthday dinner in *the Green Man* this evening; a private event, just for ourselves, I mean; not the whole community. I believe that even as we speak a birthday cake is being prepared for our May Prince…'

Needless to say, the moment that birthday cake is introduced, Colin is all for staying, and Julia reluctantly acquiesces.

And if Colin's platter of glorification hasn't been piled to the limit already, he now finds himself being targeted for feminine kisses! Yes; as they thread the crowd, laughing women dance up to him and plant big wet kisses on his cheek, his brow, his caramelised mouth, before vanishing back into the crowd.

'Well, someone is a big hit with the ladies,' says Julia, with one of her rare smiles.

'W-why are they doing that?' asks Colin, red-faced but not displeased.

'Why, they are seeking the blessing of the Prince of May,' replies David, 'so that they will become fruitful and bear children.'

'My goodness Colin Cleveland, you are quite the stud,' Julia, still smiling.

'What's a stud?' asks Colin innocently.

But then someone hits him over the head with a balloon, and while this is probably the most inoffensive object you could ever be hit over the head *with*, when Colin turns to learn the identity of his assailant, he sees the Green Man, armed with his balloon-on-a-stick, disappearing into the crowd.

Suddenly the spell is broken and Colin feels ill at ease again.

Evening. They sit at a table in a back parlour of the *Green Man*.

The table is generously laden with food, the centrepiece being Colin's promised birthday cake, a chocolate cake (Colin's favourite), decorated with thirteen now extinct candles. Thus far only two slices have been cut from the cake, one for Colin, one for Julia.

When blowing out those thirteen candles (and he did it in one puff!) Colin had silently made the wish that his sister will be there to meet them when they get to Norton-Braisley; but now, belatedly and guiltily, Colin remembers Natasha, and wishes that he'd wished that she was okay and that he'd be seeing her again soon. A double-barrelled wish and sadly thought of too late.

There are just five of them seated at the table: Colin and Julia, David and Helen, and the village elder, the latter eating little and saying even less. The adults are drinking ale, Colin soft drinks, and Julia has been telling their hosts about the Incident and its consequences; all the events of which the isolated community of Wood Haven have been living in complete ignorance. David and Helen listen with polite interest, but seem strangely unconcerned, as though whatever might be happening in the outside world is of little consequence to themselves.

'Whatever might be happening out there do no harm to us,' explains David when Julia comments on this. 'The people of Wood Haven are watched over by Slumpy Feg.'

'Who's Slumpy Feg?' asks Colin, mouth full of cake.

'Slumpy Feg is the guardian of the woods. He is as old as the oldest tree in the woods. He is the spirit that inhabits every leaf of every one of them. You and your friend would not have been allowed to come here today if Slumpy Feg had not ordained it. You would have passed through the forest without knowing our village even existed.'

'He is a spirit then, this Slumpy Feg of yours?' queries Julia. 'He has no physical form?'

'He *can* take physical form,' replies Helen. 'He can make a body for himself from the bushes and the trees.'

'Yes, and then he becomes the Green Man,' says David. 'Hence the name of this public house.'

‘So that was Slumpy Feg at the fair today!’ exclaims Colin. ‘The one who hit me with the balloon!’

‘Not exactly. That was just a villager dressed in his image.’

‘Well, I didn’t like him,’ Colin avers, and then yawns prodigiously. ‘Tired…’

‘Yes, that will be the drug starting to take effect,’ David tells him.

‘Drug!’ Julia springs to her feet. ‘You have drugged Colin? Oh—!’

She totters dizzily, falls back into her seat.

‘We’ve drugged both of you,’ continues David calmly. ‘Just a harmless sleeping draught. We put it in the birthday cake, of course.’

‘Why-why are you doing this?’ demands Julia, groggily.

‘Why? To do the very thing you suspected us of wanting to do since you got here,’ answers David. ‘Your suspicions were right, only you got the time and the place wrong: the sacrifice will take place tonight.’

‘You’re… going to sacrifice… Colin…?’

‘Yes. You see, we’ve been lying to you this whole time. Our village has not been barren of children for the last twenty years: we have never stopped bearing children. But then, one day last winter all of them suddenly disappeared; every single child in Wood Haven, gone in an instant. It was Slumpy Feg who took them away. At first we couldn’t understand why he would have done this to us, but then the truth was made known to our wise woman here. Slumpy Feg was displeased with us. You see, in the olden times, in the years gone by, we *had* always offered up a virgin child as a sacrifice to Slumpy Feg; but latterly this practice had been discontinued, and the ritual of sacrifice had just been performed symbolically by way of our Mayday festival. But this was our mistake, you see? Slumpy Feg still demands a human sacrifice in his honour: that is why he took our children away, and that was why he caused Colin Cleveland to be brought here today. You see, if we perform the sacrifice, as in the olden days, then Slumpy Feg will return our children to us. So this is how it must be.'

Colin cannot move. He wants to get up and run, but his body feels as heavy as lead. David, sitting across the table from him, keeps swimming in and out of focus. He wants to turn his head to look at Julia, to implore her help, but he can't even do that…

'You fools…!' he hears her say. 'If your children disappeared last winter then it was because of the Incident…! It happened everywhere… Have the population of the world… I told you this…! If in your village it was only the children who vanished… that… that was just a coincidence…!'

'Slumpy Feg took our children,' insists David. 'We know this.'

'Nonsense… You're all insane… It… doesn't even make sense… Even if Slumpy Feg *did* take your children, then why would he return them to you in exchange for just one…?'

'Shut your noise, you!' comes the sharp dry voice of the village elder. 'Think ye know the ways o' Slumpy Feg, better'n we do? Like buggery do yer! An' as for *you* callin' *us* all barmy…! Ruddy cheek, that! Talk about ruddy kettle callin' t'pot black-arse! Come from Israel, do yer? Ruddy sight closer'n that, I reckon!'

'The sacrifice has to be performed in the old way,' says David. 'There is a place in the forest; Colin will be taken there. And then, at midnight, Slumpy Feg will manifest himself to accept our offering, and then he will be appeased and our children will be returned to us…'

This is the last thing Colin hears. And then sound and vision dissolve into darkness and oblivion.

Chapter Thirty-Four
'It's *Not* a Dead Tree!'

It's the pain in his arms that awakens Colin, or that he awakens to. Panic surges over him. He is bound and helpless, held completely upright, his arms hoisted high above him, bound tightly and painfully at the wrists. His legs have been similarly bound together at the ankles. Looking up, he sees that the rope binding him and holding him upright is looped over a branch of the tree under which he stands, the other end of the rope having been lashed around the trunk of the tree.

He takes stock of his surroundings. Trees silvered by moonlight, creating a chiaroscuro of light and shadow, stand all around him. Directly in front of him is a small clearing. All around him is quiet and still. He's very cold. He is still dressed in the thin white robe, but his sandals for some reason have been taken away from him. He can feel that the chaplet of flowers he had worn at the fair, but taken off afterwards, has been placed back on his head.

Here he is, cold, alone and helpless, left as a sacrifice for the Green Man, for Slumpy Feg, the spirit of the forest. He would have thought the villagers would all be there to watch him being sacrificed, but perhaps this is not allowed.

Colin knows that the children of Wood Haven almost certainly vanished because of the Incident, the same way people vanished everywhere else. No tree monster called Slumpy Feg came along and took them away. But that fact alone doesn't mean that Slumpy Feg doesn't exist—right now Colin can well believe in the existence of Slumpy Feg.

He has never heard of Slumpy Feg or any other 'Green Men' in any of those supernatural accounts described in his dad's books, but he has read other tales of creatures that are supposed to live deep in the forests. He remembers one that particularly frightened him, a forest monster they had in America called the wendigo, a really ancient monster that the American Indians have always known about. The wendigo is supposed to eat people. Is this what's going to happen to him? Is Slumpy Feg going to come along and eat him?

Whimpering, Colin tugs vainly at the ropes pinioning his arms. Where's Julia? Why has she let this happen to him? She said she was going to look after him! She promised…!

But Julia ate the poisoned birthday cake as well, and she went to sleep just like he did… They wouldn't bring her out here; they don't want to sacrifice her, so she's probably still back in the village, wherever that is…

Or maybe not! The Wood Haven people don't need Julia for anything, do they? She's just in the way. What if they've already killed her…?

And then he hears the noise. A loud wooden crack like a branch being snapped. At the far side of the clearing, directly in front of him, stands a large old tree. The sound seems to have come from that tree. Even as he looks there comes another crack. There is no sign of movement. Could it just be the sound of wood settling? He remembers his dad telling him once how wood expanded and contracted when it got hotter or colder, and that this was why you sometimes heard household furniture creaking during the night. Perhaps it's normal for trees to do the same…

But now follows a whole succession of loud cracking noises that don't sound natural at all, more like the cracking of a set of wooden knuckles. And then, as Colin watches, comes an even louder crack and something tears itself away from the tree, a thin stick-like shape emerging from the trunk at about six feet up and angling down to the ground. Colin's mind struggles to process what he sees. Is it the bark? Is it the bark peeling away from the tree? Does bark even do that on its own?

But then the stick moves again, moves with volition, with a life of its own. And then, with an awful tearing noise a Shape detaches itself from the tree, a hideous lumbering Shape.

Colin's knees buckle and only his bonds keep him from falling to the ground. His terrified eyes try to make something out of the Shape, to discern a familiar form… It appears to have a head; a gnarled and knotted bulbous excrescence that could pass as some half-formed parody of a head. But the body… Colin searches in vain for signs of a familiar human form. There are what could be called limbs, projecting from a thicker 'torso', but there is no sense or symmetry to them.

Colin's reeling mind tries to reject the impossible sight, and meanwhile, with awful cracking and dragging noises, it slowly advances across the clearing towards him.

This thing, this Shape, it must be him; it must be Slumpy Feg.

The Green Man isn't green at all: not a leaf in sight, just a gaunt, misshapen skeleton of branches.

Colin feels dizzy with terror. Sound rushes in his ears and his vision starts to blur.

And then the thing stops in its tracks. Still over twenty feet away from Colin all sound and movement from the creature abruptly cease.

What is it doing? Why has it stopped?

New sounds reach Colin's ears. Off to the right, the sound of movement through the foliage, muted conversation. Turning his head in the direction of the sounds, he sees two figures emerge from amongst the ferns, one in front of the other moving towards the clearing. As they advance Colin recognises the bearded form of David as the leading figure, and behind him—Julia!

They step into the moonlit circle of the clearing, Julia pushing David in front of her with one hand, while with the other she holds a kitchen knife. (The knife they cut his birthday cake with?)

The first thing Julia sees is Colin and she smiles at him, relief written on her features; but the first thing David sees is the Shape—at least that's how it seems because, terror-stricken, he starts screaming and babbling, turns to flee, and collides with Julia. A brief struggle follows, and then David, his incoherent babbling terminating with a grunt of pain, drops to the ground. Has Julia stabbed him? No; wrong hand. She must have punched him in the stomach.

She rushes over to Colin. 'I am glad that you are alright, Colin,' she says, and with the knife, quickly saws through the rope where it angles down from the horizontal branch. The taut rope snaps, and Colin, no longer held aloft, drops to the ground.

In a moment Julia is at his side, supporting him. 'Are you unhurt? Come, I will untie the ropes from your wrists and ankles.'

Meanwhile Colin stares at her, speechless with horror. She hasn't seen it! From the way she's acting, she hasn't seen the Thing! She thinks it's all over; she's working at the rope binding his wrists like she's got all the time in the world!

Mutely, frantically, Colin nods his head towards the clearing, whimpering the words he cannot form.

Julia registers his expression with puzzlement.

'What is wrong with you?' she asks. 'The danger is over. You are safe now.'

Colin wildly shakes his head, renews his frantic head-nodding. Perceiving what he wants, Julia turns her head to the clearing, where the still motionless Shape stands in full view.

She looks back at Colin, apparently none the wiser. 'What?'

'*Behind you!*' Colin forces the words out, shrill and half-stifled.

Julia looks round once more, and then back at Colin.

'What is behind me?'

'*There.* Can't you see it?'

Another look. 'All I see is a small dead tree.'

'It's *not* a dead tree!' desperately.

David certainly knows what it is. Prostrate and quivering, he whimpers unintelligibly, a terrified acolyte who finds himself for the first time in the presence of his master.

'What is it, then?' asks Julia.

'*Slumpy Feg…*'

Suddenly, accompanied by a whiplash sound, something snakes across the ground towards the prostrate man. His babbling turn to screams; and with horrible rapidity he is being dragged across the ground towards the creature.

And now Julia reacts. She gathers Colin in her strong arms and springs to her feet. David's screams become shrill with terror, as the creature now comes to life, reaching out with tendril arms, folding itself over the doomed man.

Julia runs. With Colin in her arms, his own arms grasped around her neck, she runs, striking off into the forest.

With her precious burden, she runs and she doesn't stop running until she can run no longer and the horror in the clearing has been left far behind.

His name, softly breathed in his ear, gently pulls Colin from his slumber. He awakes as he fell asleep, wrapped in Julia's arms, lying on the bare earth at the foot of a tree. Julia, with her flightsuit unzipped to the crotch, sharing her body heat with him. It is morning, a damp mist hangs in the air. In spite of his situation Colin still feels cold. His feet are frozen.

They are still in the forest, but several miles from the scene of last night's horror. Julia, Colin in her arms, had kept on running until she could run no longer, and even after that they had walked together for some time, before exhaustion had forced them to halt for the remainder of the night.

'Today we will reach Norton-Braisley,' Julia tells him, as they both sit up, and stretch their limbs. 'The worst is over.'

'I wish I had some proper clothes…' says Colin.

'Ah, yes. Well, if we find any on the way, we will appropriate them for you.'

With no breakfast to detain them, they make immediate preparations for moving on. Julia chafes some life into Colin's frozen feet, and then generously donates her boots to him. She then picks up a coil of rope from the ground and hoists it over her shoulder. This is the rope with which had been tied and which had still been attached to him when they made their desperate flight.

And now, having each privately micturated, they set off: Julia walking barefoot, smoking her first cigarette of the day, while Colin plods awkwardly along in boots ridiculously too large for him. The morning remains chill, and as they proceed the fog grows thicker.

They have been walking for about half an hour when out of the fog suddenly looms a wall blocking their path; a brick wall of no recent origin, at least twelve foot in height. The trees come to an abrupt stop just short of this wall, and a well-defined path runs alongside it. This path they are now forced to change direction and follow. Thus, they continue for some time, encountering no gate or termination of the wall.

Suddenly Julia stops. 'Perhaps, Colin Cleveland, it would save time if we were to scale the wall,' she says, eyeing its summit speculatively. 'With the rope that we have, it should be possible to accomplish this.'

'But don't we need one of those ropes with the metal gripping thing on the end?' questions Colin.

'A grappling hook? Yes, it would make it a lot easier if we had one of those; but even with just the rope I believe we can still scale this wall. Yes... I have a plan. I will first tie the end of the rope around your waist and then you will climb up onto my shoulders. This way you should be able to reach the top of the wall. If you find there is broken glass or any other impediment up there, then we shall abandon the plan; but if there is not, you can climb up onto the top of the wall. Once there, I, holding the end of the rope from here, can lower you down the other side of the wall.'

'But then how will you get over?' asks Colin.

'Hopefully you will find something on the other side to tie the rope around; a tree would be best; and then I will be able to scale the wall.'

'What if there isn't anything to tie the rope around?'

'You will determine if there is before I lower you down; if there is nothing, then we abandon the plan. You will come back down the wall on this side and we will proceed as we are.'

'Okay...' says Colin, not over-enthused. The wall looks very high and moreover he feels like he's not exactly dressed for this kind of activity.

'Good! You had better take those boots off first. I will wear them until we are over the wall.'

Colin takes off the boots—by the simple process of stepping out of them—and Julia returns them to her own feet. She now squats down against the wall, and Colin climbs up onto her shoulders and she slowly stands erect.

'I can feel the top of the top of the wall now,' reports Colin.

'Can you feel any obstruction: glass or spikes?'

'No, it's smooth.'

Colin pulls himself up onto the summit of the wall. Stradling it, he examines the terrain, as much as the fog will allow him to see. The ground is turf, dotted with trees and shrubs.

He reports this to Julia. 'It looks like a park or a big garden. Can't see any buildings…'

'Is there any tree or bush close enough to the wall for you to tie the rope to?'

'Yes, there is. There's a silver birch tree right in front of me.'

'Excellent! I will now lower you down the wall. Take hold of the rope in both hands and just ease yourself off the wall. You won't fall; I have hold of the rope; I will lower you slowly. Call out when you reach the ground.'

Colin obeys and soon his feet are on *terra firma*.

'Now untie the rope from around your waist and tie it round the silver birch tree.'

Colin does this. The silver birch tree makes him think of his own, back in the garden of his home in Eastchester. Having secured the rope to the tree he reports this to Julia. The becomes taut and presently Julia appears on the lip of the wall. She lowers herself over the edge and drops to the ground.

Julia stands up, turns to Colin, and as she opens her mouth to speak, the wail of a siren from some nearby source suddenly interposes. To this sound is joined that of urgent voices and running footsteps rapidly approaching.

Shadowy figures appear in the mist, taking shape as they close in on Colin and Julia. The shapes resolve themselves into uniformed men carrying rifles. Grey uniforms with coalscuttle helmets, uniforms Colin recognises from World War Two films he has seen.

Germans!

They have climbed into an Enemy base!

Chapter Thirty-Five
'Erection-Suppressor!'

The soldiers, six in number, surround Colin and Julia.

'*Hände hoch!*' snaps one of them. 'Hands up!'

Colin puts his hands up. He looks at Julia and receives a

further shock: in fact, he barely recognises the woman. Her face is completely transformed; her skin pale as death, her eyes glassy with a fixed look of abject horror—an expression so irreconcilable with the fearless, self-sufficient woman Colin has come to rely upon, she seems a completely different person.

A smile, and not a nice one, spreads across the first soldier's face as he looks at Julia.

'Vhy, it's 2480!' he exclaims. 'So, you heff come back to uss! But vhy scale the walls, 2480? You could heff just announced yourself at the front gate—' He breaks off. His smile widens. 'Vait: don't tell me that you actually didn't know? That you climbed offer ze back wall not knowing you hed returned to the very place from vhich you hed escaped?'

Julia, still a frozen statue, offers no response.

The soldier bursts into a roar of laughter, laughter which is soon taken up by his comrades.

'You alvays did have soch a terrible sense off direction, 2480!' he says.

'Ja, und such terrible lock, also!' adds another.

A low moan starts to issue from Julia's parted lips. Rising rapidly in pitch and volume, it becomes a sustained wailing scream. Her terrified expression becomes further contorted with a look of stark insanity and she clamps the hands she has raised in the air to the sides of her head.

The smile vanishes from the first soldier's face. 'Silence, 2480!' he barks, levelling his rifle at Julia. 'Cease that noisse at vonce! Cease und desist!'

But Julia is too far gone to even hear the order. Colin looks on with horror as she starts swaying from side to side, wailing and gripping her head, lurching around in some mad Dance of Despair.

The first soldier strides up to her, reverses his gun and drives the stock into her face. This seems to act as a signal and the others join in. They descend on Julia like a pack of jackbooted hounds, clubbing her with their rifles, and, when she falls prostrate at their feet, kicking her.

'Stop it, stop it!' screams Colin. Tears streaming from his eyes he runs forward, starts pummelling the back of the nearest soldier. 'Let her go! Let her go!'

'Silence, girl!' snarls the soldier, turning on Colin and shoving him back violently. 'You dare to interfere?' To the other soldiers. 'That is enough for now. The Herr Director vill vish to interrogate 2480. Und you—' turning back to Colin; 'you vill com wiff us also, girl.'

'I'm not a girl, I—'

'Silence! Now, move!' snarls the soldier, indicating the direction with a jerk of his rifle barrel. 'Move, girl! *Schnell! Schnell!*'

Julia, battered, bleeding, and barely conscious, has been hauled to her feet by two of the soldiers, and Colin is now marched and Julia dragged across the park, Colin still trying to process this rapid turn of events. Witnessing Julia's inexplicable transformation and then her savage beating has left him in a state of shock; and then, on top of all this there is the additional bewilderment of the guards here being well-acquainted with Julia. From what Colin can gather it seems that this place is a prison camp and that Julia escaped from it—but then how did she come to be in an aeroplane the day he met her? And what about her story of having just flown to England from Israel…?

His eyes turn to Julia; supported and dragged along by two of the soldiers, head hanging, her face bruised, swollen and red-bearded, it's hard to tell if she's even conscious.

The rear of a large building emerges from the fog before them; a substantial country house. They march round it and onto the gravelled forecourt of the front entrance. On the wall above the portico hangs a vast swastika banner; and with the black cross emblazoned upon the white oval against a background of vivid crimson, it is undeniably an arresting image—and just as it was intended to be, for, whatever their faults (like making the trains to death camps run on time) the Nazis were certainly ahead of the game when it came to crowd manipulation and making an impression.

The prisoners and their escort now mount the steps, pass through the porticoed entrance doors where two more soldiers stand sentinel, and they enter a commodious, tiled hallway. Here, Colin is steered towards a pair of open doors off to the right and pushed through them.

'You vill vait here, girl, until you are summoned!' the soldier tells him.

Colin turns to protest, but the doors are slammed shut in his face. He hears a bolt slide into place and then the sound of retreating footsteps as Julia is dragged away.

The room into which he has been introduced is a large front parlour. He is not alone. About a dozen individuals occupy the room, all dressed in the striped shirts, trousers and caps of convicts. Beneath the latter, all of them exhibit shaved heads. Either standing or sitting around the room, they regard the newcomer through listless eyes.

Colin deduces the room to be some prisoners' common room, albeit a surprisingly comfortable and well-furnished one. He would have expected more spartan accommodation. Dominating the room, on the wall facing the window, is a large framed photograph of an obese man in the black uniform of a Nazi officer.

One of the convicts, a thin, middle-aged man of placid appearance approaches Colin.

'And who might you be, my dear?' he inquires, his quiet voice matching his appearance.

'I'm Colin,' says Colin.

'Oh!' surprised. 'I beg your pardon, but I thought you were a girl. The dress…'

'It's not a dress, it's a robe,' says Colin. 'Where have they taken Julia?'

The man perks up at the name. 'Julia? Were you with Julia? Oh dear; so they've recaptured her, have they? Oh dear, oh dear…' shaking his head. 'Well, if that's the case, she'll have been taken to see the director. Yes, the director. Oh dear, oh dear…'

'Do you mean that Julia was a prisoner here with you and she escaped?' inquires Colin.

'Yes. Yes, she was. Escaped last week, she did. Yes, last week…'

'But how long had she been here before last week?'

'How long has she been here? Well, that's hard to say, hard to say. One day just rolls into another, you see. A long time, though; yes, a long time…'

'But when I met her, she told me she'd just come here from Israel!'

'Israel?' The man giggles. 'Israel? Ha-ha, that's a good one! Israel! No, no; she may be Jewish; but Israel? No, no, no; she's as English as you or I. Never even been to Israel, as far as I know.'

So none of it's true?' demands Colin, indignation rising within him. 'Julia's not from Israel, and she's not a spy for…' he's forgotten the name, '…for the Israeli spy people? She's just been a prisoner here all the time?'

'Yes, I'm afraid so,' replies the man. 'Although they prefer it if you say "patient", rather than "prisoner"; and after all, that's what we are: we're all patients here.'

'Patients? Why do you call yourselves patients? This is a prison camp, isn't it?'

'Goodness me, no! Whatever gave you that idea? This is a mental hospital; yes, it's a mental hospital. We're all detained here under the mental health act.'

'Mental hospital?' Colin is starting to feel giddy. 'You mean where they keep mad people?'

'Well, yes. But you needn't be alarmed; we're not all raving lunatics.'

'But if this is a mental place, then how come there's all those soldiers?'

'Soldiers? Oh! You mean the orderlies.'

'Orderlies?'

'Yes: orderlies. They keep us all in order. Every hospital has orderlies.'

'Then how come they're dressed as soldiers?'

'Oh, that was the director's idea. Come: I'll introduce you.'

They cross the room and stop before the framed enlargement of the fat man in Nazi uniform, who, stern and moustachioed, gazes off-camera, standing to attention.

'This is our director,' says the man, pointing to the plaque attached to the bottom of the frame.

Colin reads the inscription aloud. '"Institute Director, Dr Josef Noebbals,"' pronouncing the last name "No-balls."

The man titters at this. 'Yes, that's right. Dr Noebbals. Ha, ha, ha! Yes, he's the one in charge around here, and he's the reason why things here are the way they are. It wasn't always like this. No, no; it wasn't always like this. But you see, our director, he's a keen collector of Nazi memorabilia. Yes, that's his hobby; or rather, it *was* his hobby: but then, after the Incident his hobby started to get out of hand, and then, before we knew what was what, in came the guns and the uniforms and the stripey pyjamas and all the rest of it.'

Colin is still completely at sea. 'But... if those soldiers... if they're not really German soldiers... then... what about the Incident...? The conspiracy...? The Germans and Japanese taking over the world...?'

'Germans and Japanese taking over the world? Where did you get that one from? Oh, I know! It was Julia, wasn't it? Yes! Did she tell you that? Is that what she said?'

'Yes, she did!' hotly. 'You mean none of it's true? It's not the Germans and Japanese who made the Incident happen?'

'I don't know who caused the Incident; I don't think anybody does. At least, nobody around here knows. I very much doubt if it was Germany and Japan, though. No, that was just a story that Julia told you. Just a tall story.'

'That means she lied to me about everything!' exclaims Colin, aggrieved (and probably with himself as much as with Julia.)

'Oh, don't be too hard on Julia,' says the man. 'She would have believed what she was telling you herself. Yes, the first person she would've fooled with her tall stories would've been herself. It comes from being in this place, you see. Julia didn't like it here. I mean, none of us like it here, but Julia especially.

You see, the director,' indicating the portrait, 'he's always had a particular dislike for Julia. Always bullying her, shouting at her, confiscating her cigarettes, sending her to solitary for every little misdemeanour. Yes, he was very hard on poor Julia. That's why she escaped, you see. Couldn't stand it anymore, couldn't stand it.'

'Oh…' says Colin, subdued. 'And now she's back again…'

'Yes, and the director, he's not going to let her off lightly. Furious he was, when she escaped. Absolutely livid. Had us all on bread and water for a week. Yes, he's not going to let her off lightly, now he's got her back… Hm… I wonder if he'll operate…?'

'Operate?'

'Yes. Operate.' The man taps the side of his head. 'Brain operation. He's a skilled surgeon, the director. He operated on me, he did. Yes, he performed the operation himself.'

'A brain operation? Was there something wrong with your brain?'

'Yes! Or at least, the director thought so. I used to write books, you see, a long time ago. Yes, I used to write books. Perhaps you've heard of me? Rampion Quarles. Does the name ring a bell?'

'I think so…' answers Colin diplomatically.

'Yes. Well, the director, he didn't like my books, you see; didn't like them at all. Said they were liberal and degenerate. So, he operated on my brain, and now I can't write books anymore. It's gone, you see: my imagination; completely gone away, it has. Couldn't think up a story even if I wanted to…'

'But that's horrible!' protests Colin. 'Doesn't it upset you that he did that to you?'

The man ponders this. 'Hm… Yes, I suppose it *would* upset me; it would upset me a great deal. In fact, I'm sure I'd be devastated; completely devastated. Yes; yes, I would be inconsolable… But it's the pills, you see, the pills they make me take. The pills keep me happy; yes, the pills keep me happy…'

And the man smiles placidly while two tears trickle down his wan cheeks.

Now comes the sound of the door being unlocked and in walks the first soldier from before. He marches straight up to Colin.

'The Herr Director vill see you now. Follow me.'

Colin has followed his conductor across the hall, along several corridors and has arrived at a door bearing the name Dr Josef Noebbals, before it occurs to him that he doesn't actually have to be here at all. It was alright letting himself be bossed around when he thought this place was a Nazi prison camp and that he was a prisoner of war, but now that he knows it's just a mental hospital, they shouldn't be telling him what to do at all; they may be allowed to order the patients around, but he's not one of the patients, is he?

Before Colin can arrange these thoughts into words, the soldier has knocked briskly but subserviently on the door, and being bidden enter, has opened the door and announced: 'Here is the suspect to see you, Herr Director.'

Suspect? What's he suspected of?

'Sehr gut. Show him in,' comes a voice from within the room.

Colin hesitates in the doorway.

'Enter,' orders the soldier tersely.

'But I—'

'Enter, you *schwein-hund! Schnell! Schnell!*'

Colin enters. Dr Noebbals, looking just as fat and pompous as his photograph, sits at his desk. On the wall behind hangs a painting of the *Führer*. An unsurprising adornment in the office of a deranged Nazi memorabilia collector you might think; except that this particular painting is somewhat unorthodox, in that the subject is smiling impishly and tipping a wink at his audience.

Noebbals dismisses the soldier, before turning his attention to Colin.

'Vat iss your name, girl?'

'My name's Colin and I'm not a girl.'

'Vhat? Not a girl? Then vhy are you wearink a dress? Explain!'

'It's not a dress, it's a—'

‘Silence! You think I do not know a dress vhen I see one? Impudent boy! Do not attempt to deceive me! This iss your first und last varnink!’

‘But I’m not trying to—’

‘Silence! Do you know who you are talking to?’

‘Yes. You’re Dr Noebbals—’

Noebbals springs to his feet. ‘Swine! My name iss pronounced ‘Nurbals’, pig-dog! ‘Nurbals’! Insolent cur! You dare to mock my name? And while standing there violating all the laws of decency and acceptable behaviour by vearink vomen’s clothink! Gender dysphoria! Oedipus Complex! Bed-vetter! Erection-suppressor! Clearly you are unfit to be released back into the community! You shall be detained here until you can be cured—and as your case is incurable, you will be detained here indefinitely! Orderly!’

The soldier reappears.

‘Take this person avay! See that he is issued mit the regulation priso—pyjamas! Und guard him carefully: he iss ein ferry dangerous sexual deviant!’

The soldier clicks his heels. ‘Jawohl, Herr Command—Director!’

And Colin finds himself being led away at gunpoint.

Chapter Thirty-Six
‘...Cigarette...’

3579. One of those easy to remember pin numbers. And it’s Colin Cleveland’s pin number, emblazoned on the back of his regulation stripy pyjamas.

Colin is on cleaning duty, issued with bucket and mop, listlessly cleaning the tiled floor of B-wing’s main corridor. The pyjamas aren’t the least drastic change to Colin’s appearance since we last saw him: beneath the matching cap that goes with them we can see that his head has been shaved, another regulation of this institution.

And it is listlessly that he goes about his work, because Colin is in a state of acute dejection. He has been a patient here for over a week now, and to be a patient in this particular mental institution would be enough to render anyone clinically depressed.

Two orderlies, dressed in the ubiquitous field grey, appear at the end of the corridor. Hands clutching belts, they amble towards Colin with studied insouciance.

Colin's hands tighten on the mop. Eyes down, he continues mopping the floor.

The orderlies come to a halt right where Colin is mopping, forcing him to suspend his work.

'Is this all you haff done, 3579?' inquires the first orderly. 'You should haff finished B-wing by this time. You are a slow vorker, 3579, ferry slow.'

'Ja, but perhaps he cleanss der floors slowly to ensure that he cleanss them thoroughly,' suggests his comrade.

'Perhaps so,' agrees the first. 'Let uss examine his vork…'

The two orderlies make a show of scrutinising the section of the corridor that has already been cleaned.

'Hmm… Vhy, this hass not been cleaned thoroughly at all!' declares the first orderly. 'Look at this mess right here!'

'Vot mess?' asks the second.

'Vhy, right here. Look!' Unbuttoning, the first orderly micturates on the floor. 'Do you not see it?'

'Vhy, yes!' agrees the second. 'This iss indeed ferry inefficient vork! Vot haff you got to say for yourself, 3579?'

3579, saying nothing, starts mopping up the pool of urine.

'Insolent swine!' shouts the second orderly, snatching the mop from Colin. 'Answer vhen you are spoken to! Vot haff you got to say for yourself?'

Colin still has nothing to say for himself, knowing that whatever he has to say will be the wrong thing.

'Insubordinate scum!' grates the first orderly. 'I vill teach you to ignore my comrade!'

Taking the mop from his companion, the first orderly beats Colin repeatedly with the wooden haft, punctuating the blows with imprecations, 'Scum! Wretch! Filth!' until Colin is flat on the floor, dazed and lying in the pool of urine.

'Don't just lie there!' snarls the assailant. 'You heff vork to do! Get up! Schnell, schnell!'

Colin, still racked with pain, struggles to rise.

'He iss half asleep,' declares the second orderly. 'This vill help brink him round.'

And so saying, he unbuttons and directs a stream of urine into Colin's face.

'Vakey-vakey! Rise und shine!'

Colin finally attains the vertical, and the two orderlies, satisfied for the time being, depart laughing down the corridor.

'Got a spare fag?' asks the jittery woman.

'No, I haven't!' snaps back Colin.

Jittery woman retreats, leaving Colin sitting on a chair, defences firmly up.

With the exception of Colin, all of the patients here are smokers (they're mental health patients, so of course they are), and one of the staff's preferred methods of torturing them is to strictly ration their supply of cigarettes, and, upon the slightest pretext, real or manufactured, to withhold it completely.

When not being put to work, Colin has to sit in the common room with the other patients (he would much rather be alone in his room, which of course is why he's not allowed to stay in his room), and he sits in a self-imposed isolation, repelling any verbal advances. The patients aren't threatening in the same way the orderlies are, but they make Colin feel uncomfortable, and they are constantly badgering him for cigarettes. Even after he's told them that he doesn't smoke, that he never has any cigarettes, the same patients will come back and ask him the same question over and over, day after day, the jittery woman being one of the most persistent offenders.

The most 'normal' seeming of the patients is Rampion Quarles, and Quarles has repeatedly tried to befriend Colin, to engage him in conversation; but when Quarles comes up to him Colin raises his shields to maximum. He has a grudge against Quarles. He has taken a powerful dislike to Quarles. In fact, he considers Quarles to be responsible for his entire miserable predicament. Quarles had set him up, hadn't he? Telling him the wrong way to pronounce Dr Noebbals' name like that! *That's* why he's been made a prisoner here! Locked up in the loony bin with all the loonies! Just because he got the director's name wrong…!

Although the dress might have had something to do with it as well…

And then one day Julia comes back.

Pushed stumbling into the common room by escorting orderlies, she blearily takes in her surroundings, her expression nervous, confused. Colin perks up at the sight of her, smiles, trying to catch her eye. Julia doesn't seem to notice him. She doesn't even seem to recognise her surroundings. Her head has been freshly shaved, and the injuries to her face have completely disappeared, so long is it since Colin last saw her. This is the first time he has seen her wearing her patient's striped pyjamas.

Since her recapture, Julia has been confined to A-wing, the 'special ward' where severe cases are kept in solitary confinement. Off-limits to all other patients, Colin has never set eyes on A-wing, but he imagines white, padded rooms and patients confined in straightjackets. Julia has been undergoing a course of 'special treatment', personally supervised by Dr Noebbals, who, according to Quarles, has always especially disliked Julia.

And the first thing Julia's eyes focus on is the director's framed photograph. She turns from the image with a look of stark terror, swiftly crosses the room and sits on the floor in a corner, hugging her knees.

Colin gets up and walks over to her. The other patients in the room, having observed Julia's arrival with nothing more than mild curiosity, have by now lost interest completely, returning to their own thoughts, their internal or in some cases external monologues.

Seeing Julia sitting huddled in the corner like this isn't exactly an encouraging sight for Colin, but he still has hopes. Julia was strong once. Julia had rescued him from Slumpy Feg the tree man. Colin had slept in the same bed with Julia and she had smelled nice and the muscles in her arms and legs had been strong.

And she has already escaped from this place once. Maybe she can do it again.

'Julia…?' he says hesitantly, squatting down beside her. 'It's me: Colin… You remember me, don't you…? Julia…?'

Julia makes no response, stares at the floor.

'Julia…?' cautiously touching her shoulder.

She turns her head slowly, looks blankly at Colin.

'It's me…! How are you, Julia? You—'

Even as he speaks, she turns her head away again.

'Julia…?'

Still hugging her knees, she starts to rock back and forth. Words form, whispered words, the same three syllables repeated over and over. Colin, straining his hearing, tries to distinguish the words. The same three syllables…

Let's escape… Is that it: let's escape? Is that what she's saying?

…Let's escape…

…Let's escape…

Colin leans in closer, listening intently. The vowel-sounds and sibilants now take shape.

'…Cigarette…

'…Cigarette…

'…Cigarette…'

Chapter Thirty-Seven
'Nice Skinhead You Got There, Mate!'

By dawn's early light the rough hand of an orderly shakes Colin abruptly from sleep.

'Vake-up, 3579! Vake-up!'

'Wha-what is it...?' blearily.

'2480 vishes to speak to you! Get up! *Schnell, schnell!*'

2480! 2480 is Julia! Has she come out of her trance? Is she speaking at last?

So excited is Colin as he slips on his shoes and follows the orderly that he doesn't even stop to wonder why a member of staff should care less that one patient wanted to speak to another one, let alone go to all the trouble of acting as messenger boy. He is wide awake and full of a sudden optimism. Julia is back to her old self! She wants to speak to him! She escaped from this place once already: maybe she's come up with a new escape plan!

Colin's burst of optimism doesn't last long. It dissolves when he sees that there are other orderlies loitering outside Julia's room, and that they appear to be amused about something. The smiles beneath those coal-scuttle helmets broaden when they catch sight of Colin and his escort.

What's going on? wonders Colin, suspicion clouding his brow. Why are they all standing there outside her room? Is he being set up for something? Has Julia summoned him so urgently like this just to ask him if he's got any cigarettes?

'Make haste, 3579!' urges one grinning orderly. '2480 is avaiting you most impatiently!'

And Colin is pushed through the open doorway.

Julia doesn't want a cigarette. Stone cold and hanging by her neck from the ceiling, she will have quit smoking by now. She hangs there pale and naked, her pyjamas having been utilised to form the noose around her neck. He only recognises the pendant corpse as Julia's from her body, limp and pasty-hued as it is; the face, popeyed and purple, is unrecognisable.

For a moment Colin stands as frozen as the corpse in front of him. And then his knees buckle under him and he falls to the floor, landing on his backside, much to the renewed merriment of the orderlies.

A corpse. A thing. Not Julia; not anymore. Just a thing. She was already half-gone, her mind broken by Dr Noebbals' course of treatment; and now the remnant that was left of her has also departed, and Colin doesn't need to be told that she left of her own volition.

Colin flees. Scrambling to his feet, he fights his way through the laughing orderlies and flees back to his own room, throwing himself on his bed. He wants to retreat, retreat into his Doomsday Defence mode, but he knows that in this place he will not even be allowed that luxury. The orderlies will be back soon to turf him out of his room; he has no safe haven in this place. Safety and comfort no longer exist. They have been eliminated by people who laugh at death and despair.

And Julia *did* have an escape plan; the final escape. She carried out her plan and made the final escape. Then maybe he, Colin, should also—?

Sounds of a disturbance outside disrupt his meditations. And no ordinary disturbance. Explosion, shouts, gunfire. The klaxon wails into life.

Colin goes to the window of his room, which looks out on the front of the grounds. He sees thick white smoke rising into the air in the gardens between the building and the outer wall. An object falls, explodes, more white smoke billows upwards. Gas grenades.

Orderlies pour out through the main entrance and charge towards the smoke, firing their rifles. Machine-gunfire from unseen assailants. Colin sees an orderly fall, screaming.

They are under attack.

Everything's coming apart at the seams. A new menace has arrived, possibly even worse than the current one. Maybe it's them: the unknown Enemy; the people behind the Incident, finally making their move, taking the world by force.

The screams and gunfire intensify, and when it becomes clear that the attacking force is winning the day and have entered the building, Colin takes refuge under the bed, and for additional protection, squeezes his eyelids tight shut. He hears shouts, footsteps ascending the stairs. It sounds like the invaders are making a sweep of the building.

The door bursts open.

'No-one in here!' reports a voice; a young voice, the accent English.

'Yeah? Hang on a minute…'

And then:

'Alright then, you. Come out from under there. We ain't gunna hurt you. We're here to bloody rescue you, ain't we?'

The voice sounds familiar… Colin crawls out from under the bed and stands up. Before him are two boys his own age, dressed in British Army battledress, circa World War Two, and armed with Sten guns.

'Fuck me, if it ain't Colin Cleveland!' exclaims one. 'Nice skinhead you got there, mate!'

The two soldiers are Bradley and Ferret.

Chapter Thirty-Eight
'Ever Read *War of the Worlds*, Cadet?'

'…and when Chorley found out you'd scarpered—Christ, he went fucking mental! Foaming at the mouth, he was! Accusing all of us of helping you to get out: he was even accusing his mate Maclean! Christ, if he'd found out it was me who helped you, he would've fucking murdered me! Anyhow, he broke up the gang. He just didn't care anymore. All he could think about was finding where you'd got to and getting you back! I tell you, mate: that

bloke's got a serious bee in his bonnet about you. Major bee in his bonnet. I just hope you don't run into him again, that's all.'

'I did *run into him again.'*

'Did you? And what happened?'

'I got away from him again.'

'Good for you. Well, you're safe enough now, with us. Colonel Martin, he won't let Chorley get his paws on you. Yeah, you stick with us. He's a bit bonkers, is the Colonel, but he's not like Chorley; he won't... you know... He's trained all us kids to be his barmy army, so's we can take on the aliens. He's got this country house and he's turned the whole place into a great big training camp. Well, you'll see for yourself when we get there...'

Enter Colin Cleveland, decked out in World War Two khaki battledress, with tin hat on his head, the webbing over his shoulders pipeclayed to perfection, the boots on his feet polished to a shine. Unaccustomed to the cumbersome footwear, he walks rather clumsily, coming to a halt at a door bearing the legend 'Colonel Martin, DSO.'

He knocks hesitantly. Apparently his knock is a bit too hesitant, because it is dignified with no answer. Colin tries again, this time knocking more firmly.

'Enter.'

Colin walks in. A man in officer's uniform sits at a desk facing the door. The man is middle-aged and sports a clipped moustache. A large-scale map of Northern England has been fixed to the panelled wall behind him.

'I'm here,' says Colin.

The Colonel looks at him dryly. 'No, Cleveland. You're a cadet in my army now. You salute and say "reporting for duty, sir."'

Colin manages an awkward salute. 'Reporting for duty, sir.'

'Louder!'

'Reporting for duty, sir!'

'That's better. At ease, Cadet.'

Colin hesitates.

'That means you can put your arm down and relax.'

Colin complies.

'Good. Before you start your training, I want to have a word with you regarding the Enemy. You know who the enemy is, don't you, Cadet?'

'Aliens,' says Colin.

'Aliens, *sir!*'

'Aliens, *sir!*'

'Good. Yes, the Enemy are aliens. Extraterrestrials. I know it sounds a bit hard to believe. Science-fiction stuff, right? *War of the Worlds*, and all that. Ever read *War of the Worlds*, Cadet?'

'No sir. Seen the film, sir.'

'Well, you should read the book, it's a damn sight better. Knew how to spin a good yarn, that Wells fellow, even if he was a socialist. Don't know if our lot are actually from Mars, but they're aliens, alright. No-one else could've pulled off what's been done here. Just look at the Incident. The sudden disappearance of half the population, and the permanent disruption of all radio signals. Clearly these acts are the first stage of a planned invasion from beings possessing a superior technology. We're being softened up, Cleveland. Law and order have disintegrated; the Government, if it even still exists, has become completely ineffective. Chaos and fear prevail across the British Isles. Have you seen the flying saucers?'

'Yes, sir. Friend of mine was taken on board one.'

The Colonel looks interested. 'Was he, now? What was the fellow's name?'

'Natasha, sir.'

'And what did he have to report about his abduction experience? This could be valuable intelligence.'

'Didn't remember anything, sir. Suffered from missing time.'

'Missing ti—? Ah, yes; happens in these cases, doesn't it? Those flying saucer wallahs, they mess around with your memories. Where is this friend of yours?'

'Don't know, sir. Believe she was abducted again.'

'Ah, the Enemy have got him, have they? Too bad. Well, maybe we can get him back. That's what all this is about,

Cleveland; this show here. We're getting ready to make a pre-emptive strike against the Enemy. The raid on the mental hospital yesterday: that was just a training exercise. I mean yes, it was high time someone put paid to that rascal Noebbals and his nest of vipers; high time someone released those poor souls they were torturing back into the community—but Noebbals was just small-fry: a penny-ante dictator. The real object of that raid was to give my platoon their first taste of action in the field—and the men acquitted themselves splendidly: operation a complete success. And now, our next objective will be a direct attack on the Enemy.'

'How will you do that, sir? Do you know where their base is?'

'Yes, I do, Cadet. At least, we have located *one* of their bases; and it's not too far from this location, either…'

Lying on his stomach, propped up on elbows, Colin surveys the compound through a pair of binoculars (or 'field-glasses,' as the Colonel insists on calling them.) The knoll affords them a full view of the installation, while the foliage screens them from observation. A single building, huge and sprawling, flat-roofed, featureless and windowless, it looks like a vast aircraft hangar. The only visible means of ingress and egress are a row of huge shutter doors along the front wall of the building, from which a road leads to the entrance gates. There is no sign of life. Not a guard to be seen, either at the gate or patrolling the perimeter fence.

'Know what that building is, Cadet? Ever seen it before?' asks the Colonel, lying by Colin's side.

'No, sir.'

'No? Well, it's the Amazon warehouse. *That's* where the Enemy are.'

'You mean Amazon's run by aliens?' exclaims Colonel, forgetting the 'sir' in his surprise.

'No, Cleveland; I mean the Amazon warehouse has been *taken over* by aliens. With me?'

'Yessir! Is it here that they park their flying saucers, sir?'

'Good question, Cadet; but as far as we can tell, no, they don't.

We've had this place under twenty-four surveillance, and the only traffic that has ever entered or exited that building has been wheeled traffic. In fact...' looking at his wristwatch, '...Yes, it should be just about time. Keep those glasses trained on the front entrance, Cadet.'

Colin does so. At first nothing happens, but then one of the shutter doors slides open and a grey articulated lorry appears—one of the suspected food-delivery trucks. Quickly followed by a second lorry it drives along the access road towards the gates, which swing open to allow egress. Behind the second comes a third identical truck, and then a fourth, and then a fifth... A whole fleet of lorries emerge from the warehouse, and Colin soon loses count of their numbers. Driving in tight single-file, each vehicle the same distance behind the one in front, they drive out through the gates and onto the trunk road. Finally, the procession comes to an end, the shutter door descends, and when the last lorry has passed through the entrance gates they swing shut.

Colin lowers the field glasses.

'Seen any lorries like those before, Cadet?' asks Colonel Martin.

'Yessir.'

'And you know what their function is?'

'Delivering the food to the shops, sir.'

'Correct! And those trucks are the only vehicles that ever come in or out of that enemy installation. They come and go in huge convoys, like the one you've just seen; and they come and go like clockwork, always at set times. So, what d'you think must be going on inside that installation, Cleveland?'

'It's where they make the food, sir.'

'Correct! Or where they process and package it at least. Yes, the Enemy have turned that warehouse into a huge food-packaging factory, supplying grub to the supermarkets all across the country. What we don't *know* is who's operating the factory, or who's driving the lorries. Is the whole show just being run by the Enemy themselves? Or have they got a prison-labour force working in there? That's what we need to find out, and the only way to do that is by getting inside the place. So: how do we do that? Launch a full-scale assault? What do you think of their defences, Cadet?'

'Can't see any, sir.'

'No; neither can I. We've been watching this place for weeks and there's never a guard in sight, human or… whatever it is the aliens are. (And that's another thing we don't know: what the blighters actually look like; nobody's ever seen one.) Yes; aside from the barbwire fence, no visible defences—but you can bet they'll still have 'em; they're not going to just leave themselves vulnerable to attack. That's why I've come up with a different plan, Cadet; a plan that will get us right inside that installation without even being stopped…'

'…And this, Cleveland, will be our Trojan horse.'

They stand in a lofty outbuilding which has been converted into a workshop. On the concrete apron stands an articulated lorry, its bodywork in the process of being spray-painted grey by squad members wearing masks and overalls.

'I've told you how those convoys of lorries coming in and out of the enemy base run to a strict timetable; well, we've learnt that timetable. And when D-day arrives, this bus here will join one of the convoys returning to the warehouse—and that's how we're going to get inside. Any questions?'

'Are you sure that's the right shade of grey they're using, sir?'

''Course it's the right shade! No difficulty matching the colour! We've got eyes, haven't we? Tricky thing was the windows. The Enemy vehicles use tinted glass. Found the right model of truck easily enough; trouble was: didn't have the tinted windows. Couldn't find replacements either. We've had to paint on a coating; does the job, as you can see; only drawback is that it's tricky seeing *out* through the bally glass, as well as in! Well, we'll manage! Sergeant Boon's an excellent driver.

'Now, Cleveland: D-day for Operation Pipe-Cleaner's set for ten days from today: you want to take part in the sortie, don't you? 'Course you do! But we can't have cadets on active service!

Not allowed. So if you want to be in on the show, you need to get your first stripe! Solution: a crash course in training! I'll take charge of it myself! Can you handle a crash course, Cleveland? 'Course you can! Well, let's get cracking!'

The redbrick mansion house has been converted into headquarters for Colonel Martin and his platoon of youngsters, and the surrounding parkland is the training ground. The once pristine lawns have been churned into mud; trees have been blasted by shell-fire; networks of trenches crisscrossed with barbed wire have been dug. There are gun emplacements, guard towers and wooden fortresses. A row of what Colin first thought to be corpses hanging from gibbets, are actually just straw dummies used for bayonet practice.

And there is the assault course. Colin's first task, under the Colonel's supervision, is to tackle the assault course.

He's done his limbering up exercises, and is as ready as he'll ever be. Before him stands the first obstacle of the course, a scramble net, alarmingly high.

The Colonel stands off to the right, stopwatch at the ready.

'On your marks…'

Colin braces himself.

'…Get set…

'…Go!'

Colin sets off. Never the fastest of runners, Colin is slowed down further by the heavy army boots. He reaches the net, puts his foot in the first loop and commences climbing.

'No, Cleveland!' roars the Colonel. 'You should jump at the net! Don't start from the bottom!'

Colin pauses. Does the Colonel want him to start again?

'Well don't stop now! Keep climbing!'

Colin resumes climbing.

'Faster, boy! Faster! It's called a scramble net for a reason!'

Colin does his best to climb faster, but he has never been very good with heights, and the further from the ground he advances the more anxious he feels.

‘Keep going, Cadet! Keep going!’

Colin reaches the summit, both of the scramble net and his anxiety. The ground is so far away! With trepidation, he swings a leg over the top. The net bends alarmingly.

‘No, boy! Don’t *climb* over the top, *roll* over!’

It is too late for that now. Having got both legs over, Colin begins his descent, relaxing as he lessens the distance between himself and the ground.

‘That’s enough! Jump!’

Jump? He must be more than ten feet from the ground. Reluctantly, Colin lets go of the net. He falls, lands and rolls.

Back on his feet, he runs to the next obstacle, a smooth log raised on hurdles above a pool of water. He climbs onto the log, and arms out at his sides, commences walking across.

‘Faster, Cadet! Imagine you’re under enemy fire!’

Colin increases his pace, totters and falls into the water.

‘Never mind! No, don’t go back! Onto the next one!’

The ‘next one’ is a heavy net spread across the ground. The object is to crawl beneath it, flat on the ground. Colin worms his way under the net and starts inching forward.

‘Faster, boy! And keep your backside down! Do you want to get a bullet in it?’

Emerging at last from the net, Colin runs for the next obstacle, a six-foot wooden fence.

‘Jump and vault!’

Colin jumps for the fence, hauls himself and vaults over. And lands in two feet of muddy water, gasping for breath.

‘Don’t just stand there, Cadet! Move! Move!’

Colin runs on…

Chapter Thirty-Nine
'What the Devil's Going On...?'

D-day has arrived.

Colin, having completed the physical training programme without collapsing, and learnt how to hold a Sten gun the right way round, has been awarded the rank of private in Colonel Martin's (barmy) army, and can now take part in the raid on the Amazon warehouse, which has been designated Operation Pipe-Cleaner. (It being a time-honoured military tradition to give these operations completely irrelevant names.)

Much to his own surprise, Colin has adapted well to military life. The atmosphere could hardly be described as being feminine and nurturing, but his fellow recruits (not least of all his former tormentors Bradley, Janice and Ferret) have all been friendly and supportive, nor is there that miasma of toxic masculinity which permeated the air at Orville College. (Not so surprising, considering that roughly half of Colonel Martin's 'men' are actually girls.)

And compared to his last place of residence, it's practically paradise.

Looking back on that time, on his ordeal at the sanatorium, the thing that saddens Colin the most is when he thinks about Julia, and that never-to-be-forgotten morning when he saw her hanging body.

If only she had waited; if only she had waited just one more day.

But from Julia also comes hope, because although she was wrong about the Enemy being Nazis, it now seems like she was right about prisoners being forced to work in food-making factories; and what she had said about Natasha and Miss Lantier being made to work in one of the factories: that might be true as well! So Natasha and Miss Lantier might be there at the factory they're going to attack soon!

Seventeen hundred hours. The troops assemble in the briefing room, seating themselves in the rows of chairs facing the podium, Colin sitting alongside Bradley, Ferret and Janice. (Goobie and the twins, the other former members of Chorley's gang of thieves, are not here, having elected to stay in Eastchester when the gang broke up.) Colonel Martin stands on the podium, large-scale map on the wall behind him, pointer stick at the ready.

'Right,' says the Colonel, when everyone has settled down. 'This is your final briefing for tonight's show, so pay close attention. As you know, the objective of Operation Pipe-Cleaner is to infiltrate the Enemy installation. What happens once we're inside will depend entirely on the situation we find there. But first, I'm going to go over just how we *are* getting inside: as you know, the convoys of trucks that go in and out of that installation work to a strict timetable—and we know that timetable. Now we are *here*,' pointing to a mark on the map, 'and the Enemy base is *here*, forty-two miles nor' nor'-west of us as the crow flies, forty-eight miles by road. *This* is the road which passes the Enemy base, and the lorries either approach from the eastern or westerly direction, depending on where they're coming from. The convoy due to return tonight will be approaching from the easterly direction. At precisely twenty-two hundred hours the convoy will be passing this intersection *here*. Our lorry will be stationed there waiting for them. When the last of the trucks has passed the intersection, our vehicle will join the convoy and we'll follow them all the way back to their base. Sergeant Boon will be driving our lorry and I shall be riding shotgun. Now, there is room for one more soldier to sit up front in the cab; I suggest you draw lots to decide who gets the honour. The rest of you, of course, will be sitting in the trailer. In there you won't be able to see what's happening of course, but we've established a communication link between the cab and trailer, so you won't be completely in the dark.' (This 'communication link', as Colin has been shown, consists of two polystyrene cups and several metres of plastic tubing.) 'Any questions so far?'

A trooper raises a hand. 'What happens if we get stopped at the gate, sir? They might work out that they're one truck too many.'

'Good question. Well, if we *do* get stopped at the gate, then we will have to launch our attack from there. I'll give the order and you'll all pour out of the back of the truck guns blazing, just like we've practised. But I calculate the chances of us being stopped at the gate to be very slim. For one thing, the gate is automatic, there are no guards posted there. I think it more likely that, if they *do* work out they're "one truck too many," it won't be until after we're inside the building—and by then it will be too late to stop us.

'This brings me to the second part of the operation: what we do after we have achieved our primary objective and have penetrated the Enemy stronghold. Our actions will be dictated by what the situation is inside the Enemy base, and as we can only speculate as to what that situation might be, we can only speculate our possible courses of action. What we do know is that those lorries deliver the food to the supermarkets around the country; therefore it seems safe to assume that the food is being produced or at least packaged inside the installation: in other words that the installation is primarily a factory. Now, I have no definite proof, so this is pure speculation on my part, but I believe that the factory is being operated by a slave-labour force of human prisoners. If this proves to indeed be the case, then our *second* objective will be to effect the rescue of those prisoners. Ideally, our goal would be to secure the entire installation, overcoming the enemy, capturing them or causing their retreat. If overcoming the Enemy proves to be impossible, if they have the advantage of numbers or firepower, then we ourselves will effect a retreat, taking the liberated prisoners with us. We will most likely need to requisition additional transport in order to achieve this; that will depend on their numbers.'

A hand goes up.

'Yes, Private.'

'What about the aliens, sir? What are they going to look like?'

'That, Private, is one of our main disadvantages, because unfortunately we still have no idea what the aliens look like. But remember,' addressing the whole room, 'however frightening in appearance the Enemy may turn out to be, and whatever superior technology they may possess—doesn't mean the blighters can't stop a bullet! So, when you find yourself facing the Enemy, keep your fingers on your triggers and give the devils what for!'

The Colonel looks at his wristwatch. 'Right. I'd say that concludes this briefing. Time for you men to get some grub; after that you can stand down for a couple of hours. We will assemble at twenty-one hundred hours for embarkation, and zero hour set for twenty-two hundred hours. Alright, platoon dismissed!'

A scraping of chairs.

It is Colin who picks the winning number, and now he sits in the cab of the lorry between Colonel Martin and Sergeant Boon, the latter a robust blonde girl, renowned (particularly among the boys) for being the owner of the biggest set of tatas in the platoon.

They are parked at the side of the road waiting for the convoy of delivery trucks. All eyes are fixed on the intersection ahead. Night has fallen and the surrounding terrain is heavily wooded.

Colin is still worried that their lorry isn't painted the right shade of grey.

The Colonel sits with the window beside him wound down, listening intently. 'I think I hear 'em,' he now announces.

Colin pricks up his ears. Yes, he too can hear the sound of engines, faint but growing more distinct.

'Yes, it's them alright. Start her up, Sergeant, but keep the lights doused until they've passed the intersection.'

Sergeant Boon turns the ignition and the sound of their own engine for a moment drowns out those of the approaching vehicles. But soon they can hear them again and then, driving fast and in tight formation, the fleet of lorries sweeps past the intersection. Three pairs of eyes count them as they pass: three, four, five... and then ten, the expected number, marks the end of the procession, and Sergeant Boon shifts the gears and accelerates forward. Their headlights, illuminating the road ahead are (thank goodness!) clearly visible, in spite of the tinted coating which has been applied to the windscreen.

Smoothly taking the corner, they increase speed and rapidly close in on the taillights of the last of the fleet of lorries. They have now joined the convoy and are *enroute* towards their target, the former Amazon warehouse.

'You're doing fine, Sergeant; you're doing fine...' says Colonel Martin. And then, more briskly: 'You know who I reckon's driving those trucks in front of us, Cleveland?'

'Aliens, sir!'

'Wrong, Cleveland! I reckon it's prisoners from the factory, that's who! But if it's prisoners driving the lorries, then why don't they just use the opportunity to escape? Why are they meekly driving back to their prison? That's what you're thinking, eh?' (Colin wasn't.) 'Well, I'll tell you why: it's because those drivers will have loved ones, friends and family, working in the factory, and they know it'll be the worse for them if they don't come back from their delivery rounds.

'That's one theory, anyway. You know who else might be driving those trucks, Cleveland?'

'Aliens, sir!'

'Wrong again, Cleveland! I mean quislings! Quislings!' Colin is none the wiser, and says so. 'Quislings means traitors, Cleveland! Turncoats; collaborators! Human beings who've betrayed their own species and gone over to the Enemy! Nasty thought, I know; but you'll find there're always some rotten apples in the barrel.'

The wooded terrain has now given way to moorland. Colin can see the headlights of the leading trucks as the road curves to the left ahead of them. And further off, appear the lights that mark the location of their target, the former Amazon warehouse.

'This is it, men, this is it...' murmurs the Colonel. He reaches behind him for the speaking tube (polystyrene cup and plastic cable) and advises the soldiers in the back of their situation.

Very soon they are passing alongside the chain-link fence marking the perimeter of the warehouse installation and the trucks are slowing as they turn in through the gateway. One by one the trucks turn the corner, and now it is their own turn.

The gates remain open for them and now they are inside the compound. Colin half expects their arrival to be greeted with the sound of alarms, but nothing happens, nothing to suggest they have been detected. They follow the access road leading form the gates to the warehouse building, where one of the shutter doors has been raised to allow entrance to the returning convoy.

Following the truck in front, Sergeant Boon guides their truck through the doorway and now they are in a well-lit concrete chamber with a loading bay at the far end and parking spaces for the lorries on either hand. The trucks in front of them peel off to the right and left, parking themselves in two neat rows, cabs facing the walls. Sergeant Boon follows suit, steering their truck into the innermost parking space on the lefthand side. They come to a halt and Sergeant Boon extinguishes the engine.

'Now we'll see what we're dealing with,' says the Colonel. 'Weapons ready, men!' Colin and Boon take up their Sten guns. The Colonel picks up the speaking tube again. 'We're inside,' he announces. 'Get ready to move on my order.'

They wait, eyes fixed on the driver's side door of the truck beside them.

Nothing happens. The cab door doesn't open. The inner doors of the loading bay remain closed. Nobody appears, either from the lorries or from inside the building. Complete silence reigns.

A minute passes.

'What the devil's going on…?' mutters the Colonel. 'Are *none* of them getting out?'

'Don't see any movement, sir,' reports Boon, who has been studying the wing mirror. 'Perhaps we've been detected, sir.'

'Then why hasn't the alarm been raised, eh?' demands the Colonel. 'Why are they all just sitting in their lorries? It doesn't make sense, dammit!'

Another minute passes.

'Well, we can't just sit here all bally night waiting for them to make the first move,' declares the Colonel, picking up his Sten gun. 'Right: here's the drill. You two get out and cover the door of the truck next to us. Soon as you're in place, I'll open the door on my side and order the blighters to surrender. Understood?'

Colin and Boon express their comprehension. Boon opens the driver's side door and jumps down, Colin following. They run around to the neighbouring truck and, taking up positions right and left of the door, train their guns on it. The reflective glass of the side window reveals nothing of the cab's interior.

The passenger door of their own truck swings open

'Alright: come out from there!' orders Colonel Martin crisply, gun pointed at the other cab.

Nothing happens.

'I said come out! We are armed and have weapons trained on you.'

Still no response.

'Alright, Sergeant: open that door!'

Jumping up onto the footboard, Boon pulls the handle of the door and swings it wide open.

The interior of the cab is empty.

Chapter Forty
'Run for it!'

All of the lorries prove to be empty.

The platoon, summoned from the back of the lorry, quickly inspect each of the parked vehicles: there is no sign of an occupant in any of them. The roofs and floors of the cabs are closely examined for concealed exits. The trailers are also carefully checked. Nothing. There seems to be no way in which the drivers of the other lorries could have exited their vehicles without being seen or heard by Colin, Boon or the Colonel—and yet the lorries are all empty and there is not a soul to be seen; the raiders appear to have the place to themselves.

It's uncanny. A feeling of extreme unease assails Colin; and he's not alone in this, as he can see from the anxious looks being exchanged by his comrades. It feels like they've walked into a trap. The very lorries themselves, in their two neatly-parked rows, now look appear sinister and threatening. (That is, with the exception of their own lorry. Parked alongside the vehicles it is supposed to be imitating, Colin can now see that he was right all along and that they *have* painted it the wrong shade of grey: their lorry is lighter in hue than the others.)

Bradley sidles up to him. 'You seriously tellin' me you never saw anyone get out of any of the lorries?'

'Yes!' Colin tells him. 'We didn't see anyone!'

'No-one?'

'No-one!'

Bradley, incredulous, turns to Ferret and Janice for support, Ferret sharing his look of disbelief, while Janice just looks as stolidly indifferent as usual.

'Alright, alright!' calls out Colonel Martin over the increasing mutter of conversation. 'Stop that nattering and fall in on the double!'

The squad falls in, standing to attention in front of their commanding officer.

'That's better,' says the Colonel. 'This is no time to be getting the jitters, men! I know it's a deuced queer state of affairs, but there has to be a reasonable explanation somewhere.'

'Maybe there was no-one in the trucks in the first place, sir,' offers Sergeant Boon.

'What do you mean, Sergeant?' barks the Colonel.

'The lorries might be self-driving, sir. Automatic.'

The Colonel rubs his chin with a gloved hand. 'Hm. Automatic... That could be—But no! No, that's not going to wash, Sergeant; not going to wash. Trucks that can drive themselves: yes. But how do the bally things unload themselves when they reach their destinations?'

'Could be people waiting there to unload them, sir.'

The Colonel's eyes widen.

'By Gad, I think you're onto something there, Sergeant! Good man!' Smiling, he surveys his assembled troops. 'Yes! That has to be the explanation! Self-driving lorries. Well, this is it then, men!

We're inside and the blighters don't know that we're inside! Now to strike while the iron is hot! Remember our objectives: locate the captives, subdue the Enemy, and secure the installation! And as I said at the briefing: when we do make contact with the Enemy, however nightmarish and disgusting the blighters may turn out to look, *don't let yourselves be intimidated by their appearance!* Right! Now follow me!'

And, having successfully revived all the dormant fears of his platoon on that particular subject, Colonel Martin (who, let it be said to his credit, is not one of those officers who leads his troops from behind), leads them up onto the raised area of the loading bay and to the double doors at the rear. Passing through these, they find themselves in a storage area. Stacks of cardboard boxes on either hand, while in front of them a wide central aisle leads to a second set of doors.

Still there is silence. Still there is no sign of movement.

They pass through the second set of doors and find themselves in a huge, lofty chamber. Row upon row of conveyor belt production lines stretch out before them as far as the eye can see. The conveyor belts are inactive and the room appears only half-lit, as though the lighting has been reduced for the night hours.

'Funny,' says the Colonel. 'I would've expected them to have their production lines running 24/7 for an operation as big as this. Well, if the captive workforce have all been dismissed for the night, what we've got to do is find out where they're billeted.'

'Permission to speak, sir.'

'Yes, Sergeant Boon. Go ahead.'

'What if there *isn't* a workforce, sir? The production line looks like it might be completely automated.'

'Automa—? By George! You might be right at that, Sergeant! Yes, it does seem like these blighters go in for automation, don't they? Automated transport, automated production line! Good man, Sergeant! Well, if you're right and there are no prisoners to liberate, that makes our job a jolly sight easier! All we have to do is locate and subdue the Enemy: and with everything automated and no prisoners to guard, chances are there won't be too many of

’em around!

‘Alright, men! They’ve got to be hiding around here somewhere! Fan out and advance! Split up into units of three or four, and stay in sight and sound of the unit next to yours! We haven’t got the luxury of radio, remember? Right, men: forward!’

The platoon divides and advances between the rows of conveyor belts. Colin finds himself with Bradley, Ferret and Janice, his erstwhile school bullies. With Sten-guns at the ready they advance between two of the conveyor belt production lines. In the murky distance of the vast chamber rises the cylindrical form of a huge metal tank or vat.

So there aren’t any prisoners working here after all, thinks Colin. Then Natasha won’t be here, or Miss Lantier. Colin had been hoping for a reunion.

Suddenly there is noise and movement all around them: the conveyor belts have come to life!

‘What the fuck?’ exclaims Bradley.

Guns at the ready, they rapidly survey the area around them, Colin moving more awkwardly than the others. They see other groups of soldiers in a similar state of confusion and alertness, but no sign of any newcomers. As Sergeant Boon has hypothesised, the production line is operating automatically.

Cornflakes. Box after box emerges from the whatsit, moving rapidly along the conveyor belt. Colin passes the whatsit. He can’t believe what he sees: grey blobs, like grey paste or jelly are coming along the conveyor belt and, disappearing into the covered section, are emerging from the other end as boxes of cornflakes!

‘What is that grey shit?’ demands Bradley. ‘And how does it turn into boxes of cornflakes?’

‘It’s not just cornflakes; it’s everything!’ retorts Ferret. ‘Look over here!’

They look. On the conveyor belt opposite the same thing is happening; blobs of grey gunk dropping from the pipe at regular intervals and proceeding into the covered section; only here the blobs are coming out the other end converted into shrink-wrapped frozen chickens.

Moving along, they see the same thing happening again and again. Cans of baked beans. Multipacks of potato crisps. Bottles of detergent. Bunches of bananas. All being produced from the same grey gloop. Colin sees that the pipes dispensing the gloop form an intricate network high above their heads, leading back to that huge metal cylinder standing in the dim recesses. That tank must be full of the stuff!

And now, a new disturbance: shouts coming from across the factory floor; shouts and now gunfire!

'Something's going on over there!' cries Bradley. 'Come on!'

They thread between the conveyor belts heading towards the sounds of disturbance. Colonel Martin's voice can be heard, barking orders, although too far away for the words to be discerned.

And now another sound, much closer. The sound of moving wheels and a whirring electric motor.

'Look out!' yells Bradley

Speeding towards them between the rows of conveyor belts, a forklift truck, driverless, prongs raised for the attack!

Bradley opens fire. Bullets, flashing sparks, ricochet off the truck's bodywork, but do nothing to slow its progress.

'Run for it!'

They run. The driverless vehicle isn't giving up easily, it follows in dogged pursuit! Two aisles later a second forklift appears, blocking their path.

'Christ, they're everywhere!'

They turn back, but their original pursuer is closing in fast!

'This way!'

They vault over the nearest conveyor belt. Colin, who is last, slips and finds himself being carried along by the conveyor belt. Before he has chance to right himself, he is suddenly picked off the ground and lifted him high into the air! It's one of those mechanical arms!

'Help!' cries Colin.

The arm carries him along the production line to where other grabbers are loading packets of cornflakes (it's always cornflakes!) into large shipping cartons, and then sealing them with tape. Colin is dropped into an empty box which, rapidly closed and sealed, plunges him into darkness.

Helpless, he feels himself being lifted, moved forward and then set down again. And then, to the accompaniment of an electric motor, he is moving forward again. He's been loaded onto one of the forklift trucks.

A short journey follows, and then he is set down once again. Now he hears other boxes being put down all around and on top of his own. He's trapped; he's being literally boxed-in!

The sound of metal doors being closed, and then the deep-throated roar of an internal combustion engine igniting. He feels the floor beneath him vibrating. He has been loaded into one of the lorries!

The vehicle starts to move forward, gaining speed. What's happened to the others? Why haven't they come to help him? The lorry slows and makes a turn, then gathers speed once more. Turning out through the factory gates.

Where is he being taken?

Chapter Forty-One
'That's a Really Big Weapon You've Got There!'

Colin would never believe he could have fallen asleep. Situated as he was, trapped and helpless in his cardboard prison cell, being driven to an unknown destination and to an uncertain fate, he would not have believed that he could actually have fallen asleep—but when he wakes up, he is forced to acknowledge that fall asleep is what he must have done.

The first thing that hits him is that his situation has changed. He's still trapped inside his box, cramped and into total darkness, but he is no longer in motion. Has the truck arrived at its destination? And has it been unloaded while he slept? Or, is he still inside the truck?

He listens. Nothing. Not a sound.

Perhaps he *has* been moved, and perhaps there are no longer other boxes stacked on top of his own. Experimentally, he pushes against the upper surface of the box. The flaps are still sealed but they give a little to the pressure of his hand. Yes! It seems like there are no longer other boxes stacked on top of his own! Extracting his knife, he finds the join of the two upper flaps and inserts the blade of his knife. A crack of light appears. Very bright light.

Eagerly, Colin slices the seal all the way across and pushes up the flaps. Intense light floods into the box. Colin screws his eyes shut against the glare. Holding a hand up to shield himself and blinking his eyes, his vision adjusts to the sudden influx of light.

Blue sky! This is what he sees when his vision clears. What he had at first assumed to be artificial light is actually the light of day!

Gripping the edges of the box, Colin slowly raises his cramped and aching body until he is standing completely upright.

He is in a field, a grassy meadow. Looking around him, he sees trees and fields and hills, and in the distance a road. He is alone. His box stands solitary in the meadow.

Relieved and bewildered in equal portions, Colin climbs out of his box and sets about working some life into his leaden limbs. Why has he been left out here in the middle of nowhere?

The only explanation that presents itself is that this is someone's idea of a joke.

His thoughts now turn to his comrades! Did they make it out of the warehouse or not? Were they killed, captured, or did they manage to escape? Perhaps they are all back at the base right this minute, wondering what has become of him…

And what *has* become of Colin? Just how far is he from the base? How far did the lorry travel last night? How long was he in there before he fell asleep? He's not sure. All things considered, he could be just about anywhere in the country, miles and miles away from where he was before.

Well, the first thing he needs to do is get his bearings; to find out where he is. Only then can he decide on his next move. Shouldering his rifle, Colin makes his way across the meadow to the road, and choosing the direction that feels like the right one, sets off along the roadside. The sun climbs the cloudless sky, rapidly warming the air. Colin soon begins to feel uncomfortably warm. He needs food and drink.

After an uncomfortable hour of footslogging, houses appear ahead of him, the first he has seen today. It soon becomes clear that these dwellings mark the outskirts of a town or village. He sees a signboard, announcing the town's name: Afternoon Dream. Funny name for a town. Sign looks brand new, as well. Coming up to it, Colin spots another, older signboard lying face-upwards on the verge; it reads Mansford. That must have been the old name… Wonder why they changed it…

Walking on, Colin finds himself amongst airy streets of modern houses. Everything looks clean, the streets, the gardens of the houses all well-tended; but so far he has seen no people. Colin knows from past experience that in this post-Incident world, you never know what surprises each town you come to is going to have in store for you. But then, surely people who would give their town a nice name like Afternoon Dream aren't going to be bad people? You wouldn't think so, would you? And anyway, even if there is any danger here, Colin can deal with it, can't he? This is the new Colin Cleveland we're talking about! He's a trained soldier now! He's got his Sten-gun!

He hasn't progressed much further when he discovers the first inhabitants: two young girls appear in the road ahead of him. They both just stand there in the road, watching him as he draws nearer, giggling and whispering to each other. The sight—in spite of the giggling which seems to be at his expense—is a reassuring one. The town must be safe if children are allowed on the streets, mustn't it? The two girls look to be aged eight and six respectively; both are pretty, blonde, wearing flowery cotton summer dresses.

Colin stops before them.

'Hello,' he says.

'It's a handsome soldier!' exclaims the older girl, grinning all over. 'Are you back from the wars?'

Colin draws himself up. Of course! He must look very smart in his uniform to these girls!

'Yes, I've been fighting the Enemy,' he announces proudly.

'Ooh,' says the older girl. 'What a brave soldier! Fighting the Enemy! And that's a really big weapon you've got there!'

The younger girl giggles.

'Yes, it's an assault weapon,' Colin tells her.

'I know it is!' The girl runs her hand along the barrel of the gun. 'Ooh, it's so long and hard! I bet it can pump out a lot of rounds!'

The younger girl giggles, cupping her hands over her mouth.

'And I bet it's seen a lot of action, hasn't it?'

'Well, I've only used it for practice, really,' confesses Colin. 'I haven't used it for real.'

The two girls burst into gales of laughter. Colin grins uncertainly. What has he said that's so funny?

'Oh, dear,' says the older girl. 'So your weapon hasn't seen any real action yet? That *is* a pity.' She turns to her friend. 'Isn't that a pity, Flo?'

The younger girl giggles her concurrence.

'And what a waste!' proceeds the older girl. 'If you've got a weapon like that, then you ought to be using it as much as possible! That's what it's there for, isn't it?'

'I'm not sure about that,' demurs Colin seriously. 'I think you should really only use them in emergencies.'

This provokes another fit of laughter from the girls.

'What?' demands Colin, blushing but not knowing why. 'What did I say?'

'Oh, nothing, nothing,' splutters the older girl. She collects herself with an effort. 'So, what's your name, Mr Soldier Boy?'

'Colin,' says Colin. 'What are your names?'

'I'm Lottie,' says the older girl; 'and this is Flo,' indicating her friend.

'And is this town alright?' asks Colin. 'I mean, it's safe here, is it?'

'Oh yes! Afternoon Dream's as safe as houses,' Lottie tells him. 'Did you come here for a reason? Or are you lost?'

'I'm lost,' confesses Colin. 'I want to find out where I am so I can get back to Colonel Martin's army base. And I'm really hungry and thirsty, too. Do you know where I can get something to eat and drink?'

'Oh, we've got plenty to eat and drink. But you need to go to the Town Hall first,' announces Lottie. 'Everyone has to go to the Town Hall first, when they come here.'

'Why's that?'

'Just is. That's how we do things in Afternoon Dream. You've got to be registered.'

'But I don't want to *stay* here,' explains Colin. 'I'm just passing through.'

'Doesn't matter. You've still got to report to Town Hall.'

'Can you take me there, then? I don't know where it is.'

'Yes, we'll show you the way,' affirms Lottie. 'Come on, then! Forward march!'

The two girls take up position either side of Colin, Lottie on his right, Flo on his left, and they set off down the street, the girls walking with exaggerated marching steps, giggling and mimicking military music.

Colin feels embarrassed, not to mention vaguely suspicious. Are they just playing around like little kids do—or are they taking the mickey out of him?

A couple of streets later they come to a three-storey building fronted by a carpark which a sign announces to be the town hospital. They are walking past when a cry alerts Colin. A man in pyjamas has burst through the main doors and is running across the carpark towards them. Three female nurses appear in hot pursuit.

'Oh dear,' says Lottie. 'Looks like we've got a runner.'

Colin and his guides have stopped. The man is running directly towards them. He is bald, skinny, looks to be in his thirties. He seems to be running with difficulty; his pursuers are rapidly gaining on him.

'Help me!' gasps the man. 'For God's sake, help me!'

He staggers and falls. Before he can raise himself, his pursuers are on top of him. Two of the nurses pull him to his feet, pinion his arms. The man's wild eyes meet Colin's.

'Help me!' he cries. 'Don't let them take me back!'

'What's going on?' demands Colin, brandishing his gun and trying to sound authoritative.

The head nurse looks at Colin and then at Lottie. 'Who is this male?'

'He's new. He just walked into town,' answers Lottie.

'Then you should take him to the Town Hall.'

'That's what we're doing.'

'Don't concern yourself with this,' the head nurse says to Colin. 'This man is a disturbed patient.'

The nurses turn to escort their prisoner back to the hospital.

'For pity's sake,' wails the man. 'I don't want to die…'

'Bye-bye Mr Floppy,' Lottie calls after him. 'It'll be over before you know it.'

Flo giggles and the man is led away.

'What was all that about?' asks Colin.

'Oh, he was just a dud,' replies Lottie.

'A dud? I don't understand.'

'It doesn't matter,' is the airy response. 'Come on, Soldier Boy: quick march.'

They resume their progress as before, the girls with arms and legs swinging.

Colin wonders about the man he has just seen. He talked about not wanting to die… Was the man just mad or was he really in danger? Could it be that the hospital here is another evil one, like Dr Noebbals' sanatorium…?

Ahead of them a trio of young girls playing hopscotch in the road. The girls suspend their game when they see the trio approaching.

‘Cor! What have you got there, Lottie?’ inquires one of the girls.

‘It’s a Soldier Boy,’ replies Lottie. ‘We’re taking him to Town Hall.’

They stop when they reach the hopscotch players. The girls look Colin up and down.

‘He really is a soldier!’ enthuses the same girl. ‘Has he shown you his cock, yet?’

Colin’s eyes saucer. *What* did she just say?

‘Oh, no,’ replies Lottie. ‘He’s a “good little boy”, if you know what I mean,’ with a meaning wink.

‘Oh! One of them!’

The girls all giggle.

Leaving the hopscotch girls behind, they enter the shopping district, and now there are more people about. They all seem to be female: women and girls; Colin doesn’t see any men. And as he passes them, these women look at Colin with gleaming eyes and sly, calculating smiles on their faces.

Colin feels increasingly uncomfortable.

A large building with a clock-tower faces the town’s market square; this proves to be their destination, the Town Hall. They mount semi-circular stairs and enter a vestibule. Colin spots a water cooler.

‘Can I have a drink?’ he asks.

‘Of course you can.’

Colin takes one of the flimsy cups, fills it with water from the spigot, gulps it down. He looks at the girls.

‘Can I have some more?’

The girls giggle. ‘You don’t have to ask, stupid! Help yourself.’

Colin drains two more cups and pronounces himself satisfied.

‘Now where do we go?’ he asks.

‘Upstairs. You’ve got to meet the chief councillor. She’ll want to see you first.’

‘She?’ echoes Colin. ‘Everyone here seems to be women. Apart from that man at the hospital. Where are all the men?’

‘Oh, we keep them locked away,’ announces Lottie.

More childish giggling.

They ascend a staircase, traverse a corridor and arrive at an imposing door. Lottie knocks and, without waiting for a response, opens the door.

Facing the door is an ornate desk. And seated at the desk is a woman Colin knows very well: a woman with short brown hair and an oval face.

The recognition is mutual.

‘Why, Colin Cleveland!’ exclaims the woman. ‘I thought you ’ad perished months ago!’

‘Miss Lantier!’

Chapter Forty-Two

‘I Shall Be Your Instructress!’

Yes, the woman behind the desk, apparently chief councillor of the town of Afternoon Dream, is none other than Miss Lantier, Colin’s former French French teacher! (Still French but no longer teaching the language.)

Something seems wrong; something that quickly dampens Colin’s feeling of elation. Here they are, Colin and Miss Lantier, suddenly reunited after having been separated for many months, during which time each has been unsure of the other’s fate; and yet Miss Lantier’s reaction seems oddly restrained. Yes, she is surprised to see him, having believed him to have been killed by the Road Ragers in Kettleworth; but she clearly doesn’t feel the same elation that Colin himself feels (or did feel.) He remembers the occasion of their last reunion: that time he had made it back to the school in Eastchester after escaping from Chorley’s headquarters: she had been all over him on that occasion! Hugging him and kissing him (‘I was so distraught!’); and that reunion had come after a much shorter separation than this one. But she doesn’t leap from her chair, run to embrace him and smother him with kisses; instead she just sits there, smiling at him with that same calculating look he has seen on the faces of the women he has passed in the street just now.

And that is this lack of reaction that dampens Colin's feelings of joy.

But then a sudden thought sends them rocketing back up, and he blurts out excitedly: 'Is Natasha here as well?'

'Alas, no,' is the disappointing reply. 'I really wish Natasha was with us, but she disappeared the very same day I last saw you, and I 'ave not seen her since. We escaped from Kettleworth in a car you see, and we were driving on to the next town, when the car's engine suddenly died. We got out to ascertain what was wrong and then—well, I do not know what 'appened, because one moment it was day and then suddenly it was night, and Natasha: she 'ad vanished; *poof!* She was nowhere to be seen.'

'That's cuz you were both abducted by aliens!' exclaims Colin excitedly. 'And they put you back in different places!'

'And 'ow do you know this, Colin?'

Colin explains.

'And so, you think they came back for her…' says Miss Lantier, thoughtfully. 'It's true I have long suspected there might be a connection between the flying saucers and the incident with the car that day… I wonder what has become of Natasha? I so wish she could be 'ere with us in Afternoon Dream; I know she would approve of the world we have created here…'

'You've created a world…?' echoes Colin, confused. 'How come, Miss Lantier? How did you get to be in charge of this town?'

'Ah! Well, that is a long story, Colin Cleveland, and one which I will unfold in due course.' She gets up from her chair and, walking round her desk, approaches Colin. 'There are many things you will need to learn now that you will be staying here.'

'I'll be staying here, then…?'

'But of course! That was decided the very moment you set foot in this town. But first of all, you won't be needing this—' She takes the gun from Colin. 'Or this,' removing his helmet. 'You seem to have been playing soldiers, yes? Well, that is all over now. Let me ask you something: as you walked through this town, did you perceive any males?'

'Yes, I did see one,' says Colin.

Miss Lantier is taken aback; but then Lottie explains the incident outside the hospital.

'Ah! I see: one of the failures… Well, apart from 'im you did not see any men walking the streets, yes? Only women and girls, yes?'

'Yes.'

'*Bon*. Well, there is a reason for this, Colin: you see, in the town of Afternoon Dream, males are not at liberty to walk the streets as they wish; in fact, they are not at liberty to do anything at all; and this is because in Afternoon Dream males have no human rights; males are just property, slaves. And you, Colin; you, the moment you see foot in this town you relinquished your own human rights, your own personal freedom. We women are the only ones with freedom and rights in Afternoon Dream; we are the masters, and the males are the slaves—and you Colin,' placing a solemn hand on his shoulder; 'you are now also a slave. You comprehend?'

'I think so…' says Colin. 'Does that mean I'll have to do work…?'

'Yes, Colin, it does. You will have to work very hard indeed. And it is work of a kind I believe you have never performed before,' (giggling from Lottie and Flo); 'but you need not fear, for I will personally instruct you in the performance of your new duties.'

'Okay…' says Colin. 'What kind of work is it…? I mean is it… difficult…?'

'No, Colin, I do not believe you will find it difficult, once you get the 'ang of it. Do you recall zat morning at the picnic site, when you observed Natasha and Paul together in the woods? *That* is the kind of work you will be doing, Colin Cleveland,' leaning closer; 'and *I* shall be your instructress!'

The look on Colin's face! 'We-well, m-maybe I shouldn't stay here, then…' he stammers. 'M-maybe I should just g-go b-back to

Colonel M-Martin…?'

'No, Colin; you cannot just leave here. Have I not made this clear? You cannot choose what you wish to do, you have no freedom to choose anymore: you are a slave; you are *my* slave. You cannot choose for yourself; you cannot make decisions for yourself; you can only obey. In this town women command, men obey. Understand?'

'Well, I… I… I think, I…'

'*Bon!* Now I will take you home and we shall commence your training at once! Or at least, as soon as you have bathed. You have a distinctly unwashed aroma about you.'

It is the first opportunity to relax in a bath that Colin has had for some time. At Colonel Martin's base there had only been showers; at the mental hospital there had also only been showers (infrequent and usually cold); his last bath had been at the *Green Man* pub in Wood Haven—and on that occasion, although he didn't know at the time, he was being prepared for sacrifice. And on *this* occasion, he is also being prepared for sacrifice, albeit a sacrifice of a very different kind, which is why although Colin is immersed in a warm bath, fragrant and foamy, is physically relaxed, his mind is not.

As you ought to have realised by now, Colin is no male chauvinist; and the idea of living in a female-dominated society and being Miss Lantier's slave is, in principle, a very appealing one. As a slave he would be protected, he would be looked after, he would be saved from that whole stressful business of having to make decisions for himself—but why does his job involve having to do all that dirty stuff? That sex stuff? *This* is what Colin wonders. And if you're wondering *why* this is what Colin wonders; why he's not champing at the bit like you'd expect any normal, healthy teenage boy to be—well, it's basically because Colin is a touch behind most boys his age when it comes to the S-word. In fact, when back at the sanatorium, Dr Noebbals had accused Colin of being an erection-suppressor, he had actually made a sound diagnosis for once. Yes, Colin has yet to attain the onanistic stage of development—or in other words, of the only orgasms Colin's body has ever performed, Colin himself has never experienced the full benefit, having slept through the performance.

Miss Lantier's home is a swanky modern bungalow on the outskirts of Afternoon Dream. She and Colin had made their way here by e-scooter. Except in the case of emergencies, motor cars are banned on the streets of Afternoon Dream; and not solely on account of the petrol shortage. As Miss Lantier had explained, why should the lives of pedestrians be needlessly endangered by the presence of fast-moving motorised traffic on the roads? In a small town like this in which nobody ever needs to get anywhere in a hurry, fast-moving motorised traffic is just unnecessary.

The bathroom door now opens and in walks Miss Lantier, a stark-naked Miss Lantier. Colin jumps (as far as someone recumbent in a bath-tub can be said to jump) splashing water all over the place.

'Do not disturb yourself,' says Miss Lantier. 'For the moment, I only wish to speak with you. Remain as you are.'

Disturbed already, Colin tries to relax. Wide-eyed, he takes in Miss Lantier's naked form, inevitably comparing it with the only other naked female body he has ever been this close to, that of Julia, his bedfellow that night in the farmhouse. Miss Lantier is of course much smaller than Julia was, smaller both in height and thickness of limb; but although she doesn't look as physically powerful as Julia, her frame is still supple and athletic. Her skin is paler in hue—and also much smoother than Julia's was, as, aside from her pubic hair, Miss Lantier exhibits no body hair.

'I promised to explain to you how I came to be in this town and how I rose to prominence here, did I not?' begins Miss Lantier, seating herself on the toilet seat. 'And although I am in no way obliged to honour any promises made to a slave, I will do so in this case, as I wish you to understand exactly how things have come to be as they are in this town.' Miss Lantier pauses, her face assuming a look of concentration. For a moment it appears to Colin as though she is making a mental effort to recall some important fact she has forgotten, but then a heavy splash in the toilet bowl advises him of the truth, and the heady aroma which quickly fills the room confirms it.

Reaching for the toilet roll, Miss Lantier resumes: ‘It began with the Incident of course; that goes without saying; or to be more exact, it began with the disappearances. Mansford (as this town was still called at the time) experienced the disappearances the same as everywhere else: ’alf of the population suddenly vanished. But in Mansford there was a disparity: many more men than women vanished that night. Why was this? I do not know. I suspect that it was nothing more than coincidence. But zis was the starting point, this disparity. You see, after the initial period of panic and unrest had passed, and things began to settle down, the women started thinking. They began to think about how greatly they outnumbered the men. Of course, the first thing that happened was that they started sharing the men. This is natural; the women craved sex and, as there were not enough males from them to ’ave one each to themselves, they started sharing. And this sharing the men for sex, it began to alter the way the women regarded the men; to change the way they treated them. They started to see the men more and more as merely objects designed for the satisfaction of their physical desires—and along with this feeling, their appetite for sexual gratification began to increase exponentially.

‘This was the stage things ’ad reached when good fortune brought me to this town. Fresh in my mind at zis time were our experiences at Orville College. Our time in that place had started me thinking. The society they had created at Orville College was in essence a very good one—except that there the genders were the wrong way round. By doing what they had done, those boys had merely taken the existing corrupt order of female oppression to extremes—by reversing the genders and enslaving the men, you turn that corrupt order on its head.

‘Before the Incident I had always believed that the solution to the problem of sexual discord was to create a world of complete gender equality: men and women interacting and cooperating in all aspects of life, and with friction between the sexes reduced to a controllable minimum. That is what I thought then. But now, things, they are different. The existing order of things has been overturned, the future is uncertain. New worlds are being created, microcosmic societies. So, why not create a world designed solely for the pleasure and convenience of women?

'This is what I had been thinking. So, imagine my surprise and delight, when arriving here, I discovered the very world I had been contemplating already existing in an embryonic state. When I explained my project to the women here, they embraced it with open arms. We inaugurated the Reduction of Men, completely rescinding their human rights and declaring them to be nothing more than the sexual possessions of the women. This transition proved very easy to achieve; the women had numerical superiority, and as many of the men were already beginning to regress into rutting beasts, the majority of them acquiesced without demur to their state of sexual servitude.

'But very soon the very imbalance of the sexes which had helped to create this Utopia, started to become a problem. With our sexual appetites increasing ever more and more, there were just not enough men to satisfy us. The solution was obvious: we needed to acquire more men—and this is what we 'ave been doing. On occasion, travellers like yourself will wander into the town and be appropriated; but this method cannot always be relied upon, and so we organise raiding parties in which we make midnight attacks upon neighbouring towns and villages to abduct any suitable-looking males. Of course there 'ave been some problems: some of the men we have acquired have proved to be 'duds'. This is our term for males who cannot adequately perform their sexual duties. These unfortunates are taken to the hospital, where every effort is made to increase their potency; those who fail to respond to therapy we have no recourse but to put painlessly to death.

'And of course,' studying a sheet of toilet paper; 'we have had to change the name of the town: "Mansford" had become amusingly inappropriate. It is I who chose the name Afternoon

Dream. And so, Colin, this is the society we have evolved: a matriarchal utopia in which everyone is content, the slaves as much as the masters. And why should they not be? Have men not always been preoccupied with the gratification of their sexual urges? Have they not always measured their own worth by their ability to perform the sexual act? Have they not always rated sexual achievement above any other form of achievement? There is a clichéd scenario in science-fiction story-telling: the Planet of Women; the world where the women are intelligent and dominant, while the males are a subject race of barbarians; a scenario originally created by male writers and with intentions anti-feminist; but perhaps what they had conceived was nothing more than the true natural order of things. Perhaps men were never intended to develop rational, higher thought; perhaps their doing so was just a catastrophic mistake in the course of human evolution. Think about it. With men, instinct and intellect have always been at odds with one another, and with the former often triumphing over the latter. With us women conversely, instinct and intellect have always existed in harmony. So yes, perhaps this demonstrates that males were never intended to evolve more than a rudimentary intelligence, enough to perform simple tasks, and to understand and obey the commands of intellectually-superior women. And perhaps their rising to supremacy by repressing women first by brute force and later by creating a society in which women were denied all means of advancement; perhaps this has all been some evolutionary cul-de-sac; a wrong turning.'

Miss Lantier rises from the toilet, flushes it, and moves to the basin to wash her hands.

'And so, Colin Cleveland, you are to be my house-slave, my pet. I will feed you, shelter you and protect you; but you exist solely for my pleasure, my amusement. It only remains now for me to instruct you in the performance of your duties—and that instruction begins now.'

Chapter Forty-Three
'My House-Slave, My Pet'

The dog days of summer.

If we look into the front room of Miss Lantier's bungalow, we see Colin Cleveland dusting the bookshelves with a feather duster. He wears fashionable street clothes: jeans and t-shirt, sneakers. His hair has grown back to its original length and has been fashionably styled. He smiles while he works, and we see that his mummy's-boy face has a look of unworried self-assurance about it, as though all his former anxieties have been lifted from his shoulders.

And this is exactly what has happened. Colin Cleveland's End of the World Anxiety, his fears for the future, have been expunged from his system; he has embraced the 'living for the moment' ethos of the women of Afternoon Dream. Or more precisely, in Colin's particular case, he is living for his mistress, Miss Lantier. To please her, to make her happy, to earn her praise, has become his mission, his joy, his whole *raison d'etre*.

Yes, Colin is a slave who is happy in his servitude. As Miss Lantier had predicted, he has adapted to the society of Afternoon Dream with such ease and facility, he might as well have been born and raised there. And perhaps it is for this reason that Colin, unlike many of the other slaves, has retained his intelligence and personal identity, and has not begun to regress into a caveman. He is still himself: more mature, sexually experienced, single-mindedly devoted to his mistress, but still essentially Colin Cleveland.

He has not actually seen much of the other slaves, caveman or otherwise. House slaves are not allowed to meet or to mingle in their free time. For one thing slaves do not have any free time, and for another, the mingling of slaves might lead to male-bonding, and male-bonding is an unhealthy institution, one that has been abolished in Afternoon Dream. From what Colin hears, most of the slaves are stupid and happy, but there are exceptions:

some who cannot or will not adapt. They obey and they perform their duties, because they have no choice but to obey and perform their duties; but they remain sulky and discontented.

Rika's house-slave was one of these unfortunates. Colin has met Rika's house-slave because Rika, who is chief clinician at the hospital, is Miss Lantier's lover. Love is one institution that has *not* been abolished in Afternoon Dream; but the women here reserve their love for one another; love is an emotion not to be wasted on mere men; men are just possessions, and although some of the men, Colin being a prime example, may be ardently in love with their mistresses, the most they can hope for in return is the affection of an owner for her pet. And while Colin does receive no shortage of that kind of affection from Miss Lantier, he still could not help feeling jealous when Rika had first appeared, and he had witnessed at first-hand Miss Lantier's much more powerful love for her. Colin's ill-concealed jealousy had been a source of endless mirth for the two women, but nevertheless he had taken the trouble to cure him of his jealousy, by means of mutual intimacy.

As well as Rika, Colin has also been intimate with Gerald, Rika's slave, this being something the slave-owners like to watch. And this is how Colin had come to be acquainted with the recalcitrant slave. Colin had disliked the man from the start, considering his sulky demeanour to be the height of ingratitude—and now Gerald has gone: he has escaped, run away; a rare event in Afternoon Dream, but not unheard of.

Colin, it goes without saying, has no intention of running away; the thought has never so much as crossed his mind. Why would it? For Colin, running away from Miss Lantier, from Afternoon Dream, would be like fleeing from paradise into purgatory.

Nevertheless, fleeing from paradise is just what Colin will shortly be doing, although not through choice. Miss Lantier isn't around to protect her property at the moment, and this absence is about to be exploited by an unexpected arrival.

He could never tell what it was that alerted him. There is no movement, no sound to attract his attention. He senses a change in the atmosphere; a feeling that something is here that was not here before.

He shivers in spite of the heat, and turns his head to face the window.

And there; there at the window grinning in at him is Chorley!

Chapter Forty-Four

'We'll 'Ave Ter Put 'im in the Bleedin' Boot!'

'Hello there, Colin old mate! 'Ow yer been keepin'?'

Chorley. His hair has turned so grey as to be almost white, but otherwise just the same: the same red baseball cap, the same Punchinello grin, the same humorous twinkle in the eyes.

Colin stands horror-stricken.

'What's with that look, then?' says Chorley, assuming an injured expression. 'If I didn't know any better, I'd say yer wasn't best pleased ter see yer old mate Chorley.'

Chorley. Colin had all but forgotten the man's existence. His sudden advent is so unexpected that he struggles to accept the evidence of his own eyes.

'Nothin' to say for yerself?' continues Chorley. 'Well, 'ow about inviting your old mate inter yer 'ouse?' No reply. 'No? Then I tells yer what: I'll just go ahead an' invite meself in, eh?'

Chorley disappears from the window. Colin knows the front door is unlocked. During daytime the front door is always unlocked. There is nothing Colin can do to stop Chorley from just walking into the house. Colin turns and runs. He runs through into the kitchen, where to his further consternation, he sees the bulky form Maclean entering through the back door. Like Chorley, he now sports grey hair, but looks otherwise the same as before. His lugubrious features register no surprise upon seeing Colin; but when Colin tries to dodge past, Maclean grabs him, pinions his arms and marches him back into the living room, where Chorley now stands waiting.

'So yer've reacquainted yerself with me pal Maclean, 'ave yer?' he says. 'That's nice, that is. Yer see, I considered yer might be so overwhelmed at seein' yer old mate Chorley again that yer might lose yer 'ead an' go an' do a runner, so's that's why I 'ad Maclean 'ere cover the rear exit, as it were.'

Colin says nothing.

'Still got nothin' to say?' proceeds Chorley. ''Aven't seen us fer all this time, an' not a word to say. Well I never,' shaking his head sadly. 'Yeah, it's been months, ain't it? since you left us in that bleedin' 'aunted 'ouse. Yes, that was very obligin' of yer, that was; leavin' us there. Didn't think ter come back fer yer old mates, did yer? Well, well, never mind: we got out by ourselves any'ow, we did. Eventually. But as yer can see,' pointing to his grey hair; 'we did not emerge unscathed. As fer the details, well I won't go inter them right now.'

Colin says nothing.

'You've changed a bit yerself, 'aven't yer?' continues Chorley, looking Colin up and down with appraising eyes. 'Yeah, you look like yer've been doin' a spot o' growin' up since I last clapped eyes on yer. Yes… Y'know, since we got outer that bleedin' 'ouse, we've been lookin' all over for yer, me an' Maclean 'ave. Up an' dahn the 'ole bleedin' country, we've been. Ain't that right, Maclean?'

Maclean grunts his assent.

Colin at last finds his voice. 'H-how did you find me…?'

'Ah! Well, that was a stroke o' luck, that was,' says Chorley brightly. 'Run into a bloke what knows you, we did. Former resident o' this 'ere burrer, name o' Gerald. Seems 'e didn't like it much 'ere, so 'e skipped town. Which reminds me: we can save all this natterin' for later, cuz right now we gotta get you out o' 'ere before that French tart gets back. Come on, Maclean.'

They know about Miss Lantier! Colin breaks free from Maclean and runs for the window, the closest avenue of escape. Fast as he is, he no more than gets one foot on the sill when

Chorley and Maclean grab him and pull him back.

'No yer don't, sunshine!'

Colin struggles with all his might. Never has a convict fought so valiantly against being rescued from incarceration! However, it is a case of two large men against one small boy, and between them they are able to drag the struggling Colin across the room and out through the front door.

'Bleedin' 'ell! 'E's bloody stronger than 'e used ter be, an' no mistake!' exclaims Chorley. 'You been in the bleedin' army or somethin'?'

Colin's fist swings and catches Chorley under the jaw. He makes another bid for freedom, but is caught again. The two men start dragging him towards their car, which is parked a few doors further down the street. Colin vainly screams for help, but many of the houses around here are untenanted, and it seems that no-one hears him.

'We'll 'ave ter put 'im in the bleedin' boot!' declares Chorley. ''E'll be too much of an 'andful in the back seat!'

With Maclean holding Colin, Chorley opens the boot, starts throwing out the clutter stored within. Amongst the junk is a roll of duct tape. Chorley displays it triumphantly.

'This'll do the trick!' He turns to Colin. 'Now, 'old still.'

Colin has no intention of holding still. Knowing that he is about to be made helpless, he only redoubles his attempts to escape.

'Alright, then,' says Chorley. 'If yer wanna play it like that, then yer doesn't leave me no choice. This is fer yer own bleedin' good!'

He drives his fist into Colin's stomach. Colin jack-knifes. The pain is excruciating. He falls to the road, and is powerless to resist as the two men first tape his wrists together behind his back, then secure his ankles. A final piece of tape is placed over his mouth, and Colin is hefted and folded into the car boot.

'Stop!'

It is Miss Lantier, on her e-scooter, racing towards them. She is the last thing Colin sees before the lid descends, consigning Colin

to stifling darkness and wretched misery.
Miss Lantier!

It has been the author's policy throughout this chronicle to only describe those events of which Colin is either a direct participant or a first-hand witness; and so, much as I would love to, I cannot describe the thrilling chase that ensues as Miss Lantier sets off in determined pursuit of Colin's abductors. But, given that Colin's abductors are driving a motor car with a two hundred horsepower internal combustion engine, while Miss Lantier is riding on an e-scooter with a maximum speed of fifteen miles per hour, it's not a chase that lasts very long.

Colin cries horizontal tears of frustration. The stifling atmosphere of the boot increases as the car ejects mile after mile of road. He is being slowly roasted and what with the confinement and the tape over his mouth, he finds it increasingly hard to breathe. Why did this have to happen? He is being taken away from paradise; from a comfortable life of simple animal pleasure in which he didn't have to worry, didn't have to think; where he was pampered, petted and cared for. Why hadn't Miss Lantier come back in time? Why hadn't she come back in time to save him?

Miss Lantier's French class. Stiflingly hot in the classroom. Must be near the end of summer term. Colin is broiling in his World War Two battledress. Why is he wearing his battledress in class? Did he get dressed in the wrong clothes? Then he sees that all the class are all wearing battledress. All except Miss Lantier, who is stark naked of course, like she always is. But then Miss Lantier's not in Colonel Martin's army. She doesn't have to take part in the attack. It's time to charge! The Enemy are right across the field! Fix bayonets! Charge! Bayonets fixed, they charge across the blasted ground. Black flying saucers fly low overhead, raining death on them. Heat and explosions all around Colin. Who's that in front of him? Natasha! He's found her at last! He runs after her. An explosion right in front of him. It knocks him off his feet. He's falling, the air is burnt away, he can't breathe—

Blue sky fades in, and Chorley's concerned face is looking down at him. He is lying on soft turf and he can smell a river close by.

'Sorry, mate,' says Chorley. 'There I was, so concerned abaht getting' you clean away from that den of iniquity, I bloody forgot it'd be like an oven for yer locked up in that boot…!'

Chapter Forty-Five
'I Want To Go Back!'

'…And we went to this town where everyone was angry all the time; an' I mean *really* angry, like 24/7. All red-faced and shoutin' an' swearin' at each other, they was. Funny thing was they never got violent or nothin'. It was all jest verbal, like; jest the shoutin' an' swearin'. They shouted an' swore at me and Maclean an' all, the 'ole time they was 'elpin' us stock up with supplies, an' then, when we went, they shouted an' swore at us while they waved us bon voigee. Bonkers place, it were.'

'I'm not interested.'

It is evening and they are sitting round the table in the old-fashioned kitchen of an old-fashioned farmhouse they have found tenantless. On the table lies the remains of the meal they have just eaten, and Chorley is now making himself comfortable with a bottle of scotch, while Maclean makes himself less comfortable, drinking only sparingly—and as for Colin, he can't really be described as being comfortable at all, having been securely tied with ropes to the chair on which he sits.

Colin has proved an obdurate and ungrateful rescuee. After recovering from his near-asphyxiation in the boot of the car, he had immediately taken to his heels, displaying the homing instincts of a cat by making a beeline towards his recent town of residence. But he had only run about one hundred metres before being recaptured, because he was still too week to run very fast. He had been dragged kicking and screaming back to the car where that convenient roll of duct-tape (perhaps the car's previous owner had been a serial killer) had been utilised once more, although this time Colin had been given more comfortable quarters on the back seat of the car.

And now, he sits wrapped in a cloak with chilly sullenness, rebuffing all Chorley's attempts to engage him in conversation.

'An' then there's them Cyber Flashers. Did you ever run inter them? Gangs of 'em, there are, roamin' the countryside; wearin' these raincoats, an' indecently exposin' themselves at everyone they meets. They calls 'emselves Cyber Flashers cuz they're blokes what used ter like sendin' dick pics all the time, back when they still 'ad the internet. And cuz they can't do that no more, they go around in these packs, flashin' at everyone instead! Bonkers, ain't it? Bloody bonkers! Some people, eh?' Chorley shakes his head, chuckling.

'Don't care,' says Colin sulkily.

Chorley sighs, turns to Maclean. 'You think he'd show a bit more gratitude, wouldn't yer? After we gone to all the trouble of rescuin' 'im from that den of iniquity.'

'Oh yes,' sneers Maclean. 'Must've been hell on Earth for the poor kid; having to spend all his time having sex with a load of beautiful women like that.'

Chorley bursts into laughter. 'That's a good one!' he splutters. ''E's a card, Colin, ain't 'e? Yer must o' been missin' that sense o' humour of 'is!' And then, after recovering his composure: 'No, but seriously. We knows what was goin' on in that place: we got the 'ole story from that geezer Gerald; an' 'ee didn't like it there, did 'e? 'E got outer there first chance 'e got, dint 'e? Cuz he knew that what them women was doin', that was just abuse, that was. Slavery and abuse. *'E* knew. But you, Colin, old mate, you don't get it cuz yer still too young. That French bird, she got round yer, cuz she used ter be yer school teacher like; an' you trusted 'er, dint yer? Brainwashin'; that's what it was: brainwashin'. But it ain't right, is it? It ain't right, turnin' people inter slaves like that, robbin' 'em of their dignity. It jest ain't right. Don't yer see?'

'Women have the right to avenge themselves for the countless centuries of abuse, repression and degradation they have suffered at the hands of men. All men carry with them the accumulated guilt of their forefathers and must suffer and endure the punishment that is their just desert.' Colin reels off these words, rapidly, mechanically, and then falls silent again.

'Well, I'll be...' Chorley's voice trails off. Clearly words have failed him as to just what it is he will be. He turns to Maclean for support. 'Did you 'ear that? Did you 'ear it? Brainwashing. Brainwashing, pure an' simple. If that don't prove it, I dunno what does.' To Colin: 'Don't yer see? You been brainwashed, talkin' like that; brainwashed by bra-burners—an' a bunch of nymphomaniac bra-burners at that! Lumme! Well, I'm glad I got you outer that place, and when that there brainwashin' starts to wear off, I reckon you'll be glad an' all.'

'No I won't,' Colin, doggedly. 'Let me go. I want to go back!'

Chorley ignores the request. 'D'you know where you are?' he inquires. 'I mean right now. No? Well, I'll tell ya where you are: just a stone's throw away from Norton-Braisley, that's where we are. Remember Norton-Braisley? That place you was so keen to get to before, on account of your sister bein' there? Do you even remember yer bleedin' sister? I bet you ain't been thinkin' of much of late, 'ave yer? No, cuz all you can think about is that French tart who's been screwin' yer bloody brains out. But what about yer sister, eh? Yer own flesh an' blood...? You get it now? D'yer see what bein' in that place 'as done t'yer? It's gone an' made you forget about everythin' that's important to yer, that's what it's done!'

This time Colin offers no short, sharp response. The thrust has struck home.

'Y'see?' Chorley, triumphant, reading his expression. 'Well, tomorrer we're gunna take you to Norton-Braisley, me an' Maclean, jest like we always said we would; an' it's only gunna take us about an hour. So, you jest think about that one for a bit; you jest think about that...'

'...So yer seriously tellin' me that all this booze in this 'ere bottle was made outer this grey gunk…?'

'Yes, and not just the drink; the bottle as well.'

It's much later now, and Colin has become more communicative, not because he has become reconciled to his situation, but because there's little else to do (and he has hopes that a degree of cooperation might lead to him being freed from his restraints.) He has just been telling them about the ill-fated raid on the Amazon warehouse in which he took part.

'An sho it ain't the real thing, then? Ish all fake?'

'No, it *is* the real thing,' Colin tells him. (He knows this because back in Afternoon Dream, after they'd heard Colin's story, they had analysed samples of the supermarket food, and found it all to be normal: no additives or abnormalities, everything natural that should be natural. It seems the grey substance doesn't just imitate food, somehow it becomes the real thing. Primordial soup, Miss Lantier called it.)

Chorley, by now much the worse for drink, is in ebullient spirits. 'Blimey…' he says, eyeing Colin blearily. 'You been through it all, ain't yer? You been 'ere, there an' bleedin' everywhere… You been in the loony bin; you done mitary… military shervish; an' you been a bleedin' shex shave…slave, in a town what's run by women… Rather you 'an me…' He trails off, stares into his empty glass. 'Still!' he exclaims, apparently finding inspiration in that helpful drinking vessel. 'Still, it washn't all with women, wash it? Eh? Eh? 'Eard a thing or two from that bloke Gerald, we did! Kissun tell! You done it withim an' all, ain't yer? Eh, eh?'

A drunken lascivious grin has spread itself over Chorley's face, an all too familiar drunken lascivious grin, a grin Colin remembers from that night in the warehouse, back in Eastchester. Time, and the rapid march of events has done much to cure Colin of the after-effects of that night—but one thing it has not cured him of is his aversion for the other person involved.

He does not like the way the conversation is going.

'Sho… C'mon then: wish one d'yer like best, eh? With a bird or with a bloke? Wish one yer like besht?'

‘I only did that because Miss Lantier wanted me to,’ says Colin, frowning.

‘What? Yer did it just cushee told yer to?’ says Chorley, with incredulity, real or affected. ‘Jusht cushee an’ ’er leshbo mate wannid ter watch?’

‘Yes! I’d do anything that makes Miss Lantier happy! Anything!’

Chorley sits back in his chair. ‘Well, then… An’ would yer like ’ave duunit with anyone yer Mish Lannier told yer to do it with…? Would yer… Would yer ’ave dunnit with… with ol’ Chorley….?’

Colin’s face wrinkles with distaste.

‘Don’t be stupid! Miss Lantier would never want me to do anything with you! She *hates* you! She hates you!’

Colin spits out the words, and Chorley bridles. ‘Whadjer mean she *’ates* me? She ain’t never even bleedin’ *met* me, ’as she? Not unlesh you count today, an’ wither at the other end of the bleedin’ street, we washn’t exactly introduced, wash we?’

‘Yes, but I’ve told her all about you!’ retorts Colin.

‘Oh, yeah: you *told* ’er, ’aven’t yer? You bleedin’ *told* ’er!’ Chorley leaps to his feet, knocking his chair over backwards. ‘Spreadin’ lies abaht me be’ind me back! Thash what you been doin’, ant yer? Badmouthing me! Jusht like you did wi’ that girl you used ter fancy, that Paki bitch! Told ’er a lotter liesh abaht me an’ all, dint yer?’

‘I only said what was true!’

‘No you dint!’ snarls Chorley. ‘You twished it… twishted it all arahnd! You… you—’

‘Give it a rest, for Christ’s sake!’ Maclean has risen to his feet. He grabs hold of Chorley’s arm. ‘You’ve had way too much to drink and you don’t know what you’re talking about! So just give it a rest and go to bed! Come on: I’ll take you upstairs.’

Chorley, swaying on his feet, flails his arms, trying to shake off Maclean’s restraining hand. ‘No! I don’t bleedin’ wanna go ter bed! I wanna… I wanna…!’

‘Oh, come on! You’re about to pass out drunk anyway! Let’s

get you to bed!'

Chorley, his rage subsiding as quickly as it arose, allows himself to be guided out of the room, muttering confused half-sentences. Colin hears their footsteps ascending the stairs.

Presently, Maclean returns, and silently unties Colin, escorts him upstairs to the airing cupboard, shoves him inside, ties him up again and shuts the door.

Chapter Forty-Six
'Try Asking Him What Happened to that Girl of Yours!'

And so Colin spends the night locked in a cupboard, lying foetal in cramped darkness, his wrists and ankles bound together.

He has a lot to think about. Chorley's words and this alleged proximity to Norton-Braisley have opened up the gates of memory. For the past few weeks Miss Lantier has been his goddess, his world, the sole focus and concern of his mind and his body. To make her happy, to pamper to her every whim, has been his only reason for existing. Everything else, anything that didn't relate to Miss Lantier, had just drifted out of his conscious mind, dismissed as unimportant, irrelevant.

But now his sister has been called back to his mind (and what *she'd* have to say about his relationship with Miss Lantier…!) and from her the rest of the tapestry of his recent life has rewoven itself. Natasha. To think he could even have forgotten about her… Natasha who was always the love of his life. He feels like he has betrayed her, betrayed her through neglect. Natasha with her beautiful raven hair, so straight and so black; that smile of hers, so warm and so genuine; her beautiful hands, brown on one side, pink on the other, her feet the same… How could he have forgotten about her? And where might she be right now? The aliens who took her away might have brought her back by now. It probably happened ages ago. Aliens don't abduct people for good;

they always bring them back again. They probably put Natasha back close to where she was when they took her, near Kettleworth and Heatherly… What would she have done? What would Natasha have done, after she got back and she couldn't find either him or Miss Lantier? Might she have gone to Norton-Braisley to look for him? Had Colin ever told Natasha that Norton-Braisley was where his sister was, and that he'd thought about going there to find her? He searches his mind… Maybe that last night they were together, that night at the bungalow in the woods… Had he told her about his sister then…?

His thoughts slip away from him, Natasha dissolving into Julia, Julia into Miss Lantier, and he warmly melts into the women's combined embraces…

Colin is awoken by the opening of the cupboard door and the sudden irruption of daylight.

'What did you lock 'im in the bleedin' cupboard for?' demands Chorley.

'You told me to make sure he couldn't escape!' retorts Maclean.

'Yeah, but you still could've put 'im in one of the bleedin' bedrooms, for cryin' aht loud! He couldn't have escaped from any bleedin' room tied up like this! Gor blimey!'

After breakfast, they set off on their journey to Norton-Braisley.

Another canine day, the air stagnant and oppressive beneath a colourless hazy firmament. The road they are travelling takes them across parched moorland. And soon they will be in Norton-Braisley, the city which—on and off—has been Colin's objective ever since he left Eastchester behind. The imminence of his arrival at this long-sought destination seems hard to credit; it also forces Colin to confront the possibility, long pushed aside but always there at the back of his mind, that the sister he hopes to be reunited with might not even be there…

And even as his mind looks ahead, picturing what might happen when he reaches Norton-Braisley, another part of him just wants to jump out of the car and start running back towards Afternoon Dream. Miss Lantier has imprinted herself on Colin to such a degree that her lodestone influence over Colin is not one that is going to be vanquished overnight; and he is painfully conscious of the fact that every mile the car travels takes him further and further away from her.

Meanwhile silence prevails within the car. With Chorley feeling ill-disposed towards Maclean, Maclean feeling ill-disposed towards Colin, and Colin feeling ill-disposed towards both of them, they are not a convivial party. And now the car, perhaps infected by this atmosphere of general ill-disposition, chooses this moment to malfunction. A single cough, and then the smooth noise of the engine becomes a terminal rattle. Simultaneously smoke starts to escape from under the bonnet.

'Oh, now what's 'appened?' groans Chorley.

Maclean slams on the brakes, kills the engine.

They all get out of the door and Maclean opens the bonnet. More smoke billows out.

'Well, what's wrong, then?' demands Chorley, hands on hips.

'I don't know, do I?' is the sulky response.

'Whaddaya mean yer don't know?' retorts Chorley. 'Yer surpposed to know abaht motors, ain't yer?'

'I know how to drive them,' says Maclean. 'I can change the oil, I can recharge the battery, but I don't know how to fix the engines.'

Chorley throws his arms up. 'Well that's jus' bloody marvellous, ain't it?' he exclaims. 'Knows 'ow ter drive but knows bugger all abaht engine maintenance. So whadda we do now, Einstein? 'Ow far are we from where we're going?'

'We're miles from anywhere,' Maclean tells him. 'Middle of nowhere.'

'Oh, that's jest beautiful, ain't it?' declares Chorley, eyes ranging over the bleak landscape. 'It jus' gets better an' bleedin' better, don't it? So now we've got ter 'oof it ter bleedin' Norton-Braisley, 'ave we?'

'As if you care whether we get there or not,' mutters Maclean.

'An' whass that surpposed ter mean?' requests Chorley. ''Course I care whether we get there! It's where Colin wants ter go, ain't it? Ter find 'is sister.'

'Yeah,' snorts Maclean. 'And the only reason you've been willing to take him there is because you know damn well that he's probably not going to find his sister when he gets there. Because you don't *want* him to find his sister, do you?'

''Course I do! Why shouldn't I want 'im to find 'er?'

'Oh, come off it! If Colin meets up with his sister, do you think she's gunna put up with you hanging around? Like that's going to happen! She'll just take one look at you and give you your marching orders.'

A silence follows, during which Chorley surveys his comrade with no friendly expression. And then he says, speaking slowly: 'Yer gettin' a bit lippy there, old son. An' I can't say I care fer it; I can't say I care. I calls that ungrateful, I do. I calls that no way ter pay yer old pal back, after all 'e's done for yer.'

Maclean slams down the bonnet cover. He looks Chorley in the eye and his usually morose features tremble with anger. 'After all you've done for me? All *you've* done for *me?* What the hell have you *ever* done for me? It's always been *me* waiting hand and foot on *you*, hasn't it? Maclean do this, Maclean do that! You made me your dogsbody while we were inside, and I've been your dogsbody ever since we got out! And what did I ever get in return? You were never grateful, never. Not one word of thanks. You just took me for granted, like it was right for someone like you to be waited on by someone like me! You're bloody toxic, that's what you are! A parasite! You're too selfish to even know what a friend is. And if that wasn't bad enough, you became fixated on this little squirt here! No feelings for someone who's been with you through thick and thin, who's shared a cell with you for five bloody years; *oh* no! One look at that skinny schoolkid's mummy's-boy face, and that's all you can bloody think about! You broke up the gang because of him, and you've had us chasing up and down the whole bloody country looking for him! Well, you've got him now, haven't you? You've found him!

Congratulations! He's all yours, isn't he? So, what do you need me for? I'm just the fifth bloody wheel, aren't I? Well fine; you can have him if he wants you! Which, by the way, he bloody *doesn't*. I've had enough; I'm getting out of here! Goodbye and good bloody riddance!'

And with this, and without waiting for a reply, Maclean turns and sets off along the road, back the way they came, walking with dogged footsteps.

'Get back 'ere!' Chorley yells after him. 'Where'd yer think yer going?'

Maclean, already a fair distance away, stops and turns round—but it's Colin he addresses.

'And you: why don't you try asking him what happened to that girl of yours! Yeah, that morning she disappeared, when you were so sure she'd been abducted by aliens! Ask him what really happened to her! Go on: ask him!'

Having fired this parting shot, Maclean resumes his retreat along the road.

This Parthian shot has found its target. Colin stares at Chorley, and Chorley refuses to meet Colin's eye. A suspicion, vague and unformed, that has been nagging at Colin's mind since the night before, begins to assert itself, to take on form.

'What was that about Natasha?' asks Colin, his voice quiet, controlled. 'What did he mean?'

Chorley shrugs uncomfortably. 'Didn't mean anything, did it? Just tryin' ter stir things up, 'e was. Don't pay 'im no mind.'

Colin slowly shakes his head. 'No… No, he *did* mean something… That morning… at the bungalow in the woods… Natasha disappeared… and then… and then *you* turned up… You saw her, didn't you? While I was still asleep: you saw Natasha! What did you do to her?'

'I didn't do nothin'!' snaps Chorley, throwing Colin a nervous glance and then quickly looking away. 'It's just Maclean stirrin' things up, I tell yer! I never set eyes on that girl in me life!'

'You're lying!' Colin's voice trembles, on his face a look of growing horror. 'Natasha's mixed-race; she's got brown skin.

When we were in Eastchester and I first told you about her, I never mentioned that. I know I didn't, because I remember thinking how, from her name, you probably just thought she was white. And last night, when you were calling her names, you said she was Pakistani. She's not Pakistani, but someone who saw her might think she was. That means you must've seen her. You've *seen* her!'

'Alright, I *saw* 'er! So bleedin' what? Christ! Only reason I never told yer abaht it was cuz I didn't wanna 'urt yer feelin's! But if yer really wanna know what 'appened, then fine: I'll tell yer! Truth is, she ran off; that's what happened! She went an' deserted yer, she did! That boyfriend o' 'ers turned up, an' she ran off with 'im! Ran off an' left you be'ind cuz she's no bloody good fer yer! *That's* what happened!'

'You're lying!' screams Colin. 'That wouldn't have happened! Natasha and Paul didn't like each other anymore! They *hated* each other! You did something to Natasha, didn't you? You did something! When I woke up that morning, I knew something was wrong! I could feel it! I couldn't find Natasha anywhere, and then *you* turned up! And you already knew I was there, didn't you? Cuz you'd been there before; you'd been there before and you'd met Natasha! What *happened?* You... you killed her, didn't you? You *killed her!*'

'It was your bloody fault!' snarls Chorley, at bay. 'It was you badmouthin' me what set 'er off! She went mental, she did! She 'ad this bloody great knife an' she came at me with it! It was self-defence!'

'I don't believe you! She wouldn't have just attacked you like that!'

'I'm tellin' yer she did! We was drivin' around, lookin' for you, and there she was, standing at the edge of the road, outside that 'ouse. We stopped to ask 'er if she'd seen you, and then she worked out 'oo I was an' she totally lost it, she did! Started callin' me all these bad names, tellin' me that she 'ad you now, an' she wasn't gunna let me get my filthy 'ands on you again! An' she came at me with that bloody great knife! That's what she did! An'

I struggled with ’er, an’ I got the knife outer ’er ’ands an’… an’ it was over in a second, it was! Just like that. It were self-defence, I tell yer! It were *self-defence!*’

By now, tears streaming from Colin’s eyes. His whole body trembles as he mutely shakes his head.

‘An’ then… Well, we ’ad to get rid of—we ’ad to ’ide ’er, didn’t we? We didn’t want you seein’ what ’ad ’appened… An’ then, when we got back, there you was, sittin’ on the doorstep… An’ I was all ready to tell yer that she’d gone an’ run off wi’ that boyfriend of ’ers; but turns out I didn’t ’ave to, cuz you’d got that bee in yer bonnet about ’er bein’ taken off by one o’ them flyin’ saucers…’

Eyes imploring, he takes a step towards Colin. Colin, still crying and shaking his head, backs away from him, edging round the side of the car.

‘Now don’t do that, mate…’ begs Chorley. ‘You don’t need ter be scared of old Chorley… It was an accident… I never wanted it to ’appen like that… It was an accident… No-one’s ter blame… I mean, I wouldn’t do nothin’ ter upset yer, would I…? Not on purpose, like… All I ever wanted ter do is ’elp yer… That’s all… I jest wanted to be yer pal and to ’elp yer… So, don’t back away from old Chorley… Don’t back away… I ain’t gunna ’urt yer… I mean, I… I love yer, I do; I bloody love yer…’

Colin turns and runs.

Chapter Forty-Seven
‘Colin… I’m Beggin’ Yer…’

Six months ago Colin had run away from Chorley, and six months ago Colin hadn’t believed he could outrun his pursuer for long. But that was then, and Colin has been through a great deal in these past six months and he is stronger than he was before.

Along the road he runs, with Chorley some distance behind.

All this time he has been with that man… All of that day, the day he actually killed Natasha, right up until he had left them in the haunted house… And now, since yesterday, when Chorley came back into his life and snatched him away from Afternoon Dream and Miss Lantier… All this time he has been in the company of Natasha's murderer and he hasn't known it…

Illogically, Colin thinks with guilt and regret of that birthday wish he forgot to dedicate to Natasha's safety, and that if he *had* made that wish, then maybe Chorley would never have killed Natasha (an event which happened several weeks prior to his birthday) and she would still be alive today…

Breasting a rise Colin sees the road ahead curving off to the right, while before him a gravel track branches off from it, crossing the heath towards some rising ground where a grove of trees mark the horizon.

Colin takes to the gravel track, towards the cover of the thicket.

Chorley calls after him.

He reaches the thicket. Beyond the trees the ground opens up, the gravel road sloping towards a gritstone quarry, a vast amphitheatre girt by towering grey cliffs. A landscape of hills and defiles, and the rusting forms of dormant mechanical behemoths, it offers a wealth of hiding places and Colin heads towards it.

'Colin!'

Colin looks back. Chorley, way behind him, has paused, clearly out of breath.

'Come on, Colin! Let's just stop this runnin' arahnd! It's jest stupid, it is!'

Colin's only answer is to keep running. He joins the furrowed track descending the cliff-face. Down to the bed of the quarry. Ahead of him are two long wooden huts, scattered around them a litter of machine-parts. Colin races towards them. Behind the cover of the nearest hut, he stops, peers round the corner. Chorley is lumbering down the track; he already looks exhausted.

Colin tries the door of the hut. Locked. He looks around and selects a rusting, unidentifiable piece of machinery and takes cover beneath it, lying flat on the ground.

He waits, and soon Chorley appears, panting and dripping with sweat. He staggers to a halt, stooping to catch his breath.

'Alright then,' he pants. 'I don't... see yer runnin' so... yer must be hidin'. Now, let's jus' stop... playin' silly buggers, eh? It's too bleedin' 'ot fer all this malarkey! Now jest... be a smart boy an' come on out!'

Colin stays where he is.

'Oh, come on, mate!' expostulates Chorley. 'I know why you're mad at me, but it was self-defence, weren't it? An accident! 'Ow many times do I 'ave ter keep tellin' yer that...? An' she was no good fer yer, any'ow! She wouldn't uv stayed with yer...'

He pauses again, looking around, while Colin watches from the shelter his hiding-place.

'Alright then,' says Chorley, finally. 'If yer really wants ter play 'ide an' seek, then alright: I'll come lookin' for yer.'

Chorley moves to the nearest hut and tries the door. Finding it locked, he begins a systematic survey of the discarded machine-parts, hunkering down to check underneath every one of them. His search brings him ever closer to Colin's hiding place.

Time to move.

While Chorley is hunkered down, inspecting a rusting dumper truck, Colin slithers out from his place of concealment, starts running deeper into the quarry.

'Oi!' comes Chorley's voice. 'C'mere!'

Colin looks back. Chorley is in pursuit once more.

'Stop runnin' fer Christ's sake!'

Colin runs on, scrambling over piles of slag and shale, skirting round cranes and excavators. Ahead a conveyor-belt raised on a network of metal supports intersects his path. Running horizontally at first, the belt then angles upwards to feed a huge silo standing against the cliff face. Colin can see no sign of a second access road on the surrounding cliff-face; the only exit from the quarry is the road by which he entered.

Unless...

Snatching another glance over his shoulder, Colin sees Chorley still pursuing him, slipping and stumbling over the rough terrain.

Colin, redoubling his efforts, puts on a spurt, his objective the conveyor belt. Reaching it, he mounts the support structure and starts to climb the jungle gym of spars and girders. Reaching the summit, he hoists himself up onto the conveyor belt.

He looks down. Chorley has reached the foot of the structure. He looks up at Colin.

'Get down from there, yer daft…!' pants Chorley. 'You tryin' ter kill yourself or somethin'?'

Colin offers no reply. He sets off along the conveyor-belt, running as fast as he can along its concave surface. It stretches off ahead of him, its course horizontal for some distance, before inclining skywards. His eyes follow its course up to the silo. Yes, the roof of the silo looks to be about level with the top of the cliff.

Reaching the end of the horizontal section, Colin looks back—and sees Chorley. With terrifying tenacity Chorley has come after him; he has actually climbed the support structure, and is pulling himself up onto the track.

Chorley is not giving up.

Colin starts to ascend the diagonal section of the track, endeavouring to increase his speed; but as he climbs, and with the ground falling away on either side of the conveyor belt, Colin is assailed by stabs of vertigo. Increasingly unsure of his balance, he is forced to drop down on all fours. Thus he continues his ascent, the fierce heat of the sun, unrelieved by the gauzy curtain which serves only to diffuse the strength of its light, hammer down on his back, while the metal trough of the track burns the palms of his hands.

Finally, he reaches the summit where the conveyor belt terminates at the lip of the opening at the top of the silo, the maw into which it feeds its mineral freight when in motion. Colin rises unsteadily to his feet. Now he has to climb up onto the roof of the silo. Anxious as to how far behind Chorley might be, he looks down. He looks down and the sight of Chorley doggedly ascending towards him disturbs him less than the dizzying perspective of the track plunging down to the ground alarmingly far below. Vertigo hits him, his legs buckle and he drops to his hands and knees, holding onto the edges of the conveyor belt for dear life.

But he can't stay like this. Chorley is closing in. Subduing his fears, he rises to his feet once more. The opening in the silo is larger than he anticipated, taller than himself, so that the lip of the silo roof is only just within arm's reach. He will have to pull himself up, and with the opening yawning before him, no hope of a foothold to assist him.

But there's no time to waste. He reaches out, gains a purchase on the roof, first one hand and then the other, and with a supreme effort, heaves himself up onto the roof of the silo. Unsteadily, he stands up. He looks down, sees Chorley closing in fast. He needs to hurry now. Chorley, much taller than he is, won't have any difficulty climbing up onto the roof.

He turns to face the cliff wall. From down on the ground, the silo had looked as though it had been positioned flush with the cliff-face; but now he sees that it isn't nearly as close as he had anticipated: there is a gap of about six feet between them; and to Colin that six-foot gap seems more like a yawning abyss.

With the thought that he has climbed all this way just to reach a dead-end, panic surges over him. Chorley is just below him now. Colin would rather just jump to his death than have to face Chorley up here. He knows he would. He would just throw himself into the void.

Well, if he's going to fall anyway, he might as well fall while attempting to jump the gap between the silo and the clifftop.

No time to lose. He runs. He launches himself at the cliff. For a split-second he feels the pull of the yawning abyss, but then he lands on blessed solid ground, falls and rolls. Much to his own surprise he has cleared the gap with ease.

But it sn't over yet. Chorley is now on the roof of the silo. He stands there, panting, wiping the sweat from his face with his sleeve. Chorley, his hair turned white, but otherwise looking just as he looked the first time they met: the same red baseball cap, the same cracked brown leather jacket, the scruffy trousers and shoes.

His eyes lock with Colin's. And then, without a word, he runs across the silo roof and he throws himself at the cliff.

He almost makes it. He lands half on half off the precipice, but before his hands can find purchase, he is slipping backwards. Colin rushes to the cliff-edge. Chorley hangs from the cliff by the fingers of his hands. Once again and for the last time, their eyes meet, Chorley's wide, desperate and entreating.

'Come on, Colin…' croaks Chorley. 'Jus' gimme a hand, mate. Can't hold on fer much longer…'

His fingers start to slip.

'Come on, Colin… I'm beggin' yer…'

Colin stands frozen.

Chorley's fingers lose their hold and he plummets.

Soundlessly, Chorley falls. Colin is unable to tear his eyes away. He sees the man's body impact against the side of the silo with a hollow clang, and then, rebounding, slammed into the cliff-face. Like a ragdoll he falls the rest of the way, broken limbs cartwheeling in the air. And then the body hits the ground, bouncing off a large boulder before coming to rest on a bank of loose shale, arms and legs splayed at unnatural angles, the neck broken, the head twisted sideways, a pool of blood spreading rapidly around it.

Part Three
Journey's End

Chapter Forty-Eight
'*We're* The Ones Who Disappeared'

Three black flying saucers, flying low and in formation, pass overhead. The alien vessels are not quite silent after all; a steady humming sound, so quiet as to be almost off the audible scale, accompanies their effortless movement across the ether.

Colin continues walking. The road curves round the shoulder of a hill, beyond it intersecting with an A-road. The moorland gives way to wooded country; isolated houses appear. Colin follows the road across a motorway overpass, and then through a plantation of trees, a great river appears before him, spanned by a suspension bridge. Seagulls wheel in the sky overhead, the air echoes with their cries. Beyond the suspension bridge a city rises on an eminence on the opposite bank of the river; an industrial city, crowned by the crenelated remains of a castle. The city is Norton-Braisley. Colin has reached his destination.

Colin follows the road down to the suspension bridge. Here he pauses. The length of the bridge is clear, but at the extreme end an obstruction of some kind appears to completely block the road. He starts walking along the bridge, keeping to the middle of the road. As he closes the distance, the obstruction across the road reveals itself to be a barricade, solidly constructed from miscellaneous materials. A narrow aperture extends along the front of it.

'Halt!' The amplified voice stops Colin in his tracks. The muzzle of a rifle has appeared through the loophole.

'Hands in the air!'

Colin raises his hands.

'What do you want here? State your business!'

'I'm looking for my sister.'

'Where have you come from?'

'I've come from Eastchester. My sister went to the university here, so I've come here to find her.'

'What's your name?'

'Colin Cleveland.'

'And your sister's name?'

'Carol.'

A pause. And then:

'Alright. Walk towards the barrier. Keep your hands in the air.'

Keeping his hands in the air, Colin walks towards the barrier. The rifle remains trained on him. Off to the left, a door, previously invisible, swings open.

'Walk towards the door. Take one step inside and then stop. Do not lower your hands.'

Colin walks to the door and takes a single step over the threshold into a gloomy interior. He stops. The door swings shut behind him and a pair of hands quickly and efficiently frisk him.

'He's clean,' announces a voice, female.

Two young men appear from the semi-darkness in front of him, both are holding guns, but they are not pointed at Colin and the men are smiling. The woman who frisked him comes forward and joins them.

'Sorry about all that,' she says. 'But we can't be too careful. You might not have been as harmless as you looked.'

'What about my sister?' asks Colin, eagerly. 'Is she—?'

'Yes; she's here. We just called her. She's on her way over right now. Come on.'

Colin is led through a narrow passageway and out into the open. He looks back at the barrier, which is in fact a substantial makeshift guardhouse. Out here there are sandbags, crates of equipment, a parked military jeep. There are a number of people about, all of them carrying weapons.

Colin turns to the woman. 'What's going on here? Are you fighting the aliens?'

'We're resisting them, yeah,' answers the woman.

Norton Braisley: the main rebel base. That was what Julia had told him. But Julia was mad, she made up stories; how could she have—?

'Here she comes.'

A jeep is driving towards them from the city, at the wheel of it a dark-haired girl in her late teens, a girl very familiar to Colin. He is surprised to see that she can drive a car now.

The jeep pulls up at the guardhouse, and the girl jumps out, and, all smiles, races over to Colin and throws her arms around him.

'Colin! Ohmygod I don't believe it!' hugging him, rubbing his back. Colin responds passively to this embrace, not resisting it, but without marked enthusiasm. The girl steps back and holding Colin at arm's length, scrutinises him with puzzled concern.

'What's up, Colin?' she asks. 'You look dazed or something…'

'I… I…' Colin's mouth moves, but he struggles to form words. 'I… it… a lot's happened…'

'I bet it has! How come you're all the way up here? And on your own, as well! What happened to Mum and Dad?'

'Mum and Dad disappeared…' says Colin. 'When the Incident happened…'

A heavy sigh. 'I thought they might've. Look, let's get back into town; you look totally knackered, and we've got tons of catching up to do. But don't worry about Mum and Dad. They're alright.'

Colin's eyes widen. 'What? Do you know where they are then? The people who disappeared? You know where they all went to?'

Another sigh.

'Listen, Colin: those people didn't go anywhere. Mum, Dad, all of them: they're still where they always were. It's *us*, Colin: *we're* the ones who disappeared. Come on.'

She takes her brother by the hand and leads him back to the jeep.

Samurai West

disappearer007@gmail.com

Printed in Dunstable, United Kingdom

65515998R00167